THE ELEVENTH SON

THE ELEVENTH SON

A NOVEL OF MARTIAL ARTS
AND TANGLED LOVE

Gu Long

Translated from the Chinese by

Rebecca S. Tai

HOMA & SEKEY BOOKS
PARAMUS, NEW JERSEY

Library of Congress Cataloging-in-Publication Data

Gu, Long, 1937-1985
[Xiao Shiyi lang. English]
The eleventh son : a novel of martial arts and tangled love / Gu Long ; translated from the Chinese by Rebecca S. Tai.— 1st American ed.   p. cm.
ISBN 1-931907-16-1 (pbk.)
1. Gu, Long — Translation into English. I. Tai, Rebecca S. II. Title.
PL2874.L8X5313 2004
895.1'352—dc22
2004011832

Published by Homa & Sekey Books
3rd Floor, North Tower
Mack-Cali Center III
140 East Ridgewood Avenue
Paramus, NJ 07652

Tel: 201-261-8810; 800-870-HOMA
Fax: 201-261-8890; 201-384-6055
Email: info@homabooks.com
Website: www.homabooks.com

Editor: Shawn X. Ye

Printed in the United States of America
1 3 5 7 9 10 8 6 4 2

Contents

Note from the Translator

THE TITLE OF the novel, *The Eleventh Son*, is the literal translation of the hero's name—Xiao Shiyi Lang. First published in Chinese in 1973, the novel is set in ancient China and centers around a problematical romance filled with moral dilemmas, which, in turn, brings out the other theme of the story—contempt for human hypocrisy. The protagonist, Xiao Shiyi Lang, is an infamous bandit who allegedly kills without blinking. The self-righteous swordsmen who hunt him down are so-called Ideal Gentlemen who do noble deeds and uphold justice. As the story unfolds, however, we realize that the well-respected gentlemen are merely hypocrites who care about nothing but their own fame and reputation, and Xiao, named the Great Bandit by these gentlemen, is the only man who truly respects truth and follows his conscience. On the other hand, Xiao's fateful romance with a beautiful married swordswoman lands him in a moral quagmire. He finds himself in danger of becoming one of the hypocrites he despises.

Chinese readers new to Gu Long's work often find his distinctive style quite challenging to their concept of how a typical novel should be written. When *The Eleventh Son* was first published, its format was a dramatic departure from conventional novels of the time. It featured extremely short paragraphs—so short that most of them consisted of only one or two sentences. This format not only gave the narrative a fast and poetic rhythm, but it also amplified the interaction between characters. Although the style was controversial and stirred considerable critical analysis, it became immensely popular. Gu Long soon became a household name. Millions of copies of his novels have been sold. Many of them have been adapted for cinema or TV, and a great many academic papers dedicated to the research of his works have been published. Gu Long's status as a pioneering figure in the history of modern Chinese fiction is firmly established.

Those who have never read Chinese martial arts fiction often assume that books of this genre are simply tales of macho fights and, therefore, are meant for unsophisticated readers who have a taste for violence. On the contrary, martial arts novels are widely read by Chinese of every gender, class, profession, and level of education. Highly entertaining as they are, the interactions between characters are no less sophisticated than any other type of fiction. *The Eleventh Son* has several thrilling scenes involving the many styles of kung fu and saber fights, but it also has spellbinding schemes, unexpected twists, tender and unforgettable romance, and incredibly astute observations about human nature.

About Gu Long

Syong Yaohua, better known by his pen name Gu Long (1937-1985), is one of the most popular martial arts novelists in the world of Chinese literature. Born in Hong Kong, he settled in Taiwan with his family when he was thirteen. He published his first novel at the age of twenty-three. A prolific writer, he wrote sixty-nine novels in a career spanning twenty-five years. Millions of copies of his books have been sold in Taiwan, Hong Kong and Mainland China in the past few decades.

Gu Long's distinctive writing style sets him apart from other novelists. His narratives feature short paragraphs, flavored dialogues, and cinematic images. Well read in both Chinese and western literature, he incorporated elements used by many admired Eastern and Western writers. The result is a highly innovative style, which had never been seen on the landscape of Chinese martial arts fiction. His style has been described by many critics as an intricate blend of prose, poetry, and drama. You can make a contrast between Gu Long's writing style and that of most other contemporary novelists as you would traditional Chinese landscape paintings and classic European oil paintings. While the latter is colorful, meticulous about detail, and generally realistic, the former is more sketchy, dreamlike, and poetic—leaving much more room for imagination. Ever since his celebrity status was established, Gu Long's unique style has been widely imitated by newcomers to this genre.

Those who are familiar with modern Chinese kung fu movies are used to seeing their heroes and heroines punch and kick antiheroes throughout the entire storyline. However, readers of *The Eleventh Son* will be surprised to find that the martial artists (both male and female) seldom fight. Although highly skilled in particular styles of kung fu, they fight only when it is necessary and their speed is more useful than any combination of complicated moves. Truly outstanding kung fu masters are expected to defeat their opponents in a very short time. It didn't make sense to Gu Long that the fights involving his protagonists should be dragged out for several pages of script. Furthermore, he sometimes portrayed martial artists who do not always need weapons or even fists to fight. Gu Long felt that the mind is often a more useful weapon in creating an invincible hero or heroine, and many of his martial artists become legends because of their extraordinary wit, in addition to their expertise in kung fu. Readers, therefore, see more duels of intelligence than clashes of swords in Gu Long's stories.

Before Gu Long's work became so popular with readers, Chinese martial arts novelists typically devoted lengthy descriptions to the protagonist's *process* of learning extraordinary kung fu. Gu Long doubted the necessity of such a formula and believed it made every story predictable and unexciting. After writing a few novels that followed this convention, he skipped this kung fu learning process and introduced heroes and heroines that were outstanding martial artists at the very beginning of every story. He felt that where or how they learned their kung fu was less important than how they used it for the good of mankind, as presented in the plot.

Another striking feature of Gu Long's work is the lack of background information. Unlike other Chinese martial arts novelists based in Hong Kong, who frequently use China's rich history as their majestic backdrop, Gu Long rarely explained the historical background of his stories. His readers are never told the exact Chinese dynasty in which his stories are set, because of the political climate in which he lived. Although Taiwan is currently a democratic entity, during the era of the Cold War, the fear of Communists prompted the government to impose martial law for over three decades. Freedom of speech was suppressed. Many writers had their books banned because of unfitting references to history. Given that Chinese history is full of events in which peasants rebelled against tyrannous regimes, novelists who specialized in ancient Chinese martial arts stories were more likely to get into trouble than writers of most other genres, as the heroes in these stories are usually rebels fighting against the authorities.

Under the shadow of censorship, Gu Long had to be cautious. He deliberately left the backgrounds of his stories vague and focused on the depiction of his characters. He figured that no matter how much or how often politics changed, human nature would always be the same. Though kung fu plays an important role in his novels, the characters he created are usually ordinary people with ordinary emotions, who just happen to be distinguished martial artists. They are not invincible super heroes. Readers may not remember the details of accomplished martial arts feats, but they will always remember how the heroes and heroines have laughed, cried, loved, and hated.

Title Clarification

As mentioned at the beginning of the introduction, the title of the book, *The Eleventh Son*, is the literal translation of the hero's name: Xiao Shiyi Lang. Most Chinese names consist of two or three characters: one for the surname and one or two for the given name. Some longer surnames have two characters. In that case, the full names will have three or four characters. Xiao Shiyi Lang is an uncommon name in that its given name alone consists of three words. *Shi* means "ten," *Yi* means "one," and *Lang* means "man" or "male." *Shi* and *Yi* spelled together mean "eleven."

The reason the protagonist is given this name is because he is a son and the eleventh child of his parents. In ancient China, it was a common practice for parents to name their children based on gender and birth order. A son was called *Lang* and a daughter was often called *Niang*, which means "female." This explains why Feng Siniang, another important character in this novel, is given her name. *Si* means "four," and *niang* means "female." Why eleven? Why didn't Gu Long use other numbers, like six, nine, or thirteen? In fact, Gu Long tried many other numbers. Eventually, he settled on "eleven," because it sounded the most poetic in Mandarin when it was spoken with the surname Xiao.

Birth order is not the only reason Chinese parents use numbers to name their children. Sometimes, they use a certain number because a child is born on that date or because a fortune-teller says it's auspicious.

Rebecca S. Tai
May 2004, Taipei

Acknowledgements

I WOULD LIKE to give my deepest thanks to Peter Redgrave, who encouraged me to pick up this project and was always the first to read the manuscript as it developed, offering extensive and thoughtful comments. Without him, this book would never have been completed. Peter, I am truly blessed to have you as my friend. I will always cherish the time we spent together on this project.

My many thanks go to Chen Hsiao-Lin, copyright proprietor of *The Eleventh Son*, for authorizing my English translation, and my appreciation to Heather Redgrave and Erik Ethornquist, for their valuable suggestions.

Thanks also to Nancy Johanson, for professionally and meticulously copyediting the manuscript.

Shawn Ye, my editor at Homa & Sekey Books, deserves my heartfelt gratitude for making the publication of this book possible.

Special thanks to my husband, JT, who supported and encouraged me every step of the way.

Rebecca S. Tai

Chapter 1

The Hands of a Lover

IT WAS A fine sunny day in early autumn.

The rays of the sun shone through the thin paper window, touching her fine, silky skin.

The water was slightly warmer than the sunlight. Feng languished in the tub, resting her delicate feet on the high edge. The sunlight touched her soles as gently as a lover's hands.

She was greatly pleased.

After traveling for more than half a month, what could be more relaxing than a hot bath? Her whole body melted into the water. Only her half-opened eyes remained free, to admire her feet.

This pair of feet had climbed mountains, waded through water, walked in the burning desert for three days, and crossed frozen rivers.

This pair of feet had kicked three hungry wolves and a bobcat to death, squashed countless vipers, and kicked Cloudy Sky, the notorious bandit of Mount Qilian, off a cliff.

Yet, this pair of feet was still delicate, exquisite, and flawless— without a single scar. Even those young ladies of noble households, who never stepped out of their mansions, might not have such perfect feet.

She was more than satisfied.

Water was still heating on the stove, and she added more to the tub. Although the water in the tub was hot, she wanted it even hotter. She liked the excitement generated by heat.

She liked all kinds of excitement.

She liked to ride the fastest horses, climb the highest mountains, eat the spiciest food, drink the strongest liquors, and use the sharp-est knives ... to kill the most vicious men.

Some have said excitement makes people age faster, but this saying didn't apply to her. Her breasts were still firm, her waist still slender, her abdomen still flat, her long legs still slim, and her skin still wrinkle free.

Her eyes were still bright and her laugh was still alluring and radiant. Whoever saw her would find it hard to believe that she was already thirty-three years old.

In the past thirty-three years, Feng Siniang had never allowed herself to be mistreated. She knew what to wear for each occasion, what to say to any sort of people, what to eat with a particular liquor, and she knew which kind of kung fu would kill which kind of people. She knew about life and how to enjoy it.

Few people were like her. She was unique. Some envied her; some were jealous of her. She was completely pleased with herself, except for one thing: she was lonely.

No excitement of any kind could dispel her feelings of loneli-ness.

Now, the last thread of her fatigue had dissolved in the water. She picked up a white silk washcloth and stroked her body with it.

When the soft silk touched her skin, it always brought indescrib-able joy, yet she wished it were a pair of hands—the hands of a man she liked.

However soft the washcloth was, it could not match a lover's hands; nothing in the world could take the place of a lover's hands!

Gazing at her smooth, translucent, and nearly flawless body, she felt a prick of unspeakable sadness.

All at once, several huge holes were torn into the window, the door, and the wooden walls; a head was thrust through each hole, each with a pair of lustful eyes.

Some were giggling wildly; some were gawking with their eyes almost popping out, completely speechless. At the sight of a beau-tiful naked woman, most men act like dogs. Ravenous dogs. The hole above the window had the best position, being closest and offering an unsurpassed view. The head protruding from this hole had a fat ugly face and a large rounded lump on the top, giving the illusion of one head atop the other. The sight of it was revolting, but the other heads didn't look any more pleasant.

Even a man in the bath would be terrified by the presence of so many intruders, yet Feng did not seem ruffled at all. She sat comfortably in the tub and cleaned her hand with the silk washcloth.

Without lifting her eyes, she gazed at her elegant fingers and scrubbed them carefully. When she was through, she offered the hint of a smile to the staring men. "Haven't you seen a woman take a bath before?"

All of the men broke into loud guffaws. A young pimple-faced man, who had stared with the widest eyes and laughed the hardest, bragged, "Not only have I seen women bathing, but I'm an expert in bathing women. If you let me scrub your back, I guarantee you'll be more than satisfied."

"Wonderful!" Feng flashed him a bewitching smile. "It happens that my back is itching. Why don't you come in?"

With narrowed eyes and laughing with excitement, the young man bashed the window open, eager to leap in, but he was pulled away by the big guy with the large lump on his head. Wiping the grin from his face and red with anger, the young man glared at the big guy and snarled, "Brother Xie, you already have several wives! Why fight me over this chick?"

Before the young man could finish speaking, the big guy slugged him, sending him flying.

"My goodness, if you scrub my back as hard as you hit people," Feng said, "I don't think I can stand it."

Xie glared at her, his eyes as hideous and vicious as those of a serpent, his voice more rasping than that of a rattlesnake. "Do you know what kind of place this is?" he hissed.

"If I hadn't, I wouldn't have come."

Feng smiled again before continuing. "This place is Mount Jumbled-Rocks, also called Bandit Mountain, because everyone living here is a bandit. Even the keeper of this small inn is a bandit, although he looks like an honest man."

"If you knew what kind of place this was, why did you come!" Xie demanded.

"What does it matter? I didn't come to pick a fight. I just came to take a bath."

Xie grinned with malice. "Why here?"

Her eyes twinkling, she said softly, "Perhaps I like to have bandits watch me bathe. It's exciting, no?"

Suddenly, Xie whacked the windowsill with the flat of his hand, crushing the big pieces of wood and demonstrating he was rather good at Iron Sand Palm.

Remaining unfazed, Feng simply sighed and murmured, "It's a good thing I didn't ask this uncivilized man to scrub my back."

Xie flew into a rage. "Stop beating around the bush. Why did you come here? Spit it out!"

"You're right," she smiled. "I wouldn't have come here merely to take a bath."

His eyes glinting, Xie said, "Did someone send you to collect information?"

"Of course not. I came to visit an old friend."

"Your friend isn't here."

"How do you know?" She laughed. "Who says I can't make friends with bandits? Did it occur to you that I might be a bandit, too?"

His face darkened. "Who is your friend?"

"I haven't seen him for quite a while," she said unhurriedly. "But I heard he's been doing quite well in recent years and has become the leader of the bandits in the region of Guanzhong. I wonder if you know him."

His face fell again. "There are thirteen gangs in this region, and each has its own leader. Which one are you talking about?"

"The chief of the thirteenth gang."

Xie was stunned for only a moment, before bursting into laughter. Pointing at her, he sneered, "How could you possibly be a friend of *our* chief?"

"Why couldn't I?" she asked, in a docile voice. "Do you know who I am?"

Xie stopped laughing and began to size her up. "Who are you?" he asked, his voice cold. "Could you possibly be ... Feng Siniang, the Enchantress?"

Brushing his question aside, she asked, "Are you Xie Bude, also known as Two-Headed Snake?"

He grinned, feeling smug about being recognized. "That's right. And whoever sees me—Two-Headed Snake—has to die. No one can get away."

"If you are Two-Headed Snake, then I have to be Feng Siniang."

Hearing this, Two-Headed Snake felt as if his head were bursting.

Was the naked woman sitting in the bathtub really Feng Siniang—the notorious and much feared Enchantress?

He almost couldn't believe his own ears, but he knew he had better believe it.

His feet started to move backward and the other men retreated even faster.

Suddenly, they heard Feng shout: "Freeze!"

Everyone froze and she smiled again, in her lovely and charming way.

Her voice was warm. "After ogling at a bathing lady, did you think you could get away so easily?"

"What do you want with us?" Two-Headed Snake asked.

Though his voice was quivering, he stared with widened eyes. When they settled on her bare breasts, he became emboldened and grinned maliciously. "Do you want us to take an even closer look?"

Amused by his inference, Feng chuckled. "Well, evidently you think that because I'm still undressed, I wouldn't dare go after you."

"That's right. You can't kill while you're sitting in the bathtub ... unless you carry weapons into the water."

Feng raised her hands, laughing. "Do these hands look like they can kill?" They appeared as delicate and graceful as orchids.

"No way," replied Two-Headed Snake.

"I agree, but the funny thing is ... sometimes they do."

She waved her hands in the air, and, all of a sudden, a dozen silver rays shot out from among her fingers.

A chorus of painful screams filled the air. A silver needle became imbedded in each eye of every man. No one had seen where they came from and no one had been able to dodge them.

Feng sighed again and murmured, "Have you ever heard the saying that whoever peeps at bathing women will get *needle-eyes*?"

The howling men rolled frantically on the ground with their hands over their eyes.

Their cacophony of yowls did not make Feng cover her ears. She continued to examine her own hands.

After a long while, she closed her eyes and sighed. "Such fine hands should be doing embroidery, not killing. What a pity!"

Suddenly, the squalling stopped, almost simultaneously.

Feng shouted, "Hua Ping, is that you?" She frowned.

All was quiet outside, except for the noise of the tree branches, swayed by the wind.

After several moments, she heard a click—the sound of a saber being inserted into its scabbard.

A smile spread over her lips. "I knew it was you. Who else can kill seven people so quickly? Who else can wield a saber so swiftly?"

No response came from outside.

"I know you killed them to end their suffering," she said. "It's just that I wonder ... since when have you developed such a soft heart?"

At length, a voice replied. "Is that Feng Siniang?"

"I'm glad you still recognize my voice," she said, smiling to herself. "That means you haven't forgotten me."

"Other than Feng Siniang, who would hide weapons in the bathtub?"

"So you were peeping at me, too." Feng giggled softly. "How else would you know I was taking a bath?"

Hua didn't seem to hear her question.

"If you wanted to look, why didn't you come in?"

He seemed to draw in a deep sigh. "Since you moved out to the borderlands a few years ago, everyone has been pleased with the ensuing peace. Why did you come back?"

"Because I missed you."

Hua fell silent again.

"You don't believe I have missed you? Why else would I come to see you?"

Hua sighed again.

"Why are you sighing?" Feng asked. "You think I have an ulterior motive? You're so prosperous, you don't want to see old friends anymore?"

"I'll see you when you're dressed."

"I'm dressed. Come on in!"

At last, Hua emerged through the doorway. His pale face became even paler, when he saw that Feng was still sitting in the tub, naked.

She giggled. "When someone wants to peek at me bathing, I kill him. But if you *don't* want to look ... I insist that you do."

Although Hua was not tall, no one would think he was short, because he was full of vast, fiery energy.

Dressed in a long black cape, he revealed the red hilt of his saber.

This saber had made him the leader of the bandits in Guanzhong.

"I heard that you killed First Sword of Taiyuan, Gao Fei, a few years ago," Feng said. "True?"

"Um-hmm."

"I heard that Twin Swords of Taixing, the Ding brothers, were also defeated by you. True?"

"Um-hmm."

Hua was not only unwilling to look at Feng, he was also unwilling to talk.

She laughed. "Both Gao Fei and the Ding brothers were among

the finest fighters and you killed them, which shows that your saber is even faster than before."

Hua did not even mutter this time.

"I returned to Guanzhong to see exactly how fast your saber is," Feng said.

"You want a demonstration?" he asked, his voice hoarse, and immediately on guard.

"Don't worry." She smiled radiantly. "I didn't come to fight a duel. I don't want to kill you or be killed by you."

It took Hua a while to regain his composure. "In that case," he said coolly, "you don't have to see my saber."

"Why not?"

"My saber is used to kill, not to be viewed."

With her eyes twinkling, she said, "What if I insist on seeing it?"

It was quite a while before Hua finally agreed. "All right, I'll let you."

His words were spoken slowly, but no matter how slowly, it wouldn't have taken long to speak so few of them. Yet, by the time he was through, Hua's saber had appeared and been returned to its scabbard again, and in that flash, a wooden bench near the door had been chopped in half.

Hua's saber was, indeed, stunningly fast.

Feng chuckled again, shaking her head. "What I want to see is how you use your saber to kill, not to chop firewood. Do you have to keep your saber techniques secret, even from an old friend?"

"Me keep secrets?"

"Although you can use either hand to wield the saber, who in the martial world doesn't know that you are a lefty? Your left hand is at least twice as fast as your right one."

Hua blanched again. After a long pause, he asked, "Do you have to see me use the saber with my left hand?"

"Yes, I insist."

At a loss for what to do, Hua sighed, "All right ... *look*!" He flung off his cape.

Feng had been laughing, but now she stared, mute. Noted for

his Left-Handed Divine Saber, Hua Ping was renowned as the fastest saber in China. No more. His left arm had been severed at the shoulder. After a long silence, Feng let out her breath. With a quivering voice, she asked, "Was it chopped off?"

"Um-hmm."

"By a sword or an ax?"

"Saber."

"A saber?" she gasped. "Whose saber could be faster than yours?"

Hua closed his eyes. "Only one man," he said.

Although he looked somewhat depressed, he didn't seem bitter. He was obviously so awestruck by the man's swordsmanship that he almost believed his amputation was justified.

Feng could not refrain from probing further. "Who?"

Staring into the distance, Hua spoke the name distinctly, word by word: "Xiao Shiyi Lang."

Xiao Shiyi Lang!

The sound of the man's name caused an instant, uncharacteristic change in Feng's facial expression. Was it anger, joy, or sadness? It was hard to tell.

"Xiao Shiyi Lang ... Xiao Shiyi Lang.... " Hua murmured. "You should remember him."

"That's right," she said, nodding slowly. "I remember him. Of course, I remember him."

Turning his eyes back to hers, Hua asked, "Do you want to see him?"

Feng glared at him, snarling, "Who said I want to see him? Why would I want to?"

"You'll have to turn to him sooner or later." Hua sighed.

"Bullshit!" Feng shot back angrily.

"You don't have to lie to me. I know you came back to China for a specific reason."

"Who said that?" She stared with widened eyes.

"I don't know exactly what you're up to, but it must be a heavy task. You're afraid you can't take it on alone, so you came to me for help." He grimaced. "Unfortunately, I'm not much use to you now."

"Even if your guess is correct, so what?" Feng said defiantly. "I can always find someone else for help. Why is Xiao Shiyi Lang the only candidate? It's not as if all the top fighters in the Martial Order were dead."

The Martial Order referred only to the circle of established martial artists, while *the martial world* included not only martial artists but also gangsters, as well as all kinds of itinerants such as street performers, circus artists, fortunetellers, magicians, prostitutes, pimps, charlatans, beggars, thieves, bandits, etc.

"Who else can help you?" asked Hua.

Feng rose to her feet, still naked, and cried, "I'll find someone! You'll see."

Hua closed his eyes again. "Who else is on your mind? Flying Doctor?"

"You said it. He's my next choice."

Her eyes glistened with animation. "Flying Doctor is not inferior to Xiao Shiyi Lang in any way. His Lightness Kung Fu is second to none; he can run and leap faster than anyone else. Besides, the strength of his fingers can probably overwhelm ten Xiao Shiyi Langs combined."

Legend has it that Flying Doctor, Gongsun Ling, could use a finger to stop a galloping horse. His Lightness Kung Fu, known as Swallow Thrice Skimming Water, was without equal in the Martial Order. Moreover, he was a distinguished medical doctor. Many people respectfully referred to him as Triple-Title Gongsun.

The place where Gongsun lived was unique. It was a tomb built of stone slabs. His bed was a coffin. He thought this was convenient, because, once he died, he wouldn't have to be moved.

A strange lad answered the door. Feng fired a round of questions at him. "Is Mr. Gongsun at home? Where did he go? Is he coming back today? When do you expect him?"

The lad uttered a short reply, consisting of only three words. "He's not in."

Feng was so mad she wanted to slap him in the face.

In fact, she knew the only thing that would keep Flying Doctor away from home was probably a visit to his patients.

Although Flying Doctor had a peculiar temperament, he was not compassionless.

She also knew that Flying Doctor wouldn't stay anywhere else for the night. He always slept in his coffin, in case he died in his sleep.

She could have stayed there and waited for him to come back, but she was a living person. It gave her the shivers to sit on a coffin in a tomb.

She preferred to sit by the road and wait for him.

It began to grow dark. A chill autumn breeze was blowing.

At the top of a small cliff by the trail, Feng found a nice spot and lay down. She gazed at the dark sky, waiting for the first star to rise.

Few people notice how the first star rises, but this was Feng's style. She could always find something interesting to do. She never wasted her time.

Alas! How many people appreciate such quiet pleasures?

It was late and the stars were finally out.

In the shadow of evening, Feng heard the sound of heavy footsteps. Two bearers, carrying a palanquin, trotted along the trail. A gaunt old man in a blue gown sat inside.

The haggard old man seemed to be dozing.

The two bearers appeared tired, too, as they puffed and panted like old bulls. When they approached the hill, the one trotting in front turned his head and said, "It's a long way to the top of the hill. How about taking a break, before we continue?"

"I've been getting really tired," said the other one. "How about trading places on the way up?" On an uphill road, the bearer in the back usually takes all the weight.

"Bastard, you are being lazy," the one in front jokingly scolded. "Did you see Little Sweet Melon again last night? You will die on her belly, sooner or later."

As the two men talked and laughed, their pace began to slacken.

Feng could not tell if the old man was really asleep or simply pretended that he didn't hear anything. His eyes remained closed.

When they reached the bottom of the hill, the bearers stopped and slowly lowered the palanquin.

Then, without warning, almost simultaneously, the two men each pulled a pair of long swords from within the supporting bars of the palanquin. They aimed two swords at the old man's chest and the other two at his back.

Chapter 2

Legs of Flying Doctor

THE OLD MAN was none other than Flying Doctor.

The two bearers were martial arts masters, in disguise. With lightning speed, the four swords lunged toward Flying Doctor from four directions—above, below, in front, and behind—instantly trapping him in the center, with no room for escape. It appeared that no matter how he might try to dodge them, he was about to be stabbed by at least two swords.

Though a martial arts veteran herself, not even Feng had expected such a vicious attack. It was too late for her to come to the rescue. She was afraid Flying Doctor would become a dead doctor, this time.

Surprisingly, in a split second, Flying Doctor leaned to one side, with two swords shaving past his body. The other two pierced his clothes, but both were clamped tightly in two of his fingers. It was as if his fingers were cast in iron. As hard as the two bearers tried, they could not dislodge their swords.

With a heavy clank, the two blades were snapped in two.

Astonished, the bearers somersaulted and landed several yards away.

With his eyes closed, Flying Doctor waved his hands. He sent the two snapped blades flying like blue rays toward the two fleeing bearers, who screamed in terror.

Blood spurted from their bodies, like arrows. Though the bearers were dead, their bodies were launched forward, leaving two streaks of crimson on the ground.

Following the screams came deathly silence.

Then, the crisp sound of clapping hands was heard.

"Who is it?" Flying Doctor snarled.

His eyes snapped open and peered intensely at the cliff where Feng was looking on. He saw her beautiful face and disarming smile.

"It's you." He frowned.

Feng smiled pleasantly. "It's been many years since we last met. I'm surprised to see you're not only more active, but you've also made incredible progress in kung fu."

His eyes drew together in an even deeper frown. "Why are you being so courteous? What do you want?"

"When I'm courteous, people say I'm up to something," Feng lamented. "When I'm not courteous, people say I'm rude. Alas! How difficult it is to act properly!"

Flying Doctor listened quietly, showing no emotion.

"The truth is, I just stopped by to see you," she said. "After all, we're old friends, aren't we?"

He remained silent.

Feng flew off the small cliff and stood in front of him. "I haven't been injured or offended by you. Why would I demand anything?"

"Have you taken a good look at me?"

"Of course I have."

"Good, then. Good-bye!"

Feng blinked and then giggled like the tinkle of a bell. "You are indeed an old fox. Nothing escapes you!"

Flying Doctor smiled, too. "To match the Enchantress, I have to be an old fox."

She used her eyes to point at the corpses on the ground. "Do you know who they are and why they wanted to kill you?"

"I've been around for quite a few years and killed countless people," he replied nonchalantly. "It's natural that someone would want to kill me. I won't bother to make an inquiry."

"I know you aren't afraid of death." Feng grinned. "But if these young upstarts had killed you, wouldn't that be a great pity? Aren't you afraid that your commanding reputation would be ruined?"

Silence ensued. Flying Doctor scrutinized her with intensity. "What do you want from me?" he grumbled.

"If you do a favor for me, I'll help you find out who was behind the surprise attack," she said, hands clasped behind her back. "You know, intelligence gathering is my specialty."

Flying Doctor sighed and smiled grudgingly. "I should have known you wouldn't seek me out for a good cause."

"But this time, it *is* for a good cause," Feng said, solemnly.

She squatted in front of Flying Doctor's palanquin. "It is a great cause. When this task is accomplished, both you and I will benefit from it."

After a period of silence, a weary smile flickered across his face. "I would like very much to help you. Unfortunately, you are too late."

"Too late?" She grimaced. "Why?"

Flying Doctor flung off the blanket covering his legs, leaving Feng in such shock; it was as if someone had poured ice water over her head.

His legs had been severed at the knees!

Flying Doctor's Lightness Kung Fu had been unequaled. When he applied his Swallow Thrice Skimming Water, he could capture flying birds barehanded. Now, his legs had been amputated.

The sight was even more shocking than Hua Ping's missing arm. "What happened?" Feng's voice trembled.

Flying Doctor's face was grim. "They were chopped off."

"By....?"

He spoke the name, one word at a time: "Xiao Shiyi Lang."

Xiao Shiyi Lang! Xiao Shiyi Lang, *again*!

Feng held her breath for a long time. Suddenly, she stamped her feet, screaming, "I don't want to see him. Why is everyone telling me to see him?" She detected a pattern in the treachery.

"You should have turned to him in the first place. With his help, whatever you want to do can be easily achieved."

"What about you? Don't you want to get even with him?"

"It's true that he injured me, but I don't hate him," Flying Doctor replied, with a shake of his head.

"Why not?"

Closing his eyes again, Flying Doctor became quiet.

A long silence followed. "I know you don't want to talk," Feng said at last, with a sigh. "Very well. In that case, I will take you home now."

"No, you don't have to."

"Why not? How can you get up this hill, in your condition?"

"Men and women mustn't have physical contact. I don't want to trouble you. Please go."

"What's the big deal about men and women having physical contact?" She stared straight into his face. "I don't care how you think a woman should behave. I never pay attention to those stupid restrictions."

Ignoring his protest, she lifted him up and carried him on her back.

Flying Doctor smiled wryly, not knowing what to do with such a woman.

In the shadow of evening, the tomb looked even more mysterious and frightening than usual. A dim light radiated from inside. From a distance, it looked like a will-o'-the-wisp.

"I don't understand why you have to live in a place like this," Feng complained. "Aren't you afraid of ghosts?"

"Sometimes ghosts are easier to live with than the living," replied the doctor.

"That's true. At least ghosts won't chop off your legs." Her voice was sarcastic.

Though there was a light in the chamber, no one was in. The peculiar-looking lad was nowhere to be found. What's more, the coffin had disappeared!

What burglars would be interested in such a place?

Feng couldn't help but laugh. "What a funny thief! He stole nothing but your coffin. Even if someone in his family had died, he didn't have to come all the way here—"

She broke off when she noticed Flying Doctor trembling and sweat dripping from his brow.

"Did you hide something in the coffin?" she asked, sensing something was wrong.

Flying Doctor nodded.

"You wouldn't have hidden money in the coffin, because you're not a miser," she mused aloud. "In that case...."

Her eyes flashed. "Aha!" she blurted. "You thought no one would steal your coffin, so you inscribed all the secrets of your medical skills and martial arts inside. You wanted those secrets to be buried with you when you die."

Nodding his head again, Flying Doctor seemed paralyzed.

"I don't understand why people like you are so selfish," Feng sighed. "Why aren't you willing to teach others what you have learned?"

At that moment, they heard the sound of panting from outside. The strange-looking lad appeared at the doorway.

His whole body was soaked with blood and his right arm was ... *missing*. Staring at Flying Doctor, he managed to utter a few words: "Xiao ... Shiyi ... Lang!"

With that, he collapsed and died. His left hand clutched a boot.

Xiao Shiyi Lang! Xiao Shiyi Lang, *again*!

Stamping her feet and muttering angrily, Feng said, "I didn't know he had become such a *monster*. I never imagined that he would do something so ... appalling."

"I don't believe this is his doing," observed Flying Doctor. "This is not like him."

Feng's eyes fell on the boot.

The boot was made of curried leather. The craftsmanship was elaborate. What struck her was that the surface was decorated with colorful beads. Decent ordinary people wouldn't wear such shoes. Most martial artists wouldn't wear them, either.

"It's true that he never wore such shoes," Feng said thoughtfully, "but, who knows what he has become?"

"His character would not change."

Feng regarded Flying Doctor with a mixture of bemusement and curiosity. "This is odd. He chopped off your legs, and you're leaping to his defense."

"He came to me in good faith. We had a duel, and he beat me fair and square. I know he's an honorable man who wouldn't do anything underhanded."

"It sounds like you know him better than I do," Feng said, with a soft sigh. "But why did this boy speak his name before he died?"

Flying Doctor shifted his eyes. "The boy didn't know Xiao Shiyi Lang, but you do. If you track down the murderer, you'll find out who did this."

"I see." She laughed. "You want me to catch the thief for you."

Flying Doctor hung his head, looking at his legs ruefully.

"All right, I'll go after the thief," Feng said, compassion for him in her eyes. "But I can't guarantee I'll catch up with him. You know I'm not very good at Lightness Kung Fu."

"With a coffin on his back, the thief can't run very quickly," the doctor said. "Otherwise, the boy wouldn't have been killed. He must have caught up with that crook and held on to his leg."

"Why did he assume Xiao Shiyi Lang's name? Why did he kill this boy?" Feng murmured, thinking of a motive. "Otherwise, even if he had stolen eight hundred coffins, I couldn't have cared less."

The bright moon was cold, the mountain desolate, and the wind strong.

Feng had always disliked using her Lightness Kung Fu against the wind, afraid that the wind blowing in her face would produce wrinkles.

Nevertheless, she dashed and leaped while facing the wind. Not because she wanted to catch the murderer, but because she wanted the cold wind to efface the image from her mind.

The first time she saw Xiao Shiyi Lang, he was only a teenager. Bare-chested, he was braving the rushing torrents in an attempt to scramble up Longqiu Falls.

He tried again and again. Once, he almost made it, only to be pummeled by the rushing water. His body landed on the rocks with a thud. His head gashed open, his body bruised, he rose to his feet, covered in blood.

Without stopping to dress his wounds, he clenched his jaws and lunged forward again. This time, he made it all the way to the top of the falls. He stood there clapping and laughing.

His victory was seared into her memory.

No matter how fierce the wind, it could not dispel her image of him.

Feng bit her lip hard, and it hurt. She had tried not to think about him, but the saddest thing about being human is that you often can't help thinking about the last thing you want to remember.

A shadow swayed in the wind.

Absorbed in her thoughts, Feng didn't notice. She raced on, with her head hanging low, until she came upon a face. The face was upside down, its bulging eyes bloodshot and staring in a fixed position. The sight was terrifying.

No matter how bold, anyone would be caught off guard by the sight of such a face. Feng backed away a few steps, lifting her head. The man hung upside down from a tree branch. She could not tell if he was still alive.

Just as she was about to check the man's breath, his eyes started to roll and his throat to gurgle, as if he wanted to talk.

"Were you ambushed?" she asked.

Unable to nod, he blinked and croaked, "It was a bandit ... a bandit...."

He blinked again.

He was not old, but his chin was covered with unshaved blue stubble. Though dressed gaudily, he had a mean-looking face.

"In my opinion," Feng scoffed, "you look like a bandit, too. If I save you, I might become your next victim."

Though his eyes made him look malicious, he managed a nervous grin. "If you help me, I'll pay you generously."

"But, you have been robbed. What can you pay me with?"

The man couldn't answer. His face produced cold sweat.

Feng smirked. "I don't think you look like a decent man, but ... I can't leave you to die."

"Thanks ... thanks a lot." He was relieved.

She smirked again. "I don't need your thanks. I just hope that after I save you, you won't take an indecent interest in me."

The man repeated his thanks, but his eyes fell on her chest. The curves of her firm breasts were vaguely visible under her clothes. Knowing most men were like that, Feng wasn't offended.

She leaped onto the branch of the tree. Just as she was about to unravel the tangled rope, she noticed that his tied foot was wearing a sock ... but no shoe. The sock was stained with blood.

Turning to the other foot, she found it wearing a boot ... a boot made of curried leather and decorated with elaborate beads!

Feng was stunned.

A long pause transpired. "Ma'am! You said you'd help me. What are you waiting for?" said the man.

She narrowed her eyes. "I still think it's ... inappropriate."

"Why?"

"As a woman traveling alone, I have to be cautious. It's midnight, and there's no one else around. After I save you, what if you want to ... hurt me? What would I do?"

The man strained to smile. "Ma'am, please don't worry. I'm not an evil man. Besides, judging from the way you leaped onto the branch, you don't seem to be easily harmed."

"But I should still be careful. I've got to ask you some questions first."

"What about?" he grumbled, obviously impatient.

"What is your surname? And where are you from?"

He replied hesitantly, "My surname is ... Xiao, and I'm from ... the north."

"What did the robber look like?"

"Truthfully," he sighed, "I was hung up before I could see his face."

She frowned. "How about the coffin? Was it snatched away, too?"

Pale, the man looked uncomfortable. "What coffin? Ma'am, I have no idea what you're talking about."

Feng bounded off the branch and gave him seven or eight quick slaps, leaving his face swollen and loosening some of his teeth. With a trickle of blood around the corners of his mouth, the man snarled in rage, "Who are you? Why did you hit me?"

"That's exactly what I'm asking you," Feng sneered. "Who are *you*? Why did you steal Flying Doctor's coffin? Who sent you here? Why did you assume Xiao Shiyi Lang's name?"

The man's head jerked with each question. His face twisted and his eyes spewed maliciousness. He glared at her, his teeth chattering noisily.

"You don't want to talk, do you?" she asked, her voice cold. "All right, let me. I'm Feng Siniang. Whoever is at my mercy confesses everything."

A look of horror flickered across his face. "*Feng Siniang*? So ... you are Feng Siniang!"

"Since you know my name, you should know I speak the truth."

The man drew a long breath and muttered, "I never thought I'd meet Feng Siniang, the Enchantress. Well, well, well, well...."

At the fourth "well," he suddenly bit down.

Feng immediately rushed to unclamp his lower jaw, but it was too late. His eyes had turned up and his face had turned black; his lips had curled into a cryptic sneer and his eyes nearly bulged out of their sockets. He stared at Feng and hissed, "Can you make me talk ... now?"

The man would rather swallow poison than tell the truth about himself. Obviously, he was afraid that if he survived, the punishment waiting for him would be worse than death.

"It's a good thing you killed yourself," Feng sneered. "Whether you talked or not has nothing to do with me anyway."

Questions remained though.

Who had hung this murderer upside down? And ... what had happened to the coffin?

To her amazement, the coffin had returned to Flying Doctor's tomb.

Could it have walked home by itself?

Unable to believe her eyes, Feng darted across the floor. "How did this coffin get here?" she demanded.

Flying Doctor's face beamed. "Someone sent it back."

"Who?"

With a mysterious smile, Flying Doctor said slowly, "Xiao Shiyi Lang!"

"Xiao Shiyi Lang? It's *him* again!" Feng cried in exasperation. "So it was he who hung the man upside down. Why didn't he grill the man about his motives?"

"He knows there is no use in interrogating certain types of people."

"Then why did he leave the man dangling? Did he intend to leave the man to me?" Feng was irritated.

Flying Doctor grinned but did not answer.

Her eyes swept around the room. "Where is he?"

"He left."

She glared at Flying Doctor. "He knew I was here. Why didn't he wait for me?"

"I said you didn't want to see him, so he left."

Her lips curled into a sneer. "That's right. Every time I see this man, I get upset. Where did he go?"

"You don't want to see him anyway." Flying Doctor smirked. "What's the point in asking?"

Left speechless, Feng jumped up and kicked the table over, screaming, "You old fox! I wish he would come back and chop off your hands!"

She stormed out of the chamber.

Flying Doctor sighed deeply and murmured to himself, "Why is a woman in her thirties still acting like a child? This is odd...."

Chapter 3

The Sound of Singing in the Night

FILLED WITH BAMBOO-LEAF-GREEN wine, the green porcelain cup looked like a huge piece of translucent jade.

The bright moon hanging in the sky was like a plate of ice. It was full and complete. Were people?

Feng's face was flushed and she was slightly inebriated. The moonlight shone through the window. As she gazed up at the moon, she remembered something that sobered her almost immediately.

Is today the fifteenth day of the month?

July fifteen, in the lunar calendar, was her birthday. After this day, she would be one year older.

Thirty-four! What a terrible number! she thought.

When she was fifteen or sixteen, she used to think that once a woman was over thirty, life became meaningless. A woman in her thirties was like an old chrysanthemum in November, simply waiting to wither.

Yet she was thirty-four now. She didn't want to believe it, but she had to. Why was time so relentless?

There was a bronze mirror in the corner of the room. She gazed at the face reflected in it.

The face was youthful. It had no wrinkles around the eyes, even when she smiled. Few would believe it was the face of a thirty-four-year-old woman.

Although she could fool everyone else, she couldn't fool herself.

She turned and poured herself a large cup of wine. The moon cast her long shadow onto the floor. Two lines of a well-known poem came to her mind:

Raising my cup I invite the Moon,
Then turn to my shadow, which makes the three of us.

She had never understood the loneliness and sadness it described... until now.

From far off, she heard the sound of a baby crying.

She had once loathed the sound of crying babies, but, now, how she wanted a baby! How she wanted to hear the crying of her own baby!

Her face reflected the moonlight, and a few glistening tears slipped down her cheek.

Several times, in the past few years, she had thought about finding a man and getting married ... but, she couldn't. Most men made her sick.

Her youth was fading. In a few years, perhaps even those she considered disgusting wouldn't want her. Alas! A woman of thirty-four....

She heard the loud laughter of a man passing by her door.

The laughter was raucous and seemed slightly intoxicated.

What would this man be like?

He was certainly vulgar and ugly, and he probably reeked of alcohol.

Nevertheless, if this man barged in now and begged her to marry him, she might say yes.

Does a woman become less picky when she is thirty-four than when she was twenty? She mused, her lips curling into a wistful smile.

It was getting late. The sounds outside had died down.

The tones of the night gong echoed in the distance. The sounds were dull, yet they marked the passage of time ... and life.

It's time to go to bed, Feng told herself.

Just as she rose to close the window, the sound of distant singing came drifting in with the night wind. The haunting voice, desolate and poignant, sounded familiar.

Xiao Shiyi Lang!

Nearly every time she saw Xiao, he was humming this tune. It made him seem aloof and distant.

Aroused by an inner excitement, and without hesitation, she placed a hand on the window frame for support and leaped out, darting toward the source of the voice.

The long street was quiet.

In front of every household door, the road was scattered with drifts of ash where paper money had been burned. When a gust of wind arose, the ash dispersed, swirling into the air. In the dark, no one knew exactly how many ghosts might be waiting to snatch the burned money.

July the fifteenth was also the Ghost Festival, supposedly when the gates of hell are opened wide and the spirits are let out. Was it true that the world was filled with every kind of spirit at this very moment?

Between clenched teeth, Feng murmured, "Xiao Shiyi Lang, you are exactly like a ghost. Why don't you ever show yourself?"

She didn't see any sign of ghosts around her. Even the sound of singing was gone.

"That man really is a ghost," she grunted, feeling bitter. "If he didn't want to see me, why did he let me hear his singing?"

She suddenly felt incredibly weary and morose. All she wanted to do was go back to her room, have a few more drinks, and sleep until tomorrow. Maybe everything would be different tomorrow.

Maybe the most important reason that keeps people going is there is always a tomorrow.

When Feng saw candlelight radiating from her room, she felt a hint of warmth in her heart, as if she were returning ... home.

When one comes home and closes the door, it seems as if all worries were left outside. This is what a home is for....

But is this my home? Of course not, she thought. It's little more than ... a room in an inn.

Feng drew a sigh. She didn't know where her home was or when she would have one.

When she reached the doorway, she heard someone in her room reciting a verse:

When I have left the border one thousand miles behind me,
Mr. Xiao will be just like another stranger.

Then the voice said, "Feng Siniang ... my Feng Siniang. I'm afraid you've forgotten me, haven't you?"

Feng came alive instantly. She dashed into the room, yelling, "You damned....! You finally showed up!"

The wine in the goblet on the table was gone.

A man was lying languidly on the bed, with his face covered by a pillow.

He was dressed in faded blue. A blue cloth band was tied casually around his waist and a saber was tucked casually into the band.

This saber was much shorter than regular ones. Its scabbard was made of shabby black leather, but at least it looked newer than his boots.

He lay with one knee up, his other foot perched upon it. There were two big holes on the sole of the shoe.

Feng leaped up and kicked his shoe, shouting, "Lazy bastard! Lazy and dirty! Who said you could sleep on my bed?"

The man in the bed sighed and grumbled, "I just took a bath last month, and here you are saying that I'm ... dirty."

She couldn't help but giggle a little, but she sobered up again, immediately. Grabbing the pillow covering his face, she tossed it into the air. "Sit up and let me see exactly how ugly you've become in the last few years."

Although the pillow was gone, the man's face was still covered with his hands.

"Have you become too ugly to be looked at?" she said.

The man in the bed separated his fingers, revealing eyes that were sparkling and joyful. "Whoa! What a ferocious woman!" he said. "No wonder you're not married yet. It seems that other than me, no one would dare to marry you—"

Before he could finish, Feng had slammed one of her hands down.

The man in the bed suddenly pulled back. His whole body stretched flat against the wall, like a paper doll sticking to a flat surface. He stayed there, refusing to come down.

His bright eyes were still laughing. His eyebrows were bushy, his nose straight, his short beard so thick it looked like it could puncture skin.

This man was not really handsome, but the glistening eyes and the bright smile gave him an aura of animal energy ... untamed, but charismatic.

"Xiao Shiyi Lang, you haven't changed at all, not even one little bit," said Feng, sighing softly and shaking her head. "You are still a one-hundred percent asshole in every sense of the word and in every way."

"I thought you wanted to marry me—an asshole!" Xiao grinned. "It appears that I was mistaken."

"Me marrying *you*?" she shrieked, her face burning with anger. "You think I'd want to *marry* you? Even if every other man in the world were dead, I would never marry you."

Xiao expelled a long sigh. "Whew, am I ever relieved."

He slid from the wall, landing on the bed with a thump. "Honestly speaking," he said with a laugh, "when I heard you were looking for me, I was a little scared. I'm only twenty-seven. If I wanted to marry, I'd find a young girl of fifteen or sixteen, instead of an old hag ... like you."

Feng was furious. "You call me an old hag? How old do you think I am?"

With a flourish, she withdrew a sword from her sleeve.

In a matter of seconds, her sword had lunged toward him seven or eight times.

Xiao was even faster. He scrambled back to the wall and climbed to the ceiling, staying there like a giant gecko. He waved his hand at her. "Please, don't move. I was only joking. Actually, you're not old at all. You don't look a day over ... forty-something, at most."

Feng tried to keep a straight face, but she couldn't hold back her laughter. She wagged her head at him. "It's lucky for me I don't see you often. Otherwise, I would have died getting mad at you a long time ago."

Xiao flashed her a broad smile. "Too many people flatter you. Isn't it fun to have someone teasing you for a change?"

After he came down, his eyes rested on the sword Feng was holding.

The sword was a little over a foot in length. Its blade was very thin and had a greenish-blue shine. This kind of sword was most suitable for a woman. Madame Gongsun, the most famous swordswoman in the Tang Dynasty, used a similar one. She taught sword dances in the Imperial Music Institute. Even the renowned poet Tu Fu had written a poem to extol her prowess:

> *A fair lady there was*
> > *Madame Gongsun;*
> *The dance of her sword*
> > *marveled the world.*
>
> *Beholders, many as mountains,*
> > *were filled with awe;*
> *Even the heaven and the earth*
> > *breathed to her rhythm.*
>
> *She flashed, like the Nine Suns*
> > *whirling down to the Archer;*
> *She flew, like graceful gods saddled*
> > *on gliding dragons.*
>
> *She moved, like rolling thunders*
> > *as the storm rages;*
> *She ceased, like cold light shimmering*
> > *off placid rivers.*

This poem was a testament to the superiority of Madame Gongsun's swordsmanship. She was a petite woman. If she had not used this kind of sword, she would not have been able to dance so deftly.

While Xiao was staring at her sword, Feng was studying his eyes. Without warning, she moved her hand, slashing the wine cup on the table with the weapon.

With a clang, the green porcelain cup was cut in half.

"Excellent sword!" exclaimed Xiao, in admiration.

"Although this sword can't cut iron as if it were clay, it comes close," said Feng, with the shadow of a smile. "Count Carefree cherished it so much he was reluctant to let anyone else view it."

The edges of Xiao's mouth curled upward. "Yet ... he gave it to you?"

Feng raised her head high. "Exactly."

"Does that mean he is ... interested in you?"

"So what?" Feng smiled humorlessly. "Is there some reason he shouldn't be interested in me? Am I that ... old?"

After studying her for a moment, Xiao spoke in a serious voice. "It's not easy to draw the attention of a man like Count Carefree. I was just wondering ... how many concubines do you think he's had before you?"

Her anger surged. "You're full of shit!"

She raised her sword and Xiao braced himself again.

But then Feng lowered her sword slowly, slanting her eyes at him. "If you're so smart, then you should know the story behind this sword."

"It appears to be Blue Jade, used by Shen Ruolan, Madame Gongsun's first disciple."

Feng nodded. "You *do* know something."

"But, it is one of a pair. Since you have Blue Jade, you should have Crimson Glow as well. Unless...." He broke off.

"Unless what?"

Xiao smirked. " ... unless Count Carefree was reluctant to give you both."

She glared at him defiantly. "If I wanted his *head*, he would put it on a platter and offer it to me, not to mention two measly swords."

"Really?" Xiao laughed. "In that case, where is Crimson Glow now?"

"I have it with me. I don't mind if you want to take a look at it."

"Actually, I don't want to, but if I refuse, you'll probably throw another tantrum."

Xiao grinned and added, "Remember what happened that October, a few years ago? It was still very hot, but you came to see me in a mink coat. You were sweating and insisted that you simply *had* to wear more clothing, because you had caught a cold."

"Bullshit!" Feng snorted. "You think I was trying to show off?"

Xiao grinned. "Lucky for you, you had something to show off. I have nothing to show off but myself."

"You're such a clown!" Feng scolded, playfully.

She took out the other sword. Its sheath was inlaid with pink gems. Taking the hilt into his hand, Xiao shook his head and remarked, "To no one's surprise, things used by women always smell of rouge and powder."

As he spoke, he started to draw the blade.

To his bewilderment, Crimson Glow was broken!

Feng didn't seem disturbed. She eyed him calmly. "Surprised?" she said.

"How was such a fine weapon ruined?" Xiao asked.

"By a saber."

Xiao raised his eyebrows. "What saber? How could it be so sharp?"

"I know that every time you hear about a fine saber, you itch for it," Feng said, casually. "But this time, I won't tell you about it, in case you say I'm a showoff."

Xiao rolled his eyes and stood up. "I just remembered I haven't eaten. Let's go. I'll treat you to a midnight snack."

There was a small noodle shop at the end of the street.

This particular noodle shop had been in business for more than ten years. Rain or shine, it opened every day, even on holidays and festivals.

As a result, the town's night owls were especially fond of it. When their wives threw them out, they could always come for steaming beef noodles.

Old Zhang, the boss, was very old and had graying hair. At this moment, he was sitting in his shop eating noodle soup. The paper lantern hanging at the door was blackened by greasy smoke. It was yellowish black, like Old Zhang's face.

Customers who frequented his shop knew that he never showed even a flicker of expression. Aside from asking for payment, he usually remained mute.

"How about eating here?" Xiao inquired cheerfully.

Feng frowned. "All right," she agreed, hesitantly.

"Don't scowl. I guarantee you have never had beef noodles as delicious as these."

Seating himself at a shaky old table near the door, Xiao called out to the boss. "Old Zhang! I have a guest today. Serve us something nice."

Without lifting his head, Old Zhang gave Xiao a sidelong stare, as if to say, "What's the hurry? Wait until I have finished my soup."

Xiao whispered, "This old man is a strange bird. Better not offend him."

The legendary Xiao Shiyi Lang was afraid to offend an old man who ran a noodle shop? Who would believe this! Feng was greatly amused.

After quite some time, Old Zhang brought over two dishes and a jug of wine. He set them forcefully onto the table and then turned away.

Feng could not help laughing. "Do you owe him money?"

Xiao held his head high. "I did owe him a chunk of change, but I paid him back yesterday."

Gazing at him thoughtfully, Feng said, "Everyone in the martial world affirms that Xiao Shiyi Lang is the finest and the most professional thief of the last five hundred years. None of them knows that, in reality, Xiao Shiyi Lang is so poor he can only afford to treat his guests to cheap noodles, sometimes on credit."

Xiao laughed aloud. "I know it and you know it. Isn't that enough? Come, let me make a toast ... to you."

Xiao was an enigma. Some cursed him, some hated him, some loved him ... but few understood him.

He didn't expect to be understood and he didn't worry about his well-being.

If you were Feng Siniang, would you love him?

Feng had remarkable drinking skills. When most people drink too much alcohol, they tend to get confused and bleary-eyed.

But she was different. The more she drank, the brighter her eyes became. No one could tell if she was intoxicated or not. That's why few people dared to match her drinking, even though her tolerance for spirits was really not so high.

Chapter 4

The Deer Carver

"DON'T YOU WANT to hear the story of the saber?" Feng asked, her eyes as bright as lamps and focused on Xiao.

"I don't want to hear it," came his response.

Feng was visibly surprised. She remained quiet for a moment. "Why not?"

"If I said I wanted to hear it, you wouldn't tell me," Xiao said, with a deadpan face. "On the other hand, if I don't want to hear it, maybe you'll want to tell me—"

Before he could finish, Feng started to laugh at the top of her voice. "You are full of the devil! People call me the Enchantress, but when the enchantress meets the devil, she is completely powerless."

Xiao kept drinking, without responding. He knew he must not counter. If he showed too much curiosity, Feng might change her mind again and refuse to talk.

Since Xiao had no comeback, Feng had to continue with the conversation. "As a matter of fact, whether you want to hear it or not, I will tell you. The saber is called Deer Carver."

"Deer Carver?"

"That's right. Deer Carver."

"The name is fancy. Why haven't I heard of it before?"

"Because this saber was made less than six months ago."

Xiao raised his eyebrows. "A newly-forged saber can cut fine weapons made long ago? Is it possible that the man who made this saber is as good as the distinguished swordsmiths of the late Zhou Dynasty?"

Instead of answering his question, Feng asked, "After such masters as Ganjiang, Moxie, and Ou Zhizi, there was another renowned swordsmith. Do you know who I'm talking about?"

"Madame Xu. Right?"

Feng smiled. "Exactly. You're not ignorant after all."

Madame Xu was not a woman. Xu was the swordsmith's surname and Madame was his given name. As a matter of fact, the sword used by Jingke to assassinate the first emperor of the Qin Dynasty was made by Madame Xu.

Xiao's eyes gleamed. "Was the Deer Carver made by Master Xu— Xu Luzi?"

"You know about him, too?" Feng said, in slight surprise.

Xiao nodded. "Xu Luzi is a direct descendant of Madame Xu. You mentioned Madame Xu; that must mean *Master* Xu is related to the Deer Carver."

Feng's eyes revealed her admiration and exhilaration. "You're right. The Deer Carver really was made by Master Xu. He devoted his best efforts and his entire life to making this particular saber. In ancient China, the deer was used to symbolize the coveted throne. Master Xu drew his inspiration for the name of the saber from the famous verse:

The Qin Empire has fallen and lost the deer.
It is fair game now for anyone to hunt.
Only the final victor will cut off the prize and win the deer.

What Master Xu means is that only the greatest hero is worthy of the Deer Carver. The name shows his absolute pride in it."

Xiao's eyes sparkled. "So ... you have seen the saber?" he asked hastily.

Feng closed her eyes and drew a long breath. "It was, without a doubt, an extraordinary sword. Compared to it, Crimson Glow was almost like ... scrap metal. It cut Crimson Glow so easily."

Xiao threw back a cup of wine and then smacked the table. "I wonder if I'll ever have a chance to see such a fine saber."

Feng's eyes glistened. "Of course you will."

"But I'm not personally acquainted with Master Xu. Why would he allow me to see it?"

"Xu Luzi doesn't have it anymore."

"Really?" Xiao was surprised. "Where is it now?"

"I don't know," she said flatly.

Xiao was truly stupefied this time. He raised his cup, but quickly put it down. He rose to pace around the table and then sat down again. He picked up a piece of beef in his chopsticks, but forgot to put it in his mouth.

Feng burst into laughter. "I didn't know I could make you blow your cool like this. I suppose it's more difficult for an adolescent to remain calm."

"Are you calling me an adolescent?" Xiao said, winking at her. "I remember you being two years younger."

"Kid, your nose is brown," Feng teased him. "I'm your senior by five years, four months, and three days. You should respectfully address me as 'big sister'."

Xiao smiled wryly. "Big sister, you have a marvelous memory."

"Little brother, hurry and pour a cup of wine for your big sister."

"Yes, big sister. As you wish."

When Xiao had filled her cup with wine, she smiled and said, "Ah, that's more like it, my good little brother."

Though still laughing, she couldn't conceal the hint of sadness in her eyes, where tears were gathering. She threw down her cup of wine and said, "The Deer Carver is on the way to Guanzhong, as of this moment."

Xiao almost spilled his wine on the table. "Is it being escorted the whole way?"

"Do you think they *wouldn't* put such a prized saber under heavy guard?"

"Who's escorting it?"

"Zhao Wuji—"

"*Zhao Wuji?*" Xiao frowned. "You mean the chief of the Supreme Boundless Gate?"

"Who else?"

Xiao pondered quietly for a while and then nodded, as if he had formed some sort of plan.

Feng had been watching him closely to detect any subtle change in his facial expression. "In addition to Zhao Wuji," she continued, "there are other fighters, including Tu Xiaotian—also known as the Knight of Guandong, the only fighter left in the Hainan Sword School. And there is Hai Lingzi—"

"*Enough!* The three of them are plenty," Xiao declared.

"But they don't think so. They also enlisted the help of Sikong Shu, known as One-Armed Hawk King. He slaughtered the eight notorious bandits of Mount Heaven, with only one arm."

Xiao made no response.

Feng was still staring at him. "I don't think anyone in the world would be bold enough to wrest the saber from the escort of those four."

Suddenly, Xiao broke into a loud guffaw. "So *that's* the reason you're telling me all this. You're challenging me to capture the saber ... *for you!*"

Her eyes twinkled. "Do you dare?"

"If I capture the saber for you, the saber is yours," Xiao said, with another laugh. "There's nothing in it for me."

Feng bit her lip. "Do you know why they're escorting the saber to Guanzhong?"

"I don't know, and I don't want to know." Xiao shook his head. "One thing's for sure ... they aren't doing it to give me the saber."

"Even if you're afraid to take the saber, don't you at least want to see it?"

"No."

"Why not?"

"If I see the saber, I'll probably get the itch for it. Once I feel the itch, I'll want it for myself. If I fail, I'll be killed."

"What if you succeed?"

"If I succeed, you'll ask me for it. Although I would be reluctant to part with the saber, it would be hard to say no to you. In that case, I might just as well not go see it."

Feng started to her feet. "I didn't know you were such a coward," she said with bitter contempt. "I was wrong about you. That's all right, if you won't go, I'll go by myself. Let's see if I'll be crushed without you."

Xiao smiled wryly. "Whenever you fancy something, you must have it. I wonder when you'll get rid of this awful habit."

The town was not big, but because it was near the border, it was prosperous. Anyone who wanted to enter the district of Guanzhong, from north of the Great Wall, had to pass through it. Among the common travelers were ginseng, fur, or horse traders from the northeast, and merchants and fortune-seekers from the Mongolian Desert. Most of them stayed one or two nights, when they came through.

It was the lavish spending of these travelers that had brought unwholesome prosperity to the town.

The town was particularly famous for two things.

The first thing was food. There were few men who didn't like its great food. There were all kinds of cuisine to satisfy all kinds of preferences.

The lamb hot pot was better than that served in Beijing. Compared to the stewed pork balls prepared by the chef of Kuiyuan Rain, a renowned restaurant in Hangzhou, those served at Five-Blessing Chamber, at the end of the main street, were equally delicious. Even the most critical gourmets could have their taste buds pleased.

The other thing was women. There were even fewer men who didn't like its women. There were all kinds of women to satisfy all kinds of men.

Two is not a large number, but these two specialties were enough to keep most men in the town for quite some time.

Endeyuan was an Islamic restaurant. Its boss, Ma Huihui, could make a hundred and eight different dishes out of a single cow. Moreover, he was one of the best wrestlers around.

Endeyuan didn't have a big and ornate façade, but Ma Huihui was its best advertisement. With his shiny bald head and his wide belt, he often stood in front of the restaurant to greet customers. Most people from the martial world, who passed through the town, made a point to go to Endeyuan for a few drinks.

Ma's face normally glowed with vitality. On this day, he appeared particularly excited.

Even before dusk, he kept coming out of the door to gaze into the distance, as if expecting important guests.

Around six o'clock in the evening, a black carriage, drawn by four horses, appeared from the other end of the road. It did not slow down, though the street was busy. Fortunately, the driver was very professional and the horses were obviously well trained. It was going very fast, but the carriage did not cause any trouble.

Although there were always many vehicles on the road, such a majestic carriage was a rare sight. While the pedestrians scrambled to get out of its way, they couldn't help trying to get a closer look.

They heard a loud neighing. The driver yanked on the reins, and the carriage pulled up in front of Endeyuan. Ma rushed out to greet it, opening its door with an ingratiating smile.

The spectators were mystified. Though Ma was a practical businessman, he had seldom humbled himself in this way. Why was he so deferential to the men in the carriage?

The first person out of the carriage was a middle-aged man with fair skin and a sparse beard. His round face was all smiles.

He was slightly overweight and dressed in a floral green silk robe, long but fitted. Gentle and gracious, he looked like a nobleman traveling incognito. Smiling, Ma brought his two fists together in salute. "Lord Zhao, it has been a long journey. You must be tired. Please come in."

The middle-aged man smiled and returned the salute with his fists. "Manager Ma, you are too kind."

When veterans of the martial world heard how Ma addressed this man, they had a fairly good idea of who he might be.

Could it be Zhao Wuji, the chief of the Supreme Boundless Gate, renowned for his Supreme Boundless True Qi and Eighty-one Variation Boundless Sword?

Who would be the next person to step out of the carriage?

The second person out of the carriage was a white-haired old man holding a long-stemmed tobacco pipe. He was plainly dressed in a gray cotton-padded jacket. The lower half of his cotton-padded trousers was tucked into his white socks. He looked like a clumsy country bumpkin, yet his bright and penetrating eyes gave him an aura of grandeur.

Ma bowed with another smile. "Since we last met, Lord Tu, you seem to have become stronger and stronger."

The old man returned the salute and smiled, too. "I've been blessed by my friends' good wishes."

This old man's surname was Tu. Was this Tu Xiaotian, also known as Knight of Guandong? Having been famous for four decades, he was considered the finest in assaulting the body's meridian points. He could use his pipe to attack thirty-six major meridian points and seventy-two minor meridian points on the human body.

The first two passengers were impressive. And the third?

Murmuring to each other, the spectators were getting more and more curious.

The third man stepping out of the carriage was a lanky Taoist priest with high cheekbones and an aquiline nose.

Though he was a priest, he was richly dressed. His purple robe was embroidered with gold thread. An oddly-shaped long sword was slung across his back. Its hilt was decorated with cat's-eye; its sheath was made of green shark's skin. The priest's slanted eyes were slightly turned up, as if he had never looked at anyone seriously.

Ma was even more courteous this time. He bowed and said, "I have heard so much about you, Father Hai. Your excellent reputation precedes you. It is a great honor to meet you."

The old man did not bother to even glance at Ma. He nodded and said simply, "Fine. Fine."

Father Hai. Was it Hai Lingzi?

The sword techniques of the Hainan School were noted for their mystique and speed. The swordsmen of this school were all rather eccentric and seldom mingled with others.

The Battle of Tongye Island, which had taken place seven years earlier, had been a sensational event. The master of Tongye Island and all thirteen of his disciples were killed. Out of the nine top fighters of the Hainan School who had challenged Tongye Island, only Hai Lingzi had survived the bloody fight. Since then, Hai was more famous and haughtier than ever.

What had brought him, Zhao, and Tu together?

The strangest thing was that, after they disembarked from the carriage, they did not walk straight into the restaurant. Instead, they all stood beside the vehicle, waiting for a fourth passenger.

A long time later, the fourth man finally emerged.

When this man emerged, everyone was taken aback.

His appearance was bizarre.

He was less than five-feet tall, but he had a massive head with disheveled hair. His shaggy eyebrows were so thick they almost merged. His left eye glistened like a bright star, but his right eye was as ashen as a dead fish's. His bushy mustache covered a blood-red mouth.

His right arm was severed at the shoulder, but his left arm was so long it almost touched his toes.

He carried a rectangular yellow bundle in his hand.

This time, Ma dared not even glance at the man. "Your Lordship," he said humbly, "when I heard you were coming, I selected a fine ox."

The one-armed man's nod was barely perceptible. "An ox is better than a cow. I only wonder whether it's dead or alive."

"It's alive and kicking, of course." Ma smiled ingratiatingly. "It's meant for Your Lordship to eat fresh."

The one-armed man seemed amused. "Excellent. Excellent. My grandson, you know how to please me."

He referred to Ma as his grandson, and yet Ma seemed pleasantly surprised. Those who did not know this one-armed man felt shame for Ma.

Some of the spectators, however, had guessed the identity of this man. They were proud of Ma. It was an honor to be referred to as a grandson ... by the One-Armed Hawk King.

Behind Endeyuan, there was a garden reserved for very important guests. In the garden was a miniature mountain surrounded by a few big trees. Tied to one of the trees was an ox.

This ox was enormous and had horns as sharp as knives.

The yellow bundle that One-Armed Hawk King had been carrying was now nowhere to be seen. He was circling the ox while muttering, "Excellent! Excellent!"

Tu Xiaotian smiled. "Brother Sikong, since you're satisfied, what're you waiting for?"

The Hawk King grinned. "You old bastard, you want to see my trick again, right?"

He waved his left arm in front of the ox's eyes. The frightened bull lowered its head, aiming his horns at the Hawk King's belly.

"Fantastic!" shouted The Hawk King.

In the blink of an eye, he had ducked under the ox's belly. He reached his hand upward, tearing into the ox's gut.

The ox sprang violently and snapped the rope. It lunged forward, leaving a trail of blood along the way as it careened into the wall. The hole torn into the wall trapped the ox. After struggling frantically for a short while, the ox collapsed and died.

When the spectators returned their attention to the Hawk King, they saw an enormous blood-dripping heart in his hand. With an audible chortle, he opened his mouth and sank his teeth into it, making a loud crunching sound.

It was a chilling sound.

Hai Lingzi frowned, turning away from the spectacle.

The Hawk King laughed harshly. "There's no need to frown. You're not ready to eat a fresh ox's heart yet. To reach this state, you'll have to spend eight, maybe ten years practicing the Strength of Hawk's Talon."

A look of contempt flickered across Hai's long face. "I don't need to learn the so-called Strength of Hawk's Talon," he said, in a monotonous voice.

The Hawk King glared at him. "You don't *need* to? You look down on my Strength of Hawk's Talon?"

Without warning, the Hawk King reached for Hai with his bloody hand.

Startled, Hai somersaulted and landed several yards away, his face ashen.

The Hawk King laughed aloud. "Kid, you don't have to be afraid. I was merely playing with you. Your master and I are good friends. I wouldn't hurt you."

Hai was in his fifties. It was an insult for him to be called a *kid*. His hands were shaking with anger, but he couldn't muster enough courage to draw his sword.

The cruelty, accuracy, and speed demonstrated by the Hawk King, in his Strength of Hawk's Talon, had been intimidating.

Seven dishes were served.

Ma Huihui's culinary skills were excellent. He was able to make beef taste like tender chicken, or like game, and sometimes even like tofu.

He could make beef taste like anything other than beef.

Ma served up the eighth dish himself, with a smile. "Though the food is not so good, the wine is not bad. Please enjoy the drinks."

The Hawk King slapped his hand on the table. "The wine is not good either," he snapped.

Ma was taken aback.

Luckily, Zhao Wuji explained. "Although the wine is excellent, it would taste even better if there were a lady to pour it for us."

"Exactly." The Hawk King grinned broadly. "You went to school for a few days after all. You know that good wine and beautiful women should always come together."

Ma grinned, too. "I thought of this myself. However, I'm afraid that our ordinary beauties won't meet your satisfaction."

The Hawk King frowned. "I heard this place is renowned for its women. Isn't there at least one extraordinary beauty?"

"There is one extraordinary beauty, but only one...." Ma muttered.

The Hawk King slapped the table again. "One is enough. Mr. Hai is a priest. Zhao Wuji is well-known for being a henpecked husband. Mr. Tu is too old. Don't worry about them."

"That's right." Tu laughed. "Find one for Mr. Sikong and that will be plenty. I will simply watch. For an old man like me, it's enough to merely have a look."

Zhao laughed, too. "For a henpecked man, it's better not to have even a look, but I will feel sorry for myself if I don't get to see what she is like. Manager Ma, please take care of this for us."

"I will be on my way," Ma mumbled. "It's just that...."

The Hawk King stared at him. "It's just ... what?"

Ma smiled respectfully. "This lady is famous for being difficult. She may not answer our call."

"That's all right." The Hawk King laughed. "I like difficult women. There must be something special about them. That's what makes them haughty."

Ma broke into a grin. "In that case, please wait a few moments."

"I don't mind waiting," said the Hawk King. "I have no patience, *except* for women."

Chapter 5

An Extraordinary Beauty

ALMOST TWO HOURS had passed. The alleged extraordinary beauty had not come.

Tu drank another cup of wine and shook his head. "She is, to be sure, a difficult woman."

The Hawk King shook his head, too, but he chuckled. "You don't understand women at all. No wonder you have been single all your life. Do you really think this woman is difficult?"

"Isn't she?"

"She's not being difficult. She's just playing hard to get."

"Hard to get?"

"Exactly. She knows men like challenges. The longer they have to wait for a woman, the more curious they are ... and the more desirable they assume her to be. Those women who respond eagerly don't excite men as much."

"What a shrewd observation!" Tu clapped and hooted. "I had no idea that Brother Sikong is a scholar of women, in addition to being a martial arts master."

The Hawk King snickered. "Understanding women is harder than learning martial arts."

Suddenly, he stopped laughing and perked up his ears. "Here she comes!" he whispered gleefully.

Then they heard soft footsteps from outside the room.

Even Hai turned, eager to see what this extraordinary beauty looked like.

The door was open, but a curtain blocked their view.

Below the curtain was a pair of feet.

The shoes worn on these feet were made of common blue cloth, but they had delicate shapes, making the feet appear exquisite.

Though the Hawk King could only see the woman's feet, he was already satisfied.

His large head swayed and his one glistening eye fixed on the shoes, almost popping out.

Someone outside said, "May I come in?"

The voice was aloof, yet as pleasant as the singing of a nightingale.

The Hawk King laughed. "Of course you can come in. Please do."

The feet didn't move. Instead, a hand reached from behind the curtain.

The fair-skinned hand had long tapered fingers. The fingernails were trimmed neatly and not polished with ground balsam, as with many other women.

The hand was not only pretty, it was distinctive.

The sight of it was enough to convince everyone that this woman was indeed extraordinary.

The Hawk King kept nodding and grinning. "Good! Great! Wonderful!"

The men saw the hand push the curtain open.

At length, the exceptional beauty revealed herself.

Tu had thought a woman this arrogant would be luxuriously dressed, heavily made up, and wearing lots of jewelry.

He was wrong.

This woman was dressed in a fitted light blue gown. She didn't seem to be wearing any makeup, and the only jewelry she wore was a small pair of pearl earrings.

Tu was surprised. He hadn't expected a prostitute to be dressed so plainly. Basically, she wasn't dressed up at all.

Though Tu wasn't a young man anymore, he knew little about women. In contrast, this woman knew men well.

She knew that the less she dressed up, the more she would stand out as a refreshing beauty.

There is something ironic about men's expectations. They like a whore not to act like a whore, but, rather, to act like a noble lady or the girl next door.

On the other hand, when they meet a decent woman, they wish she would act like a whore in bed.

As a result, those prostitutes who are decent women are usually tremendously popular. Similarly, those decent girls who act like whores in private are eagerly sought after as well.

Though Zhao was frightened of his wife, every henpecked man fools around sometime. Just as there is no cat that doesn't steal food, so there is no man who doesn't fool around.

He had met many prostitutes. As far as he could remember, when they walked in, they usually wore a sweet smile. A professional smile, of course.

But this woman was different.

Not only didn't she smile, she didn't talk either. After she came in, she simply sat on a chair, as quiet as a wooden doll.

Indeed, she was a striking beauty.

She didn't seem to be very young, but she was definitely not old either. Her eyes were sparkling and attractive.

The Hawk King narrowed his eyes and beamed. "Good. That's fine. Please have a seat."

"I'm seated," the woman snapped, without glancing at him.

"You're right. You're sitting. The way you sit is quite beautiful."

"Go ahead and have a good look. I'm here to be ogled."

The Hawk King gleefully smacked the table. "Old man, look! See how interesting this woman is? Even her words are well-presented She is bold enough to rebuff me."

If someone else had rebuffed him, he would have smashed open his skull. Yet when this woman rebuffed him, he was amused.

Alas! How remarkable women are!

Tu smiled, too. "Ma'am, could you tell us your name?"

"Seniang," she replied.

"Seniang?" The Hawk King laughed. "No wonder you are so unhappy. You miss your mother. Is she as pretty as you?" *Se* means "to think" or "to miss," and *Niang* means "female" or "mother." He was teasing her.

Without saying anything, Seniang rose and started toward the door.

"Wait! *Wait*!" he bellowed. "Where are you going?"

"I'm leaving."

"Leaving! You're leaving?" He scowled. "But, you just got here!"

"Though I'm a fallen woman, my mother is not," she said icily. "I'm not here to listen to you mock her."

Seniang knew men. She knew that the more distinguished and eminent a man was, the more he liked disobedient women, as he met too many people who were subservient to him.

Only those who seldom had contact with women liked submissive females who were eager to please.

It was true that the Hawk King didn't get angry with her. In fact, he grinned even more broadly. "Right, right, right! From now on, whoever makes fun of your mother, I will break his neck."

Grudgingly, Seniang reseated herself.

"So, you don't like to be teased," Zhao said. "What do you like?"

"I like everything, and I dislike everything."

The Hawk King chortled. "Well said. When you talk, you sound more pleasing than when others sing."

"Your talking is charming." Zhao grinned. "I believe your singing must be even more charming. Could you sing us a song and delight our ears?"

"I cannot sing," she said.

"Then ... could you play us the zither?"

"No."

"How about playing the banjo?"

"No."

Zhao broke into a laugh. "Then ... exactly what *can* you do?"

"I'm here to be your drinking companion. I can drink."

"Wonderful!" The Hawk King laughed heartily. "That's enough. I like women who can drink."

Indeed, Seniang was a very good drinker. Zhao planned to get her drunk. He wanted to see what she would be like in that condition.

The more Seniang drank, however, the brighter her eyes became. She didn't seem to be getting drunk at all. Zhao stopped challenging her.

The Hawk King did not force her to drink. He was a man who knew how to appreciate beauty. He wanted his woman to be tipsy, but not dead drunk.

He also knew the importance of timing.

When it was about time, he pretended to be drunk.

Zhao knew what was expected of him. "Brother Sikong," he said with a smile, "you must be tired from our long journey. I suppose you are overcome by alcohol by now, as well?"

The Hawk King immediately stood up. "Yes, you're right. I'm drunk and sleepy."

"Manager Ma has reserved a nice, quiet room for you behind the restaurant," Zhao said. "Ma'am, would you mind escorting Brother Sikong to his room?"

Seniang gave him a cold stare but didn't refuse. She held the Hawk King's arm and started to walk, as if accustomed to such things.

Tu spoke sarcastically. "I thought she was somewhat different. Evidently, she is like all the other women."

"Basically, all women are alike," Zhao said. "Women like her become whores to make money. What's the point in refusing?"

"It's just that the way she sells her service is quite ... unusual," Tu said.

The room Ma had prepared for the Hawk King was definitely quiet.

Upon entering it, Seniang pushed the Hawk King away. "You should have sobered up by now," she said, her voice icy.

"How can anyone sober up so fast?"

She was not to be humored. "You were not drunk. Do you think I didn't notice?"

The Hawk King sobered up a little. "Sober is drunk. Drunk is sober," he said with a laugh. "Life is like a stage. Does the difference matter?"

He found the kettle and drank some water from the spout. "Wine is thicker than water," he mumbled. "Water doesn't taste as good as wine."

Seniang's stare was aloof. "Now that I've walked you back here, what else do you want?"

He picked up one of her hands, grinning nastily. "You don't know what a man wants at a time like this?"

Shaking off his hand, she retorted, "What makes you think I'm that kind of woman? What makes you think I'd do something like that for you?"

The Hawk King laughed. "This does."

He took out a gold ingot, threw it onto the table, and glanced at her sideways. "Do you want it or not?"

"If it weren't for the money, who would want to be used like ... a wine jar?"

"So you want money," he laughed. "Well, that's easy."

He held her hand again, but she shook it off once more. "Yes, I want money, but I like to pick the right men."

"What do you want? A handsome man?" he asked, agitated.

"I have seen too many handsome men. I want a real man."

The Hawk King flashed a broad grin. "In that case, I am your best choice. I am a real man."

Seniang eyed him up and down. "I want a remarkable man. Are you remarkable?"

"Of course I am."

"Let me see what's so remarkable about you. If you can convince me, I'll be happy to follow you even without the money."

He laughed loudly. "As you don't know me, you don't know what's so remarkable about me. In the martial world, whoever hears my name does whatever I ask."

"Everyone can brag."

"You don't believe me? Let me prove it to you."

He cut off a corner of the table with his hand as if cutting tofu with a knife.

"Your kung fu is not bad," said Seniang. "But ... that's not enough."

He snickered. "Whether it's enough for you or not, I can't wait any longer. Come here!"

He pulled her closer, holding her to him in an embrace. Seniang closed her eyes without struggling. "You are strong. If you want to rape me, I can't resist. But a real man makes a woman follow him of her own will."

His mouth had stopped moving, but his hand was very busy. Though he had only one hand, he groped faster than men with two.

"How dare you say you're a real man?" Seniang sneered indignantly. "It turns out that you simply terrorize women. Men who enjoy bullying women are not only shameless but worthless. I didn't think you were that kind of man."

The Hawk King panted and snarled. "What kind of man did you think I was?"

"Although you're ugly, you seemed like a hero. That's why I came here with you. If someone else had gotten drunk and collapsed on the floor, I wouldn't have bothered to help him up."

She gave a soft sigh. "It looks like I was wrong about you. I cannot blame anyone but myself. Very well. Let's get it over with. This won't take too long anyway."

The Hawk King's hand stopped groping; he appeared to be confused.

After a moment, he started to his feet, shouting, "What on earth do you want me to do?"

Seniang sat up, pulling her clothes back on. "I know you're good at martial arts and you kill people. Everyone is afraid of you. But none of that really counts as remarkable."

"What does?"

"I heard people say that the more competent a man is, the more he is able to control his temper and hide his talent. Over a thousand years ago, Han Xin was forced to crawl between a street thug's legs. He endured this humiliation and eventually succeeded in helping Liu Bang establish the glorious Han Dynasty. If he had killed the thug in a mad rage, who would admire him today?"

The Hawk King laughed. "Do you want me to follow Han Xin's example and crawl between your legs?"

Seniang released an amused giggle.

With a straight face, she was merely a wooden beauty. Yet when a smile spread over her, she looked luscious and appetizing. Any man who was not mesmerized by her sweet smile had to be dead.

The Hawk King was not a dead man. He grinned with gawking eyes. "I—Sikong Shu—have been a hero all my life, but if you want me to crawl between your legs, I'll do it."

Seniang smiled pleasantly. "That's not what I meant. It's just that...."

Her eyes twinkled and she went on to explain, "Though I can't beat you, if you let me merely ... hit you ... and still refuse to fight back, that will prove to me you are a real man ... a manly man."

"That's easy," the Hawk King laughed. "Give me a slap in the face. What does it matter?"

"Really?"

"Of course. Go ahead and hit me. Hit me hard. It doesn't matter."

"In that case," she smiled, "I'm going to hit you. Ready?"

She rolled up her sleeve, revealing her wrist, as fair as translucent white jade.

The Hawk King stayed motionless, waiting to be hit.

This is what men are like. Poor men! In order to prove to women how macho and brave they are, they will do anything.

Seniang smiled radiantly, and slowly raised her hand.

Seniang moved her hand very slowly and gently, but when her hand almost touched the Hawk King's face, her fingers sprang out all at once, attacking four of his major meridian points.

Obviously, the Hawk King had never expected something like this to happen to him. When he realized what was going on, it was too late. He had become as paralyzed as a wooden doll.

Seniang's giggle was like the tinkle of a bell. "One-Armed Hawk King, you do have the aura of a hero. You have my deepest admiration."

The Hawk King glared at her, his eyes flashing fire. But he couldn't utter a single word, as his face was completely numb.

"Don't feel bad or angry," she said. "No matter how smart a man is, he often becomes a moron at the sight of a pretty woman. That's why young ladies can fool very cunning old bastards. Things like this happen all the time."

While still talking, she had started to search the Hawk King.

He was wearing a loose robe.

The yellow bundle he had been carrying was hidden in it.

When Seniang found the bundle, her eyes sparkled with excitement.

She opened the bundle and saw … a saber box.

The sword in the box was as shiny as newly-fallen snow!

She gazed at the saber, muttering, "Xiao Shiyi Lang, you thought I couldn't capture this saber all by myself. You underestimated me and you underestimate women. Men will never realize how powerful women can be."

Oh! What a remarkable woman!

What a remarkable woman was … Feng Siniang!

But … Feng Siniang was a woman after all.

When women see something they desire, they often ignore potential risks.

Most dirty old men know this weakness. They often use dazzling gifts to conceal their evil intentions.

Feng focused all her attention on the saber, so much so that she did not notice the wicked smirk on the Hawk King's face.

When she was turning to leave, it was too late.

The Hawk King's long arm stretched out with lightning speed

to grab her wrist. One side of her body was numbed immediately. The saber clattered to the ground.

The attack had caught her off guard.

The Hawk King chuckled derisively. "If you think I'm a moron, you underestimated me and you underestimate men. Women will never realize how powerful *men* can be."

Feng's heart plummeted, but her face still wore a smile. The only weapon she had left was her smile.

She cast a sidelong glance at the Hawk King and smiled charmingly. "Why do you have to be so upset? Isn't it exciting to be fooled by a woman once in a while? If you take it too seriously, it takes the fun out of it."

The Hawk King's returning smile mocked hers. "Isn't it also fun for women to be raped by men *once in a while?*"

He tightened his grip and Feng's entire body became anesthetized and lost strength. He turned his hand and flung her body to the bed.

With a nasty smile on his face, the Hawk King advanced toward her. She clenched her jaws and used all her power, in an attempt to kick him.

Before her foot could touch him, it was seized by his talon-like hand. He twisted it, and she was sure her ankle had broken. It hurt so much that she had to fight back tears.

Her thin blue cloth shoes were torn apart, revealing her feet— delicate, translucent, and flawless.

Captivated by the sight of her feet, the Hawk King murmured, "What beautiful feet! What beautiful...."

Much to Feng's dismay, he lowered his head and used his nose to stroke one of her soles.

There are no women whose feet are not ticklish. The Hawk King's bristly beard pricked her sole. A current of heat seemed to flow from her sole to the bottom of her heart. She was shocked, frightened, outraged, and ... disgusted.

She couldn't bear the sensation any longer.

Although almost exploding with anger, she could not help giggling through her tears. She was laughing and cursing. "Beast! Beast! You old beast! Let go of me...."

She spewed out all of the most venomous insults she could think of, but she still couldn't keep from giggling.

The Hawk King stared at her, his eyes shining with lust. He tore apart the clothes covering her chest and revealed her fair breasts.

She almost passed out. Feeling the Hawk King's body sitting on her, she could do nothing but make her legs stick together, refusing to separate them.

The Hawk King hissed, "You bitch! You asked for it and you're gonna get it!"

His hand gripped her throat.

She could barely breathe, let alone struggle or fight. She was losing consciousness ... her body was losing strength ... her legs were starting to loosen....

All at once, the nearest window was rammed open, hitting the floor with a thud.

A man in blue jumped into the room to swoop up the saber lying on the floor.

The Hawk King was a seasoned fighter. Even in this situation, he didn't lose his head. He made a reverse somersault and grabbed at the intruder's head with his long arm.

Without enough time to pick up the saber, the man in blue backed up a few steps.

With a click, the Hawk King's arm grew by almost two feet! Now his arm could reach where it couldn't before.

A surprise attack like this was nearly impossible to evade. It was the trademark skill that had enabled the Hawk King to intimidate the Martial Order.

The man in blue, however, was even faster. He spun and used the edge of his palm to cut the Hawk King's wrist. Then he kicked the saber over to Feng.

Feng held her torn clothes with her left hand and caught the sword with her right one. "Thanks, both of you!" she cried, with a triumphant smile.

She leaped out of the window.

The man in blue sighed and reached behind him. In a flash, he drew a shining saber, chopping at the Hawk King's shoulder.

His saber was stunningly fast.

The Hawk King had been around for several decades, but he had never seen anyone wield a saber so fast. He couldn't clearly see how it moved. He leaped backward, shouting, "Who are you?"

The man in blue didn't respond. Instead, he relentlessly pressed his attack. Surrounded by the interwoven lights reflecting off the blade and with little room for escape, the Hawk King managed to dodge several strokes. Then he broke into a wild laugher. *"Xiao Shiyi Lang*! It's *you*!"

The man in blue laughed, too. "Hawk King, you have a quick eye!"

In laughter, he and his saber seemed to have merged. Following a flash of his sword, he flew out of the window.

The Hawk King shouted and stormed out behind him.

All was quiet outside. The dark sky gleamed with autumn stars. Xiao was nowhere to be found!

Feng was mumbling and swearing under her breath as she changed her clothes. It was hard to tell who or what she was cursing.

Yet she didn't appear upset. In fact, she looked rather cheerful. When she observed the saber box on the bed, she couldn't resist a smile of pure delight.

She had finally gotten the Deer Carver, which she had coveted day and night.

To acquire it, she had organized her plan carefully. She had arrived at the town several days beforehand, knowing for sure that Zhao Wuji and his posse would pass through it.

She had rented a secluded house just outside the town, and then visited Ma Huihui, to ask for his help. Ma had always cherished loyalty to friends, and he owed her a favor. There was no way he could have refused her request.

But the One-Armed Hawk King had been difficult to deal with.

She would have failed and gotten herself ruined, if it hadn't been for Xiao Shiyi Lang.

The thought of Xiao made her fume.

She was fastening her last button, when she heard someone outside draw a long sigh and lament.

"I will advise everyone never to make friends with a woman or do her any favor. You try to help her, and she just runs away, leaving you hanging there alone."

When Feng heard the voice, her face burned. Somehow, she ripped out the button she had just done up. She was so angry she could have kicked a hole in the window.

But, she rolled her eyes and refrained. Instead, she started to giggle. "Exactly. I wish the Hawk King had hung you up and ripped your heart out so everyone could see how black it is."

The window was pushed ajar, revealing half of Xiao's face. He broke into a grin. "Whose heart is black? Mine or yours?"

"How dare you! *My* heart? I sincerely asked for your help, and you refused it with silly excuses. I came here and you followed me. I had almost made it, and then you showed up to grab the easy prize. So you tell me ... are you *a good thing*?"

The more Feng said, the more furious she grew. Finally, exploding with rage, she leaped up and smashed a hole in the window, as though it were Xiao's face.

Xiao had already moved. He flashed another grin. "Of course I'm not a good *thing*. I'm a *person*. How can I be a *thing*?" *A good thing* is Chinese slang that means "a decent person" when used to describe people. Xiao pretended that he didn't understand what Feng meant.

"Perhaps I shouldn't have come," he groused. "I should have let that bigheaded fellow sniff at your smelly feet and get gassed to death. It would have saved me a lot of—"

"Bullshit!" Feng shrieked. "How do you know my feet stink? Have you ever smelled them?"

"Of course not," Xiao laughed. "I'm not as enthusiastic about your feet."

Feng realized she was embarrassing herself by continuing on

this topic. Color rose heatedly to her cheeks. "Even if you did do me a favor, I'm not going to thank you. You didn't come for me, you came for the saber."

"Is that so?"

"If you had come to save me, why did you go after the saber first?"

Xiao shook his head. "This woman doesn't even know the usefulness of subterfuge," he mumbled to himself wryly. "Let me ask you," he said to Feng. "If I hadn't gone for the saber first, would he have let go of you so easily?"

No words could contest Xiao's analysis.

What Xiao had said made sense. If he had not gone for the saber and had attacked the Hawk King instead, the Hawk King might have hurt her.

"If there were a rat crawling over your favorite crystal cup," Xiao added, "would you throw a stone at the cup, possibly breaking it?"

"All right, I admit that you are silver-tongued," Feng declared, with a deadpan face.

Xiao burst into laughter. "Deep down you know you're wrong. You're just too proud to admit it."

"How do you know what I think? Are you a parasite in my belly?"

"In your heart, you've admitted your mistake and feel grateful to me. That's why you're speaking so harshly ... to cover up your feelings. That's all right. As long as you're grateful in your heart, you don't have to say a word."

Though she was still trying to keep a straight face, Feng couldn't suppress a smile.

A woman's heart is strange. When dealing with men she doesn't like, her heart can be harder than steel. When dealing with a man she is fond of, however, it is impossible to harden her heart.

Xiao had been gazing at her, seemingly hypnotized.

Feng stared back and giggled. "What are you gawking at?"

"This is something you don't understand. A woman looks best

when she is trying to resist a laugh but can't. How could I miss this terrific sight?"

"Stop playing up to me," she chided him lightheartedly. "I know exactly what's on your mind."

"Wow! Since when have you become a parasite in *my* belly?"

"You're not happy empty-handed, so you want to get something from me. Right?"

"Not really. It's just that...."

He smiled a little and changed the subject. "Well, now that you have the Deer Carver, why would you want to keep the Blue Jade?"

She laughed. "I knew you were itching for that sword. All right ... since you're being so respectful, I will give it to you."

She retrieved the sword and tossed it out the window.

Grinning, Xiao reached up with both hands to catch it. "I'm much obliged," he said.

He drew the sword, stroking it gently. "What a fine blade! Unfortunately," he muttered to himself, "it's only meant for women."

"By the way," Feng asked, "what do you want with this woman's sword?"

"I'm going to give it to a woman," he replied cheerily.

She glowered at him. "What woman?"

"I don't know yet. But don't worry. Sooner or later I will find a woman worthy of this sword."

Feng bit her lip. "All right," she said, brooding, "but could you at least let me know when you find her?"

"No problem. I'll go find her now."

Just as he turned around to leave, Feng cried, "Wait!"

He turned back slowly. "How else may I help you?" he asked.

She picked up the Deer Carver from her bed. "Don't you want to take a look at this?"

"No."

"Why not?" she asked, surprised by his terse reply.

Xiao smiled. "Because, if my guess is correct, that saber is probably a fake."

"A *fake?*" she echoed, stunned. "What makes you think it's a fake?"

"Let me ask you, Siniang. Considering Zhao Wuji, Tu Xiaotian, and Hai Lingzi ... which one is easier to deal with?"

"None of them are decent men," she said in disgust.

"Then why did they degrade themselves by imploring such a scumbag as the Hawk King to help them and by allowing him to insult them? They entrusted him with the saber and agreed to let him take all of the credit, if the mission were accomplished. Why would such a powerful figure as Zhao Wuji do something so ... irrational?"

"Why?"

"Because they used the Hawk King as a scapegoat ... a decoy!"

"A decoy?" Feng frowned.

"They knew that many people who coveted this saber would lay in ambush along the way, so they gave a fake saber to Sikong Shu. Everyone's attention would be focused on the fake sword, making it easier for them to escort the real saber to its destination."

Xiao exhaled before continuing. "Think about it. If they had not been aware that the saber was a fake, why didn't they come to the Hawk King's assistance while we were having our fierce fight?"

"Um ... maybe it was because they didn't want to disturb Sikong. Maybe they stayed somewhere else for the night. Ma Huihui only prepared a quiet room for Sikong."

Xiao shook his head and smirked. "If the saber Sikong had been carrying were the original, would they have felt comfortable leaving him alone?"

Feng was left speechless for several minutes. All at once, she drew the saber and cried, "Whatever you say, I refuse to believe this is a fake!"

The saber was polished and impressive.

But when they took a closer look, they realized its burnish was very similar to that of the cheap jewelry worn by young girls.

Xiao drew the Blue Jade. "If you don't believe me, let's test it."

Clenching her teeth, Feng flew out of the window and slashed at the Blue Jade with the coveted saber.

With a clang, the long blade snapped.

Feng was horrified. What was left in her hand dropped to the ground. Though people said she never aged, she seemed to age several years in mere seconds.

Xiao shook his head and mumbled, "Women are said to be smarter than men, but why do they fall for men's tricks?"

Abruptly, Feng stamped her feet and cried, "You *knew* the saber was a fake, yet you fooled me into giving Blue Jade to you. You're a thief ... a pickpocket!"

"It's true that I shouldn't have fooled you," Xiao sighed. "But, I know a girl. She's intelligent, beautiful, and free-spirited. I haven't seen her for quite a while. I want to give her a present to cheer her up."

"Who is she?" Feng glared at him.

Gazing at her, Xiao spoke slowly and with an affectionate smile. "Her name is ... Feng Siniang. Do you know her?"

Instantly, she felt a wave of heat rising within her. All her anger vanished. She leaned against the window limply, her lips twisting. "You ... Well ... With you as my friend, I'm doomed. You will take at least thirty years off my life."

Grinning broadly, Xiao offered her Blue Jade with both his hands. "Though you didn't get the Deer Carver, you got Blue Jade as a gift. Don't you think you should still be pleased?"

Chapter 6

The Heart of a Pretty Woman

JINAN WAS A famous city, highly populated with people from all walks of life, and nowhere in Jinan could you find more types of people and more gossip than in teahouses.

Although Feng seldom spent time in teahouses, every time she did, she enjoyed it. She liked having men gaze at her.

It's a great pleasure for a woman to be the center of a man's attention.

Not surprisingly, most of the men in this teahouse were staring at her. Few women went to teahouses, let alone beautiful women.

Feng slowly sipped her tea from a small cup with a cover. It was not fine tea. She usually didn't drink this brand, but today she seemed unwilling to put it down.

She was not really savoring the tea. She simply thought the way she drank it was graceful, and she wanted people to admire her elegant hands.

Xiao was looking at her too ... in amusement.

He had known her for many years and he knew her well.

Although she was tough and cranky, sometimes the so-called Enchantress could be as naïve as a child.

Xiao was fond of her, and he had always enjoyed her company, but somehow he never felt sad when it was time to part.

Exactly what kind of relationship they had he couldn't say.

They had come to Jinan, because the Deer Carver was coming here.

Many other well-known figures had also come to the city.

All of a sudden, the men who had been ogling Feng turned their attention outside. Some craned their necks to see, and some even stood up and ran to the door.

Is there a woman outside even more beautiful than I am? Feng wondered with surprise.

A little annoyed but also a little curious, she wanted a look, too, and she never hesitated to do exactly what she wanted.

Outside, she found everyone staring at a carriage.

This carriage was somewhat more luxurious than ordinary ones, but there wasn't anything particularly special about it. All of its doors and windows were tightly closed. Feng couldn't see who was inside.

The vehicle was not going fast. The driver was cautious. He didn't even raise his whip high, as if afraid he might lash passing pedestrians.

Though the horses drawing the carriage were moving well, they were not exactly thoroughbreds.

Everyone was still staring at this carriage, however. Some were whispering excitedly to each other, as if a big morning glory were growing out of the carriage's top.

These people would rather gawk at this old carriage than look at me! Feng was mystified. Was there something wrong with the men in this city?

"Haven't they ever seen a carriage?" she remarked, her voice filled with contempt.

The men beside her threw her a glance, but then continued to watch the carriage. Only a hunchbacked old man grinned and said, "Young lady, you don't understand. Though there's nothing special about the carriage, the person inside is a most important individual in this town."

"Really? Who is it?"

"A truly famous person. She is Miss Shen Bijun, the only descendant of the Gold Needle Shens, and she is said to be the fairest woman in the Martial Order."

A smile flooded his face as if he were sharing the glory by talking about this lady. Then he added, "Oh, I have made a mistake.

She's not Miss Shen anymore. We should call her Mrs. Lian instead. Young lady, you seem to be well-traveled. You must know Flawless Manor of Gusu, the most respected house south of the Yangtze River. Ms. Shen's husband is Mr. Lian Chengbi, the master of Flawless Manor."

"Lian Chengbi … the name rings a bell," Feng said nonchalantly.

As a matter of fact, she had heard a lot about it.

The name commanded enormous respect in the martial world of late. Even his enemies could not help respecting him.

The old man went on enthusiastically. "Ms. Shen got married a couple years ago. She came back here last month, to visit her family. The folks in this town want to see whether she has grown even more beautiful in the last two years. Unfortunately, as a cultured lady, she was taught to be modest and stay at home. In the past twenty years, I have seen her face only a couple of times."

Feng sneered again. "So, for you folks in Jinan, Ms. Shen must be the apple of your eye."

The old man didn't notice the sarcasm in her voice. "Exactly. You can say that again," he said, beaming and nodding.

"But … she's behind closed curtains. Did you get a good look this time?"

The old man narrowed his eyes into the semblance of a smile. "Even if we can't see her face, we feel happy to merely look at her carriage."

Just as Feng was becoming green with envy, the carriage turned and went out of sight. A few customers started to walk back to their seats.

Some were still talking about Shen. "Did you see that? Since returning, she has come out only once. Whoever is married to her must have done a lot of good deeds in his past lives."

"But Mr. Lian is equally outstanding. He is well-educated, well-mannered, good-looking, and he belongs to a highly respected family. What's more, I heard that he is one of the finest martial artists in China. Where could you find a more ideal husband?"

"That's what I call a marriage made in heaven."

Every word was about how wonderful Lian Chengbi and Shen

Bijun were. According to them, Lian and Shen were about the only perfect couple in the world.

Tired of hearing about this perfect couple, Feng decided to ask Xiao to pick up the tab so that they could leave. Just as she was turning toward the teahouse, she caught a glimpse of someone!

Diagonally opposite the teahouse was a bank called Yuanji.

Travelers and businessmen often found it inconvenient to carry silver ingots with them; they preferred to purchase bank notes. Notes issued by banks with good credit were accepted everywhere. Banks with poor credit did not survive long. Bank notes were popular at the time and all of the banks enjoyed excellent credit.

Most bankers were from Shanxi. People from this province were generally frugal and good at managing money. Yuanji was the biggest bank in the district.

The man Feng saw was just leaving Yuanji.

He was about thirty years old, with a square face and a square mouth, and he was dressed in an ordinary light blue silk robe and a dark blue jacket. On his feet were sturdy white socks and blue shoes. All in all, he was dressed so neatly that he looked like a freshly-made pancake. He gave the appearance of an honest and upright man who could be trusted with anything.

Nonetheless, no sooner had Feng seen him than she covered her face and turned away, lowering her head, like a tenant trying to evade her landlord.

It happened that this man also had sharp eyes. When he spotted Feng, his eyes sparkled and he called out, "Siniang! Siniang! *Feng Siniang!*"

His voice was so loud that even people from three blocks away could hear him.

Feng had to stop. "What rotten luck!" she groaned. "Why did I have to bump into this pathetic loser today?"

The man hitched up his robe, rushing across the street in her direction.

It seemed that the moment he saw Feng, he stopped seeing any-thing else. A carriage, which had just turned the corner, was coming straight at him, too fast to stop. It appeared that it was going to run him over.

The people in the teahouse gasped in horror. To their surprise, the man took a step back, holding on to the running vehicle by the yoke. It ground to a halt.

His feet were planted firmly on the ground and his arms seemed strong enough to lift a thousand pounds. A great cheer arose from the crowd on the street.

He didn't seem to hear it. Instead, he saluted the frightened driver with touching fists and apologized.

Then he ran toward the teahouse. "*Siniang*, I finally found you!" he cried, with a broad smile of relief on his square face.

Feng gave him a cold stare. "Why were you making such a fuss? People will think I owe you a ton of money, the way you were yelling and shouting."

"I ... I wasn't yelling or shouting." he said with an embarrassed smile.

"What do you want?" she snorted.

"N-nothing."

She glared at him. "Nothing? Then why did you call me?"

He nervously wiped the perspiration from his brow. "I-I just thought ... that it has been a while, s-since we last met, s-so ... I...."

Whenever he got nervous, he stuttered. The more he stammered, the more difficult it was for him to speak. He was supposed to be a man of genteel appearance, but now he looked more like a silly goose.

Feng broke into a laugh. "Even if we haven't met for a long time, you shouldn't stand in the middle of the road shouting at the top of your voice. Understand?"

Relieved by her laugh, he smiled cautiously. "Are ... are you a-alone?"

"No, I have a companion," she said, pointing at Xiao, who was still sitting inside.

The man's face fell, burning with agitation. He scowled ferociously at Xiao, as if eager to eat him up. "Wh-who is he?"

Feng glared at him. "What does it matter to you who he is? Why do you care?"

He was so tense that he blushed to the very roots of his hair. At that moment, Xiao stepped over and said, "I'm her cousin. And you are ... ?"

At the sound of "cousin," the man relaxed again and was now able to speak clearly. He brought his hands together in salute. "So you're Feng Siniang's cousin. That's wonderful. I'm very pleased to make your acquaintance. My name is Yang Kaitai."

Xiao seemed a bit surprised. "Are you Lord Yang, the owner of Yuanji, also known as Iron Gentleman?"

Yang smiled. "Yes, but I'm afraid my reputation is somewhat overrated."

Xiao returned his smile. "It's a pleasure to meet you."

Xiao was surprised, not because this man was the boss of Yuanji—one of the biggest banks in China, but because Yang was the only secular disciple of Master Tieshan, the abbot of Shaolin Monastery. Yang's Shaolin Divine Boxing was said to have reached ninety percent of its potential. Of the secular disciples of Shaolin Monastery, he was believed to be the finest.

It was hard to believe that a man so clumsy in the presence of Feng could be a top fighter whose kung fu prowess was well-known throughout Guanzhong.

Yang's eyes shifted to Feng. "Why don't you two take a seat so we can talk?" he said courteously.

"We were just leaving," Feng said.

"L-leaving? Wh-where are you going?"

Feng rolled her eyes at him. "We were simply going to find some-one to treat us to lunch."

"Why b-bother to find someone? I-I...."

She glared at him out of the corner of her eyes. "Are you going to treat us?"

"Of course. Of course. I-I heard the pork chop noodles in the restaurant next door are quite good. And their steamed buns are white and soft...."

"I can afford to eat pork chop noodles myself," Feng said dryly. "I don't need you to treat me. You may go now."

Yang wiped his brow again. "Wh-whatever you want, it would be my p-pleasure," he said, with a submissive smile.

"Well, if you're serious, we should go to Guest-Pleasing Chamber. I would love to try their pickled pork intestines."

"All r-right." Yang set his jaw. "L-let's go to Guest-Pleasing Chamber."

Every city has a few luxurious restaurants. They are especially expensive, but their business is also especially brisk. Rich people need to show off their wealth.

Dining at an especially expensive restaurant makes a person feel proud and important.

A serving of pickled pork intestines was five pennies at Guest-Pleasing Chamber, whereas the same dish might be only two pennies at other restaurants. The former did not necessarily taste better than the latter, but some people insisted that there was a distinctive difference between them.

From the time they began to walk up the stairs until the time they sat down, Yang wiped his forehead at least seven or eight times.

Feng began ordering. After she had ordered four or five dishes, Yang's face started to turn pale. He got up and said, "I-I must step out for a minute. I ... I'll be right back."

Feng ignored him and continued to order. Before Yang could reach the ground floor, she had ordered sixteen or seventeen dishes. When she finally stopped, she said to Xiao, "Guess why he left?"

Xiao smiled. "To get money?"

"That's right," she said, returning his smile. "People like him never carry more than a tael of silver."

"That doesn't matter. He's a gentleman. You shouldn't take advantage of him."

"*Gentleman*! You mean Iron Gentleman?" She scoffed. "I think he's as cheap as an iron *rooster*, who wouldn't shed even a feather for the sake of others. He's just like his father. Such people deserve to be ripped off."

"At least he's generous to you. He'd shed a whole duck ... for you."

"I want to scare him away by spending as much of his money as possible."

She curled her lips and griped, "You have no idea how annoying he is. Since we met at Lady Wang's birthday banquet, he has latched onto me, following me everywhere ... like a puppy."

"I think he seems pretty nice. He's honest, decent, and upright. He comes of a wealthy family, and his kung fu is excellent. I think you should marry him."

"Kiss my ass!" she snapped back. "Even if every other man in the world were dead, I wouldn't marry an iron rooster like him."

Xiao sighed and laughed wryly. "Women are funny. Before they marry, they want their future husbands to be as generous and open-minded as possible, but after they marry, they want their husbands to be as tight-fisted as possible. Their ideal arrangement is for their husbands to give all their money to them and not waste any on treating guests to dinner."

Yang didn't return until the second dish had been served. When he came in, a middle-aged man with a sparse beard, who was seated in another corner, rose and saluted him with touching fists.

Yang returned his salute. They were courteous to each other.

The middle-aged man was alone. He was dressed tastefully but not luxuriously. The black sword that hung at his waist didn't seem ordinary. His eyes were radiant and penetrating. It was obvious that he was accustomed to giving orders.

Feng had noticed the man even before Yang returned. "Who is he?" she asked him.

"You don't know him? That's strange."

"Why should I know him?"

Yang lowered his voice. "He is Liu Seqing, the disciple of Father Gu of Bashan. When it comes to swordplay agility, few people can match him."

Feng's countenance changed. "I heard he has acquired the essence of Forty-Nine-Hand Whirlwind Dancing Swallow Sword from

Father Gu. He is said to be even better than his master. Have you ever seen his kung fu in action?"

"He's a modest man who always keeps to himself. Few people in the martial world know him personally, but he's a good friend of Brother Jinghu from the Songshan School. That's how I got to know him."

When Yang talked about something else, he was coherent and articulate. Only when the conversation touched on the relationship between him and Feng would he become tongue-tied.

Feng cast Xiao a look, then said to Yang, "It seems that many legendary bigwigs have come to Jinan."

"That's right," Yang smiled. "In addition to Liu Seqing and me, there are Li Gang, Xu Qingteng, Zhu Baishui, and Lian Chengbi."

"Does that mean you're a legendary bigwig, too?" Feng teased him.

"I-I ... I...."

He was at a loss for words again.

Lian Chengbi, Liu Seqing, Zhu Baishui, Xu Qingteng, Li Gang, and Yang Kaitai were, indeed, renowned celebrities. Among the apprentices who had emerged in the past decade, few could compare with these six, in terms of reputation or kung fu.

None of them was an old man. Even Li Gang, the oldest of them, was only in his forties. They all belonged to highly-respected families, and they were all righteous men who did noble deeds. Even Wooden Oldster, a notorious old curmudgeon, admitted that these six were worthy of being called Ideal Gentlemen.

After he said so, everyone started to refer to them as the Six Ideal Gentlemen.

Feng cast Xiao another look. Xiao kept his eyes lowered and drank his wine without saying anything. She turned to Yang again. "What brought you to Jinan today?"

Yang wiped his sweat and stammered, "S-someone invited us to come h-here."

"Who is powerful and important enough to invite all of you?"

"The invitation was issued by Sikong Shu, Zhao Wuji, Hai Lingzi,

Tu Xiaotian, and Master Xu Luzi. They invited us to view a saber at Shen Manor by the Daming Lake"

Feng's eyes sparkled. "What saber would that be?"

"The Deer Carver."

"Aren't they getting a little carried away asking all of you to come?"

"It's said to be an extraordinary saber, which took Master Xu his whole life to make. He's planning to give it to one of us, but he can't decide who that person should be."

"So he invited all of you over to see who's the best fighter, so that he can give the saber to the champion?"

"I guess so."

"You guys came all the way here just to fight each other over a mere saber? The alleged Six Ideal Gentlemen are so shameful," she taunted.

Yang blushed to his ears. "Actually, I-I'm not really interested in the s-saber. It's just ... it's just that...."

"I know what you mean," Xiao interrupted, with a light laugh. "Master Xu issued an invitation, and if you refuse to come, it will show that you don't have sufficient self-confidence. What you really care about is your honor, not the saber."

Yang grinned broadly. "Right. That's exactly what I'm saying."

"In addition," he went on, "Master Xu is not going to give the saber to us for nothing. Whoever wins the saber has to accept two conditions."

"The saber took his entire life to make," Feng remarked. "Even twenty conditions wouldn't be too much to ask."

Yang sighed. "I'm afraid that these two conditions are more difficult to meet than any other two-hundred conditions combined."

"Oh?"

"The first condition is that whoever is given the saber must carry it with him all his life, never letting it fall into the hands of another person. Easier said than done," he said with a wry smile. "Many people in the martial world have heard about the saber. Whoever gets the saber will gain instant fame and trigger an uproar. Carrying the saber is like carrying dynamite. It will bring nothing but endless trouble."

"That's true," Feng laughed. "Even I may want to join the fight."

"Compared to the second condition, though, the first is insignificant."

"Really? What else does he want you to do? Pull down the moon for him?"

"He demands that the person who gets this saber must promise to kill the most notorious bandit alive—"

"Who is that?" Feng asked, interrupting him.

"Xiao Shiyi Lang!"

Ten dishes had been served.

Yang suddenly noticed all of the dishes on the table and his face went pale. "Too many dishes. Too much food," he mumbled. "How can we finish all of this?"

Feng chided him. "What you just said should have been said by your guests. The host should say, 'I'm sorry. The food is not very good. There's not enough food. And so forth.' Don't you know even this basic rule of entertaining?"

Yang wiped his perspiration. "S-sorry, I ... I seldom entertain."

Feng was amused and laughed. "Although you're stingy, at least you're frank."

"Brother Yang," Xiao broke in, "do you know this ... Xiao Shiyi Lang?"

"No, I don't."

"Since you don't know him at all, even if you win this special saber, how could you find it in your heart to kill him with it?"

"Although I don't know him personally, I know he's the greatest villain alive. He deserves death. I wouldn't hesitate to kill a man like him."

"Have you ever personally seen him doing anything ... evil?"

"No. Not really. I ... I have just heard a lot about him."

"Even seeing is not necessarily believing. And you have only *heard* about his evil deeds. How can you be so sure of his alleged crimes?"

Yang had no answer for that. A moment later he broke into a weak smile. "Actually, even if I wanted to kill him, I might not be able to. Many people in the martial world have wanted to kill him, but he's still alive and well."

"Exactly," Feng said. "You'd better stay away from this mess. Otherwise, you might lose your honor *and* your head."

"Honestly speaking," sighed Yang, "I don't see much chance of my winning that saber."

"Who has the best chance ... in your opinion?"

Yang pondered the question. "Li Gang was the first to become famous. His Great Slab-Smashing Hand is fairly mature, but he's too straightforward, and his boxing style lacks flexibility and variation."

"In that case, he hasn't a chance."

"He may not even beat me."

"What about Xu Qingteng?"

"Xu Qingteng is the favorite disciple of the chief of the Wudang School. He's excellent in both boxing and swordplay. His Lightness Kung Fu is impressive, too. It is said that his swordplay demonstrates such a supple grace that it can be described as otherworldly or even heavenly. It's just that...."

"It's just what?"

"He's the hereditary General of Hangzhou. He eats well and lives well. Everything he uses is luxurious. Anyone who leads a life too comfortable has difficulty making progress in martial arts."

"So ... you don't think he stands much of a chance either?"

Yang acknowledged his agreement with silence.

"How about Zhu Baishui?" Feng asked. "I heard that he's learned the specialties of both the Emei School and the Diancang School. Besides, his mother is Madame Zhu, the Thousand-Hand Goddess of Mercy. She is a renowned expert in the use of hidden weapons. As the inheritor of her kung fu, Baishui is second to none in the launching and catching of projectiles."

"He's an absolute genius, but it's said that he's so wise and philosophical that he has renounced the world and decided to become a monk. This time, he may not even make the trip."

"What if he does come?"

"He has renounced the world. Even if he comes, his heart won't be in it."

"So ... he doesn't stand much of a chance, either?"

"No."

Feng stole a glance at Liu Seqing, who was sitting in another corner drinking alone. "How about him?" she whispered.

"His swordsmanship is extraordinary. There's no doubt about it. It's just that he's arrogant and tends to underestimate his opponents. What's more, if he can't beat his opponent within a hundred moves, he has a tendency to lose his composure."

Xiao smiled. "Your penetrating analyses are impressive, Brother Yang."

"If you're so good at analyzing the others," said Feng, "why don't you give an analysis of yourself?"

Yang squared his shoulders. "It has been twenty-one years since I became my master's disciple. In the past twenty-one years, rain or shine, I have insisted on a practice session in the morning and another session in the evening ... every day. I never skip my practice. I don't want to underestimate myself on purpose. In terms of the strength of my palms and the duration of my internal strength ... in all probability, few people can match me."

Xiao drew a sigh of admiration. "Brother Yang, you are worthy of being called an Ideal Gentleman. When you comment on things, you don't inflate your own importance by belittling the others. And you don't try to act like a saint by being overly modest. And—"

"And he can't hide what's on his mind," Feng interrupted, laughing. "Whatever he feels always shows on his face. For example, when he's asked to treat guests, his long face looks even uglier than a horse's."

Yang blushed again. "I-I ... I'm just...."

"You're stingy and overly cautious," Feng continued. "Though your internal strength is profound, your boxing style lacks an aggressive spirit. You are more interested in avoiding losses than in taking risks. It's difficult for others to beat you, but it's equally difficult for you to beat others."

Feng smiled and added, "Since you can dish it out, I'm sure you can take it ... right?"

Yang's face stayed flushed for a long while. "Siniang, you are close to my heart," he said, at last.

"I'm not so sure I can be considered close to your heart," Feng countered, "but I do know your weaknesses well."

Yang sighed. "It's because of this weakness that I feel I'm inferior to Lian Chengbi."

"Have you ever seen his kung fu in action?"

"No. Not many people in the martial world have seen him fight."

"Then how do you know his kung fu is superior to yours?" Feng asked.

"It's because he doesn't display his kung fu unnecessarily. People feel that his actual strength is an unfathomable mystery."

"People say that he's a real gentleman," Xiao added. "He was labeled a prodigy at the age of six. When he was ten, his swordsmanship was already regarded as professional. At eleven, he was good enough to fight with Tagen Sinki, the chief of One-Saber Gate from Japan. He remained undefeated even after three-hundred moves. After that, even the Japanese knew of the Chinese prodigy in martial arts."

Xiao produced a slight smile before continuing. "But I have also heard that Xiao Shiyi Lang is another martial arts prodigy. His saber style is unique. Since his entrance into the Martial Order, he has never been defeated. How does Mr. Lian compare with him?"

Yang replied, "Xiao's swordplay is swift as lightning and thunder, while Lian's swordplay is as graceful as a spring breeze and the gentle moon. Both have reached perfection. But as the saying goes, 'The soft always conquers the hard.' If there is anyone who can beat Xiao Shiyi Lang, that person is Lian Chengbi."

Xiao remained calm, with a fixed smile on his face. "According to you, one of them is *yang*—the hardest, and the other one is *yin*—the softest. They seem destined to be mutual enemies."

"But Xiao is inferior to Lian in several ways."

"Oh, really? I'm all ears."

"Lian comes from a highly-respected martial arts family. He is a righteous and thoughtful man, who never actively strives for fame or wealth. His reputation is so vast that he is worthy of being labeled a genuine hero. Wherever he goes, he receives great respect. He enjoys support and many advantages."

Feng bit her lip. "How about Xiao Shiyi Lang?"

"Xiao is an infamous bandit," said Yang. "He has no family or friends to speak of. Wherever he goes, no one will help him."

Though Xiao still wore a smile, it seemed somewhat bleak and aloof. He took up the wine, drinking it dry in one gulp. Then he burst into a loud laugh. "You're quite right. You could not be more right. Xiao Shiyi Lang is just a carriage driver's son. How can he compare with such a noble man as Lian Chengbi?"

"Lian has another thing that no one else has," Yang said.

"What?" Feng asked.

"He has a wonderful helper ... a great wife."

"You mean ... Shen Bijun?"

"That's right. As the granddaughter of Gold Needle Lady Shen, Mrs. Lian is not only an expert in the use of Golden Needles, but also a wise and virtuous wife."

"Too bad she's married," Feng commented. "Otherwise, you could chase her instead of me."

Yang blushed scarlet. "I-I ... I just...."

Feng sipped her wine slowly, while mumbling to herself. "I wonder how the Golden Needles of the Shens compare with my Silver Needles?"

Then she lifted her head and said, "When are you going to Shen Manor?"

"Tomorrow afternoon. Sikong Shu, who leads the escort, should arrive by tomorrow morning."

She rolled her eyes. "I wonder who else they've invited."

"Not too many guests were invited—"

Something struck him and he caught Feng's eye. "Do you want to go?"

She chuckled sarcastically. "No one has invited me. How can I go? I'm not that bold-faced."

"I can take you with me. I'll say you're my ... my...."

She stared at him. "Your *what?*"

Yang blushed. "F-friend."

Chapter 7

Awe-inspiring Lady Shen

SHEN MANOR WAS nestled among the hills beside the Daming Lake. One could imagine the family's long and glorious history by simply admiring the pair of stone lions at the gate.

There were not many servants in Shen Manor, but all of them were well-mannered and well-trained. No guests would consider themselves coldly received.

Several years before, Shen Jinfeng—the master, and his wife had joined a mission to wipe out wandering bandits; however, both were killed in the battle of Jiayu Pass. Ever since then, not many people remained in the family, and Lady Shen, the late master's mother, had managed the Manor alone.

Shen Manor, however, had not declined in the least. In fact, its reputation had grown even greater. It was not simply because everyone felt sorry for the tragic death of the Shens and respected their heroic deeds, but because Lady Shen herself was a truly admirable figure.

Lian Chengbi had gone out of town in the early morning, to meet the escort of the saber. The man receiving guests in the main hall was Wan Chongshan, Lady Shen's nephew from her mother's side. He was known as the Swordsman of Xiangyang.

Not many guests had arrived yet. The earliest to arrive was Yang Kaitai, who was from Taiyuan of Shanxi Province.

He brought two "friends" with him. One was a striking and young, fair-skinned scholar, called Fong Shiliang. The other was his cousin, called Fong Wu.

Wan had a great deal of experience with people. He felt both Fongs had an aura of bravery and looked able-bodied. He did not think they were ordinary people.

Yet, he had never heard of their names.

Although he was puzzled, he neither mentioned it nor showed any undue suspicion. He had faith in Yang and believed that his friends could not be miscreants.

But Li Gang was different.

Li arrived early as well. After Wan introduced them to each other, Li fastened his piercing eyes on the two Fongs.

Li was noted for his Thirty-Six-Variation Great Slab-Smashing Hand. Not only did he have sharp piercing eyes, but he was also like a knife himself. An unsheathed knife.

He exuded an air of ferocity and power.

Feng Siniang felt uneasy being stared at by Li, but Xiao Shiyi Lang didn't seem to mind. He still wore a calm smile. He didn't care at all.

That was what set Xiao Shiyi Lang apart ... he didn't care about anything.

Then Liu Seqing arrived.

Next came Xu Qingteng, the hereditary General of Hangzhou. As expected, he had refined manners and was expensively dressed. His hat was decorated with a pearl as large as a pigeon egg. It was obviously a priceless object. Yet he was polite and gentle. He wasn't arrogant and he didn't attempt to intimidate others with his wealth.

Other guests arrived. Naturally, all of them were highly regarded celebrities, but Li Gang kept his eyes riveted on Xiao.

Yang sensed something was wrong. He tried to break the ice by asking, "Brother Li, have you visited the Shaolin Monastery recently?"

Li nodded slightly. "Is this Brother Fong your friend?" he asked.

"Yes, he is."

"Is Fong his real surname?"

Feng was so irritated that she couldn't keep her cool. With a satirical smile she said, "If you don't like the surname Fong, what do you think our surname should be?"

Li drew a long face. "Whatever your surname is, it has nothing to do with me. I merely despise cowards who change their names to conceal their identities. I never let such vermin off the hook easily."

Feng's features darkened. Wan Chongshan tried to ease the tension by saying, "We all know Brother Li is a righteous man. He is rather straightforward."

Xu Qingteng, trying to change the subject, forced a smile and said, "Where is Brother Baishui? Why hasn't he come?"

Wan sighed softly. "Brother Baishui shaved his head and took vows at the monastery on the top of Emei Mountain. I'm afraid he won't be coming to our meeting."

"Why did he insist on doing this?" Xu lamented. "Is there a story behind his decision?"

Li banged his fist angrily on the table. "Reasons don't matter. He shouldn't have done it. Each generation of the Zhus has had only one heir. He is the only son. Yet he chose to become a monk. As the ancient saying goes, 'There are three major offenses against filial piety, and the gravest of them is not producing an heir.' He may be well-educated, but he has forgotten this wisdom completely. If I ever meet him again, I will teach him a lesson."

Wan and Xu looked at each other, not knowing what to say.

Still fuming, Feng couldn't help sneering. "What a strange man! He sticks his nose into everyone else's business."

Li jumped to his feet, shouting, "I happen to enjoy being nosy. So what?"

Yang also stood up and yelled, "Brother Li! Keep in mind that he's my friend."

"So what?" Li shot back. "Today, I'm going to teach your friend a lesson."

Yang burned with anger and grumbled, "All right, you ... you.... Why don't you teach me a lesson first?"

Both of them rolled up their sleeves, ready for a fight. No a single person came forward to mediate the quarrel. Knowing Li's temper, no one wanted to ask for trouble.

Just then, they heard someone speak. "Did you come here to pick a fight?"

The words themselves were not really intelligent, dignified, or graceful. As a matter of fact, they were more like what a street thug looking for a fight would say.

Yet when the question was asked by this person, it sounded completely different. No one felt it sounded ungraceful or unintelligent, because ... it came from Lady Shen.

With her age, status, and position, she could say whatever she wanted. Those who were scolded by her felt honored, not humiliated. In fact, if she were too polite, they might feel uneasy.

She knew this principle well.

She knew everything well. She had heard a lot, seen a lot, and experienced a lot.

Even though she was a little hard of hearing, if she wanted to hear something, she could still hear clearly. It didn't matter how much people lowered their voices.

On the other hand, if she didn't want to hear something, she wouldn't catch a single word.

Her eyes were not as bright and sharp as before and she couldn't see faces clearly, but she could see through everyone and read their mind.

As the maidservants helped her into the hall, she was chewing on a candied date. It seemed as if all her attention were focused on the date.

It was as if the spoken words had not come from her.

Both Li and Yang blushed and bowed their heads in shame. They quietly turned aside, to roll down their sleeves.

Everyone respectfully bowed to Lady Shen.

She narrowed her eyes into a smile and nodded. "Xu Qingteng, the pearl on your hat is remarkable." she commented. "It's a pity that you fixed it onto your hat. Why don't you hang it on your nose instead, so that people can see it more clearly?"

Xu blushed, unable to respond.

Next, she beamed at Liu Seqing. "I haven't seen you for several years. You must have progressed in your swordsmanship and, now, no one can compete with you ... right? You should change your nickname to First Sword of the World. At least your sword is prettier than anyone else's."

Liu blushed, too. He had kept his hand on the hilt of his sword, afraid that people wouldn't notice it, but, now, he hurried to hide it behind his back.

Though they blushed, the men didn't really feel embarrassed. There was no shame in being chided by Lady Shen.

By doing so, Lady Shen was saying that she didn't regard them as outsiders.

In contrast, those who didn't get picked on appeared looking lost.

Yang bowed his head and mumbled, "Please forgive me for being impolite, My Lady."

She cupped her ear. "What? What did you say? I can't hear you."

Yang blushed again. "I-I was not p-poli...."

"Oh!" she smiled. "You're saying that you didn't bring a *present*. What does it matter? I know you're a miser. You don't even spend money on food and clothes for yourself. How is it possible that you would prepare a present for someone else?"

Yang stood speechless.

Li tried to explain. "I didn't really want to fight with Mr. Yang. It's just that these two people—"

"What? You mean these two want to fight?"

She took a look at Feng and Xiao, then shook her head. "I don't think so. They both look like nice kids. How is it possible that they would fight at my place? Only those who are ill-mannered and unruly would fly into a temper here. Don't you think so?"

At a loss for words, Li bowed his head and said, "Yes, My Lady."

Feng was amused. She thought the old lady was interesting. She hoped she would be as much fun when she grew to her age.

"We used to entertain many guests here," Lady Shen said. "But ever since Bijun got married, it hasn't been this busy for a long time. I finally realized that those former guests came to see her and not me. However, if you expected to see this beautiful girl of mine today, I'm afraid you will be disappointed."

She narrowed her eyes into a smile. "My little girl cannot see guests today. She is sick."

"Sick? What's wrong?" Yang asked with concern.

"Silly boy! What are you anxious about?" she teased him. "If she were truly sick, would I still be so happy?"

She winked and spoke under her breath. "Let me tell you. She has morning sickness. But don't tell the girl that I told you, or she will complain that I'm an old gossip."

The houseguests rose to offer their congratulations. Yang was grinning broadly.

Feng stared at him and whispered, "What are you so happy about? Is the baby yours?"

Yang shut his mouth, to choke back his laugh. Such a compliant man was rare.

Xiao sighed inwardly. He thought a man should never be that submissive to a woman. Women considered meek men as lacking backbone.

No matter how many people were around him, Xiao always seemed aloof. He was always an outsider who could never share other people's joy.

He was also the calmest, so he was the first to notice Lian Chengbi.

He had never met Lian, but he knew the man walking into view must be him.

Xiao had never seen anyone with such elegant manners. Lian's elegance contained an air of unattainable graciousness.

There were many handsome young men, many refined young scholars, many dignified young noblemen, and many young heroic fighters in the world, but none could compare with the man walking into view right now. Although it was difficult to describe exactly how he differed, whoever saw him would agree that he was exceptional.

Zhao Wuji was an outstanding individual as well. Whenever he was in a group of people, his charming manners usually drew the most attention.

But now, as the two men walked into the hall together, Xiao didn't even see Zhao.

Zhao's clothes were always perfectly tailored and made of the finest material. Every accessory he wore was carefully chosen and matched. No one would say his clothes were sleazy or gaudy, and, certainly, no one would say he was dressed like new money.

Not many people in the Martial Order were as well-groomed as Zhao, yet he looked like the young man's attendant, when they walked together.

If this young stranger were not Lian Chengbi, who else could he be? If he were not such a perfect individual, then he would not be Lian Chengbi!

Lian also noticed Xiao.

He didn't know Xiao, nor had he ever seen him. He couldn't have known that the young man standing on one of the stairs at the entrance of the main hall was Xiao Shiyi Lang.

But, he saw at a glance that the young man stood out from the others in many ways. In exactly what ways, he could not say.

He wanted to take a closer look at the young man, but he thought better of it. It was impolite to stare at others.

Lian Chengbi was never impolite to anyone.

The sight of Lian and Zhao stirred great excitement throughout the hall.

Then Zhao bowed to Lady Shen.

Though her face was still all smiles, her eyes showed concern. She seemed to sense something was wrong.

"I'm sorry to keep My Lady waiting," Zhao said. "Forgive me for being late."

"That's all right. Better late than never."

"Yes, My Lady."

"Where are Tu Xiaotian, Hai Lingzi, and the old Hawk King? Why didn't they come? Are they too ashamed to come see me?"

"Indeed, they are too ashamed to come," Zhao said meekly.

Alertness gleamed in her eyes. "You lost the saber, didn't you?"

Zhao bowed his head.

"It doesn't matter that the saber is lost," she said. "I was concerned that lives had been lost as well."

Zhao bowed his head even lower. "I would've been too ashamed to come, too. It's just that—"

"No need to explain. I'm certain it's not your fault. The old Hawk King must have insisted on carrying the saber himself. He must have been the one who lost the saber."

"Even so, I'm guilty of negligence. I swear I will find the saber and bring it back, or I will never be able to face anyone in the Martial Order again."

"There are not many people in the world capable of wresting the saber from the old Hawk King. Who did it? It must have been someone extraordinary."

"It was Feng Siniang."

"Feng Siniang? I've heard of her name. She's a pretty good martial artist, but I don't think she is capable of doing this. She's not that good."

"She had an accomplice."

"Who?"

Zhao breathed out a long, rasping sigh before finally saying: "Xiao Shiyi Lang!"

All of the people in the hall were ideal gentlemen. Even at the sound of such striking news, none lost their calm. No one showed a look of surprise or disappointment, and no one said a word. All were aware that at a moment like this, whatever they might say would embarrass Zhao.

An ideal gentleman never embarrasses others.

Actually, there were two people who *did* show a look of surprise. One was Yang, and the other was Feng. Yang stared at Feng, but Feng was staring at Xiao.

She was baffled. She knew for a fact that the lost saber was a fake. Where was the original?

At the sound of Xiao's name, Lady Shen frowned. "Xiao Shiyi Lang. Xiao Shiyi Lang ... " she grumbled. "Why does this name keep coming up? He seems to account for all of the misdemeanors in the world."

Then she smiled. "I want to see what this man looks like. It's no small feat for a single person to commit so many crimes."

Li Gang looked grim. "If we don't eliminate this man, there will never be real peace in the martial world. Sooner or later, I will bring you his head, My Lady."

She ignored him and turned to Xu. "Xu Qingteng, do you want Xiao Shiyi Lang's head?"

Xu pondered the question, before answering. "Brother Li is right. If we don't eliminate this man, there won't be peace in the martial world—"

Before he had finished, Lady Shen turned to Liu. "Liu Seqing, what do you think?"

"I have long wanted to fight it out with this man."

She shifted her eyes from Liu to Lian Chengbi. "What about you?"

Lian smiled, but didn't answer.

Lady Shen shook her head. "You're a fine young man, but you're much too quiet." She turned to the others. "Can you believe this? He has stayed at my place for two weeks, and I haven't heard him speak more than ten sentences."

Yang opened his mouth, as if to speak, and then shut it.

"What do you want to say? *Say* it," said Lady Shen. "Are you going to be as quiet as he?"

Yang stole a glance at Feng. "I think it's better not to speak sometimes."

Lady Shen beamed a smile. "What about you? Do you want to kill Xiao Shiyi Lang as well?"

"Whoever kills this notorious villain will win immediate fame and respect. I would be interested, too. It's just that...."

"It's just what?"

Yang bowed his head. "I don't think I'm his match."

"Good," she laughed. "You're an honest young man. I like down-to-earth young men like you. It's a pity I don't have a second grand-daughter for you to marry."

Yang blushed. He dared not look at Feng. He could imagine her facial expression.

Lady Shen turned her eyes back to Li. "See? There are many

people who want Xiao Shiyi Lang's head. It might not be easy for you to get it first!"

Feng looked at Xiao. "How do you feel?"

"I feel wonderful," Xiao replied.

"Wonderful? You feel ... *wonderful?*"

"I didn't know my head was so valuable," he chuckled. "Otherwise, I would have put it in a pawnshop."

She laughed, too.

It was quiet at night. Her laughter was like the tinkling of a bell.

Their rooms were at the rear of Shen Manor. Every guest was assigned a chamber. Lady Shen insisted that all the guests stay for at least one night.

Feng soon stopped laughing and frowned. "The saber we took was a fake, but they lost the real one. Don't you think the whole issue is bizarre?"

"No, it's not bizarre at all."

"You don't think it's bizarre? Where do you think the real saber is?"

"The real saber—"

Xiao broke off.

He heard footsteps approaching. He thought they must be Yang's. Only an ideal gentleman's feet would be so heavy.

An ideal gentleman never walks on tiptoe to eavesdrop on private conversations.

Feng frowned and murmured, "He's like a ghost that refuses to leave. Here he comes again."

She whirled and glared at Yang. "Do you expect me to thank you?"

"That ... that's not what I m-meant," Yang stammered, blushing.

"I should have thanked you. If you had given me away, those people would never have let me get away with it."

"Why sh-should I give you away?"

"Didn't you hear them say that I stole the saber?"

Yang wiped his sweat. "I know you didn't."

"How do you know I didn't?"

"Because ... because I-I believe you."

"Why do you believe me?"

He wiped his forehead again. "No reason. I just ... b-believe you."

Feng gazed at him, seeing the transparent sincerity on his square face. Her eyes misted.

Even if she were usually as cold as a statue, there were moments when her heart of stone melted. At that instant, she was deeply moved. She held his hands and said in a gentle voice, "You're a good man."

Yang's eyes misted, too. "I-I'm not too good, and I-I'm not too bad. I...."

Feng broke into a tender smile. "You're a gentleman, but you're also a fool."

Suddenly remembering something, she released Yang's hands and turned to talk to Xiao. "What do you say—"

Her smile froze. Xiao was not where he had been.

She looked confused for a few seconds, before crying, "Where is he? Did you see where he went?"

Yang was confused, too. "Where is who?"

"He ... my cousin. Did you see him?"

"No, I ... I didn't."

"Are you blind? He's a big guy and you didn't see him?"

"I ... I didn't see him. I only ... s-saw you."

She stamped her feet. "You're a fool."

She hoped Xiao had gone back to his room, but she was uncertain. She knew Xiao very well.

She knew he could disappear at any moment.

And Xiao had disappeared.

There was no one in his chamber. Beneath the candlestick on the table was a note.

The ink on the paper was still wet. She recognized Xiao's sloppy handwriting.

The note read: "Marry him or you will be sorry! I guarantee it. You will never find a nicer man."

Clenching her teeth and with red eyes, Feng started to call him names: "Asshole! Pig! Son of a bitch!"

"Isn't he your cousin?" Yang said meekly, "Why are you cursing him like this?"

"Who said he's my cousin? Are you *nuts*?"

Yang wiped his forehead. "If he's not your cousin, who is he?"

She choked down tears and muttered, "He ... he ... he's another fool!"

A fool is not necessarily a gentleman, but a so-called ideal gentleman is more or less a fool. It's not smart to be an ideal gentleman.

Xiao was humming a song. It sounded like a shepherd's song from the prairie north of the Great Wall. It sounded grand, but a little poignant, forlorn and morose.

He usually hummed this song when he was in a bad mood. What he disliked most about himself was that he did not allow himself to play the fool.

It was not a gloomy night. The bright stars twinkled in the sky. The sporadic hum of autumn insects seemed to make everything else quiet.

In the silence of night, strolling alone under such a starry sky usually helps one leave worries behind and feel serene.

Unlike others at moments like this, Xiao always thought of many things he shouldn't think about. He reflected on his childhood and all that had happened to him.

He had been an outsider all his life, always lonely and feeling out of place. Sometimes he felt weary, but he never dared rest.

Life was like a whip, beating him and driving him forward, urging him to keep searching, yet never telling him what he would find.

He had no choice but to keep walking, hoping to find something special, something ... unusual. Otherwise, life's journey would be too dull.

Chapter 8

The Hawk King's Secret

SUDDENLY, XIAO HEARD the crisp sound of clothes flapping. It was obvious to him that this person traveling during the night was fairly good at Lightness Kung Fu.

The flapping sound stopped in the dark woods ahead of him. Xiao heard someone panting and groaning in anguish.

It was also obvious that this traveler was seriously injured.

Xiao didn't stop. He kept walking into the woods. The panting sound stopped.

After a while, he heard a voice croak, "Please stop, my friend!"

Xiao turned around slowly and saw a man emerge from behind a tree. The man had a big head with disheveled hair.

It was ... *the Hawk King!*

Xiao didn't show his surprise. "How may I help you?" he asked.

Like a hungry raptor, the One-Armed Hawk King stared at Xiao with the only eye he had left. After a few seconds, he sighed. "I'm ... injured."

"I can tell."

"Shen Manor is nearby. Do you know it?"

"Yes, I do."

"Carry me there. Quickly! This is urgent!"

"Why should I? You don't know me, and I don't know you."

"How dare you be so rude!" The Hawk King was outraged.

"Who's rude? You or me?" Xiao spoke dryly. "Don't forget ... you're the one begging, not me."

The Hawk King glared at him with a vicious look, but his face was twisted in pain.

After some moments, he took a deep breath. A grim smile appeared on his face. He removed a gold ingot from his shirt. "This is for you," he said, panting. "If you help me, I promise I will reward you generously."

Xiao broke into a grin. "That's more like it. You should have said so in the first place."

He stepped forward slowly, as if he really wanted to take the gold ingot, but when he extended his hand, the Hawk King's arm and fingers sprang out like hooks to grab for his wrist.

As the proverb goes, "Centipedes die hard." Though the Hawk King was critically injured, his last blow was still powerful and fast as lightning.

Xiao was even faster. He spun around, using his foot to flick the gold ingot into the air. Then he turned his hand to catch it as he flew backward several yards. The swiftness and agility of this display were beyond the wildest imagination. Only those who witnessed it would believe that it was possible.

The Hawk King's face turned ghostly white. "Who are you?"

Xiao smirked. "I recognized you from the start, and you still don't recognize me?"

The Hawk King was stunned. "You ... you're Xiao Shiyi Lang?"

Xiao smiled. "Finally, you got it."

The Hawk King goggled at him as if seeing a spirit. Puffing, he hissed, "Good ... Xiao Shiyi Lang. How are you?"

"Not too bad."

The Hawk King stared at him for one more moment, then burst into wild laughter.

Laughing made his wound more painful and also made him sweat, but he kept laughing and laughing.

What's so funny? Xiao wondered.

Xiao had never laughed the way the Hawk King was laughing right now. "Are you having a good time?" he asked.

"Yes, I'm having a great time," the Hawk King said, laughing and breathing heavily. "It's good to know that, just like me, Xiao Shiyi Lang would fall for the tricks of others."

"Oh?"

His body contorted in pain, the Hawk King spoke in a dry, rasping voice. "Did you know the saber you took from me was a fake?"

"Yes, I did, but did you know?"

"Those three bastards couldn't keep me in the dark forever."

"And they tried to kill you, because you found out?"

"Right."

"Zhao Wuji, Hai Lingzi, and Tu Xiaotian all enjoy high social status," sighed Xiao. "Why would they risk everything they have for a saber? How are they going to split one saber among the three of them?"

The Hawk King kept coughing. "They ... they don't want the saber ... for themselves."

"Then who wants it? Are they taking orders from someone?"

The Hawk King coughed harder and harder, then started to spit blood.

Xiao's eyes gleamed. "Who can make all of them obey him? Who?" he pressed on.

Covering his mouth with his hand, the Hawk King tried to swallow the blood in his mouth so that he could say the name of this person, but he only managed to utter a word, before blood spurted out.

Xiao was about to help him stand, but, suddenly, he jumped up, disappearing into the top of a tree.

Three men dashed into the dark woods.

Like wild animals, some people have the uncanny ability to smell danger. They may not see or hear anything unusual, but when danger approaches, they always manage to get away at the last critical moment.

Such people usually become successful government officials or great combat heroes. If they choose to enter the martial world, they often become awe-inspiring heroes.

Zhuge Liang and Guanzhong both had it, and they became great statesmen.

Such generals as Han Xin, Yue Fei, and Li Jing also had it. That's how they won battle after battle.

Top fighters such as Li Xunhuan, Chu Liuxiang, Tie Zhongtang, and Shen Lang also had this quality. That's how they accomplished laudable feats and became legends. Decades later, they were still worshiped by novice fighters.

Xiao Shiyi Lang also had this instinct. People like him may not live any longer than others, but their deaths are definitely more significant.

The three people who had just entered the woods were Hai Lingzi, Tu Xiaotian, and an effeminate man in blue. He was not tall. His lifeless face was empty of expression, but his cunning eyes were bright. It was evident that he was wearing a finely made mask of human skin.

He wasn't moving faster than Tu or Hai, but he had a supple body. He appeared gracious and at ease, as if strolling in a garden.

Though the mask made his face look grotesque, his dancing eyes gave him an air of exotic charm. It was nearly impossible to resist taking a closer look at him.

What interested Xiao most was the saber that hung at the man's waist. Including its hilt, the saber was only about two feet long. The designs of its scabbard and hilt were rather plain. It had no dazzling decorations. The blade was not revealed, so he couldn't tell whether it was sharp.

But, somehow, a mere glimpse of it was enough to send a chill right up Xiao's spine!

Was this the Deer Carver?

Did Zhao, Hai , and Tu steal this saber and risk ruining their reputation so that they could give it to ... *him?*

Who was he? What kind of power did he have to make these three people listen to him?

The Hawk King's coughing was so faint that it was inaudible now.

Hai and Tu exchanged glances and let out a breath of relief.

"This old freak was tough," Tu said. "I didn't expect him to get this far."

"No matter how tough," Hai sneered, "he couldn't withstand the attack of one sword and two palms."

Tu laughed. "Actually, the blow Little Mister gave him was enough to kill him. Our help was completely unnecessary."

The man in blue chuckled. "Really?"

He walked over and stood in front of the Hawk King. Then, he unexpectedly drew the saber.

The light reflecting off the blade was pale blue, but not dazzling.

With a flash of the blade, the Hawk King's enormous head fell to the ground.

The man in blue didn't glance at the head. Instead, he stared at the saber he was holding.

Its blade was like a blue rainbow. There was not a drop of blood on it.

"A fine saber!" he muttered in admiration. "This is, indeed, a great saber!"

The Hawk King was already dead, yet the man in blue had to try the saber on him. Even Hai could not keep from frowning at such viciousness.

The man in blue slowly inserted the saber into its scabbard. "My master says that if you want to make sure a person is dead, the only convincing way is to cut off his head and closely inspect it."

He gazed at Tu and Hai kindly. "Do you think this makes sense?"

Tu produced a dry cough and forced a smile. "Yes, it makes a lot of sense."

"Whatever my master says always makes sense, even when it doesn't appear to make sense at all. Right?"

"Right. Right," Tu replied. "You are absolutely right."

Little Mister giggled. "Every time I hear nice things about my master, I feel pleased. If you want to please me, just say nice things about him to me."

Little Mister—what a strange name! Xiao thought.

The man in blue was actually called Little Mister.

Judging from his voice and eyes, he was probably rather young. Yet Tu, in his fifties, and Hai were both extremely deferential to him.

He appeared gentle, but he had cut off a dead man's head without wincing.

Xiao sighed silently. He couldn't figure out this person.

This young man is ruthless enough. How much worse is his master? he mused.

It was too disgusting to imagine.

Then he heard Little Mister say, "Now that Sikong Shu is dead, we still have something else to take care of, don't we?"

"Yes," Tu replied.

"What is it?" asked Little Mister.

Tu cast Hai a glance, muttering, "Um ... um...."

"Have you figured it out yet?"

"No," Tu said meekly.

"You're both rather old and experienced," Little Mister said, with a sigh. "How can you not think of something this simple?"

"I'm a muddle-headed old man," Tu said, with an apologetic smile. "Please enlighten me."

"You can say that again. You two could learn something from me."

Tu and Hai were at least twice as old as Little Mister, but he talked to them as if they were mere children. And strangely enough ... they were as obedient as children.

Little Mister sighed again before continuing. "Let me ask you. Sikong has been famous for many years. Isn't his sudden death going to rouse suspicion?"

"Undoubtedly," Tu said.

"If someone suspects something, then someone will want to find out the truth. He will ask, 'How did Sikong Shu die? Who killed him?'"

"That's correct."

"Let me ask you another question." Little Mister winked. "Do *you* know who killed Sikong?"

"Other than you Little Mister, who else could have been capable of this?" said Tu with an ingratiating smile.

"Are you saying I killed Sikong?" Little Mister glared at him. "Do I look like a murderer?"

Tu was baffled. "Well ... um ... No."

"If I didn't kill him, did you kill him?"

Tu wiped his sweat. "I didn't have grudges against him. Why would I want to kill him?"

"That's the point." Little Mister grinned broadly. "If you say *you* killed Sikong, people will still wonder why. They won't stop asking questions."

"I didn't kill him either," Hai chimed in.

"Of course you didn't," said Little Mister. "But if none of us killed him, who did?"

Tu and Hai looked at each other, wondering what Little Mister was driving at.

"Are you blind?" Little Mister sighed, "Didn't you see Xiao Shiyi Lang?"

Hearing this, Xiao was stunned! Does he see me hiding up here? he wondered.

Then he heard Little Mister say, "Didn't you see that it was Xiao Shiyi Lang who cut off Sikong's head, and the weapon he wielded was the Deer Carver?"

Tu's eyes grew bright. He took the hint. "That's right. That's right," he said with enthusiasm. "I saw Xiao kill Sikong with the Deer Carver. I'm such an old blockhead, I almost forgot!"

"Fortunately, you didn't really forget," said Little Mister with a laugh. "However, though *we* know Xiao was the killer, no one else in the martial world knows this fact yet. What are we to do?"

"Um ... that's right," Tu said. "We must figure out a way to make this known."

"That's just what I'm getting at. Do you have any bright idea?"

Tu frowned. "I haven't thought of anything yet."

Little Mister shook his head. "Actually, it's quite easy. Now, look!"

He drew the saber again, slicing off a piece of bark in a flash. "Sikong's blood is still warm. Dip his clothes in his own blood and write a little poem on the tree. Now listen and write down every word I say. Understand?"

"Yes," Tu responded.

Little Mister's eyes twinkled. "Now you write:

> *Carving the deer is nothing*
> *Compared with carving the head.*
> *Pare off everyone's head, if I can.*
> *Wouldn't that be a thrill!*

Then sign Xiao's name at the end. With that, everyone will know who did this. It's easy, isn't it?"

Tu laughed loudly. "Little Mister! That's a brilliant ruse! What a genius you are to come up with such a shrewd trick! Beyond that, the tone of these words is just like Xiao himself would use."

"I don't have to be too modest." Little Mister smiled. "It's true that other than me, few people could compose a poem like this."

Xiao was almost exploding with rage.

Though Little Mister was very young, he was far more treacherous than many veteran villains. If he lived a few years longer, half of the people in the martial world would probably die by his hand.

Then Little Mister said, "Have we finished our job?"

"I think so." Tu smiled.

Little Mister sighed yet again. "You gentlemen are so careless. I wonder how you've managed to survive."

Tu gave a dry cough, turning away to spit.

"Do you want us to chop Sikong's head in half?" Hai asked, his face dark and grim.

"No, that isn't necessary." Little Mister's smile was sinister. "But what if Xiao happens to pass by and finds the body and the poem on the tree? What do you think he would do?"

Hai was wordless.

"Provided he's not as stupid as you, he'll slice off the words and remove Sikong's body," Little Mister continued. "In that case, all our efforts will be wasted."

Tu stopped coughing. "That's true. I didn't think of that."

"That's why you have to listen to me. You're just not as smart as I am."

"What do you think we should do?"

"That's very easy as well. You really can't figure it out?"

Tu's smile showed his embarrassment.

Little Mister shook his head condescendingly. "If you're afraid that Xiao will slice off the words on the tree, why don't you shave them off first?"

"But...." Tu hesitated.

"Shave off this piece of wood and then send it to Shen Manor. There are still many people gathered there. Ask them to come see Sikong's mutilated corpse. When all those people have witnessed the scene, Xiao Shiyi Lang will never be able to clear his name. What do you think? Isn't that a brilliant idea?"

"Your resourcefulness is amazing, Little Mister," Tu said, his voice filled with awe. "I'm certain no one will ever outsmart you."

"You don't have to play up to me. Just obey my orders."

At this point, not only were Tu and Hai wholeheartedly obedient to Little Mister, but Xiao was admiring his superhuman intelligence.

Xiao had never met such a formidable opponent.

Xiao's biggest weakness was his love of challenges. The more dangerous a task, the more he wanted to do it. The more formidable an opponent, the more he wanted to fight him.

Then he heard Little Mister say, "There's another thing I'd like you to do, after you get to Shen Manor."

"Your wish is my command," Tu said.

"Shen Bijun is Lian Chengbi's wife. I want you to find out when she's returning to Flawless Manor, if Lian is traveling with her, and which road they're taking."

"That's not difficult, but...." Tu hesitated again.

"You want to know why I inquire about her, but you're afraid to ask, right?"

"Not really. It's just that...."

"You're saying 'it's just that' again. Please, can't you just ask me? I'll tell you. My goal on this mission is to bring two prizes back."

"One of them must be the Deer Carver," Tu ventured.

"That's right, and the other one is Shen Bijun—the most beautiful woman in the Martial Order."

Tu's face darkened immediately, as if he had lost his breath.

Little Mister laughed. "This is my job. What are you afraid of?"

"Little Mister," Tu muttered, "you may not have seen Lian's kung fu or swordplay in action. His real strength is an enigma. Plus—"

"You don't have to tell me. I know Lian isn't easy to deal with, so I need your help."

Tu wiped his brow. "I'll do anything you say, as long ... as long as it's not beyond my ability."

"You don't have to wipe your sweat," Little Mister said, smiling. "This assignment isn't difficult. Lian will definitely escort his wife home, so all you have to do is try to divert him from his path."

Wiping his forehead again, Tu said, "Lian and Shen are deeply devoted to each other. I'm afraid that—"

"You're afraid he won't jump at your bait?"

"It won't be easy."

"If I were he, I wouldn't want to part with such a beautiful wife either. But no matter how cunning the fish, there is always a way to make it take the bait."

"What's your suggestion?"

"If you want to catch big fish, you have to use attractive bait."

"What bait would be that attractive?"

"Lian is a man of great wealth and eminent reputation. He's also a distinguished scholar and a top fighter. What's more, his wife is a beautiful and virtuous woman. In your opinion, what else would he want?"

"A man this perfect must be content with life," Tu said.

Little Mister laughed. "Human beings will never be free of desire. There must be something he wants."

"You mean ... the Deer Carver?"

"Exactly."

Tu frowned. "Other than the Deer Carver, is there anything *else* that might interest him?"

"There is one other thing ... Xiao Shiyi Lang's head."

Tu's eyes gleamed and he clapped his hands. "That's it! They all think Xiao Shiyi Lang has the Deer Carver. If Lian kills Xiao, not only will he become more famous than ever, but he'll also win the saber."

"Therefore, if you want to attract Lian's attention, you must use Xiao as the bait."

After a moment's thought, Tu said, "But how can I make Lian take the bait? Please enlighten me, Little Mister."

"You *still* don't get it?" Little Mister shook his head again. "All you need to do is tell Lian that you know where Xiao *is*, and then he'll go with you."

His eyes showed a cynical smile. "A man like Lian will die for fame and honor. His wife is far down his list of priorities."

Tu laughed. "So she's not really lucky to have married a man like Lian."

"That's right. If I were a woman, I'd rather marry Xiao than marry Lian."

"Oh?"

"Men like Xiao will do anything for love, whereas Lian has far too many other concerns on his mind. It's not easy being Lian's wife."

Even in autumn, the heat of sunrays was sometimes unbearable.

There was a wine stall under a tree. The wine was cool, thirst-quenching, and satisfying. The stall also sold roasted fava beans, roasted salted peanuts, and pickled eggs to go with the wine. They didn't taste especially good, but they looked clean.

The vendor was a gray old man with a red bottlenose. Judging from his nose, he was a heavy drinker.

Although his clothes were shabby, he looked like a cheerful fellow. Others might think his life was less than ideal, but he seemed quite satisfied with it.

Xiao had always admired people like him.

As long as a man is happy and content, why should he care about what others think? Xiao thought about having a chat with him, but the old man seemed preoccupied.

Xiao could do nothing but continue to drink by himself.

Drinking is similar to playing chess in that playing chess alone is as boring as drinking alone. Xiao didn't like to drink alone.

However, this spot was at the intersection of three roads. He was certain that Shen Bijun's carriage would pass by. He wasn't sitting here simply to drink.

It wasn't a pleasant thing to be used as bait. On that fateful day, Xiao had been on the verge of coming down from the tree to confront Little Mister.

But, having been around for so many years, he had learned the art of waiting. No matter what he planned to do, he always waited for the perfect moment.

Xiao was about to drink his eighth bowl of wine.

The old man glanced at Xiao out of the corner of his eye and laughed. "Are you going to drink more? If you drink any more, you'll be too drunk to walk."

"If I can't walk, I'll just sleep here. What does it matter? The sky is my quilt and the earth is my bed. Even if I never wake up, what does it matter?"

"Don't you need to hurry back?"

"Back to where? I don't know where I came from. Where am I going back to?"

The old man mumbled to himself, "This fellow is probably already drunk. He's talking nonsense."

Xiao laughed, "Isn't a wine vendor supposed to want his customers to drink more? Just bring me some more wine."

The old man snorted and started to ladle out wine, but they saw a cloud of dust stirred up by horses in the distance. A traveling party was approaching.

Xiao's eyes sparkled. He didn't look drunk at all now.

Dressed in hunting attire, each with a hunting hawk or a hunting dog, these travelers carried bows and arrows and had game hanging from their saddles. It was obvious that they were returning from a hunting trip.

Autumn was the hunting season.

The person riding on the first horse appeared to be a young boy. He was handsomely dressed, and the horse he was riding looked to be a fast steed. He was a pleasant-looking rich boy.

The old man was excited to see so many rich potential customers. But Xiao was a little disappointed, because these weren't the people he had been waiting for.

The old man called out his selling slogans at the top of his voice: "Come and taste my bamboo-leaf-green wine. It's sweet and refreshing. One bowl will lift your spirits. Two bowls will give you fiery energy. Three bowls will take you to heaven."

Xiao smiled and said, "I have gulped down seven bowls of wine. How come I still don't feel anything? In fact, I think I'm rather drowsy."

The old man threw him a cold stare. By now, all of the travelers had stopped. The rich boy announced: "It's still a long way back home. Let's stop here and have a few drinks. The wine sounds rather good."

The boy had a round face, a small mouth, large eyes, and fine fair skin. When he smiled, there were dimples on his cheeks. He looked incredibly appealing.

Xiao couldn't help but take a close look at him. There are many rich boys in the world, but few of them are appealing, and even fewer of them are both appealing and friendly.

The rich boy noticed Xiao, too. After he sat on the rug his attendants had placed on the ground, he smiled at Xiao and said, "The more, the merrier. My friend, why don't you join us for a drink?"

"Great!" said Xiao. "I only have enough money for eight bowls of wine. I was wondering how I'd pay for the ninth. Now I've got someone ready to treat me. Fantastic!"

The boy said, "I enjoy meeting straightforward people like you." He turned to the old man. "Come on! Bring us some more wine."

The old man ladled wine into a bowl and brought it to Xiao. But he glared at Xiao and grumbled, "With free wine, you'll probably get drunk even faster."

"What's the big deal about getting drunk?" Xiao laughed. "The faster I get drunk, the more relaxed I'll feel. Cheers!"

The moment he said cheers, the wine in his bowl was gone.

While others *drank* wine, Xiao *tossed* wine down his throat. No sooner had he arched his head backward than a bowl of wine disappeared.

Clapping and laughing, the boy turned to his entourage and said, "Did you see how fast he drank his wine?"

"If they didn't see it," said Xiao, "I can perform the trick a few more times."

"My friend, you are not only direct but also funny. May I ask your name?"

"You and I met here by coincidence, and you are kindly treating me to wine. After I'm through, I'll go away. If I know your name, I'll feel compelled to treat you in the future, to return the favor. In that case, our drinking won't be fun anymore. So, about names ... well, if I don't have to tell you my name, you don't have to tell me yours."

"You're right. Our accidental encounter is karma in itself. Look! The pickled eggs seem pretty good. Let's eat the eggs with the wine. Then we'll get drunk more slowly and can drink even more."

"That's true." Xiao smiled. "If we get drunk too fast, that's not as much fun."

He picked up a pickled egg, threw it into the air, arched his head backward, opened his mouth to catch it, and swallowed it.

The boy laughed. "My friend, you drink fast and eat fast."

"I have always thought I would die young, so I do everything fast," Xiao explained. "I never waste time."

The rich boy was fourteen or fifteen years old at most, but he was a heavy drinker. For each bowl of wine Xiao drank, he drank a bowl of wine to match it, and he drank quite fast, too.

All of the boy's entourage were big, strong, able-bodied men, yet none of them could match his tolerance for spirits.

Xiao's eyes started to narrow and his tongue started to feel numb. He seemed half drunk. People who are half drunk usually drink even more and ... faster.

It's difficult for half-drunk men not to get completely drunk.

Xiao finally got drunk.

"It turns out that he's not really an exceptional drinker," the boy said, with a slight shake of his head. "It's so disappointing."

The old man smiled. "He told me that if he got drunk, he would just sleep here. He said he wouldn't mind drinking himself to death."

The boy stared at him. "He is my guest after all. How can I let him sleep here?"

He waved to his attendants. "Watch over my friend. When we leave, take him with us."

The sun had not yet set, but there was not a single traveler in sight.

The boy seemed a little anxious. He stood with his hands clasped behind his back, peering into the distance. At last, he said, "Old man, get ready. It looks like you've got some more customers."

Another traveling party appeared far in the distance.

The black carriage was old but grand. Its door was closed and the curtains were drawn. It was apparent that the person in the carriage didn't want to be seen.

The driver was a composed, middle-aged man whose eyes were full of energy. There were three other attendants riding with the carriage. They were all competent riders.

This traveling party had been going rather fast, but had to slow down as they approached the intersection. The rich boy's carriages and horses blocked half of the road.

The old man seized the chance to solicit customers. He called out, "Sweet and refreshing bamboo-leaf-green wine! Come and drink two bowls of it. If you miss this stop, it will be at least a hundred miles before you have the chance to drink such great wine."

Licking their lips, the riders were obviously interested, but none of them dismounted. They waited for the rich boy's entourage to make way for them.

Then they heard a voice in the carriage say, "We've been traveling all day. You must all be tired. Let's stop here for a while, and you can have a drink."

Filled with compassion and thoughtfulness, her soothing clear voice induced admiration from the listeners.

The riders immediately dismounted from their horses and bowed to the carriage, saying, "Thank you, My Lady."

Then the person in the carriage said, "Old Chao, why don't you get off to have a drink, too? We're not in any hurry."

The driver hesitated for a moment before finally bringing the vehicle to the roadside. By now, the old man had prepared three bowls of wine and was ladling wine into the fourth bowl. Those who had gotten their wine were about to drink.

"Wait!" Old Chao cautioned loudly. "We don't know if it's poisoned."

"Poisoned?" The old man's face burned. "You say my wine is poisoned? All right, let me be poisoned first."

He drank the bowl of wine he was holding.

Old Chao ignored him. He removed a silver spoon from his shirt pocket and dipped it into the wine jar. When he saw that the color of the spoon hadn't changed, he took a sip and then nodded his head. "No problem," he said.

The riders, who had been holding the wine, were relieved and finally drank. One of the riders said, "The wine is pretty enjoyable. I wonder whether the pickled eggs taste as good."

He picked the biggest egg and was about to put it into his mouth.

"Wait!" Old Chao shouted again.

The rich boy had not planned to talk to them, but now he could not help but let out an amused chuckle, mumbling, "He thinks the pickled eggs could be poisoned? This fellow is paranoid."

Old Chao cast him a glance and said with a grave face, "You cannot be too careful while traveling."

He took a silver knife out of his shirt and was about to cut the egg open.

The rich boy walked over to him with a smile on his face. "It's surprising to see you carry so many interesting gadgets. We should order a set, too. May I take a look at the knife?"

Old Chao scrutinized him up and down, and then handed the silver knife to him. It was difficult to refuse such a delightful young lad.

The silver knife was exquisite.

The boy stroked the blade with his fingers. "What a beautiful knife!" he exclaimed, casually. "I wonder whether or not it could kill people."

"This knife is not used to kill," replied Old Chao.

"You are so wrong." The boy smiled. "Any knife can be used to kill people."

As he said, "kill," the knife in his hand shot out like a ray of light. As he said, "people," it plunged into Old Chao's throat.

Bellowing with rage, Old Chao turned his hand to pull out the knife and lunged toward the boy, but as his blood spurted out like an arrow, his strength drained away.

After only three steps, he collapsed at the boy's feet. His eyes wide, he couldn't believe what was happening.

The boy peered down at him, saying, "I told you any knife can be used to kill. Do you believe me now?" His eyes still appeared so gentle and obliging.

The three riders were shocked. They had never dreamed that such an angelic-looking boy could be so devious.

Not until Old Chao fell to the ground did they draw their swords. Shouting in anger, they lunged toward the boy.

"None of you is my match," the boy sighed. "Why do you insist on bringing death upon yourselves?"

Eyes red with rage, the rider who had been the first to drink the wine thrust his devil-head saber at the boy's head.

"How unfortunate!" the boy sneered, with a shake of his head.

Without flinching, he used two fingers to clamp the blade. It was as if the saber had plunged into a rock.

The rider twisted his wrist, attempting to cut the boy's fingers with the edge of the blade.

With a muffled *swoosh*, an arrow pierced the rider's body and came out of his chest, with blood dripping from the arrowhead.

All of this occurred within a matter of seconds.

The other two riders were about to raise their swords and lunge forward.

At that very moment, they heard the person in the carriage slowly declare, "It's true. None of you are his match. Now stand back."

Chapter 9

Beauty of Beauties

THE DOOR OF the carriage opened and out stepped a woman.

At that instant, everyone froze and held their breath. Never had they seen such a beautiful woman.

She was not luxuriously dressed, but any clothes would look elegant on her.

She was not wearing any jewelry or makeup. She had no need for them.

No precious stone could match her splendor, and no expensive face power could add to her loveliness.

Her beauty was beyond description.

Some people would compare beauty to a flower, but no flower could be as glamorous as she was. Some people would say she was like a lady in a classic painting, but no paintbrush could capture the fullness of her grace.

No goddess in heaven could be as delicate as she. Whoever saw her once ... would never forget her.

Her presence was surreal. How could there be a beauty like her anywhere else in the world? It was as if she might vanish with the wind at any moment.

She was Shen Bijun—the most beautiful woman in the Martial Order.

For an instant, the rich boy held his breath like everybody else.

His facial expression showed peculiar changes. Like every other man, he was a little surprised, a little awestruck, and a little dazzled.

The strange thing was that his eyes also showed a look of ... jealousy.

But after this instant, he smiled again—his smile still so innocent and lovely. "People say that intelligent women are not pretty
and pretty women are not intelligent," he observed, "because pretty
women are too busy working on their faces to work on their minds."

He gave a soft sigh and finished with, "Now I know that's not
entirely true."

Shen alighted from the carriage and stood in front of him.

Though her eyes appeared angry, she was trying to control herself.

She had been taught how to discipline her emotions, her entire
life. To be a true lady, she had to hide all her strong emotions, including anger, sadness, and joy. Even when she couldn't hold back
her tears, she was expected to hide in her chamber and weep alone.

She stood there and quietly listened to the boy.

She never interrupted anyone. It was rude. She had learned to
use as much of her ears and as little of her mouth as possible.

When the boy had finished talking, she spoke. "May I ask your
name?"

"I'm a nobody. How can my name ever compare with Ms. Shen's
name? I'm ashamed to say it in front of you."

Shen didn't ask again.

She never pursued subjects others didn't wish to talk about.

"Did you kill these two people?" she said, with her eyes indicat-
ing the corpses on the ground.

"Did you see me kill them?"

Shen nodded in confirmation.

The boy smiled. "Then why do you ask?"

"Because you don't look like a brutal person."

"Thank you for the compliment! As the saying goes, 'Don't judge
a person by his appearance.' I advise you to keep that in mind."

"Did you kill them because you had a grudge against them?"

"No."

"Then they must have been rude to you."

"Even if they were rude to me, I wouldn't have quarreled with
them over such trivial matters." He smiled. "Must you push for an
answer?"

Shen frowned, but didn't speak.

They were courteous to each other, without showing agitation. Except for Xiao Shiyi Lang, all the spectators gawked in wonder at the sight of these two being so civilized to each other. Xiao was lying still on the ground, apparently blind drunk.

After a moment, Shen said, "Please begin."

The boy was puzzled. "Begin what?"

"Please begin your attack," said Shen, still calm and expressionless.

The boy's rosy cheeks turned pale. "A-attack? You want me to attack you?"

"Sir, you said you killed them for no reason, but I believe there must be a reason. Since I cannot get a satisfactory explanation, I have no choice but to use force."

"But ... but, you're a well-known swordswoman in the martial world and I'm only a ... child. How can I compete against you?"

"You're too modest. Please begin."

"I've got it. I-I've got it ... you want to k-kill me, to avenge their d-deaths." He appeared frightened. Even his voice quivered.

"It's a universal truth that murder is punished with death."

The boy put on a pitiful face. "I only killed two of your servants, and you want me to pay with my life. D-don't you think you are being too c-cruel?"

"Servants are humans, too ... are they not?"

His eyes red-rimmed, the boy dropped to his knees. "I killed them by accident. Please forgive me, my dear sister," he pleaded through tears. "You're beautiful and kind. I know you wouldn't have the heart to kill a child like me."

The boy had been talking like an experienced, seasoned adult, but now he had become a naughty spoiled brat.

Shen stood speechless.

She didn't have much experience in the affairs of the martial world. She was at a loss how to deal with someone like this.

Tears flowed down the boy's face. His voice wavering, he said, "My dear sister, if you are really so upset about what I have done, please pick two of my attendants and kill them. What do you say to that? Please! My dear sister! Please...."

Neither Shen nor anyone else had the heart to harm a youngster. At this moment, the wretched adolescent suddenly rolled over. His left foot kicked at Shen's ankle and his right foot at her belly. His hands shot out seven projectiles with lightning speed. Some of the weapons flew straight like arrows, while others emerged spinning and dancing.

His hands had been empty. No one could figure out where these hidden weapons had come from.

Still calm, Shen simply frowned and whipped her long sleeves around. Caught in the wind generated by her sleeves, the hidden weapons all disappeared.

The Golden Needles of the Shens were said to be the finest hidden weapons. Those who knew how to launch hidden weapons naturally knew how to catch them.

Shen was a kind-hearted person. Though fast and precise, she was not ruthless. Her grandmother, Lady Shen, had always thought that she was not skilled enough in launching weapons. Lady Shen was afraid that her granddaughter would be easily overwhelmed, when facing a true enemy.

Therefore, Lady Shen demanded that she spend more time practicing interception. The move Shen had just used—Cloud Wrapping Shooting Stars—was remarkably smooth. It was one of the most extraordinary kung fu skills in the Martial Order.

Shen's footwork was not only supple and graceful, it was also effective. She only needed to shift her feet slightly aside to dodge the boy's kicking feet.

The boy had an amazing variety of tricks. Though his feet missed their targets, with a *clink*, a knife sprang out of each boot.

His hidden weapons missed, but then his sleeves emitted two thin strands of smoke with a muffled *pop*.

Shen's ankle stung and went numb, as if it had been bitten by a mosquito. Then ... she smelled the faint fragrance of peach flowers.

After that, she didn't remember anything.

The boy rose to his feet, slapping the dust off his clothes. He looked at Shen, who was lying on the ground, and said with a grin, "My dear sister, your kung fu is great. It's a shame it's so pretty, and so useless."

Then he heard the sound of clapping behind him.

He spun about and saw a pair of bright eyes.

It was Xiao Shiyi Lang.

He was dead drunk a minute ago, but, now, his eyes were completely sober and clear. He grinned at the boy. "You're amazing, little brother. I've got to hand it to you."

The boy blinked and smiled too. "Thank you for the compliment. I'm flattered."

"I have heard that there was once a martial artist known as Thousand-Hand Buddha. He was compared to a hedgehog, because he had hidden weapons all over his body. No one dared touch him. It appears that you are a baby hedgehog."

The boy grinned. "To tell the truth, you have seen all my tricks. There's nothing else."

The two riders who were Shen's attendants stood horror-struck for only a moment. Then they bellowed with anger again, lunging toward the boy with their swords raised high, prepared to risk their lives.

Still talking and smiling, the boy didn't turn his head. Instead, he merely crooked his body slightly, as if bowing to Xiao.

Attached to the sash around the boy's waist was a jade pendant. The moment he bowed, a shower of silver rays shot out from the jade with a soft whir.

The two riders had taken only two steps before they saw something dazzling fly at them. It was too late. The shower of silver rays plunged into their faces.

They fell to the ground, howling in pain. Their faces stung so terribly that they started to cut them with their swords.

His face darkening, Xiao sucked in and let out a long sigh. "It seems nothing you say can be trusted."

The boy rubbed his hands and smiled. "I assure you that this was my last trick, my friend. I'm not kidding you. Come on! You're not really drunk yet. Let's have another drink."

"I don't have a taste for it anymore."

"I assure you, the wine is not poisoned."

Xiao sighed again. "I enjoy free drinks, but I'm not prepared to die of *alcohol poisoning*. If the wine were poisoned, do you think I would have drunk it?"

His eyes sparkling, the boy smirked. "Even if the wine were poisoned, you probably couldn't tell."

Xiao smirked, too. "You're wrong. Others might not be able to tell, but I can."

"Did you suspect *me* from the very beginning? Do I look like a bad person?"

"You not only look innocent and likable, but the red-nosed old man looks like an honest man as well. It didn't cross my mind, at first, that he might be your cohort."

"What changed your mind?"

"An old man who has sold wine for decades should be able to ladle it quickly without spilling, but he often spills. How could a vendor like him make any money?"

The boy shot a glance at the old man and smiled at Xiao. "If you knew we weren't honest men, why didn't you run away?"

"Do you know why I came here?"

"No."

"I came here to wait for you."

"Wait for me?" The boy was baffled. "How did you know I was coming?"

"Because Shen Bijun would be passing through."

The boy stared at him. "It looks like you know a lot."

"I also know you're a poet."

"A poet?" The boy blinked in perplexity.

Xiao smirked and said,

> *"Carving the deer is nothing*
> *Compared with carving the head.*
> *Pare off everyone's head, if I can.*
> *Wouldn't that be a thrill!"*

Then he added, "Other than you, who is capable of writing something like that?"

The boy paled.

"You don't know me, but I know you," said Xiao. "I also know you have an interesting name—Little Mister."

This time, it took Little Mister much longer to smile his lovely smile.

"You do know a lot, "he said, "but there's something you don't know,"

"Oh?"

"Though the wine is not poisoned, the eggs are."

"Oh?"

"You don't believe me?"

"If the eggs are poisoned, why am I still alive?"

"Drinking a large amount of alcohol will slow the effect of the poison."

Xiao laughed aloud. "So there's at least one advantage to drinking alcohol."

"The poisons I use are usually slow-acting. I don't like to see people die too quickly. Killing people slowly is an art, and watching them die slowly is fine entertainment."

Xiao expelled a deep sigh and mumbled to himself, "How can a teenaged boy have such a hideous heart? I wonder how he came to be."

"I don't know how you came to be either," said Little Mister, "but I know how you're going to perish."

Xiao's face broke into a grin. "You mean choking to death on an egg? Well, in that case, I might as well swallow another."

He slowly opened his hand and, lo and behold, there was a pickled egg in it.

He raised his hand, tossed the egg into the air, opened his mouth wide to catch it, and then swallowed it ... in one gulp.

"It tastes pretty good," he said. "I'll have another."

He opened his hand again and, lo and behold, another egg came out of nowhere.

He raised his hand, tossed the egg, caught it with his mouth, and then swallowed it.

When he opened his hand again, there was still another egg in it.

Everyone was mystified. No one could see how he was doing it.

"I'm neither a chicken nor a female, but I can lay eggs." Xiao smiled. "Isn't that odd?"

There was a moment's silence. Then Little Mister sighed, "I was wrong about you. You knew the old man was my subordinate. Of course you would not have eaten the eggs."

"Finally, you got it," Xiao said, laughing.

Little Mister sighed again. "People often say that getting drunk will help one release all worries. You should never have sobered up."

"Oh?"

"Worries invariably return to those who sober up."

"I don't think I have any worries."

"Only dead people have no worries."

"Am I a dead man?"

"Not yet, but soon."

"Do you want to kill me?"

"You know too much."

"You just told me you considered me your friend. How could you have the heart to kill me now?"

"When necessary, even wives can be sacrificed, let alone friends."

Xiao sighed and lamented, "It seems that friendship is becoming less and less valuable."

He rose to his feet. "Since you once called me your friend, I don't want to deceive you. It's not going to be easy for you to kill me. My kung fu is not much to look at, but it's rather useful."

Little Mister beamed a smile. "I want to see it."

Swoosh, swoosh, swoosh! Following the clicking sounds of activated triggers came a storm of arrows.

The archers were all well-trained, but by the time the arrows had been launched, Xiao had moved from under the tree.

The moment Little Mister leaped to the top of the tree, he saw Xiao's smiling eyes.

Xiao had been waiting for him.

Stunned, Little Mister forced another smile. "Your Lightness Kung Fu is pretty good."

"Well, it's not bad."

"Let's see whether or not you're good at any other kung fu."

While still talking, he threw seven moves.

His boxing was agile, swift, and ruthless. The seven boxing moves were elusive and unpredictable. It was difficult to tell which were fake maneuvers and which were real.

But Xiao could tell.

He dodged them deftly and each of Little Mister's seven moves missed its target.

Though his fists missed, with a *flick*, all of his fingernails shot out to strike the five meridian points on Xiao's chest.

Little Mister's hands, with their long tapering fingers, were as delicate as women's hands. No one had noticed that his fingernails had been sheathed with thin steel covers.

Xiao hadn't noticed this either.

With a shout of surprise, he clutched his chest and fell out of the tree.

Little Mister smiled and whispered, "If you really thought I had used up my last tricks, you were wrong."

"I want to see your other tricks."

Somehow, Xiao was back at the top of the tree.

With a smirk, he opened his hand and revealed five thin steel fingernails.

Little Mister's face turned hard. "Who are you?"

"I am nothing ... but bait."

Little Mister let out a scream and fell out of the tree.

As he fell, a light blue flame spurted from one of his trouser legs, blowing toward Xiao.

The leaves on the treetop caught fire.

But Xiao was already on the ground ... waiting.

"*Xiao Shiyi Lang*!" Little Mister was exasperated. "I'm not a good man, but neither are you. Why are you going against me?"

"I don't care for fishing," Xiao smirked, "and I don't like to be used as bait."

Stamping his feet, Little Mister cried, "All right! Let's fight it out."

He pulled out a flexible rapier from his waistband.

The rapier was thin and narrow. As soon as Little Mister shook it against the wind, it straightened and leaped at Xiao several times, like a snake. His sword style was swift and vicious, similar to that of the Hainan School.

But a closer look revealed that it was actually completely different.

Xiao had never seen such a weird style of swordplay. He moved swiftly, dodging a few attacks. Then he clasped his hands.

Little Mister's rapier was securely clamped between Xiao's palms.

Xiao pushed the rapier forward. Unable to withstand the force, Little Mister fell backward.

The moment he fell and touched the ground, he rolled away several feet, releasing a blast of black smoke. He disappeared into the dark cloud.

"Xiao Shiyi Lang," he said, through the smoke shield, "your kung fu is really useful. I am not your match."

By the time he had spoken the last sentence, he had gone quite a distance away.

But Xiao was already waiting for him.

When Little Mister looked up and saw Xiao, his face turned white, as if he were seeing a ghost. Xiao's Lightness Kung Fu was so good that he moved as swiftly as a spirit.

Xiao smiled. "You haven't used up all your tricks. How can I let you go?"

Little Mister put on a cheerless face. "I assure you, now I have."

"If it's true that you have no tricks left, it will be even more difficult for you to leave."

"Why on earth can't you leave me alone? If it's for that beautiful woman, I can give her to you."

"Thank you very much."

"Will you let me go now?"

"No."

"What—what else do you want? The Deer Carver?"

"You don't have it with you. Otherwise, you would have used it."

"If you want it, I can get it for you."

"That's still not enough."

Xiao sighed. "Do you think I can watch you kill four people and let you get away with it?"

"If you are so noble, why didn't you save them?"

"If you had not been so swift and ruthless, I might have been able to help them, and then I wouldn't want you to pay with your life now."

"You—you really want to kill me?"

"Though I don't like to kill people, how can I sleep in peace knowing you're alive? You're only an adolescent now. How much more vicious would you be in a few years?"

Little Mister broke into a smile.

He smiled frequently and his smile was usually engaging and naive, but it was different this time.

The smile seemed to transform his face into an adult one, and his eyes became unspeakably seductive and charming.

"Do you really think I'm an ... adolescent?" he said.

Meanwhile, his hands started to unfasten his waistband.

Xiao smiled, too. "No matter what you're up to, I won't fall for it."

Xiao reached out his hand. Few people could get away from him.

His boxing play was not special. It did not have any unpredictable variations. What made it stand out was that he was fast—unimaginably fast.

He placed his hand on Little Mister's shoulder.

It was difficult for anyone whose shoulder was grabbed by Xiao's hand to get away from him, but Little Mister was more slippery than an eel. He wriggled his waist, slipping out of Xiao's grasp.

A tearing sound was heard as Xiao's grip ripped open the silk robe Little Mister wore, revealing his firm and fair ... *breasts*.

Little Mister was a woman ... a mature *woman*!

She was petite, but she had a perfectly proportioned and flawless figure. No man could resist the temptation of such a perfect body.

Xiao was stunned.

Her cheeks were as rosy as peach flowers in late spring. "Oh, Xiao," Little Mister purred sweetly as she ran into his arms.

Xiao felt the intoxicating fragrance of her luscious body. He wanted to push her away, but her body felt so smooth and soft. With a woman like her in his arms, what man could harden his heart?

Little Mister reached for the back of Xiao's head.

Her fingernails were thin and sharp. While she giggled and panted faintly, her fingernails scratched the skin on the back of Xiao's neck.

Xiao, his face dark, lashed out in anger, but Little Mister had already slipped out of his arms, like a fish. "Xiao Shiyi Lang, you fell for my trick after all," she cackled. "The poison hidden in my fingernails is called Magic Puzzle Bone Melter. Your skin will rot all over in one hour. Do you want to stay here and let me watch how ugly you become when you die?"

Xiao stamped his feet and flew out of sight.

Little Mister touched her chest, laughing like the tinkle of a bell. "Let me tell you something. That really was my last trick. Every woman has it, and nothing is more effective ... when dealing with men."

Chapter 10

A Murderous Look in the Eye

SHEN FELT AS though she were floating on a cloud, riding a wave of air and still in her cozy familiar carriage.

Lian seemed to be by her side.

They had been married for two years, but Lian hadn't changed a bit. He was still gentle and sweet to her. Sometimes, she felt he kept her at a distance.

But she had no grievances. Any woman should be satisfied with a husband like Lian.

He let her do whatever she wanted and bought her whatever she needed.

He had never said a single harsh word to her. As a matter of fact, he seldom spoke.

Their life had been calm and untroubled.

But was this happiness?

At the bottom of her heart, she had always felt something was missing, but she didn't know what.

Every time Lian was away, she felt lonely.

She wished she could keep him from going out. She knew if she asked him to stay home with her, he would.

But ... she never did.

She knew a man like Lian belonged to the people. No woman could have him all to herself.

She knew he didn't belong to her alone.

Lian was a clear-headed man with strong self-control. However, every time there was a major event in the Martial Order, his calm eyes would burn with fire.

He was supposed to accompany her on the trip home, but when

he heard of Xiao Shiyi Lang's whereabouts, his eyes blazed with excitement.

He seemed even more excited than when he had first heard about his wife's pregnancy. Though he said he didn't want to go, she knew his thoughts were fixed on the manhunt.

She knew him well, so she advised him to go.

When she did that, she secretly hoped he wouldn't.

Lian went.

Though a little disappointed, she didn't complain. She knew what kind of man her husband was. She simply had to learn how to take care of herself.

While she was semi-conscious, Shen vaguely felt a hand tugging at her clothes.

She was certain it wasn't Lian's hand. Lian had never been so rough with her.

Whose hand was it then?

Suddenly she remembered everything, including that wretched adolescent! She screamed and woke up in a cold sweat.

She saw the boy's devilish eyes staring at her.

She was in the carriage and there were only the two of them.

She would rather be caged with a viper than see this fiend again.

She tried to sit up, but didn't have the strength.

Little Mister smiled at her and taunted, "What are you afraid of? I won't eat you. Better lie still. Don't get me mad, or there'll be hell to pay."

Shen clenched her jaw; she wanted to throw out all of the most vicious insults in the world, but she couldn't think of any. She didn't know how to curse.

Little Mister stared at Shen, muttering, "You're a perfect beauty. When you're not angry, you're pretty. When you're angry, you're still pretty. No wonder so many men are infatuated with you. Even I am tempted to hug and kiss you."

Shen turned ashen and her voice quivered. "How ... how dare you!"

"How dare me? Why wouldn't I dare?"

With a grin, Little Mister continued, "There's something a woman like you will never understand. When a man desires a woman, he'll do anything."

She reached for Shen's chest.

Shen froze with fear, shaking from head to toe. She wished this were just a dream, a bad dream.

Sometimes, however, reality is even more frightening than a nightmare.

Little Mister's eyes were menacing, like a hungry cat's when focusing on the mouse beneath its paws. Her hands ripped open Shen's robe.

Shen had never spoken loudly in her entire life, but now she couldn't keep from screaming at the top of her lungs.

Little Mister ignored Shen's screams. She stared at her breasts. "Beautiful! So beautiful!" she whispered. "You have a pretty face and a pretty body. If I were a man, I would leave other women for you, too."

When she said the last few words, her smile became even more sinister. Her eyes showed a murderous look.

Often, a beautiful woman cannot stand the sight of another beautiful woman. Nothing can trigger a woman's urge to kill more easily than jealousy!

Shen fainted again.

When people encounter something they can't bear, they often lose consciousness to avoid facing it. Fainting is an innate survival tactic.

When Shen was unconscious, she looked even more attractive.

Her long eyelashes covered her beautiful, dreamy eyes, and her bowed lips formed a soft sweet smile.

Little Mister gazed at her and expelled a soft sigh. "I can't bear to kill a woman like you, but I must. If I take you back ... will he still pay attention to me?"

Unexpectedly, she heard a voice from the roof of the carriage mimicking her. "I can't bear to kill a woman like you, but I must. If I let you live, how will others put up with you?"

A vent on the roof was opened, revealing a pair of thick eyebrows and a pair of luminous eyes.

Little Mister's face froze. "*You* ... you're still alive?" she gasped, in a hoarse voice.

Who else would have such bright eyes besides ... Xiao Shiyi Lang!

"I'm no mouse," Xiao smirked. "How could I have died from a mere cat scratch?"

"You're not a mouse or a human being," Little Mister said, between gritted teeth. "It's my fate to meet you. All right, come down and kill me ... if you dare."

She crossed her arms and closed her eyes as if giving up the struggle.

Curious, Xiao winked his eye. "You don't want to escape?"

"Even when I had secret weapons all over me, you cornered me. Now that I've used up my tricks, how can I get away?"

"Why don't you hold Shen Bijun hostage? You can threaten to kill her if I attack."

"She isn't your wife or lover. Even if I tear her apart, your heart won't ache. How can I hold her hostage against you?"

"Why don't you give it a try?"

"It's useless. What's the point?"

"Are you really resigned to your fate?"

"What choice do I have, in the face of Xiao Shiyi Lang?"

Xiao shook his head, laughing. "No, no, no. I don't believe you. You don't look like someone who would resign herself to fate. You must be planning some other tricks."

"What other tricks do I have to play?"

"No matter what you're up to, don't expect me to fall for it."

"Are you afraid to come down and kill me?"

"I don't have to go down to kill you."

"Then what do you want?"

"First, I want you to stop the carriage."

Little Mister knocked on the wall of the carriage. The vehicle slowed and came to a halt. "What else do you want me to do?" she asked.

"Pick up Shen and get out of the carriage."

Little Mister did as she was told. She opened the door and got out of the carriage with Shen in her arms. "Now what?"

"Keep walking. Don't turn around. Walk until you get to the tree and then put her down. I'm right behind you. No more tricks."

"As you wish."

Little Mister kept walking, without turning her head. Xiao followed closely behind her, puzzled over why she had become so obedient.

When Little Mister reached the tree, she suddenly whirled and tossed Shen's body toward Xiao. Without thinking, he caught Shen's body in his arms.

Little Mister jumped up and spun around midair, releasing three cold rays at Shen, who was still in Xiao's arms.

If Little Mister had threatened to kill Shen a moment ago, Xiao might not have cared. But now that Shen was in his arms, how could he not care?

He dodged the three hidden weapons and briefly considered whether to put Shen down on the ground. Little Mister was nowhere to be found.

He heard her sonorous voice mocking him from a distance. "Hot potato! You figure out what to do with it."

Xiao looked at Shen, still in his arms, and smirked bitterly. This *hot potato* was rather cumbersome. He couldn't just throw it away, but he didn't know whom to give it to.

When Shen regained consciousness for the second time, she found herself in a deserted temple. It was not only incredibly rundown, it was also very small.

The statue inside the shrine seemed to be of the mountain deity. The wind was howling outside. If it weren't for the fire in front of the altar, she might have frozen solid.

The wind was seeping in from all sides. The flame kept flickering. Someone was warming his hands over the fire and humming in a low voice.

He was shabbily dressed and his boots had big holes, but he seemed more relaxed than a man in a fur coat sitting in a cozy room. Shen couldn't understand how a man could be so comfortable, under these conditions.

But the tune of the song he was humming sounded unspeakably poignant, forlorn, and lonely. It didn't match his demeanor.

She couldn't keep from focusing on the man. After some moments, she remembered that she shouldn't stare.

She should evaluate her own situation first.

There was no bed in the deserted temple, so she was lying on the altar. There was a thick layer of hay beneath her. This man, though appearing boorish, had been thoughtful enough to take care of this particular detail.

But ... was he a friend or an enemy?

She struggled to sit up, trying not to make any noise.

But the man, still warming his hands over the fire, had sharp ears. The moment she moved her body, he heard it.

"Lie down. Don't move!" he said sternly, not looking up.

She had never had anyone talk so rudely to her in her entire life. Though she had a gentle temperament, she had never taken orders from anyone.

She was tempted to jump off the altar right then.

The man still didn't look up. "If you really want to go, you'd better take a look at your leg," he said. "No matter how pretty a girl, you won't be too good-looking with one leg."

Only then did Shen notice that her right leg was swollen. Enormously swollen.

She lay down without ado.

Any woman would be frightened to find her leg in such a serious condition.

The man seemed to chuckle.

"Who are you?" she asked, when she had finally calmed down.

The man stirred the fire with a stick. "I have nothing to do with you, and you have nothing to do with me. I don't want to know who you are, and you don't have to know who I am either."

"How ... how did I get here?"

"There are some questions you'd better not ask. It will only cause you trouble."

Shen was quiet for a moment. "Did you save me?" she muttered at last.

He smirked. "How can a man like me be worthy enough to save you?"

There was a long pause. Shen didn't know what to say.

The man stayed silent, too. It seemed that both of them had suddenly become mute.

The wind was still howling outside. There were no sounds. They seemed to be the only two people in the world.

Apart from Lian, Shen had never been alone with a man. With the gusty wind, the flickering flames, and this boorish man....

She felt insecure.

She couldn't keep herself from struggling to sit up again.

But no sooner had she moved than the man stood in front of her, with a cold stare. "I know a noble lady like you can't bear to stay in a place like this for long, but you have a leg injury. You have to stay here until you recover."

His eyes were large, dark, deep, and luminous.

When stared at by this pair of eyes, Shen felt flustered. Unaccountably, she felt anger rising from the bottom of her heart. "Thank you for your kindness, but it's none of your business whether my leg is injured or not. You didn't save me and you don't know me. Why should you care?"

She struggled to jump off the altar and to limp out of the temple. She was hobbling very slowly, but she had no intention of stopping.

The man simply looked at her. He didn't try to stop her. His eyes seemed to be smiling.

If he tried to stop her ... she might stay.

The pain in her leg was unbearable.

Rarely in his life had Xiao forced anyone to do anything.

As he watched Shen attempting to walk out, he was amused.

It was said that Shen Bijun was not only the most beautiful woman, but also the most virtuous, the most gentle, and the most courteous ... and she never got angry.

Yet Xiao saw her getting angry.

It was fun to see a person who never gets mad getting mad.

Shen was at a complete loss. She didn't know why she was getting angry with this stranger. Even if he hadn't saved her, at least he hadn't taken advantage of her while she was unconscious.

She should be grateful to him.

Somehow, this man had upset her. When his eyes looked at her, she couldn't keep her cool anymore. She had always been good at controlling herself, but his eyes were too untamed, too candid.

It was windy, freezing, and frighteningly dark outside. There was not a single star in the sky.

It felt more like winter than autumn.

Her leg had been numb, but now it was hurting. The burning pain irritated her, like needles piercing her heart.

She clenched her teeth, but still couldn't lift her foot.

Furthermore, it was so dark ahead that even if she could walk, she wouldn't know which way to go.

Despite her best efforts, tears started to trickle down her cheeks.

She had never been alone in the dark like this. It was terrifying. She was a delicate orchid grown in a greenhouse, not in the wild.

She leaned against a tree, about to burst into tears.

Just then she felt a hand on her shoulder. She turned and saw that same pair of large, dark, intense eyes.

Xiao held out a bowl of steaming soup. "Eat it. I assure you it's not poisoned."

As he gazed at her, his eyes were still glistening, but they had become incredibly gentle. His words were still straightforward, but they contained only compassion, not sarcasm.

She took the proffered soup, holding it in both hands.

The steam rising from the soup seemed to dispel the chill around her. It was as though she were holding not just a bowl of soup but a bowl of warmth and empathy.

Her tears dropped one by one into the soup.

The temple of the mountain deity was still small, dirty, and decrepit.

But when Shen limped into it from the darkness and cold, the deserted temple seemed full of warmth and light.

She hung her head low, unwilling to look up.

She had never dreamed that she would cry in front of a stranger.

She had never even shed tears in front of Lian.

Luckily, Xiao didn't seem to notice her. After they entered, he ambled over to a haystack in the corner and lay down. "Go to sleep," he said. "Even if you want to leave, you have to wait until tomorrow...."

His voice trailed off as he fell asleep.

The haystack was dirty, cold, and damp, but he seemed to sleep more sweetly and soundly than people sleeping on the softest and warmest beds.

He was a strange man.

Shen had never met a man like him. Somehow, she felt safe by his side.

When he was awake, he seemed rude and rough, but when he was asleep, he looked like a child.

A child feeling hurt and left out.

His thick, knitted eyebrows seemed to hide endless and unspeakable suffering, apprehension, sorrow, unhappiness....

Shen drew a soft breath and closed her eyes.

She used to think she would never be able to fall asleep beside an unfamiliar man, but, now, she slowly drifted into sleep.

Chapter 11

The Lady and the Bandit

SHEN AWOKE EARLY.

The wind had died down. The fire was still burning. Apparently fresh firewood had been added to it. Although wind seeped in through seams and holes, the temple was warm inside.

But the man by the fire was gone.

Had he left without telling her?

Shen stared at the flickering flames, feeling empty, disheartened, and alone ... as if she had suddenly lost something.

She also felt deceived and abandoned.

She didn't know why she felt this way. They were strangers to each other. She didn't know his name, and he had never promised her anything.

He could leave anytime he wanted, and he had no obligation to tell her.

But she had never felt this way before, even when her husband left home.

Why?

When people experience hardship or suffer illness or injury, they often need more compassion and warmth. They become more vulnerable and afraid to be left alone.

This was how she explained it to herself, but she found her explanation unsatisfactory.

Bewildered and distressed, she was at a loss as to what to do next. Then she heard a forlorn, lonely voice singing outside.

The singing changed her mood. Even the fire seemed to become brighter and warmer.

Xiao appeared.

Still humming his song, he carried a bucket of water with his left hand and a bunch of unknown herbs in his right hand. He had a spring in his walk and an air of instinctive energy about him.

He seemed as vigorous as a lion or a tiger, but he was not as ferocious. Not only did he seem cheerful, but it seemed he could make everyone who saw him cheerful as well.

She couldn't help but break into a smile.

Xiao's luminous eyes happened to glance in her direction.

"Good morning," she said pleasantly.

"The morning is almost over," he retorted, casting her a look and then turning away.

Though it was only for a very brief moment, she noticed that his eyes had become very gentle.

"Last night ... " she murmured.

The thought of the soup and the tears in the soup made her blush. She bowed her head. "I'm sorry to have troubled you. In the future I will—"

"I like people to repay me," Xiao said, cutting her short. "Any method is fine. But whatever you promise now is useless, so we might as well not talk about it."

She was at a loss for words.

Every time Xiao talked to her, he sounded impatient and annoyed.

As far as Shen could remember, men had always been gentle and courteous to her. Even rough and vulgar men usually tried to act civilized and upright in her presence. She had never met a man who snubbed her.

Until now.

This man didn't even want to look at her.

What was wrong with him? Couldn't he see how pretty she was?

The pot that had held last night's soup was on the fire. Empty now, it was red hot. She didn't know whether the soup had been eaten or evaporated. Xiao poured the whole bucket of water into the pot.

Following a sizzling sound, steam poured out of it.

Xiao sat by the fire, waiting for the water to boil.

What kind of man was he? Was this deserted temple his home? Why did he refuse to reveal his name? Did he have some dark secret?

Shen was becoming more and more curious about this man, but was too embarrassed to ask questions. She wished he would say something about himself. Even if he didn't want to reveal everything, a tidbit or two would do.

Xiao started to hum the same song again. He kept his eyes closed, seemingly oblivious to her presence.

If he doesn't want to talk to me, why should I stay here? she thought.

Suddenly angry with herself, she spoke up. "My surname is Shen. In the future, if you drop by Shen Manor near the Daming Lake, I will send someone to give you a generous reward. You won't be disappointed."

Xiao didn't turn to face her. "Are you going home now?"

"Yes."

"Can you walk back by yourself?"

Shen took a look at her leg, finding it more seriously swollen than last night. Even worse, the swollen part was completely numb.

She could barely lift her foot, not to mention walk.

The water in the pot was boiling.

Xiao slowly spread out the bunch of herbs, carefully selecting a few of them. Then he tossed them into the water and used a stick to stir it.

Shen stared at her leg and felt tears welling up in her eyes. She was a proud person who had never begged anyone for help.

Nevertheless, she had no choice now.

There was nothing she could do about it. Everyone gets desperate once in a while. She just had to grin and bear it or she would go crazy.

She took a long breath and said, "I ... I need you to do me a favor."

"Um-hum."

"Could you hire a carriage to take me home?"

"No."

His brusque reply baffled her. After pausing for a moment, she asked, "Why not?"

"Because we're high in the mountains and carriage horses can't fly."

"But ... how did I—?"

"I carried you."

Almost instantly, a blush rose heatedly to her cheeks. She was speechless.

"Now," said Xiao, "you wouldn't let me carry you down the mountains, would you?"

After a long, awkward silence, she finally asked, "Wh-why did you ... bring me here?"

"If I hadn't brought you here, where else could I have taken you? If you found an injured kitten or puppy on the road, wouldn't you take it home?"

Her blushing face turned pale with anger.

She had never wanted to slap a man, but if she had possessed the strength, she might have given this man a big slap across the face.

Xiao rose to his feet and walked slowly toward her. He stood in front of the altar, inspecting her leg.

Her face blushed again. She wished she could just chop off her leg. She tried to pull it closer to her, but Xiao kept his eyes fixed on it.

"Wh-what do you want?" she asked, both embarrassed and irritated.

"Your foot is as swollen as a rice dumpling. I'm thinking how to take off your shoes and socks."

She almost screamed. This man wanted to take off her shoes and socks! Even her husband had never seen her feet!

"It looks like there's no way to take them off," Xiao murmured mostly to himself. "The only way is to cut them off—"

He pulled a knife from his waistband.

"I thought you were a gentleman," Shen gasped, in a quivering voice. "It turns out that ... you...."

"I'm not a gentleman, but neither am I in the habit of taking off women's shoes."

He stabbed the knife into the altar and fetched the bucket of water. "If you want to walk home anytime soon, take off your shoes and socks and soak your feet in the water. Otherwise, you may have to stay here forever."

In those days, asking a lady to take off her shoes and socks was like asking her to take off her clothes. If a woman could take off her shoes and socks in front of a man, then there was almost nothing she wouldn't remove.

Shen didn't have a choice.

She wished this man would turn his face away, like a gentleman.

But Xiao stared with widened eyes and had no intention of turning away.

She bit her lip. "Could ... could you please step outside?"

"No."

She blushed to the very roots of her hair, and was so embarrassed that she felt like dying.

"Don't assume that I enjoy looking at your feet. Right now your feet aren't much to look at. I just need to see what kind of poison got into your foot."

He added dryly, "If the poison spreads, you may have to take off more than your shoes."

This warning was much more effective.

Shen finally put both her feet into the water.

When people soak their feet in hot water, they relax and often start to feel and think differently about things.

When Shen took off her shoes, every inch of her body was shaking, but, now, she had calmed down. It was not as bad as she had thought it would be.

Xiao wasn't concentrating on her foot any more.

He had gotten a clear look at it.

He picked out a few herbs, nipping off the most tender parts. Then he slowly chewed on them, as if to savor their taste.

Shen focused on her feet, not knowing what to think.

She couldn't believe that she had actually soaked her feet in front of a man with whom she was unfamiliar. She wished this were only a bad dream, soon gone and forgotten.

Then she heard him say, "Lift your injured foot."

Seemingly resigned, she didn't resist.

This is the principal strength of women. They resign themselves to their fates, at one time or another.

Many intelligent, pretty women are married to ugly, stupid men. They eventually manage to live with it, because they become resigned to their fates.

Many people have the strange notion that men who defy their fates are heroes.

Women who defy their fates, however, are sinners.

The wound on her ankle looked minor. It was a small red dot, similar to a fresh mosquito bite.

But the swelling had spread above her knee.

The mere thought of that devilish adolescent gave her chills throughout her entire body. When he had attacked her ankle, she couldn't have known how severe the consequences would be.

Xiao spat out the herbs he had been chewing and spread them over her wound. She didn't know whether to feel embarrassed or grateful.

The herbs felt cool and soothing.

He tore a strip of cloth from his own clothing and boiled it in the water. Then he wrung out the cloth, draped it over a stick and held it out to her. "You have probably never wrapped a wound, but it's not very difficult. You should be able to do it."

He turned his head away before he finished speaking.

She looked at his broad back, thinking that she was becoming more and more perplexed. She couldn't figure him out.

He looked boorish, but he was meticulous about detail.

His words were harsh and caustic, but she knew he meant her no harm.

He was a good man.

Why did he want people to think he wasn't?

Xiao hummed the same song again, his voice still poignant and forlorn. Anyone who saw his face now—filled with passion and intensity—would realize he was a lonely man.

Shen gave a silent sigh, then she said, "Thank you. I feel much better now."

"Oh?"

"You have good medical skills. I'm lucky to have met you."

"I don't know anything about medicine. I just know how to survive. We all want to live, don't we?"

Shen nodded slightly. "No one wants to die, unless they have no other choice."

"It's not just people. Animals also learn to survive. They know nothing about medicine, but when they're injured, they find herbs to treat their wounds and then find a place to hide."

"Really?"

"I once saw a wolf flee to a bog after it was bitten by a bobcat. At first I thought it was looking for its final resting place."

"Wasn't it?"

Xiao smiled. "It lay in the bog for two days and then it walked out. It knew there were lots of decomposed herbs in the bog. It knew how to take care of itself."

This was the first time Shen had seen his smile. It seemed that he smiled only when he talked about animals. He didn't like to talk about people.

Then, somehow, his smile became a little rueful. "In fact, humans are like animals. If no one takes care of them, they have to take care of themselves."

Human beings are like animals?

If she had heard this a few days ago, she would have thought whoever said it must be crazy, but now she understood the desolation this comparison suggested.

She had always had someone to accompany and take care of

her. It wasn't until now that she realized how terrible it was to be alone and helpless.

Little by little, she started to feel that this man was not menacing at all. More than that, she felt he deserved more compassion. She wanted to know more about him.

People often develop an intense curiosity about those they don't understand, and this curiosity, in turn, often leads to other emotions.

"Is this your home?" she asked.

"I've been staying here a lot recently."

"Where did you stay before this?"

"I've forgotten what happened before, and I never worry about what will happen tomorrow."

"D-don't you have a home?"

"Why must everyone have a home? Isn't it easier to simply wander around and make the whole world home?"

When someone says he doesn't want a home, it usually means he really does. However, "home" is not just a house. A home is difficult to build ... but easy to destroy.

Shen couldn't help sighing. "Everyone needs a home. If you have any difficulty, perhaps I can help—"

"If you just stop talking, I won't have any difficulties," Xiao said.

She was at a loss for words again.

Such unreasonable people were unusual.

At that moment, they heard footsteps and in walked two strangers.

It was uncommon for this deserted temple to have visitors.

Both of them were decent-looking and luxuriously dressed. The one carrying a saber was older, while the one carrying a sword was only about thirty years old.

It was out of the ordinary for people like them to come to a place like this.

What was even more unexpected was that, when they saw Shen,

their faces showed a look of joy. The older one stepped forward and bowed to her saying, "Are you Mrs. Lian?"

Shen was surprised. "Why, yes. You are ... ?"

"My name is Peng Pengfei, and I'm an old friend of Mr. Lian. I attended your wedding and had a few drinks at the banquet."

"Are you Lord Peng, known as Ten-Thousand Victory Gold Saber?"

Peng smiled smugly. "My name is nothing. Ten-Thousand Victory Gold Saber is really too grand a title for me."

The other man was tastefully dressed and carried a sword. Slender and tall, he looked like an elegant young nobleman. Not many men in the Martial Order looked as refined as he.

Shen was overjoyed to meet her husband's friends at a time like this. She smiled and said, "May I ask your name?"

Peng cut in and replied for him, "He's Liu Yongnan, the eldest son of Liu Sanye—Hibiscus Swordsman. In the martial world, he's known as Jade-Face Swordsman. He has met Mr. Lian a few times."

"Mr. Liu, nice to meet you. I haven't seen Mr. Liu Sanye for quite a while. Has he recovered from his asthma?"

Liu bowed and replied, "Blessed by your good wishes, he has been feeling much better recently."

"Please forgive me for not being able to return your salute. As you can see, I'm injured."

"You are too kind," Liu replied.

"This is not a good place to talk," Peng said. "We have brought a palanquin with us. It's waiting outside. Please return to Flawless Manor with us, Madame."

The two men were both gentle and polite. Shen felt that she had returned to her own world. She didn't have to put up with another man's snubbing or harsh words any longer.

Shen seemed to have forgotten Xiao's presence.

Peng waved his hand and a small but clean palanquin was brought into the temple. It was carried by two strong women dressed in blue.

Shen smiled. "I'm sorry to have troubled you. You're so thoughtful."

Liu bowed. "Mr. Lian has contributed greatly to the Martial Order. It's our pleasure to be of help, Madame."

"Please board the palanquin, Madame," Peng said.

"Wait a minute!" Xiao said, breaking into the conversation.

Peng scowled at him. "Who are you? How dare you meddle in our business?"

"If I said I'm Ouyang Jiu—the Lord of Zhongzhou, would you believe me?"

"I don't think you're worthy of that name," said Peng, with contempt in his voice.

"If you don't believe I'm Ouyang Jiu, why should I believe you're Peng Pengfei?"

"As long as Mrs. Lian believes us," Liu said evenly, "it doesn't matter whether you believe it or not."

"Oh?" Xiao countered. "Does she really believe you?"

All three of them turned to look at Shen. She coughed. "I know you all mean well; I—"

"Mrs. Lian is a gracious lady," Xiao interrupted, with a cold snicker. "Even if she suspected you of something, she wouldn't say it."

"That's true," Liu said, "and only people like you would question a gentleman's motives."

Suddenly, he drew his sword. It moved in a zigzagging pattern, cutting the stick Xiao was holding into four pieces.

Xiao remained unfazed. "That move is, indeed, Hibiscus Sword Style," he said.

Peng spoke up, "It's called Hibiscus Zigzagging. Since you have some knowledge of swordplay, you should know that, other than Mr. Liu and his father Liu Sanye, no one else in the world uses this move."

"I think it's likely that the Hibiscus Zigzagging Mr. Liu has just demonstrated is even more proficient than that used by his father." Shen commented with a polite smile.

"Why don't you ask them how they found out you were here?" Xiao said to Shen.

"It doesn't matter how they found out I'm here. I trust their chivalrous reputations."

A pause ensued. "You're right," Xiao said at length. "The words of well-respected people certainly carry more weight than the words of people like me. I should just mind my own business."

After a hesitation, Shen said, "I know you mean well—"

"He means well?" Peng scoffed. "I'm afraid not."

"He tried to stop us and to keep Mrs. Lian here," said Liu. "He must have an ulterior motive."

"That's right!" Peng cried aloud. "Let's maim him first. Then we'll take him back to be tortured and interrogated. Maybe he was sent here by someone else!"

While shouting, Peng had drawn his golden saber.

Xiao stood still, as if he were frozen.

Something crossed Liu's mind. "Wait!" he cautioned. "Perhaps he's Mrs. Lian's friend. If that's the case, we shouldn't be rude."

Peng turned to Shen. "Do you know him, Madame?"

Shen lowered her head. "No ... I-I don't know him," she muttered.

Xiao burst into wild laughter. "How is it possible that a noble lady like Mrs. Lian would know a lowly man like me? It would be a disgrace for her to call someone like me a friend."

"Exactly!" Liu yelled.

The moment he finished this word, his sword flew toward Xiao like a streak of light. In the blink of an eye, he had thrust his sword four times in a row.

Though both current experts of Hibiscus Sword Style were male, its founder was a woman; therefore, the style of this kung fu was supple and nimble, but not very powerful.

In addition, since women are not as aggressive as men, they generally put more emphasis on defense than on attack.

As a result, in this system of swordplay, attack accounted for only thirty percent, whereas defense accounted for seventy percent.

Although the first four moves appeared impressive, none of them was a solid attack. Their purpose was to test the strength of the opponent.

Xiao hadn't stopped his uncontrolled laughter, and ... he hadn't moved.

"Since Mrs. Lian doesn't know him," Peng barked, "we don't have to be lenient with him."

The Gold-Spine Cleaving Saber he was holding was heavy, at least thirty pounds. When he brandished it around, it generated quite a wind. The two women in blue huddled in the corner, in fear.

The masculine Gold-Spine Saber happened to complement the feminine Hibiscus Sword. Surrounded by the interwoven reflections of the saber and the sword, Xiao seemed to have been pushed into the corner, unable to counterattack.

Having gained the upper hand, Peng attacked even more relentlessly. "We don't have to leave him alive," he grunted.

"Right!" Liu agreed loudly.

His sword style became more aggressive. Every move was deadly.

Xiao's eyes flashed a murderous look. "In that case, why should I leave you alive?" he sneered.

He started to counterattack, his bare hands cutting into the maze of saber slashes and sword strokes.

Hibiscus Sword Style was a closely knit program. Its defense is described as "waterproof." Somehow, it was broken through by one of Xiao's palms.

To Liu's astonishment, his attacks were all blocked in an instant. He tripped over something in his panic, and an iron bowl was heard rolling across the floor.

It was Shen's soup bowl from the previous night.

The sight of the bowl and the memory of the warmth that accompanied it touched a chord within her. "He *is* my friend!" she cried aloud. "Please let him go!"

Xiao's iron-like palms had sealed off all the exits of the saber and the sword. His next move would be deadly. Liu and Peng's lives were hanging by a thread.

Yet, when Xiao heard Shen's words, he felt a heat rising from his chest and he lost his hostility against them. He couldn't deliver the deadly attack!

Peng's and Liu's distinguished reputations were built on their solid experiences of real fighting. Naturally, they wouldn't miss such a great opportunity.

They attacked ferociously at the same time, intending to deal a deadly blow to Xiao. Following a slicing sound, they left a wound on his shoulder.

Encouraged by this, Peng turned his saber to chop at Xiao's chest.

Suddenly, Xiao produced a loud bellow. Peng and Liu felt as though they were being hit with great force and their wrists went numb. Somehow, their weapons were wrested from them and ended up in their opponent's hands.

With a clang, both the sword and the saber were snapped in two. Then *pow!* A big hole was smashed through a wall of the temple.

Xiao disappeared into a cloud of dust on the other side.

A lengthy silence ensued. Peng and Liu gawked at their snapped weapons lying on the ground and at the cold sweat oozing from their palms.

Peng sucked in a rasping breath and muttered, "He was … amazing!"

Liu also drew a harsh breath. "He was amazing!" he repeated.

Peng wiped his brow and said, with an embarrassed smile, "Why didn't I recognize such a top fighter?"

Liu also wiped his forehead. "I have never seen anyone with his speed."

Peng turned his head to face Shen. "Do you know who he was, Madame?"

Shen didn't hear him. She stared at the hole in the wall, deep in thought.

Liu coughed. "I wonder whether he is really Mrs. Lian's friend," he said.

At length, Shen let out a soft sigh. "I hope he is a true friend of my husband and mine. Anyone is lucky to have a friend like him."

She said "a friend of my husband and mine" instead of "a friend of mine," because it was the proper thing to say. As a dignified married lady, with high standing in the Martial Order, she knew she couldn't do or say anything improper.

"So, Madame," Liu said, "you don't know his name either?"

"He refused to reveal his name," she said quietly. "Maybe his background conceals enormous secrets."

Peng pondered a moment. "In my opinion," he said, "that was probably Xiao Shiyi Lang."

Xiao Shiyi Lang!

Liu's face turned ghastly white. "*Xiao Shiyi Lang?* What makes you think he is Xiao Shiyi Lang?"

"Everyone knows Xiao is a villain who can kill without blinking an eye, but he's also famous for his martial arts. He's always on the move. No one knows where he is. He has a mysterious past. Very few people have seen his face."

His eyes twitching involuntarily, Peng continued, in a hoarse voice. "Don't you think that man fits the description?"

His lips bloodless, Liu just kept wiping perspiration.

"I know he isn't Xiao Shiyi Lang," Shen said, shaking her head.

"What makes you so sure?" Peng asked.

"Xiao is a notorious villain who has committed countless evil deeds. But I know this man ... he is not an evil man."

"You can see one's face, but you can't see their heart. Sinister men often pretend to be decent people."

Shen smiled. "Xiao Shiyi Lang is a man who kills without blinking. If he were really Xiao, you two would have—"

She didn't finish.

But what she implied was clear. Both Peng and Liu blushed. After several moments, Liu said with a strained smile, "Whether that was Xiao Shiyi Lang or not, our priority is to escort Mrs. Lian back to Flawless Manor."

"That's right," Peng said. "Please board the palanquin, Madame."

Chapter 12

A Marriage Made in Hell

THEY WERE ON a rugged mountain road, but the palanquin was going rather fast. The women bearers in blue had strong legs.

Shen was going home.

As soon as she got home, all her disasters and misfortunes would be left behind. She should be happy, but somehow she felt a little depressed. Peng and Liu were walking beside the palanquin, but she was in no mood to chat with them.

The thought of the young man with large eyes made her feel ashamed. "Why didn't I want to admit that he was my friend?" she asked herself. "Do I feel superior to him? In what ways do I think he is inferior? What right do I have to look down on him?"

She remembered saying that she would try to help him, but when he was in distress and danger, she abandoned him.

Sometimes, he had looked incredibly lonely. Perhaps he had been hurt like this so many times that he felt there was no one he could trust.

Most people hurt or sacrifice others to protect their own reputation and status. Am I just like most people? she mused.

Shen drew a long sigh, feeling that she wasn't as noble as she had thought.

She owed him a great deal.

There was a carriage at the bottom of the mountain.

The carriage driver wore a bamboo hat. He pulled his hat so low over his eyebrows, it was as if he didn't want to be recognized. When the palanquin stopped, the driver came forward and took a prolonged look at Shen, before bowing to her. "You must be in shock, Mrs. Lian," he said.

There was nothing uncommon about what he said, but, somehow, it didn't sound like what a carriage driver would say. Moreover, there was something strange about the way he looked at her.

Her suspicion rose, but she still wore a smile. "Thank you for your concern. I'm sorry to trouble you."

The driver bowed his head. "You are too kind."

He raised his head after turning around and said to the women bearers, "Hurry and help My Lady into the carriage. We have a long journey ahead."

"Lord Peng, Mr. Liu, there is only one carriage," Shen said. "Please ride inside with me."

"Well ... uh...." Peng hesitated and cast Liu a glance.

The driver interrupted. "I'm quite capable of escorting My Lady back to Flawless Manor. We don't have to bother these two gentlemen any further."

To Shen's dismay, Peng responded promptly by saying, "That's right. We were just about to take our leave."

"Gentlemen, you have done us a big favor. My master will not forget it," the driver said.

The carriage driver seemed to have even more authority than Peng Pengfei, Ten-Thousand Victory Golden Saber.

"Who is your master?" Shen asked, alarm flooding her.

The driver looked surprised. "Why! My master is Mr. Lian."

"Mr. Lian?" She frowned. "Are you a member of the Lian family?"

"Yes."

"If you're a Lian, why haven't I ever seen you?"

Instead of answering her question, he turned around and said sternly, "There are some questions you'd better not ask, My Lady. Otherwise, you will cause yourself trouble."

Though she still could not see his face, she spotted his grinning mouth. She felt a chill grip her heart. "Lord Peng! Mr. Liu!" she shouted. "Who is this man? What's going on?"

Peng dropped his eyes, coughed and mumbled, "Um ... Well...."

"You'd better not ask him, My Lady," the driver said. "He can't tell you anyway."

He turned to the women bearers. "What are you waiting for? Hurry and help My Lady into the carriage!"

As the women grabbed Shen's arms, one of them said, with a fake smile, "Don't worry, My Lady. Please get into the carriage."

They not only had strong legs but also strong arms. Shen struggled, but couldn't get away. "How dare you be so rude to me? Let go of me!" she yelled. "Peng Pengfei, if you're Lian's friend, how could you let them do this to me?"

Peng hung his head low, as if he had become deaf and mute.

Shen's lower body was numb and she felt weak all over. With no strength left to use her kung fu, she was dragged into the carriage.

With a sardonic smile on his face, the driver said, "You'll understand, My Lady, when you see my master."

"Is your master th-that—" she stammered.

The very thought of that *adolescent* sent a chill up her spine. Her voice shook.

The driver saluted to Peng and Liu with his fists. "Lord Peng. Mr. Liu. You may go now," he said.

He turned and climbed onto the vehicle.

Liu's face had been somewhat downcast all along. All of a sudden, he spun about and his left hand shot two dark rays at the two bearers' throats. His right hand drew out a dagger to stab the carriage driver's back, with lightning speed. The two actions, one after the other, were swift, precise, and ruthless.

There was no way the driver could evade the attack. Liu's dagger had plunged into his back all the way to the handle.

The women bearers crumpled before either could scream.

Shen was surprised, but pleased. The driver's bamboo hat fell off. She recognized his face. He was one of the adolescent's subordinates.

Now his face was contorted and his eyes popping out of their sockets. "You! How dare you—" he hissed.

He slumped forward on the yoke, and blood spurted from the wound on his back. The frightened horse, neighing loudly, reared up with its hind legs. Then it sprang forward, pulling the carriage behind it. The driver's body was run over by the wheels and cut into two pieces.

Liu jumped up to avoid the blood spurting out of the driver's body. He landed on the horse, pulling on the reins to make it calm down and stop.

Peng stood aghast for a moment. When he finally regained his composure, he yelled at Liu, "Yongnan, you—you just landed us in big trouble!"

"Oh?" Liu responded.

"Why in the world did you do that? Don't you know what Little Mister would do to us?"

"I know."

"Then why ... why did you do that?"

Liu dismounted from the horse and stared at Shen. "I can't let Mrs. Lian fall into the hands of those devils."

Shen finally stopped panting. She was so grateful to Liu that she was on the verge of tears. "Thank you, Mr. Liu. I ... I wasn't wrong about you after all."

Peng drew a sigh. "Do you mean you were wrong about me?"

Shen clenched her teeth, choking back the hateful words she wanted to say.

"I wanted to save you, too, but what's the use?" Peng said. "The three of us combined are no match for Little Mister. It's only a matter of time before he gets you."

He shuddered. Obviously, he was afraid of Little Mister.

"So it was he who wanted you to come for me," Shen said, feeling embittered.

"Otherwise, how would we have known you were in the deserted temple?"

"He was correct in his suspicion of you," she said ruefully. "I misunderstood him."

Naturally, "him" referred to Xiao Shiyi Lang.

"He isn't a decent fellow either," Liu sniffed. "I don't believe he has good intentions toward Mrs. Lian."

"Only *you* are a man of good intentions. Is that what you mean?" Peng countered.

"That's right!"

"Unfortunately, I have seen through your good intentions," Peng said, with a look of disgust.

"Oh?"

"Though I have long known that you have an enormous libido, I didn't expect you to be so audacious as to have your eyes set on Mrs. Lian. You know what? You are just a toad who wants a taste of the swan."

Shen was mortified and outraged. "Don't talk about Mr. Liu like that. I won't have it."

"You think he's a good man?" Peng said, with a derisive laugh. "Let me tell you something. In the last few years, he has raped at least half a dozen virgins every month. No one knows the eldest son of Hibiscus Swordsman—Liu Sanye is actually a filthy letch."

Shen was appalled.

"Because Little Mister knows his dirty secret, he has no choice but to obey him—"

"How about you?" Liu bellowed in anger. "You're not any better. If Little Mister hadn't discovered *your* dark secret, he wouldn't have been able to order *you* around!"

"What dark secret do I have? Spit it out!" Peng shouted in return.

"You're a rich man now, but how did you get your money? You think I don't know? People think you're running a security agency. In reality, you're worse than a bandit! Whoever commissions you to escort them is doomed. Outgoing magistrate Chang hired you to escort his family of eighteen back to his hometown, but on the journey, you slaughtered them all and took their money. Do you really think no one knows what you did?"

"Son-of-a-bitch! *Asshole!*" Peng barked.

Peng was supposed to be a decent, respectable man, and Liu was supposed to be an ever-gracious gentleman. But, now, both of them were acting like mad dogs.

"You're a promiscuous bastard," Peng said. "I don't want to die with you."

"What *do* you want?"

"I want you to give yourself up to Little Mister. I'll put in a good word for you. Maybe he'll forgive you."

"Dream on!" Liu snarled.

Liu was going to attack first, but Peng had already thrown the first punch.

Though Peng was noted for his Gold Saber, his Flood Boxing was about ninety percent mature. When Peng threw his fist toward Liu, one could almost hear the wind. It sounded intimidating.

Liu spun and took three small steps. He turned his hand and used the edge of his palm to chop Peng's shoulder.

Like his swordplay, Liu's boxing featured agility and smoothness. Peng's kung fu was slightly more mature, but the soft always conquers the hard. Hibiscus Palm happens to be the nemesis of Flood Boxing.

It was a bitter fight. It seemed that it would probably take three- to five-hundred moves for them to fight it out.

Clenching her jaw, Shen crawled back into the carriage. She opened the small window in front and saw that the horse, frightened by the ongoing fight, was neighing and slowly backing away toward the roadside.

There were cushions on the seats.

She picked up a cushion and threw it out the window at the horse's backside.

The horse let out a loud neigh and lunged away in terror!

A runaway horse pulling a carriage without a driver was about as dangerous as a blind man riding a blind horse by the lake at night.

But Shen didn't care.

She would rather die in a collision than fall into Liu's hands.

The ride was violently bumpy and her injured leg felt piercing pain.

She didn't care about that either.

She had always thought physical anguish was easier to bear than mental anguish.

It is said that when people are dying, all kinds of strange thoughts flash through their minds. However, they can never predict what those thoughts will be, until the moment comes.

She never dreamed that the first thing that would come to her mind, at a moment like this, was neither her mother nor Lian, but the young man with startling eyes.

If she had trusted him, she wouldn't have ended up in this carriage.

Then she thought of Lian.

If Lian hadn't left her alone, none of these misfortunes would have happened. She told herself not to hate him for that, but she was upset anyhow.

She couldn't help but think: If I had married an ordinary man who was completely devoted to me and put me above everything else, would I have been happier?

She thought of the young man with large eyes again. If I had married *him*, would he ...

She stopped herself from going any further.

She dared not think anymore.

Then she heard an earth-shaking crash.

The door flew open. She was thrown from the carriage and landed on the grass outside.

She fell hard and felt as if all her limbs and bones were dislocated.

The yoke had snapped. The frightened horse ran very far away. The carriage careened into a tree and broke into pieces.

If she were still in the carriage, she would have been seriously injured.

She didn't know whether this was her fortune or her misfortune. She would rather have died in the collision.

Because ... the next thing she saw was Liu Yongnan.

Liu stood there like an idiot. The left half of his face was red and swollen. He was shaking all over, as if he were possessed.

She should be the one who was frightened. What was he afraid of?

His eyes looked glassy and lifeless. It took him quite some time to finally see her.

He walked toward her.

The strange thing was that there was no joy in his face. He walked slowly, dragging his feet as if he had a ball and chain on them.

Was he out of his mind?

She struggled to sit up, but fell again. "*Stop!*" she called out, in a quivering voice, "One more step and I will kill myself right here!"

To her surprise, Liu stopped immediately.

Just as she breathed a sigh of relief, she heard someone speak behind Liu. "Don't worry. Continue walking. She won't kill herself. If she really wanted to die, she wouldn't be alive now."

The voice was gentle and pleasant.

Shen froze at the sound of it.

She hadn't heard this voice many times, but she would never forget it.

No wonder Liu was scared to death. Little Mister was right behind him. Liu wasn't very tall, but Little Mister was too small for Shen to see at first.

Shen didn't want to die. There were many reasons she shouldn't die. But when she heard Little Mister's voice, she wished she were already dead.

It was too late to want to die ... now.

In a flash, Little Mister had dashed over and stood in front of her. She grinned at Shen and said gently, "Good girl. You can't die even if you want to. Better live on. If you're lonely, I'll find you a companion."

She wore a scarlet cloak, her hair tied in a gold ring and a red ribbon. All of these made her pink face look more lovely and appealing.

But Shen acted as if she were seeing a viper. She quivered. "What do you have against me? Why don't you just let me die?"

"I have nothing against you. That's why I can't bear to see you die."

She grinned and beckoned to Liu. "Come over here! Why are you still standing there? Come on! You're an adult. You aren't shy, are you?"

Liu, hanging his head low, walked toward them one step at a time.

Little Mister hadn't killed him, but he would rather be dead, too.

He couldn't figure out what Little Mister was up to. All he knew was that, if Little Mister wanted to torture someone, he might as well commit suicide.

When he stood in front of Shen, Little Mister shook her head and said, "You were so careless! How could you let such a nice face be mutilated like this?"

She took out a snow-white silk handkerchief and gently wiped the blood off Liu's bruised face. She was as tender and thoughtful as a mother taking care of her son.

Liu tried to smile, but his face looked uglier than if he had been crying.

After wiping Liu's face, she slapped dust off his clothes. "Good, you look more presentable now," she said cheerfully. "Be careful next time. You should always protect your face, even if it means your ass will get hit. Understand?"

Liu nodded his head stiffly, as if he were a string puppet.

Little Mister shifted her eyes back to Shen. "Do you know Mr. Liu?" she asked, smiling.

Shen clenched her jaws and closed her eyes. Not knowing what tricks Little Mister was up to, she waited for the chance to kill herself.

"Open your eyes and listen to me." Little Mister's face tightened. "I ask a question, you give an answer. Understand? If you don't obey me, I'll rip your clothes off."

Shen's eyes snapped open.

Little Mister grinned. "Good. That's more like it, my obedient little girl."

She patted Liu's shoulder and said to Shen, "Mr. Liu just killed four people, including his good friend Peng Pengfei. Do you know why?"

Shen shook her head.

Little Mister glared at her. "Shaking your head is not enough. Speak!"

Shen felt as though she would explode at any moment, but she didn't know how to deal with people like Little Mister. Choking down tears, she muttered, "I ... I don't know."

"No, no, no ... No. You do know. He did it all for you, didn't he?"

"Yes," Shen responded.

She didn't want to shed tears in front of Little Mister, but tears escaped from her eyes anyway.

Little Mister smiled. "He's really devoted to you, isn't he?"

"I-I ... I don't know."

"How could you not know? Let me ask you this. Would Lian kill his friends for you?"

"N-No."

"Therefore, he is nicer to you than Lian is, isn't he?"

Shen's nerves, already on edge, could stand it no longer. "Are you human? Why are you torturing me like this?"

"It's getting windy," Little Mister whispered. "Without your clothes, you will definitely catch cold...."

Shen made up her mind and stiffened her tongue. She had heard that if you bit off your own tongue, you would die. She didn't really want to die, but she had no choice now.

But, before she could bite down, Little Mister had clamped her jaws with one hand and started to undress her with the other. "It's not easy to live, but, sometimes, it's even harder to die, isn't it?"

With her mouth clamped, Shen couldn't talk. She could only nod her head.

"Are you going to answer my questions now?"

Shen nodded again.

No one could describe how she felt now, since so few have experienced the suffering Shen was enduring.

It was more than "suffering" can describe.

Little Mister finally smiled and slowly loosened her grip. "I know you're a clever person. You won't do anything stupid again, will you?"

"No."

"If someone is nice to you, you should repay him, shouldn't you?"

"Yes."

Shen's mind went blank.

"Then how do you think you can repay Mr. Liu?"

Shen's eyes glazed over in a blank expression. "I will repay him," she said word by word.

"There is only one way for a woman to repay a man. You're a woman. I'm sure you know what it is."

Her eyes empty, Shen no longer saw or heard anything. She appeared to have become a body without a soul.

"I know you understand. Good," said Little Mister.

Then she patted Liu on the shoulder. "Since you're so nice to her, will you take her as your wife?"

Liu was stupefied. He didn't know whether he should feel shock or joy. "I- I...." His tongue was tied.

"Just say yes or no. This is very simple. What are you nervous about?"

Liu wiped his forehead. "But ... Ms. Shen...."

"Are you afraid she'll say no?" Little Mister smiled and said, "You're such a fool. She has agreed to repay you. How could she say no? Besides, rice once cooked cannot be uncooked. There is no turning back for her."

Liu swallowed nervously and his entire face reddened, but his eyes were riveted on Shen.

"As the proverb goes, 'Strike while the iron is hot.' If you say yes," said Little Mister, "I will perform your wedding ceremony right here."

"R-right here?"

"What's wrong with this place?" she said sternly. "It can be your nuptial chamber ... or your grave. It's up to you."

"Yes, I will do it." Liu nodded frantically. "As long as it's your decision, I will do whatever you say."

"Good. In that case, I will go find bridal candles for you. Keep an eye on your bride. She has only one tongue. If she bites it off, what will you suck when you kiss her?"

Little Mister nipped two branches and placed them in the ground. "These are your bridal candles."

She pointed at the wrecked carriage with a smile. "And that is your nuptial chamber. When you're in the chamber, I will even stand guard for you. I hope you never forget that I was your matchmaker."

Liu looked at the wrecked carriage and then looked at Shen. He suddenly dropped to his knee and muttered, "Little Mister ... I-I...."

"You defied my order, and I didn't punish you. Instead, I found you a beautiful wife. What more can you ask for?"

"But ... after this...."

"What happens after this is between you and her. Do you need me to teach you what to do?"

"Have you really forgiven me?"

"If I hadn't forgiven you, I would have killed you outright. Why would I have taken so much trouble for you?"

"Thank you, Little Mister." Liu was relieved.

"But ... there is one thing you should beware of."

"Please instruct me."

"You are both famous people. This marriage will soon be known throughout the martial world. When Lian Chengbi learns about this ... well, he probably won't be so easy to negotiate with as I am."

Liu's face darkened again. Cold sweat trickled down his forehead.

"Therefore," said Little Mister, "I advise you to find a place to hide after your wedding. You'd better not see anyone. Lian has many friends. He is usually quite well-informed."

She smiled and continued, "Oh, and another thing, watch out for your bride. Don't let her run away. And be careful when you sleep. She may stab you in the back."

Liu was stunned and completely speechless.

He finally realized Little Mister's intention. Little Mister was a genius in torturing people. No one else could think of such a diabolical idea.

When Liu thought about how difficult his life ahead would be, his mouth felt bitter, but he couldn't spit out this sour taste.

Little Mister clasped her hands behind her back. "But ... I can offer you a tip."

"P-please enlighten me, Little Mister."

"If you're worried about your bride, you can disable her kung fu by severing her tendons. And you can chain her feet. If you don't give her any clothes, you will be even more secure."

She grinned and added, "A woman without clothes can't go anywhere."

Liu's palms were wet and his body felt cold.

Little Mister's viciousness was almost unequaled in the world. All who offended her would find that they would rather die than live.

But she could always figure out a way to make people live and suffer. In this case, Shen was unable to die, and Liu couldn't bear to die.

She allowed Liu to live in order to torture Shen, and she kept Shen alive so that Liu would never be able to live in peace.

Seeing the look of suffering on their faces, Little Mister couldn't help but laugh. "A wedding night is a moment more precious than gold. Hurry and enter your nuptial chamber."

Liu stared at Shen's beautiful flower-like face. He knew this would be an abyss, but he had no other choice than to jump into it.

Shen's eyes were still empty and blank, as if gazing into the distance. Liu took her hand and picked her up. She didn't seem to feel anything.

Little Mister looked up at the darkening sky and cheerily recited a poem:

"Come and enjoy the beautiful views and great moments of this evening.

There are red flowers and green grass in the shade of the willow tree. Tomorrow—"

Her voice halted and her smile froze.

She sensed that someone was behind her.

The person was like a phantom. She hadn't sensed his presence until he was directly behind her, and everyone knows Little Mister was never slow to react.

She took a deep breath and exhaled slowly. "Xiao Shiyi Lang?" she probed.

"Stand still. Don't move and don't turn around," ordered the man behind her.

It was Xiao's voice.

Other than Xiao Shiyi Lang, who had such astounding Lightness Kung Fu?

Little Mister rolled her eyes and said, "Don't worry. I've always been obedient. You tell me not to move, and I won't move."

Xiao called out to Liu. "Mr. Liu, please come over, too!"

Liu had been surprised to see Little Mister so frightened of this man. When he heard Xiao's name, he was scared out of his wits.

Daring perverts are not necessarily daring men.

"Do you know Little Mister?" Xiao asked.

"Yes, I-I do," Liu replied.

"As a matter of fact, you should call her Little Girl."

"Little Girl?" Liu was confused.

Xiao smirked. "Can't you see that Little Mister is a *she*?"

Liu's eyes widened.

"How does she compare to Mrs. Lian in beauty?" Xiao asked.

Liu licked his lips. "About ... about the same, I think."

Xiao smiled. "A lecher usually has a good eye for beauty."

He patted Little Mister on the shoulder. "What do you think of Mr. Liu?"

"He is handsome and comes from a prominent family. Any girl

would be lucky to marry him," she said sweetly, with a twinkle in her eyes.

"Would you like to marry him?"

"Very much."

"In that case, I'll perform your wedding ceremony right here. The bridal candles and the nuptial chamber are ready."

Liu was dumbstruck again.

He didn't know whether it was his lucky or unlucky day. He suddenly had become very popular. Everyone wanted to marry him to a beautiful girl.

"Mr. Liu, what do you say?" Xiao asked. "Would you like to marry her?"

Liu bowed his head, stealing a glance at Little Mister. He stuttered, "I-I...."

"Don't be afraid. Although this bride is a little ferocious, as long as you disable her kung fu by severing her tendons and leaving her naked, she'll have to yield to you."

"As long as I can marry Mr. Liu," Little Mister chimed in, with a sweet smile, "even if I have to become handicapped, I will be full of joy."

"Oh, Liu ... " Little Mister purred as she ran into his arms. She threw her arms around his neck and cooed, "My dear man! Why don't you hurry and carry me into the nuptial chamber? I can't wait!"

With an alluring beauty in his arms, Liu felt intoxicated.

Right then he heard Xiao yell: "*Watch out!*"

Too late, Liu felt his neck twist as he was forced into having his back to Xiao, becoming Little Mister's shield.

Then he was thrown backward by a heavy blow to his belly.

Little Mister, as she threw her fist forward, jumped up and threw a few silver darts toward Shen, who still sat stiffly on the ground.

Xiao had known she was going to pull some trick, but he was still not fast enough.

Although he batted away the darts flying toward Shen, he didn't catch Little Mister.

He heard the tinkle of Little Mister's laugh saying, "Xiao Shiyi

Lang, you don't have to find a husband for me. When I'm ready to marry, I'll marry you. I've had my eyes on *you*."

Liu collapsed.

His internal organs had been shattered by Little Mister's fist. There was no way he would live.

Shen's eyes were still empty. She seemed to have lost her mind with the shock and become a mindless idiot.

Xiao sighed. He didn't understand how people like Little Mister were brought into the world. Her cruelty, viciousness, and cunning were appalling.

He should have killed her the minute they met again. Strangely enough, though he knew she was as sinister as a serpent, he didn't have the heart to kill her.

She came across as being so pretty, adorable, and naïve. It was hard to believe she was a devil who could kill without blinking.

Chapter 13

The Lamp in Autumn

IN THE ROOM, there was only a bed, a bench, and a table.

Xiao had stayed in this room for three days. He almost never went out.

Shen had been in a coma for as many days.

During the three days, she struggled, screamed and sobbed ... as if fighting with an invisible monster. Sometimes, she shivered with cold; sometimes, she had a burning fever.

Now, she had finally calmed down.

Xiao gazed at her, his heart full of pity and caring.

But when she came to life, he would never show these feelings.

She was beautiful but not arrogant, intelligent but not scheming. She was gentle but also stoical; no matter how much suffering she had to endure, she never poured out her woes.

She was the woman of his dreams.

He had always wanted to meet a woman like her.

But when she came to, he would still act cold and indifferent to her. Because she was someone else's wife.

Even if she were not married, she could not have anything to do with him. She was a noble lady, a member of the Gold Needle Shens, whereas he was Xiao Shiyi Lang—the Great Bandit.

Xiao knew this code well. He had always been good at controlling his feelings.

He had to.

Perhaps, he mused to himself, a man like me is destined to be alone forever.

He expelled a faint sigh and lit the lamp.

The gentle light struck Shen's face. She finally opened her eyes—
She saw Xiao.

The large-eyed young man was sitting beside her, silently gazing at her.

Was this another dream? There had been so many frightening dreams in the past few days.

She closed her eyes again, not wanting to wake up from this dream. When she opened her eyes for a second time, the large-eyed young man was still quietly sitting there and looking at her.

The corner of her mouth curved into a smile, her eyes full of gratitude. "You saved me again," she breathed.

"I have trouble even saving myself. How could I have saved you?"

"You don't have to lie to me. I know it was also you who saved me from his hands last time."

"He? Who is he?"

"You must know him. I'm talking about the ... the terrible Little Mister."

"I don't know any Big or Little Misters."

"But he must know you. And I think he's afraid of you. He knew I was in the deserted temple, but he didn't dare go by himself to get me."

"Why would he be afraid of me? Am I a vicious person?"

"The really vicious part was those hypocrites," she said, sighing. "I misjudged you."

"People like you shouldn't be wandering around in the first place," Xiao said, his voice sharp.

Rising, he walked to open the window. "You know so little yet talk so much," he added.

It was quiet outside.

In this region, there was probably no other inn whose business was worse than the one where they were staying. Strictly speaking, it was not qualified to be called an inn.

There were no lamps in the courtyard.

Fortunately, there were stars in the sky. Xiao stood in front of the window, against the background of the starry sky, appearing especially lonely.

He was humming that song again.

Looking at his broad back, Shen felt like a migrating goose that had been left behind during a storm but had found shelter under a big tree. She felt calm and secure.

Whatever he might say, she wouldn't get mad anymore.

"What's the song you're humming?" she asked, after some time had gone by.

He said nothing.

After another long pause, Shen suddenly smiled. "Isn't it funny? Someone thinks you're Xiao Shiyi Lang."

"Hmm."

"But I know you're not Xiao Shiyi Lang, because you don't look like a vicious man."

Xiao didn't turn around. "Is Xiao Shiyi Lang a vicious man?" he asked.

"Haven't you heard of the things he's done?"

A pause. "Do you know a lot about these things?" he asked.

"I only need to know one. He deserves to be beheaded for every single crime he has committed."

Silence.

At last Xiao said quietly, "Do you want to chop off his head as well?"

"If I meet him, I won't let him live to claim another victim."

Xiao gave an indifferent laugh. "If you meet him, I'm afraid you'll be the one who will not live."

Shen's face blushed.

Suddenly, they heard footsteps. An inn servant walked toward their room carrying a lantern. Following him was an old man wearing a black cap and a blue jacket, the apparel of a manservant.

They stopped in the middle of the courtyard. The inn servant pointed at their window. The old man in blue examined Xiao up and down, before speaking with a humble smile. "Excuse me, is Mrs. Lian staying here?"

At the sound of his voice, Shen's eyes grew bright. "Is it Shen Yi? I'm right here," she said. "Please come in."

The man in blue was Shen Yi, a senior manservant of Shen Manor. His family had worked as servants for the Shens for many generations. He had worked at Shen Manor even before she was born.

When he heard her voice, he ignored Xiao and ran over. He pushed the door open, entered the room, and immediately kneeled in front of her bed. "I didn't know you were staying here, or I would have come earlier to escort you home. Please forgive my negligence."

Shen was thrilled and surprised. "That's all right. I'm happy to see you. How is Grandmother? Does she know I'm here?"

"The news about what happened to you has spread all over the martial world. When Lady Shen received the news, she immediately sent me to ask around. Today, I accidentally overheard the inn servant say they had a female guest who was very ill, but as beautiful as a goddess. When I heard that, I knew he had to be talking about you."

He drew a long sigh. "Thanks to the grace of Heaven, I finally found you. If Lady Shen knew about this, she would be overjoyed, too."

It looked like he was going to burst into tears.

Shen was speechless in her elation.

"How is your injury? Are you all right?" Yi asked, wiping his eyes.

She nodded. "I feel much better now."

"In that case, let's go home so that Lady Shen doesn't have to worry any longer."

She turned to look at Xiao, who had been standing indifferently aside. "Isn't ... it a little too late?" she said to Yi.

"Days are short in the autumn. It's only around seven o'clock. Besides, I've brought a carriage for you."

She turned to look at Xiao again.

Yi finally noticed the other person in the room. "Sir, you're—?"

"It was he who rescued me," she explained. "Hurry and kowtow to him, to thank him for me."

Yi immediately scurried over and kowtowed to Xiao. "Thank you very much for rescuing My Lady. All of the Shens are much beholden to you."

Xiao looked at Yi coldly. "Are you from Shen Manor?"

"Yes, Sir." Yi replied humbly, "I have served Lady Shen for over forty years—"

Without warning, Xiao yanked him up, slapping him in the face a dozen times.

Almost all of Yi's teeth began falling out. He couldn't even cry out.

Shen was horrified. "What are you doing? He's a member of my family. Why did you do that?"

Xiao ignored her. He picked up Yi and threw him out the window. "Go back and tell whoever sent you here to come themselves. I'll be waiting."

Yi covered his mouth and yelled in a muffled voice, "Lady Shen sent me. What makes you think you have the right to hit me?"

"People like you deserve death. All I did was beat you. Get out of here, or I'll kill you now!"

Yi scrambled out of the courtyard. When he had reached the edge, he stood there cursing and swearing.

Resentful and grim, Shen was mortified. She held her temper. "Shen Yi has worked in my house for more than four decades. He has always been a loyal servant. Did you think he was sent here to harm me?"

Xiao didn't reply.

"You saved me. For that I'll be forever grateful, but why do you have to keep me here?"

"That's not my intention."

Though his voice was cold, his eyes showed a tinge of hurt and anguish.

"What is your intention?"

She struggled to retain her composure and to keep her manners, but the tone of her voice was harsh.

"Do you honestly believe I mean you harm?" Xiao asked, clenching his fists.

"If you mean me no harm, please escort me home immediately."

After an interval, Xiao took a long breath, then said, "Not now."

He looked as if he were about to say something more, but he held off.

"When are you going to escort me home?"

"Maybe in a few days."

Xiao pushed the door open and strode out.

"Wait!" Shen cried out. "I haven't finished yet. You can't leave."

But Xiao had already walked quite a long away. He didn't turn back.

Her hands shook with rage.

She used to feel guilty when she thought about him. She felt that she should repay him and make it up to him. She had sworn that she would never hurt him again.

His behavior, however, was simply too baffling and suspicious. What upset her most was that he was obviously holding something back.

On the table was a big jar of wine Xiao hadn't finished yet.

Not knowing how to vent her anger and frustration, she seized the jar of wine and drained it.

She seldom drank.

As a lady, when she did drink wine, she usually had only a sip. What she drank today, however, probably exceeded the total amount of wine she had drunk in her entire life.

After drinking more than half a jar of wine, she felt as if a current of heat had flown down her throat and become a burning fire in her stomach.

After a while, the burning fire traveled upward to her head.

Those who have little experience with drinking never understand the strange sensations generated by such "movement of heat." Her brain became blank and free, leaving her head reeling and whirling.

Her mind seemed to become sharper, but actually, she wasn't thinking at all.

She usually tried to control and restrain herself, always careful not to lose her grace or manners, not to do anything wrong or say anything wrong, not to offend anyone....

But, now, all her restraints were discarded.

What she usually considered insignificant suddenly became important.

She lay half asleep for some moments before thinking of Xiao again.

His behavior is strange, and his attitude is incomprehensible. Why did he chase Shen Yi away? Why does he refuse to escort me home?

The more she thought about it, the more resentment she felt. She couldn't stand it anymore.

More and more, she thought it was imperative that she go home as soon as possible.

Just because he refuses to help me doesn't mean I can't find someone else to escort me home, she thought.

She felt her rationale was absolutely correct. She couldn't wait another moment. She struggled to sit up in bed, calling out with all her strength, "Manager! Porter! Is there someone who can help me! Somebody! I need help...."

She had never known she could let out such loud cries.

The inn servant came to her room almost immediately and asked, "How may I help you?"

"Hire a carriage for me. I'm going home. Hurry!"

The inn servant was hesitant. "I'm afraid that I can't provide a carriage right now."

"Try to find one for me. Don't worry about the money. I can pay the charge."

The inn servant still hesitated. He turned around and asked, "Sir, are you sure you want me to hire a carriage?"

When she realized Xiao was standing right behind the inn servant, a flame of anger ignited in her and she cried out, "Whether I want to go home or not is my own affair. What does this have to do with him? Why are you asking him?"

Xiao shook his head. "You're drunk."

"Who says I'm drunk? I only drank a little. How could I be drunk?"

She waved at the inn servant. "Go hire a carriage for me. Don't listen to him. He's the drunk."

The inn servant looked at her and then looked at Xiao.

Xiao shook his head again.

Shen cried out, "You don't want to escort me home, and you won't let me go home by myself. Why? Who do you think you are? What right do you have to interfere with my life? What right do you have to keep me here?"

"You're really drunk," said Xiao with a sigh. "Have a good rest. We can talk about everything tomorrow, all right?"

"No, I'm leaving now."

"You can't go now."

She flew into a rage. "What makes you think you have the right to keep me here? Do you think just because you saved me that I belong to you? Stop your fantasy. I don't need you to save me anymore. If you don't let me go, you might as well just ... *kill* me!"

She struggled and tried to throw herself at Xiao.

Instead, she fell off the bed with a thump.

Xiao rushed over to help her up, but the moment his hands touched her, she screamed. "Help! This man is a bandit! Go get the police! Arrest him!"

Xiao's face went red with anger. Just as his hands were going to let go of her, Shen bit his hand hard. Blood oozed from the wound.

Shen Bijun bit people! Who would believe this!

Shen had bitten his hand, but Xiao felt as if it were his heart.

"I thought you were a good man," Shen panted. "It turns out you're like everyone else. You saved me for some ulterior motive. You're worse than all of them."

Xiao slowly closed his eyes, turned and walked out.

Shen thought the words she had just said were simply brilliant. She had successfully driven that man away. Usually, she couldn't do this, but after drinking the wine, she had become *inspired* and very eloquent.

She decided she would start drinking more often.

She thought there was nothing wrong with what she had said. Drunks always think they are the most sensible ones in the world. Whatever they do is always right. It's always others who are at fault.

The inn servant was still standing in the room gawking.

She panted for a while, then, suddenly, gave him a smile.

Which showed how sober and clearheaded she really was.

Bemused, he returned her smile.

"That man is truly unreasonable, isn't he?" she commented.

He coughed. "Yes, ma'am."

"I don't like to argue with people, but he is just outrageous."

The inn servant nodded frantically. "Yes, yes, yes."

Nodding slowly, she was glad to know that others were still on her side. Most of the people in the world were reasonable after all.

Nonetheless, the inn servant was walking on tiptoe, prepared to sneak away.

"Do you know Shen Manor by the Daming Lake?" Shen asked brusquely.

He had to stop and reply. "Everyone in this region knows Shen Manor."

"Do you know who I am?"

He shook his head and smiled dutifully. "This is the first time you have used our services, ma'am. Next time you come, I will recognize you."

No one likes to deal with drunks. The inn servant wanted to run away, but he had to say something to answer the customer's questions.

"To tell you the truth, I'm Ms. Shen from Shen Manor. If you escort me back to the Manor tonight, I will reward you generously."

Amazed, the servant looked her up and down.

"You don't believe me?" she said.

He muttered hesitantly, "If you are really from Shen Manor, I'm afraid that you can't go back there."

"Why?"

"Shen Manor was burned to the ground. Many people were killed or injured, and others are missing. There is not a single person left."

Shen felt as if her heart were ripped open as the realization sank in. "*What?*" she cried out. "I don't believe it! *I don't believe a word you say!*"

"I would not dare to deceive you."

She pounded the bed with her fist. "You conspire with him against me and lie to me. You and he are both evil men."

"Whether you believe it or not, everything I have said is true," he said with a shake of his head.

She turned onto her stomach, buried her face in the comforter, and cried.

The inn servant was going to leave, but stopped when he heard her crying.

Men's hearts are easily moved by the tears of a woman, especially a pretty woman.

He heaved a deep sigh. "All right, ma'am. If you insist on going to Shen Manor to see for yourself, I'll go with you."

Xiao was sullenly drinking alone.

He wanted to get drunk. Strangely enough, he couldn't.

In the last few days, he had become a different person.

He had become rather unreasonable.

He had always been a straightforward, humorous, and happy-go-lucky man; but in the past few days, he had become indecisive and tongue-tied.

Why didn't I just tell her Shen Manor has been leveled? he asked himself. Why did I have to keep the truth from her? Why do I care whether or not she can take it?

He smirked impassively and drank another cup of wine.

I'm no relation to her. Why am I sticking my nose into her business and making her hate me?

When Shen Yi had shown up, Xiao knew Little Mister must have recruited him. Since Shen Manor had been burned to the ground, how could he escort her "back home?"

Xiao hadn't explained, afraid that Shen wouldn't be able to bear the emotional impact. In the past few days, she had suffered more than her share of hardships.

He had been afraid that she would snap.

After everything I've done for her, he thought, she should at least put a little trust in me. Since she doesn't, why should I care about her?

Xiao felt that he didn't have to do any of this. He decided not to concern himself about her business anymore. He didn't like to feel miserable and misunderstood.

Hearing the noise of a horse and carriage outside, he realized the inn servant had taken Shen home after all.

He started to worry again: Little Mister must still be lurking somewhere in the dark. If she knows Shen has left without me, she'll go after her.

Xiao couldn't keep from rising to his feet, but then he slowly sat down again.

I just said I would no longer concern myself with her. Why am I worried about her again? Even her husband doesn't care about her. Why do I bother? Who am I to her?

But ... she was drunk. Maybe she didn't know what she was saying. People sober up and often regret what they said while they were drunk. I should forgive her.

Even if I save her one more time, she'll still think I have an ulterior motive or some selfish reason. When she finds out I'm Xiao Shiyi Lang, all my good intentions will be considered evil.

But, a good deed left unfinished is not a good deed. I've saved her twice. Why can't I save her again? How can I stand aside and watch her fall into the clutches of Little Mister?

Xiao drank one cup after another, sick at heart and full of conflicting thoughts and emotions.

His head had never been so unsettled.

At last, he made up his mind.

No matter how she treats me, I can't refuse to help her! he decided.

He stood up and strode out.

A cold wind blew in his face, but he felt heat rising in his chest. He started to sing at the top of his lungs, and his powerful voice made all the paper windows around him begin to clatter.

One window after another opened and revealed one surprised face after another. All of them scowled at Xiao with their sleepy eyes.

Some were cursing loudly.

"This guy must be a drunkard! A lunatic!"

Xiao didn't care. He was amused.

He knew he was neither a drunkard nor crazy.

He told himself, "As long as I keep a clear conscience, what does it matter if others call me a lunatic? As long as I'm doing the right thing, why should I care about what others think of me?"

The carriage was going fast.

A rundown carriage driving on a rugged unpaved road is as bumpy as a ship sailing through a storm.

Still, Shen fell asleep.

She dreamed that the large-eyed young man was weeping by her and then smiling at her. His smile was menacing. She was so mad that she grabbed a knife and stabbed his chest.

When the knife went into his chest, he suddenly became ... Lian Chengbi.

Blood, like a fountain, spurted out of Lian's body. So much blood flowed out that he was submerged by it, until only his eyes remained above the surface.

The eyes stared at her. They looked sad and tormented.

She couldn't tell whether they were Lian's or the young man's eyes.

Frightened, she wanted to scream, but her voice wouldn't come out.

It appeared she was going to be swallowed by the tide of blood as well.

The blood was cold ... extremely cold.

She was shaking all over ... shaking uncontrollably.

She seemed to hear someone talking. It was distant at first, but then it got closer and closer ... so close it was like someone shouting into her ears.

She woke up.

The carriage had stopped.

The door was open and the wind blew against her body. The wind was cold. As cold as the spilt blood.

Her body was still shaking.

The inn servant stood outside the door, looking at her with pity in his eyes. He called out loudly, "Please wake up, ma'am. We're here. This is Shen Manor."

Shen looked at him blankly, as if not quite comprehending the meaning of his words. She felt that her head had been filled with lead. It was too heavy to lift.

We have arrived at Shen Manor. I'm... home, she finally realized.

She almost couldn't believe it was true.

"This is Shen Manor," the inn servant muttered. "Are you going to get out of the carriage, ma'am?"

She finally smiled and spoke. "Of course, I'm going to get out. I'm home. Why wouldn't I get out?"

Unwilling to wait another moment, she scrambled out of the carriage, almost falling to the ground.

The inn servant held her arms and said, "Actually ... I think you had better not get down."

"Why not?" she laughed. "Are you going to take the entire carriage, with me in it, into the house?"

Suddenly, her voice and her laugh froze.

Her mind went numb.

Chapter 14

Gods of Thunder and Lightning

A VEIL OF mist hung over the Daming Lake.

During the day or night, autumn at the Daming Lake was always beautiful. When there was a mist, the lake was as beautiful as the pictures children see in their dreams.

Shen's chamber was by the lake. When she opened her window, she could take in the enchanting lake view. From the time she was a child, she had admired the slightly forlorn and desolate autumn view. The memory of the lake was branded in her memory.

Even after she married, she often returned to Shen Manor.

Every time her carriage approached the lake, she would keep looking out the window. When she saw her little chamber, she always felt a sweet warmth rising in her.

Now, however, the chamber was gone.

The row of houses next to her chamber was gone as well.

Everything was ... *gone!*

The ancient, grand, beautiful, and seemingly immortal Shen Manor had been reduced to rubble!

The pair of newly painted oak gates had become two pieces of charred wood. There still seemed to be smoke rising from them.

Shen felt as if she were as weightless as the smoke and the mist. Unanchored to anything, she felt she might simply vanish into the wind at any moment.

Who had set fire to the Manor?

Where was everybody? All dead? Who killed them?

She didn't cry. She didn't shed a single tear.

She seemed frozen.

Then she remembered an old and kind face, the gray hair, a smile that was more caring than serious.

Where is ... Grandmother? Is she ... dead, too? she wondered.

She ran forward, forgetting the pain in her leg.

She didn't know where she got her strength. The inn servant tried to stop her, but she pushed him away.

She ran over and fell on the rubble.

When her body touched the cold rubble, the cruel and terrible reality finally sank in.

She broke into tears.

The inn servant hurried over and stood beside her. He felt sorry for her, but he didn't know how to comfort her. After a long while, he muttered, "There is nothing anyone can do now. I suggest you come back to the inn first, ma'am. In any case, you can talk to that gentleman about what to do next."

He sighed. "That gentleman is not a bad person. The reason he didn't want you to come back was probably that he didn't want you to see any of this."

These words made Shen cry even harder.

She was sad enough, without thinking of the large-eyed young man. When she thought of him, she felt as if she wanted to throw her own heart on the ground and squash it with her feet.

Even the inn servant trusted him and understood his good intentions, she thought. Why couldn't I? He has helped me so many times, yet I distrusted him and told him off.

She wished she had never said those nasty words.

If Xiao came now, she might run into his arms, repent, and ask him to forgive her.

But, Xiao hadn't come.

The one who did come was not Xiao.

Someone coughed in the dark.

The inn servant felt a chill travel up his spine. He couldn't help but shudder.

The cough came from behind him, but he hadn't heard any footsteps. The person who was coughing seemed to come out of the mist.

It was foggy and late. Who would come here at this moment?

He wanted to turn around to look, but dared not, afraid to see a gruesome ghost who had just died in the fire.

Then he heard Shen say, "Who are you two?"

She had stopped crying and risen to her feet. Her bright eyes were staring over the inn servant's shoulder.

He was amazed that this beautiful lady could be so brave. Her face showed no fear and she looked composed. No one could tell she had just been crying.

He didn't know that Shen was used to controlling herself and never shed tears in front of others. She had burst into tears partly because she was truly grieving, and partly because she didn't really count the inn servant as a person. Though such figures as inn servants, carriage drivers, and maidservants are all human, their presence is often ignored. Therefore, they often overhear secrets unknown to others.

The wise know these people are the best source of information.

For them, "secrets" mean "extra income."

The man coughed a few more times and then said, "Ma'am, we noticed you paying homage to the deceased here. Do you have anything to do with the Shens?"

Speaking in a calm and gentle manner, he was obviously a highly cultured man.

Shen hesitated for a moment and then nodded. "Yes, Shen is my family name."

"What's the relationship between Lady Shen and you, ma'am?"

"She is my—"

She began, then stopped.

After the experience of the last few days, she had learned about the devious nature of the people in the martial world. She had also learned to be cautious about how much detail to reveal.

She didn't know these two people, and the way they showed up was strange. She hadn't recovered from her injury, so she had less than one-fifth of her original strength left. She couldn't afford to be careless.

The man waited for a moment but didn't hear the rest of her answer, so he pressed on. "Are you Mrs. Lian, ma'am?"

Shen considered and then said, "I asked who *you* are. Why don't you reply?"

She thought her reply was clever and appropriate, not realizing that she had given her identity away.

The man smiled. "So you are Mrs. Lian. Please forgive us for our lack of manners."

Two men moved past the inn servant from behind. One was tall and strong, and the other was short and thin.

The tall one was strong and had a dark face. The spear he was holding was three feet taller than he was. The ribbon attached to the spearhead fluttered slightly. He looked imposing.

The short one was expressionless and bony. His yellowish face made him look unhealthy. He used a pair of strange weapons that Shen couldn't name.

They were finely dressed, but their clothes looked wrinkled and had some black stains on them. It seemed that they hadn't changed clothes for several days.

After stepping forward and standing in front of Shen, they bowed to her.

Shen nodded slightly to return their salute, with her eyes fixed on them. "You are ... ?"

The short one spoke first. "My name is Lei Mantang. I came from Taihu."

Before Lei spoke, the inn servant thought the voice behind him must have been from this man. As it turned out, however, Lei's voice was as loud as a temple bell. He talked as though he thought everyone else was nearly deaf.

"My name is Long Guang, and my courtesy name is Yishan," said the tall one. "It's my pleasure to meet you, Madame."

Long had a bulky build and a stern face, but when he talked, he sounded gentle and graceful. The way these two talked was the exact opposite of the way they looked.

The inn servant marveled at the contrast between these two people. They reminded him of the proverb: "Don't judge a book by its cover."

"So you are Lord Lei and Lord Long," Shen said graciously.

Lei and Long were like brothers. They did everything and went everywhere together. They were referred to as the Gods of Thunder and Lightning. They got this epithet because Lei means "thunder," and Yishan, Long's courtesy name, means "a lightning bolt."

Lei Mantang, known as Thunder God of Taihu, was noted for using a pair of Thunder God Chisels. This system of weaponry was creative and flexible. It could work both on land and in the water. In addition, Lei was endowed with great strength. It was rumored that he could overwhelm ten thousand men.

Long Guang got his courtesy name, Yishan, because his Lightness Kung Fu was outstanding.

They both lived in Taihu and enjoyed chivalrous reputations. Lei had a quick temper, but he liked to help others. He was considered a genuine hero.

Shen had never met them, but she had heard a lot about them. Their names brought a smile of relief to her face.

But her relief was gone in a flash. Didn't Peng Pengfei and Liu Yongnan also enjoy a reputation for chivalry? Yet in reality, they were more despicable than beasts.

When she thought of them, her smile vanished.

Long bowed. "Our names are not worth mentioning. The title 'Lord' is too grand for us."

"What brought you all the way from Taihu?"

Long sighed, "We came here to offer birthday greetings to Lady Shen. It turned out that ... we were too late."

When she heard him say "we were too late," she felt as if her soul were struck and crushed by a bolt of lightning out of the blue.

She was going to ask them whether Lady Shen had been killed.

But she was afraid to ask now.

Lei added, "We arrived two days ago."

He didn't seem to have finished, but he didn't continue. He knew his voice was too loud, so he tried not to talk more than necessary.

Struggling to control her grief, Shen asked, "You mean two days ago ... this place was—"

Long nodded. "When we arrived, the Manor was ablaze. Dead and wounded were lying everywhere. We did all we could, but we still couldn't put the fire out."

He looked down at the filthy stains on his clothes, which he had apparently gotten while fighting the fire. Furthermore, he hadn't slept for two days, and he hadn't been able to change his clothes.

She was devastated to hear "dead and wounded were lying everywhere," but since there were some *wounded*, that meant some must be still alive.

"Who are among the wounded?" She still held a glimmer of hope.

"The Four Knights of Ludong were visiting your house at the time," Long replied. "The first and the third brothers were killed. The second and the fourth brothers were seriously injured."

The Four Knights of Ludong had the surname Shen as well. They were distant relatives of her family. Every year, they prepared handsome gifts and attended Lady Shen's birthday celebration. For some reason, they arrived a little late this year and got caught in this disaster. Even Shen Tiansong, the eldest and strongest of them, was killed.

Shen knew the four brothers. In fact, she was very familiar with them.

She bit her lip and asked, "Other than two of the Shen brothers, who else was injured?"

Long slowly shook his head. "Other than the two of them, there was no one else."

The words seemed to mean that no one else was injured, but they really meant no one else was alive.

Shen couldn't control herself anymore. "My gr-grand—"

Unable to finish her question, she collapsed to the ground.

"Shen Tianzhu and Shen Tianju are both on the boat over there," Long said. "You might want to rest there, so that we can discuss what to do next."

When she looked up, she saw the vague silhouette of an off-shore boat.

She peered into the distance, then nodded slightly.

"Can you walk unescorted?" Long asked.

She looked at her leg and sighed deeply.

"I'm sixty years old," Lei said. "If you don't think it's too serious a breach of propriety, please allow me to hold your arms and help you walk."

"Wait!" she exclaimed.

Her voice was weak, but it still carried an air of authority.

Lei stopped and widened his eyes, with a look of question on his face.

She bit her lip and said, "Are the second and the fourth Shen brothers really on that boat?"

Instantly, Lei's yellowish face grew red with anger. "You don't believe us?"

"I-I just...." she muttered, blushing.

It was rude to show distrust of others. If it were not for the horrendous things that had happened to her of late, she would never have done this.

"So many terrible things have happened to you," said Long with a faint smile on his face. "It's natural for you to be particularly cautious, since you don't really know us."

His words seemed polite and thoughtful, but they had a slight tone of sarcasm.

Still blushing, she said, "That ... that's not what I meant. It's just that ... I wonder how seriously injured they are. Can they still talk?"

"They are still alive. Of course they can talk," said Lei with a grave face.

Long sighed. "The fourth Shen brother hasn't closed his eyes for two days, and neither has he closed his mouth. He has been repeating a name over and over again."

She couldn't resist asking, "Whose name?"

"The murderer's name."

Shivering, she emphasized each word of her question. "*Who ... is ... the ... murderer?*"

The tone of her voice was filled with so much hatred that it made the inn servant shudder.

"Since you don't trust us," Lei said coldly, "you may not believe us, if we tell you. You might as well go and see for yourself, Madame."

Long added, "There's no one around. Perhaps you will feel more secure on the boat."

Long looked like a boorish man, but his words were clever.

He was really saying, "Since there's no one around, if we harbored any evil intentions toward you, we could perform them here. We wouldn't have to wait until we get to the boat."

No matter how inexperienced with people Shen was, she understood what these words implied. Even if she still had a few doubts about them, she couldn't bear to refuse their kind offer. Besides, she honestly felt she could trust them.

She took a breath and looked down at her leg ruefully. "But ... but how could I trouble you?"

Lei let out a "humph" and inserted his Thunder God Chisels into his waistband. He turned and strode to the carriage, stopping in front of it. Then he effortlessly tore the carriage apart.

The horse neighed and was about to dash off.

Lei picked up a board with one hand and grabbed hold of a wheel with the other. The horse was still kicking its legs in the air, but it couldn't get away.

The inn servant gawked openmouthed, with his tongue hanging out. He was astonished to see that the small, ugly, dry-boned man could be so strong!

Inwardly, Shen also marveled. Lei carried the board over and put it down in front of her. "Please use this as a palanquin, and let us carry you over there."

He was so strong that he could probably knock her down with a single finger, but he kept his cool and showed his consideration for her.

Having no doubts about them anymore, she felt ashamed for having been so impolite.

She was glad there were still some good people in the world after all.

It was a medium-sized passenger barge.

The cabin was clean and tidy. There was a soft, comfortable bed on either side. Each bed had a person in it.

The man on the left had an ashen face. Eyes closed, he was groaning. He was covered with a silk comforter. She couldn't see where he was injured.

Yet, there was no doubt that he was Shen Tianzhu, the second eldest of the Four Knights of Ludong.

The face of the man on the right was pale and bloodless. He stared at the roof of the cabin with vacant, stony eyes. He kept mumbling and muttering the same words over and over: "Xiao Shiyi Lang, you cold-blooded murderer! Xiao Shiyi Lang, you cold-blooded murderer!"

His voice was filled with bitterness, hatred, and dread.

Shen sat there listening to him repeat these words. Her delicate and beautiful face became unbelievably formidable.

She gritted her teeth. "Xiao Shiyi Lang, I won't let you get away with this. I won't let you get away with this."

Her voice and Tianzhu's echoed each other, chilling all those who heard them.

Lei said with hatred, "How dare Xiao Shiyi Lang commit such a heinous crime? Now, all of us want to see him dead. Madame, you're not the only one who won't let him get away with this. None of us will let him remain on the loose."

His voice was sonorous, but Shen didn't seem to hear a word of it.

She stared blankly into the distance, muttering repeatedly: "Xiao Shiyi Lang, I won't let you get away with this!"

Suddenly, Long winked at Lei and dashed out of the cabin. Although he was bulky, his Lightness Kung Fu was excellent. No wonder he got the courtesy name Yishan—a lightning bolt.

A moment later, they heard a scream of terror come from the lakeshore.

The scream seemed to belong to the inn servant. It was sharp and short. Apparently, his throat was grabbed, as soon as he shrieked.

Frowning, Lei rose to his feet and pushed open the cabin door.

Long quickly returned to the prow of the barge.

"Who's following you?" Lei demanded.

"What are you talking about? Are you seeing double?" Long retorted.

Though he sounded confident, he couldn't keep from turning his head to look.

He saw a pair of gleaming eyes!

The eyes were staring sternly behind his back from less than three feet away.

Long was considered a first-rate expert in Lightness Kung Fu, but he had been unaware of this man following him.

Lei's face changed color. He reached for his waist, pulling out the pair of steel Thunder God Chisels, which were used mainly to attack the meridian points. "Who are you? What are you doing here?" he yelled.

His shouting was as loud as thunder, shaking the table and making the tea spill.

Shaken by the shout, Shen slowly turned her head.

Long backed into the cabin, his face filled with fright. He was holding the hilt of the flexible rapier hanging from his waist, but he didn't dare to draw it.

A man was sticking to him like a shadow. Every time Long moved one step backward, the man moved one step forward. The man's piercing eyes were fixed on Long's face.

The man wasn't old, but he wore a beard, and a short saber hung from his waist. He carried a body in his arms.

"Brother, why don't you attack him?" Lei asked.

His teeth clattering, Long still didn't dare to draw his rapier.

With a dead body in his arms, the man had still been able to trail behind Long like a shadow without Long's being aware of it. This man's ability in Lightness Kung Fu was frighteningly hard to believe.

The others present did not understand its full implications. Only Long realized how astonishing this man's Lightness Kung Fu was. With his palms covered with cold sweat, he couldn't muster the courage to draw his rapier.

Lei stamped his feet and lunged forward.

Shen spoke up. "Wait! He's my friend."

She was surprised to find that the man who had followed Long into the cabin was the large-eyed young man. When she saw him, she felt as if she were seeing family.

Taken by surprise, Lei stopped.

Long backed off a few more steps, sitting down in his chair with a thump.

Xiao didn't look at him anymore. He slowly walked in and put down the body. He gazed at Shen, seemingly unable to take his eyes off her face.

Joyfully surprised, she couldn't keep from rising. "Why ... why did you come?"

Having said this, she seemed about to fall.

Xiao quickly reached out and caught her arms to keep her from falling. "I don't know why I came," he said with a rueful smile.

Those words were a little cold, but she understood clearly what they implied.

I wronged him and blamed him, she thought, but he still couldn't stop worrying about me.

Although she dared not think further, she couldn't suppress the warmth rising within her. Her face, which had looked terrifying just a moment ago, became gentle again.

The soft light of the cabin seemed to make her rosy cheeks glow. She looked incredibly charming and pretty.

Lei and Long gawked in wonder.

Who was this guy?

Mrs. Lian was usually dignified and composed. Why did she seem so intimate with him?

Shen bowed her head in shyness. After a moment, she suddenly let out a scream. "It was *him*! Who killed him?"

She was astounded to find that the body Xiao had carried in was the inn servant who had come along with her.

The inn servant was just a good-hearted ordinary man, who had absolutely nothing to do with the killings and revenge in the martial world. Who killed him? Why?

Xiao didn't speak, but he slowly turned his eyes toward Long.

Shen followed his gaze and saw Long's face pale.

"You killed him? Why?" she asked, in a husky voice.

Long coughed. "Since this gentleman is your friend, Madame, it's not proper for me to be straightforward. However, I assure you, I am not the one who killed this man."

Long might not have remarkable kung fu, but his words were remarkably cunning.

As expected, she turned back to Xiao. "In that case, who is the real killer?"

"If my brother said he didn't kill him, then he didn't kill him," said Lei indignantly. "The Gods of Thunder and Lightning may not be extraordinary men, but we never lie."

"Brother," Long said, "everyone knows we don't lie. You don't have to explain."

"Madame," Lei said, "since my brother didn't kill him, isn't it obvious to you who killed him?"

Shen stared at Xiao. "Did you kill him? Why?"

His face darkening, Xiao said, "Do you honestly believe I killed him? Do you think I lied to you?"

"You ... I-I don't know," she muttered.

A bleak smile flickered across Xiao's pale face. "You certainly don't know. You don't know me at all. Why would you trust me? I'm just a—"

Just then a voice cried out, "I know you. *I know you*—"

Tianju struggled and sat up. His eyes were filled with fright and shock, as if he were seeing a man-eating ogre.

Lei's countenance changed. "You know him? Who is he?"

Tianju reached out his shaking hand, pointing at Xiao. "He's the murderer! He's ... Xiao Shiyi Lang!"

So the large-eyed young man was none other than Xiao Shiyi Lang—*the murderer*! As if struck by lightning, Shen glared at him. "You—*you're* Xiao Shiyi Lang?"

Xiao expelled a very long sigh. "That's right. I am Xiao Shiyi Lang."

Shen was chilled to the bone. Even her fingers were cold as ice. "You ... you're the *killer*?"

After a long pause, Xiao said, "It's true I have killed people, but I didn't—"

Before he could finish, Tianju yelled out hoarsely, "He slashed me, and he killed Lady Shen. The saber he's carrying is the murder weapon!"

Shen suddenly let out a wild cry and drew the saber hanging from Xiao's waist!

She thrust the saber at Xiao's chest!

Either he couldn't or wouldn't dodge it. Anyhow, Xiao simply stood there, watching the blade plunge into him.

The blade was cold as ice.

He could almost feel the ice-cold blade pierce his skin and flesh and shave past his ribs.

It felt as if the saber had pierced his ... heart!

He stood motionless, as if numbed with shock.

She was stunned, too.

It amazed her that she could stab and injure Xiao Shiyi Lang at all.

She had seen Xiao's kung fu in action. She knew that if he had lifted his fingers, the saber would have been knocked away. Even if she didn't get hurt, there was no way she could harm him.

So, why hadn't he parried her advance? Why hadn't he dodged it?

Xiao still stood there and silently stared at her.

His eyes didn't reveal any anger; instead, they were filled with sadness.

She had never known a person's eyes could show such poignancy.

She should have been proud of herself for injuring Xiao Shiyi Lang—the Great Bandit, but, somehow, her heart was full of pain.

She was uncertain. What if she had killed the wrong person!

The saber was still imbedded in Xiao's chest.

"Bravo! Xiao Shiyi Lang ... who'd have known you'd end up like this today!" Tianju laughed triumphantly. "Come on! Stab him again! I want to see him die by your hand."

Her hands were shaking.

Tianju yelled wildly, "He is the man who killed Lady Shen. What are you waiting for?"

She clenched her teeth and pulled out the saber.

Blood spurted out like arrows, splattering on her.

It appeared that every inch of muscle in his body cringed, but Xiao remained still.

Now his eyes were not only full of sorrow but also despair.

Why didn't he parry it? Why didn't he dodge it?

Would he rather die by her hand?

Her hands shook. Tears trickled down. She couldn't will herself to raise the saber and stab him again!

"Madame!" Lei yelled. "If you can't do it, I will!"

Following his shout, he aimed his Thunder God Chisels at Xiao's chest and lunged forward.

This move looked as powerful as a lightning bolt.

With his eyes still fixed on Shen, Xiao didn't even glance at Lei. He simply turned his hand over and smacked Lei's face.

This move didn't look special, but somehow Lei couldn't dodge it. He attacked with his chisels forward, but he was smacked before his chisels could even touch Xiao's clothes.

Splat! Whoosh!

Lei was thrown through the window and into the lake with a splash.

Long's face turned green. He was scared out of his wits.

Tianju's jaw dropped. He couldn't yell anymore.

Everyone had heard about Xiao's superiority in kung fu, but no one could have imagined that he could use a casual slap to knock out the famed Thunder God of Taihu.

Shen felt even more distraught.

He's seriously injured, yet the strength of his palms is still overwhelming. Before he was wounded, why didn't he evade my attack? If he's really the murderer, why didn't he kill me?

As these thoughts flashed through her mind, she broke out in a cold sweat.

Tianzhu, who had been lying down unconscious, suddenly slid off the bed like an eel. He was so agile, he didn't appear to be injured at all.

His eyes, flashing with resentment, glowered at Xiao.

When Shen saw Tianzhu's eyes, she cried out in fright. "Watch out!"

The moment she cried "Watch out!" Tianju pulled out a flexible rapier from under the comforter. He jumped up and lunged his rapier at Xiao's head.

Long picked up the long spear lying in the corner with his left hand, and pulled out the rapier hanging from his waist. The combined use of spear and sword had made Long famous.

The spear was long and masculine, and the flexible rapier was short and feminine. Few other people would use these two together. Long aimed the spearhead at Xiao and used the rapier to protect his own belly, the former used mainly for attack and the latter mainly for defense. The combination of these two ensured all his weaknesses were covered.

The choice of weapon is closely related to a person's personality. Long had a bulky build, but in reality he was quite timid and afraid of death.

He vigorously practiced Lightness Kung Fu, in order to get away quickly, when necessary. His weapons and kung fu styles placed a priority on defense. His spear was long so that when he attacked, his body stayed far away from his opponent. He used his other hand to wield the rapier close to his body, to ensure he was perfectly shielded.

Meanwhile, Tianzhu had rolled across the floor, sending seven silver darts flying at Xiao's back with a shriek of wind.

Xiao's chest was bleeding profusely. The tip of Shen's saber was less than six inches away from him. Long's spear was coming from the left, Tianju's bronze rapier was coming from the right, and Tianzhu's silver darts were coming from behind.

In the blink of an eye, he was completely surrounded. There was no hope of escape. But he remained motionless, looking intently at Shen.

She unexpectedly turned her saber to parry Tianju's rapier.

Even she didn't understand why she had decided to defend Xiao.

But she was too weak. She went limp immediately after deflecting the rapier.

At that instant, Xiao's once despondent eyes flashed a glimmer of light.

No sooner had she fallen to the floor than she heard a crack, some whops, and three howls of horror. In a flash, Tianzhu, Tianju, and Long were either dead or wounded.

During that instant, Xiao's right hand had shot out, grabbed Tianju's wrist, and snapped it.

He clamped Long's spear under his arms, and yanked him forward by an unstoppable force. As Xiao pulled the spear and flung Long behind him, Long became a shield and was hit by the seven silver darts of Tianzhu.

Tianzhu was too shocked to react. In a split second, Xiao had spun his hand and sunk the spear into Tianzhu's belly.

After the three screams, Tianzhu and Long were both dead. Tianju lay on the floor groaning and clutching his right wrist with his left hand.

Xiao's feet hadn't moved.

However, he *was* human. Even though Shen had missed his heart when she stabbed him, and even though she had been too weak to use much strength, the tip of the blade had gone in several inches.

No flesh could bear such a deep stab wound.

Solely relying on the power generated by his intense sorrow, he had managed to hold out this long. Now that all his opponents had fallen, he couldn't hold out any longer.

He wanted to help Shen get up, but he collapsed onto the table before he could do so.

"Excellent kung fu! Your kung fu is superb!" someone said, laughing aloud. "If you can withstand another attack from my chisels, you will have my utmost admiration!"

It sounded like ... Lei Mantang!

With laughter and the whirling sound of wind, Lei flew in through the window. Dripping wet, he recklessly aimed his chisels at Xiao.

Shen cried out and threw her saber over to Xiao.

Xiao caught the saber and thrust it forward with what strength he had left.

Lei seemed unafraid of death. Xiao's saber went into his chest all the way to the handle, but he didn't appear to feel it at all. Instead, he continued to lunge at Xiao.

Was he immortal?

To Xiao's astonishment, Lei struck one of his major meridian points. He instantly went numb, sliding off the table to the ground.

Even if Xiao were made of iron, there was no way he could get up now.

Lei stood in front of Xiao and snickered. "You want me dead? I want you dead, too. If I have to go to hell, I'll take you down with me."

He seemed to be floating. His toes were barely touching the floor. He was soaking wet, his face was contorted, and he had a saber in his chest.

Three of the four lamps in the cabin had been knocked over. The flickering light from the remaining lamp in the corner reflected off Lei's grotesque, twisted face.

This could not be a human being. It must be some abhorrent spirit.

Xiao remained composed, but Shen was nearly scared out of her mind.

"Xiao Shiyi Lang," Lei said, "why haven't you died yet? I'm waiting for you. *Die!*"

Lei's face had stiffened and his eyes were popping out of their sockets. His lips weren't moving but his voice came out of nowhere.

Xiao suddenly smirked. "Don't wait. I'm not going to die."

Surprisingly, Lei laughed ... like the tinkling of a bell.

The voice, sweet and musical, rang clearly throughout the cabin.

This ghost-like Lei emitting such a laugh was a hair-raising sight.

But Xiao merely heaved a long, long sigh and smiled wryly. "Oh, it's you. It's you, *again!*"

Lei abruptly crumpled.

Not until he had fallen did Shen notice there was another person behind him.

The tinkle-bell laugh had come from this person.

She was luxuriously dressed, her fair and delicate face wearing an enchantingly sweet smile. It was none other than ... Little Mister!

The sight of her frightened Shen more than the ghost had.

Lei had been almost dead. Little Mister had picked him up and manipulated his body like a string puppet.

"That's right. It's me again. I'm a stubborn ghost that will haunt you forever."

Gracefully, she sauntered over to Xiao and bent to caress his face. "I miss you terribly. I can't go one day without seeing you. You can't make me stay away from you ... unless you kill me. Oh, no, that won't work either. Even if I were dead, I'd stick to you forever."

Her voice was bright and sweet. It sounded more delightful than singing.

"You—are you a *woman?*" Shen's voice cracked in astonishment.

"Didn't you know? How could a man be cruel to you? Only a woman can be ruthless to another woman. Don't you understand?"

Shen was stunned beyond words.

Little Mister sighed and shook her head. "Ms. Shen is gorgeous, but she doesn't know a thing about the chemistry between men and women. My dear Xiao, why do you like her instead of me?"

Xiao smiled. "I—"

As soon as he started talking, a violent pain from his chest shot through his body. Sweat trickled down his face. He couldn't utter another word.

"Oh! You're injured," exclaimed Little Mister. "Who stabbed you? Who could have been so cruel?"

"I did. Go ahead and kill me!" Shen yelled, feeling anger rising inside her.

"You did?" Little Mister blinked. "Oh, you shouldn't have! He tried so hard to protect you, and yet you wanted to kill him? You don't look like a heartless woman."

"If I get the chance, I'll try to kill him again," Shen said.

"Why?"

"*I hate him!*" Shen said in a shaking voice, her eyes red. "He killed my family. I—"

"He killed your family? Who said that?"

"Two of the Four Knights of Ludong and the Gods of Thunder and Lightning. They were all witnesses."

"He saved you many times," sighed Little Mister, "yet you believe those people instead of him."

"But—but he confessed to me that he's Xiao Shiyi Lang."

"That's true, he *is* Xiao Shiyi Lang, but he is *not* the person who burned down your house and killed your grandmother."

Bewildered, Shen said in a wavering voice, "If he didn't do it, then who did?"

"I did, of course," Little Mister said, laughing. "Other than me, who is capable of such things?"

Shen trembled.

Little Mister continued. "The Four Knights of Ludong and the Gods of Thunder and Lightning were all working for me ... to deceive you. I thought they might have difficulty convincing you of their story. Xiao Shiyi Lang has been so nice to you and has done so much for you, how could you believe the words of those bastards so easily? As it turns out, you may not look stupid, but you are a foolish ingrate!"

Each of these words pricked Shen's heart like a needle.

She had her doubts early on, but she had refused to admit that she might have killed the wrong person. She didn't have the courage to accept such a possibility.

Now, with these words from Little Mister's mouth, it must be true. Even though she didn't want to admit it, she had to.

I misjudged him! I misunderstood, yet another time! she cried out in her heart. I swore I would believe him. Why did I wrong him all over again?

She thought of the anguish and despair in his eyes and all that he had done for her—

She wished a bolt of lightning would strike her down and kill her.

"You want to die again, don't you?" said Little Mister. "But even if you were dead, how could you make it up to him for everything he has done for you? If it were not for him, you would have died many times."

"If you want to kill me, why don't you do it now?" Shen said, her face covered in tears.

"I planned to kill you, but I changed my mind."

"Why?"

"I want you to see him every day and think about what you did—"

"I don't want to see her anymore," Xiao said suddenly. "The sight of an ingrate like her upsets me. If you really like me, send her away immediately! The farther, the better."

After he finished speaking, his pain caused perspiration to pour from his forehead like rain.

Xiao's words made Shen's heart ache even more. She knew he was trying to persuade Little Mister to let her go.

Despite the way I treated him, he is still trying to save me, she thought. I hurt him, wronged him, and almost killed him, but he doesn't hate me.

She had never imagined that Xiao Shiyi Lang, the Great Bandit, would be such a person.

Little Mister understood Xiao's intention as well. "I would've let her go for your sake. Unfortunately, I can't."

"Why not?"

"You know she's the person my master wants. Even if I can't take her back alive, I have to take her body back, to avert punishment."

"You still plan to go back?"

"I would've liked to run to a faraway place and live happily ever after with you, but...."

Little Mister sighed. "I can't avoid going back. You have no idea how powerful my master is. Even if I ran to the end of the world, he would find me."

"Who is your master?" Xiao asked, struggling to continue. "Is he really that ... powerful?"

"Even if I tell you, you wouldn't believe how powerful he is."

"I'm not bad either."

"With your kung fu, maybe you could last twenty or even up to thirty moves, but he would definitely kill you in forty."

"Don't you think you underestimate me too much?"

"No one in the world can withstand his attack for more than twenty moves. If you can survive twenty moves, you will be considered very good."

"I don't believe it."

Little Mister chuckled. "Whether you believe it or not, I won't tell you his name. The more you want to know, the more I'll refuse to tell you. The more I refuse to tell you, the more you'll want to know. You'll have to stick to me and pester me every day for the answer. The more you stick to me, the happier I'll be."

Xiao was silent for a moment and then closed his eyes, without saying another word.

The wound in his chest throbbed with every word he said, giving him acute, excruciating pain. The only reason he had managed to endure the pain was that he had been trying to trick Little Mister into revealing her master's name.

Little Mister was incredibly cunning and as vicious as a viper. Zhao Wuji, Hai Lingzi, the Four Knights of Ludong, and the Gods of Thunder and Lightning were all first-rate warriors, but they had all been obedient to her. She was the most outstanding figure Xiao had ever met.

Her master must be incredible.

Xiao appeared calm, but, in reality, he was very anxious.

He once thought there was no task in the world beyond his ability, but now he couldn't think of a way to get Shen to safety.

Chapter 15

A Wanderer's Home

IT WAS CLOSE to dusk.

A faint pink glow hung low in the west, but the sunshine was still bright.

Golden light fell upon the chrysanthemums in the valley.

There were thousands and thousands of chrysanthemums ... some yellow, some white, some gray, and some of them even black.

Under the autumn setting sun, no flowers bloomed more beautifully.

Autumn is the season of chrysanthemums.

Shen had never seen such gorgeous chrysanthemums, or so many. Not until she came to this place did she realize that those she had seen were not worthy of their name.

Surrounded by mountains on four sides, the valley was shielded from the cold northern air. Though it was late autumn, the breeze felt gentle.

The valley was filled with intoxicating fragrances.

A Persian rug was placed on the grassy hill. On the rug were all sorts of fresh fruit and a big plate of steamed red crabs ... redder than rouge.

Shen was wearing a silk gown that was softer than the wind. She reclined on a couple of silk cushions, facing the gorgeous sunset and splendid scenery, sipping sweet wine chilled by the brook and enjoying the relaxing breeze. Her heart, however, was distraught.

Little Mister left her more and more perplexed.

In the past fortnight, Little Mister had provided her with the most exotic delicacies, the finest grape wine, the most luxurious and comfortable clothes, the best carriages, and the fastest horses. Little Mister had taken her to the most beautiful places and let her enjoy a most extravagant lifestyle.

Shen's heart, however, was filled with nothing but apprehension. She couldn't figure out what Little Mister was going to do with her. Increasingly she found her truly chilling.

What worried her most was Xiao.

Every time she saw him, he appeared cheerful, but she could see his once sparkling eyes were becoming dimmer and dimmer. His raw energy was slowly slipping away.

What kind of suffering was he enduring?

Had he recovered from his injury?

Sometimes she felt guilty for thinking more and more about Xiao and less and less about Lian.

She had to find an explanation for herself:

It's because I blame myself for making him suffer, and because I may never be able to repay him for what he has done for me.

Xiao appeared, slowly strolling among the chrysanthemums below.

His hair hung on his shoulders, loosely bound with a ribbon. He was dressed in a large scarlet robe, embroidered with a lifelike dark dragon. When his robe flapped in the wind, the dragon seemed to be dancing and almost ready to fly out of the clouds.

Xiao's cheeks had become thinner and his beard had become thicker, but from a distance, he still looked imposing and dignified, like an emperor of ancient times.

Little Mister always leaned against him, wrapping her arms around his arm. Against his broad chest, she appeared even more delicate and beautiful.

Sometimes, Shen felt Little Mister's femininity and Xiao's masculinity were a perfect match.

She may look feminine, but at heart she's a venomous serpent ... a ferocious wolf, Shen thought. Whoever has the misfortune to cross her path will be swallowed in one gulp.

Shen clenched her teeth, her heart full of bitterness.

But when she saw Xiao smiling at her, her bitterness vanished. Why? She didn't know.

Little Mister smiled, too, ever so sweetly. "See!" she said to Xiao. "I told you to go change your clothes. You just latched onto me. It's your fault that we've kept the others waiting. How embarrassing!"

These words pricked Shen's heart like needles.

Xiao was latching onto Little Mister?

Was he enthralled with her?

She's probably trying to irritate me, Shen thought. I won't fall for her trick. Besides, Xiao isn't special to me. I have no reason to be offended.

Shen lowered her head, trying to appear calm.

They sat down across from her.

"Don't you think the chrysanthemums here are beautiful?" Little Mister cooed sweetly to Xiao. "Some people say that flowers are for women, because they have a feminine charm, but chrysanthemums are different."

As she spoke, she cracked open the shell of a crab with a little silver hammer, picked out the meat with a small silver spoon, and gently placed it into Xiao's mouth. "Chrysanthemums are masculine. Their solemn pride is like a poet or a hermit. They don't bloom with all the other flowers in the spring, which symbolizes their refusal to go with the current. They aren't afraid of the wind in the autumn, which shows their resilience."

She poured a cup of wine and put it to Xiao's lips. "I brought you here, because I know you must like chrysanthemums. Your personality is like a chrysanthemum's."

"The only way I admire chrysanthemums," Xiao said, "is by cooking their petals with fish and chicken in a pot of water, and then washing it all down with bamboo-leaf-green wine."

He smirked and went on. "Others may admire flowers with their eyes, but I prefer to use my mouth."

Little Mister chuckled. "You're such a killjoy."

She leaned against Xiao. "But that's why I like you. You do everything differently. The world may see another great poet, like Li Po, or another legendary warlord, like the Great King of Chu, but it will never see a second Xiao Shiyi Lang. Any girl who wouldn't fall for a man like you must be an idiot."

She turned to Shen and grinned. "Don't you agree, Mrs. Lian?"

"I don't know," replied Shen resolutely. "I'm not a young girl myself, and I have never done a study of men."

Little Mister didn't get mad. Instead, she smiled even more agreeably. "If a woman doesn't truly understand men, how can men truly like her? I used to wonder why Mr. Lian would leave such a beautiful wife at home all by herself. Now I finally realize...."

She didn't elaborate, but what she implied was clear.

Shen didn't want to be angry, but her face turned pale anyhow.

Little Mister poured another cup of wine. "The wine is pretty good. It's grape wine imported from the Xiliang Nation. Why don't you try some? If you never drink, your whole life will be meaningless."

Shen kept her mouth closed ... tightly closed.

She was afraid if she opened her mouth, she'd say something nasty.

"Are you upset, Mrs. Lian?" said Little Mister. "Come on! Don't be."

She cast a suggestive glance at Xiao. "If I were sitting on Mr. Lian's lap, you would have reason to be annoyed. But him ... ? You wouldn't feel jealous and get mad at me over him, would you?"

Shen was so outraged her fingertips went cold. She couldn't keep from lifting her head—

She had been too embarrassed to look at Xiao, but when she looked up, she naturally turned her eyes to his face.

She found his face ghostly pale, his eyes full of pain, and the corners of his eyes twitching uncontrollably.

Xiao was clearly enduring serious anguish.

He wasn't a man who would reveal his pain easily.

Shen forgot about Little Mister's sarcastic teasing. "Your injury... Has your wound healed?" she asked in a quaking voice.

"What wound?" Xiao laughed. "I forgot about it long ago."

She hesitated for a moment, but, suddenly, lunged forward.

Her leg still hurt badly. Sometimes, it was numb beyond feeling, but other times it hurt enough to awaken her from her sleep.

Her wound had drained almost all her strength. Every time she wanted to stand up by herself, she would fall over.

But now, she forgot all of that.

She sprang forward and pulled Xiao's robe open.

She let loose a horrendous scream.

Few people have heard a scream so haunting, so poignant, so heart-wrenching—

Xiao's entire chest was festered with pus. The flesh around the wound had rotted and turned black, emitting a sickening odor.

Shen finally realized why he always wore a loose robe and used lots of perfume.

He was trying to cover up the odor.

Even the most strong-stomached person wouldn't be able to stand the sight.

Her heart was shattered.

She knew little about the medical arts, but it was clear how bad his condition was. No flesh and blood could bear this kind of pain.

However, every time she had seen him, he had talked and laughed as usual.

Was he really a man made of iron?

What terrible suffering was he enduring ... while he laughed?

For whom was he doing this ... and why?

Thinking about all of this, Shen leaned on his shoulder and cried.

Little Mister shook her head. "What's the matter? Why are you crying? Come on! You're an adult woman old enough to bear children. Shedding tears so easily will make people think you're a crybaby."

Glaring at Little Mister, Shen bit her lip so hard that blood trickled from it. "You—you have a cold heart!" she said, in a gravel tone.

"*I* have a cold heart?" Little Mister said, chuckling. "Have you forgotten who inflicted this wound on him? Exactly who is cold-hearted? You or me?"

Shen shook with anger. "You have seen how his wound festers. Why didn't you do something?"

"All he cares about is you," sighed Little Mister. "He would sacrifice his own life to save you. And how does he treat me? Every time he sees me, he looks as if he wants my life."

She sighed again. "If he treated me half as well as he treats you, I would rather have been stabbed thousands of times than to hurt a single hair on his head. *You* are the one who injured him. How do you have the nerve to ask *me* to treat his wound?"

"It's bad enough that you refuse to have him treated, but why do you make him drink wine and eat such seafood as fish or shrimp?"

"What's wrong with that? I want to be nice to him. I know he likes drinking, so I found the best wine for him. I know he likes great food, so I prepare the freshest seafood for him. I'm as thoughtful as any wife could be to her husband's needs."

"But you know both wine and seafood aggravate the wound. Eating these things will surely make him worse. You are killing him!"

"All I know is that I didn't hurt him. I feed him the best food and the finest wine. Nothing else is my concern."

Shen ground her teeth, speechless.

Xiao had been silently gazing at Shen. For some reason, his lackluster eyes suddenly brightened.

He smiled and spoke. "As long as a person lives well, what does it matter if life is short? Are long-lived people always happier than the short-lived? For some people, the longer they live, the more they suffer. For them, isn't death better than life? Living happily for only a day is more meaningful than suffering for a hundred years."

"Exactly!" Little Mister clapped and laughed. "This is what a real man would say. Xiao Shiyi Lang is Xiao Shiyi Lang after all! If he were afraid to drink wine, because of some small wound, then he wouldn't be Xiao Shiyi Lang!"

She stroked Xiao's face gently. "For as long as you live, I will treat you well and try my best to make you happy. Whatever you want to do and wherever you want to go, I will take you."

Xiao smirked. "Will you really treat me so well?"

"I mean it. As long as you're happy, I'm happy."

She gazed at the sunset in the west. "I want you to live happily for a few more days. Even if for just a few days...."

The sunset was magnificent.

Which only meant one thing: *darkness was not far off*!

Shen stared at the splendid scenery under the sunset, with tears streaming down her cheeks.

Xiao's thoughts seemed to have drifted to a distant place. "I'm neither a poet nor a scholar," he said. "I'm just a country boy who grew up in the wilderness. In my eyes, the most beautiful place in the world is a boundless field or a barren mountain. Even the marsh gas and the mist, which hangs over the bog, is more lovely than all of the flowers in the world."

Little Mister broke into a chuckle. "You're a strange person. You do think differently from everyone else."

Xiao smiled. "You like me because I'm strange, don't you?"

"That's right," she said, leaning on his knee. "That's why I let you do everything as you wish. If you really want to go to a place like that, we can leave right now."

Xiao inhaled deeply. "If I could go back to a place like that, even if I died right then, I would have no regrets."

"All right, I promise you. I'll make sure you get back there alive, and then—"

Xiao finished her sentence, "Then you'll let me die there, right?"

They were in the bare and desolate mountains.

Toxic vapors hung in the valley.

Lies are usually pleasant to hear. Women as vicious as a viper are usually striking beauties. Deadly poisons are usually as sweet as honey. The lethal miasma, generated by the peach blossoms in the valley, was alluring.

On the other hand, honest advice is often grating on the ear, and good medicine tastes bitter.

Why do things work this way?

Are we all the sport of fate? Or is Heaven testing our morality?

Shen didn't get it.

If the way of Heaven is fair, why do good people often suffer all their lives and bad people often enjoy wealth and luxury?

If it were true that good will be rewarded with good and evil with evil, why would people like Little Mister continue to live carefree and happily, while Xiao had to die?

On one side of them was a barren cliff face and on the other side a fathomless abyss.

Xiao was humming that song again. At that moment, at that place, the tune sounded especially poignant and full of sorrow.

However, his expression was calm and serene, as if he were a wanderer who had finally come home.

Regarding him with interest, Little Mister asked, "Did you really grow up here?"

"Um-hmm."

"It's not easy to live in a place like this," Little Mister remarked.

Xiao's lips curved into a bleak smile. "Living is always more difficult than dying."

"I have heard, from ancient times until now, the most difficult thing is to die in the right place at the right time. Sometimes dying isn't as easy as you think."

"Only those who don't want to die find it hard."

"You really want to die?" Little Mister blinked. "I don't believe it."

"To tell the truth, I've never thought about this question seriously. I don't know whether I want to live or to die."

"But if dying is so easy and you really want to die, why have you lived this long?"

Xiao didn't answer.

"Do you want to keep going up?" she said. "It looks like the end of the road. We can't go any further."

After a long interval of silence, Xiao muttered, "You're right. I've reached the end of my road. Why would I want to climb any higher? Why ... ?"

Suddenly, he smiled at Little Mister. "I want to stand here alone for awhile and think about my childhood."

"Can you stand on your own?"

"Why don't you let me try?"

Little Mister rolled her eyes and then finally loosened her hands, which had been wrapped around his arm. "Watch your feet!" she said with a smile. "If you fall off the cliff, I won't be able to recover your body. I've seen the living Xiao Shiyi Lang, and I'd like to see the dead Xiao Shiyi Lang as well."

Xiao smiled, too. "The dead are more obedient than the living, but they're definitely not as pleasant-looking. If you see my body, it'll make you nauseous. Why would I want to disgust you?"

He turned his head and smiled at Shen. Then, unexpectedly, he jumped into the deep, deep abyss.

Shen's body went cold.

Xiao meant what he had said. He had come here to die!

It's my fault! It's all my fault....

The words rang in her ears like thunder!

He's dead, yet I still have the nerve to live! she thought, becoming hysterical. How can I ever repay him? How much longer can I live? Who is going to save me ... ?

Then she thought of Little Mister's ruthlessness. Without hesitation, she used all her strength, to push away the maids holding her, and leaped into the unfathomable gloom.

Curiously, while she was falling, she didn't think of Lian at all.

She didn't think about what Lian might feel after she died.

Nor did she wonder whether Lian would grieve for her.

Little Mister stood at the edge of the precipice, peering impassively into the miasma and marsh gas hanging in the valley.

After a long while, she picked up a rock and threw it.

After another long time, she heard a loud plop from below.

Her face finally broke into a smile.

Her smile was so innocent, so lovely ... like that of a child.

Sometimes, dying is not an easy thing.

Shen didn't die.

When she fell, she passed out, so she didn't feel any pain.

Only when she regained consciousness did she start to feel pain.

At the bottom of the abyss was a limitless bog. There were no trees, flowers, or grass. There was no life. There was only mud, smelly water, and fog-like marsh gas.

She was almost totally submerged in mud.

But she didn't sink. The bog was like a huge bucket of paste. She hadn't died, even though she had jumped off a high cliff.

Curiously, though she was soaked in such foul water, she didn't feel at all uncomfortable. On the contrary, she felt quite relaxed. Even the wound on her ankle didn't seem to hurt.

It appeared that the muddy water in the bog had an extraordinary healing power, which relieved her pain.

The shock of this finding reminded her of a story Xiao had told her.

He had said, "I once saw a wolf jump into a bog after it was bitten by a bobcat. At first, I thought it was looking for its final resting place. It lay in the bog for two days, and then it walked out. It knew there were lots of decomposed herbs in the bog, which would cure its wound. It knew how to take care of itself."

Her heart beat faster.

She seemed to hear Xiao whispering into her ear: "In fact, humans are like animals. If no one takes care of them, they have to take care of themselves."

Was this the bog where the wolf had come to have its wound cured?

If the bog could cure the wolf's wound ... could it cure Xiao's as well?

She realized then ... he hadn't come here to die!

This deep valley was in the middle of nowhere. She didn't see any life around her. Soaked in dirty and smelly muddy water, she didn't know whether she could survive and walk out. Nonetheless, never in her life had she been happier or more thrilled.

Xiao must still be alive!

She was so excited that she almost wanted to cry out with joy, but it occurred to her that Little Mister might still be up there, so she kept her mouth shut.

She could only shout in her mind: "Xiao Shiyi Lang! Where are you? *Xiao Shiyi Lang!*"

As long as she could see Xiao again, all her sacrifice and suffering were worth it.

She struggled to move her limbs and to raise her head.

As long as she could see him, she would no longer feel lonely, desperate, or helpless.

However, her motion made her body sink deeper into the mud.

The mud was extremely thick and sticky, so she hadn't submerged completely.

Nevertheless, as soon as she struggled, a terrible force in the mud started to drag her downward. The harder she struggled, the faster she sank.

She was almost completely swallowed by mud, and she found it hard to breathe. The dense mud grabbed her throat like a pair of devil's hands.

If she sank one or two inches deeper, even her nose and mouth would be covered by mud.

She couldn't cry out even if she wanted to.

She didn't know how much longer she could last, but she knew it would be only a matter of minutes.

When she was at the top of the abyss, she was resolved to die, but, now, she fervently wished she could live a little bit longer.

If she lived just a few more minutes, maybe she'd be able to see Xiao again.

But then she thought: What does it matter if I don't see him again? As long as I know he didn't die because of me and as long as he can live on, even if I die right now, I would rest in peace. I thank the grace of Heaven that I'm allowed to die peacefully with a good conscience. What more can I ask?

Only then did she think of Lian.

She knew, however, that Lian would be able to take very good care of himself. With or without her, he would live on, prosperously and glamorously.

Then she thought of the baby in her belly.

Maternal nature makes most women care more about their babies than about themselves. The manifestation of maternal love is the main reason the human race survives.

If the baby has not yet come into the world, however, then it's a different story.

Women don't have as much affection or love for babies that haven't come into being.

When they're pregnant, their maternal nature hasn't been completely activated.

This is human nature.

Maternal love may be noble, absolute, unselfish, intrepid, compassionate, and ask for nothing in return.

But human nature has weaknesses.

Shen closed her eyes.

If a person can die in peace and serenity, death might be better than life. After all, not too many people in the world can die without regrets.

It wasn't that Shen didn't want to live, only that she knew she couldn't live anymore.

This was a desperate place; she was in a desperate situation; she felt completely desperate.

Then she heard a familiar voice—Xiao's voice.

It whispered, "Don't move. Please don't move."

The voice seemed close to her ears.

Thrilled, she was tempted to turn her head to look.

But Xiao said, "Don't turn your head to look at me. Try to relax. Relax your entire body. Imagine you're lying on a comfortable bed or in your mother's arms, completely carefree. Don't think about anything. No one will harm you."

He spoke every word slowly. His voice seemed to have a magic power that made her calm down and trust him wholeheartedly.

"Can I talk?" she asked.

"Yes, you can, but talk softly and slowly. I can hear you."

His voice was getting closer.

"I can stay still, and I can also relax," Shen said, "but I can't stop myself from thinking."

"What are you thinking about?"

"I'm thinking, if we will sink as soon as we move, doesn't that mean that we'll be stuck here forever? Can you think of a way to get out of here?"

"There's a way."

"Good. As long as you're certain there's a way to get yourself out of here, I'm relieved. It doesn't matter what happens to me."

Before finishing her words, she saw Xiao's luminous eyes.

They used to be defiant and stern eyes. Sometimes she had seen mischief or sarcasm in them. Most of the time, she had seen sorrow and loneliness.

Now, they were filled with joy, relief, gratitude....

She blushed.

When she spoke those words, she wasn't looking at Xiao. That was why she was able to reveal her true feelings. If she had seen him, she probably wouldn't have been bold enough to say the same things.

Xiao was very close to her now.

She could almost feel his breath.

Xiao also avoided her gaze. "You couldn't see me then, right?"

"Um-hmm."

"I haven't moved my body at all, or I would have sunk. Since I didn't move, how did I get here?"

She didn't know.

"The bog looks like it's filled with dead mud. In fact, the mud keeps flowing, but it flows very, very slowly, so we can't feel it."

He added, "I stayed still, so the flowing mud carried me over here. If you struggle, you will only sink. That's why you've stayed here."

Shen didn't speak.

But she thought of something cheerful: If I hadn't struggled, but had ridden along with the mud, how could I see you now?

"The land isn't far ahead," Xiao said. "As long as we can hold out until then, we'll be saved. It won't take long. I believe you can do it ... do you?"

He couldn't help turning to look into her eyes.

Shen also stared into his.

She still didn't say anything, but her eyes seemed to be saying, "I'll do it ... for you."

What her eyes said came from the bottom of her heart. This kind of voice could not be seen with eyes or heard with ears.

There aren't too many people who can pick up this kind of voice.

It can be heard only with the heart.

Xiao heard it.

After a long, long silence, Shen sighed. "Now I realize I was wrong."

"Wrong about what?"

"I thought the way of Heaven was unfair and made fools of us on purpose. Now I realize that Heaven has eyes after all."

"That's right," Xiao said. "No matter what we do, we should always keep in mind that Heaven's eyes are watching."

No sound. No movement. No life. Everything seemed to be dead.

The bog seemed dead, too. No one could feel it flowing.

Can it really take us to solid land?

Shen thought about this question, but she didn't ask. She wasn't really worried.

Her mind at peace, she was content. Time seemed to have stopped. To die or to live? She didn't care.

The only thing she was afraid of was that Xiao's luminous eyes would see through her.

She was afraid that he could hear her breathing faster and her heart pounding faster and faster.

She had to find something to talk about.

What to talk about?

Xiao suddenly asked, "Do you know who saved us this time?"

"It was you, wasn't it?"

She noticed Xiao breathing very fast, too.

"No, it wasn't me," Xiao said.

"It wasn't you? Then who was it?"

"It was the wolf."

During that instant, there was a distant look in his eyes. "The first time I came here, it was a wolf that brought me."

"I've heard you talk about that."

"The wolf made me realize that there is a healing power in this bog, which can cure wounds. The wolf also taught me how to survive ... how to endure patiently."

"Those two things must have been hard to learn."

"If you want to survive, you have to learn to endure—endure being alone, endure loneliness, endure contempt, and endure pain. Happiness can be found only in endurance."

Shen remained silent for awhile. "You've learned a lot from wolves," she observed.

"That's right. Sometimes I think wolves know more than humans do and are more worthy of respect."

"Worthy of respect?"

"Wolves are great loners. They run with a pack to hunt for food, but as soon as they're fed, they disband."

"And you respect them because they like to be alone?"

"Because they're more capable of being alone, they're also more faithful than humans."

"Faithful?"

She had never heard people use this adjective to describe wolves.

"Wolves are the most faithful couples in the world," Xiao said. "The male wolf and the female wolf never separate while they are alive. If the male wolf dies, the female will never look for a new mate, and vice versa."

His eyes showed his typical biting sarcasm. "But what about people? How many husbands in this world are faithful to their wives?

Many abandon their first wives and brag about having several. Women are a little better, but not much. Once in a while, when a widow shows up, who has kept her chastity for her deceased husband, people set up a memorial archway to extol her virtues. They don't realize that every female wolf deserves a memorial archway."

Shen was silent again.

Xiao continued, "The most revered relationship in the world is between husband and wife. If people can't be faithful to their own spouses, how can they be faithful to anyone else? Don't you think wolves are more faithful than humans?"

After an interval, Shen said, "But wolves sometimes eat other wolves."

"How about people? Don't people eat other people, too?" Xiao countered. "Besides, wolves eat their own kind only when they're starving, but people eat other people even when they're not the least bit hungry."

Shen sighed. "You know a lot about wolves, but very little about humans."

"Oh?"

"There are faithful people and lovely people. Furthermore, there are always more good people than bad ones. As long as you get to know someone, you will find that they have an endearing side. People are not as despicable as you think."

Xiao fell silent.

He didn't know why he was talking about these things.

Was he hiding his true heart like Shen was? Was he afraid to be exposed, so he talked like this on purpose?

Or ... was he using these words to admonish himself?

"Why do you only talk about wolves?" Shen asked. "Why don't you talk about yourself?"

"Me? What is there to talk about?"

"For example, why is your name Xiao Shiyi Lang? Do you have ten brothers and sisters?"

"Um-hmm."

"In that case, you're not alone at all."

"Um-hmm."

"Where are your brothers or sisters?"

"Dead. They're all ... dead!"

Xiao's eyes suddenly filled with sorrow and hatred. Whoever saw his eyes now could well imagine that he must have had a tragic past.

Shen felt a sting in her heart—

During that moment, she felt that Xiao was still a child, a helpless and lonely child who needed someone to love and care for him.

She didn't know why she felt this way.

The mud was really moving.

Shen could see land.

She was surprised to find it so beautiful.

Thousands of years ago, this place must have been a bog, too, so the soil was especially fertile.

Hidden deep in the valley and surrounded by mountains on all sides, this place was shielded from the cold wind. Spring was eternal. It looked like a secret paradise Heaven had carefully reserved for the suffering world.

Plants that had withered everywhere else thrived here. Exotic flowers that had difficulty growing elsewhere flourished in this valley.

Even the water in the stream flowing down the hill tasted particularly sweet and refreshing.

Shen usually liked to be clean, but now she forgot the mud all over her body. Upon stepping onto this land, she gazed in wonder at everything that met her eyes.

She stood in place for a long while. Then she took a long breath and said, "I didn't know there could be a place like this. Only someone like you could find it."

"I didn't find it. It was—"

"I know." Shen laughed softly. "It was the wolf that found it."

Then she found a hut nestled among the flowers and shrubbery beside the stream. A bush of light purple flowers grew out of its roof.

"There are people living here," she said, with a tinge of disappointment in her voice.

Xiao gazed at her. "Other than you and me, I doubt there is anybody else here. You may be the second person to set foot here."

Shen seemed to blush a little. "Have you ever brought anyone else here?"

He shook his head.

"But that hut—"

"I built it. If everyone must have a home, it can count as mine. I fell in love with this place the first time I came here. From then on, every time I felt tired or bored, I came here to stay for a month or two. When I left, I always felt like a changed man."

"In that case, why don't you stay here longer? Why don't you live here forever?"

Xiao said nothing.

There was a light in Shen's eyes. "There are flowers, fruit, clean stream water, and fertile soil here. Whoever lives here doesn't have to worry about anything. Why don't you just live here happily for the rest of your life? Why do you go out and get into all kinds of trouble?"

It was a while before Xiao answered. "Perhaps because I'm a born drifter."

He smiled as he said it, but his smile was sad and lonely.

Shen suddenly got it!

No amount of suffering and trouble was as unbearable as loneliness.

No matter how pretty the flowers, how sweet the fruit, how refreshing the water in the stream, they could never fill the emptiness in one's heart.

"I feel I'm inferior to the wolves in many ways," Xiao said wistfully. "There are certain things they can do that I never can."

"Because you're a human, not a wolf," Shen said. "If a wolf tried to imitate humans, he would be considered an odd bird by his own kind, too. Right?"

Xiao answered after some moments of silence. "You're right.

Humans are humans. Wolves are wolves. If wolves shouldn't imitate humans, why should humans imitate wolves?"

Then he broke into a smile. "I haven't been here for quite a while. The dirt in the house must be three inches thick. I'll go clean the house. You ... Can you walk by yourself now?"

"It appears Heaven is fair to humans and wolves." She smiled back at him. "After soaking in the mud for half a day, my injury seems to have become less painful."

"Good. If you'd like to, then, why don't you go wash yourself in the stream. I'll wait for you in the house."

I'll wait for you in the house.

This was a common utterance, but when Xiao said this, he couldn't have known how much it meant to Shen.

She had spent more than half of her life waiting.

When she was little, she had often sat on the stair at the gate and waited for her parents, who were always away on some sort of heroic mission. She had often waited for days or even months. She waited for her father to come back with a kind smile on his face, and she waited for her mother to hug her gently, lovingly....

Until the day she realized her parents would never come back.

On that day, she didn't see her parents. She saw two coffins instead.

Then, as she grew up, she still spent every day waiting.

She always awoke early in the morning, but she had to lie in bed waiting for her nanny to wake her up and take her to give the morning greeting to her grandmother.

After the morning greeting, she wouldn't see her grandmother again until lunchtime. Then she would wait for dinner. The happiest part of her day was the few hours after dinner.

During those hours, her grandmother would let her sit on the small stool at her feet while she told her many tales and stories. She'd give her some tips about how to use the invincible Golden Needles of the Shens. Sometimes, she'd peel a loquat fruit or a tangerine and feed it to Shen. Sometimes, she'd even let Shen touch her thinning gray hair and wrinkled face.

However, those moments were fleeting. Then Shen had to wait until the next day.

The older she grew, the more time she felt she spent in waiting. When she was older, she didn't look forward to the short happy time after dinner as much as before.

What was she waiting for? She didn't know.

Perhaps, like every other girl in the world, she was waiting for an ideal husband who would ride up on a white horse and take her away in a bridal palanquin.

She was luckier than other girls. She finally did have a great husband.

Lian was an absolutely ideal husband. He was gentle, handsome, wealthy, well-educated, and excellent in martial arts. Few other young men could compare with him in terms of reputation and social status.

Whoever became his wife should not only feel content but appreciative.

And Shen was truly content.

However, she still kept waiting. She often leaned against the window frame, waiting for her well-known husband to return. She often waited for days or months.

While she waited, her heart was always filled with trepidation. She was afraid that what would come back would not be her gentle and loving husband but a coffin.

An ice-cold coffin!

There were probably few people in the world who knew more about waiting than Shen.

The more she experienced it, the more afraid she was of waiting.

Unfortunately, she was always waiting for others and no one had ever waited for her.

Now, finally, someone was waiting for her.

No matter how long she stayed outside or what she did there, when she went back to the house, there would be someone waiting for her.

It was only a small simple hut, and the person waiting for her was not family, but it was enough to make her feel warm and secure.

She was neither alone nor lonely.

The water in the stream was cold, but her body felt warm.

She had seldom felt such happiness.

Aside from a wooden bed, there was almost nothing in the house. It looked indescribably desolate, indescribably empty. When Xiao came back here, he usually felt at peace ... at first.

Gradually, he would become restless.

He could have made some furniture, utensils, or other accessories, to make the hut look less desolate, but he never had.

Those things might fill the emptiness in the house, but not the emptiness in his heart.

Until now.

The hut looked as bare as before, but his heart was no longer empty or lonely. He felt as if he had really come home.

This was the first time he had thought of this place as *home*.

He finally realized how rewarding and enjoyable the feeling of *coming home* was.

He was waiting, but his heart felt at ease.

Because the person he was waiting for was coming soon, without a doubt.

As long as there is a caring and thoughtful woman in the house, it doesn't matter how simple the house is. Only a woman can turn a house into a home.

Only a woman can make a man feel the warmth of home.

Therefore, the world cannot do without women.

Most men have the malady of laziness.

The only thing that can cure a man of this malady is a woman— a woman he loves.

Xiao became very diligent.

A table and some chairs appeared in the house. The bed acquired a soft straw mattress. Even the window sported a bamboo curtain.

Xiao didn't sleep in the house. Every night, he slept on a rock outside. However, he still looked upon the hut as his home, and for that reason, he had to make his home enjoyable and inviting.

This was the first time he'd ever had a home.

The table now had a vase, and the vase was filled with flowers.

When they ate, they had cups, plates, bowls, and dishes. In addition to an endless supply of fresh fruit, they sometimes had fried fish, a plate of well-roasted hare meat, or a cup of grape or strawberry wine. They didn't have any salt, but they still enjoyed their food.

Xiao had skillful hands.

He could carve a chunk of wood into a pretty vase or a nice goblet.

He caught fish in the stream or hares in the bush and turned them into dinner. Shen knit a tablecloth of fine straw, which made their dinner table look more elaborate.

Their injuries healed rather quickly.

It wasn't the healing power of mere mud, but also the power of affection. The latter was even more magical and more amazing. All the miracles in the world can be attributed to it.

One morning, Xiao opened his eyes when Shen placed a grass-knitted 'quilt' on him.

She blushed when she saw him opening his eyes. "Dew is heavy at night. It's a little cold outside...." she muttered, lowering her head.

Gazing at her, Xiao seemed to forget how to speak.

She hung her head even lower. "Why don't you build another hut? While I sleep inside, how can I feel at peace knowing that you suffer from the coldness of the wind and dew outside?"

As a result, Xiao became even busier.

A framework went up beside the hut.

Humans aren't really as smart as they think they are. They often indulge their present fantasies, forgetting to think about how long their happiness can last.

Chapter 16

Time to Bid Farewell

One day when Xiao went to draw water, he found Shen sitting by the stream looking down at her own belly.

She didn't notice Xiao standing beside her.

He couldn't resist asking, "What's on your mind?"

Startled, she looked up at him with a strange expression on her face. After a moment, she gathered herself and forced a smile. "Nothing. I'm not thinking about anything."

Xiao didn't press on.

He regretted asking the question.

He knew when a woman says, "I'm not thinking about anything," she is thinking about many things—things she doesn't want anyone to know about.

These things, however, are usually easy to guess.

He knew what Shen was thinking about.

The next morning, Shen found the nearly completed new hut torn down.

The few jars of freshly brewed wine, which were not drinkable yet, were also gone.

Xiao sat under the tree, looking slightly intoxicated. He appeared to have been awake all night.

Shen's heart raced as an ominous feeling came over her.

"Wh-why did you tear down the hut?" she murmured.

"No one's going to live in it. Why shouldn't I tear it down?" he said, without glancing at her.

"Wh-why is no one going to live in it? You—"

"I'm leaving."

Shen's body went cold. "Leaving? Why are you leaving? Isn't this your home?"

"I told you before, I have no home. I'm a born drifter, and I usually stay here less than two months before I want to get out again to look for more trouble."

Feeling as if her heart had been pricked by a needle, Shen couldn't help but ask, "Do you really mean it?"

"Why should I lie? I've never been used to this way of life."

"What's wrong with this way of life?"

"What you think is right is not necessarily right for me. You and I are different people. Unlike you, I'm a man who loves adventure and excitement."

Her eyes brimmed with tears. "But I—"

"You should leave, too. You have to leave ... sooner or later."

Shen tried to refrain from crying, but tears slipped down her face anyway.

She caught Xiao's meaning.

He's not really leaving, she realized. It's just that he knows it's time for me to leave. There's no way I can stay here forever. I have to leave eventually. How long can I escape from reality?

She took a deep breath. "When do we leave?" she asked.

"Now."

"All right."

With that, she turned around and ran back into the hut. Soon the sound of her crying was heard.

Xiao's face was still expressionless.

The breeze blowing against him was still warm.

But ... his heart was all but frozen.

Xiao picked some peaches and pears in the valley and sold them to a rich household in town for a few taels of silver. He didn't ask a high price, but the money he got was enough to pay for their journey.

Then he hired a mule cart for Shen to ride in.

He sat on the yoke.

Shen realized that every penny Xiao Shiyi Lang, the Great Bandit, spent was honest money he had earned with his own hands.

He had robbed, but he did it only to help those in need.

She realized that Xiao Shiyi Lang, the Great Bandit, was this kind of man.

If she hadn't seen it with her own eyes, she wouldn't have believed that there was someone like him in the world.

Her understanding of Xiao was getting deeper and deeper, but the distance between them was getting greater and greater.

While in the valley, they had been close, so close that they could hear each other's heart beating.

No sooner had they left than the distance between them widened.

Are we really from two different worlds? she mused.

In the inn at the bottom of the hill, they were the only guests.

Now she was waiting again.

And for what?

For their parting—for nothing but parting.

A carriage stopped outside. Xiao got off the carriage and rushed in. His face was pale, but he seemed excited.

When Shen saw him return, she felt warmth rising inside her and she went out to greet him cheerfully. "I'm surprised to see you return in a carriage today."

For most men, few things are more lovely or pleasant than the smile of the girl he loves.

When Shen smiled, Xiao usually couldn't take his eyes off her face, knowing he wouldn't be able to see it much longer.

Today, however, he didn't even cast her a glance. He simply said, "I hired this carriage for you."

'F-for me?" she responded in surprise.

Women are much more sensitive than men. When she saw Xiao's facial expression, she sensed something was wrong and her smile stiffened.

"That's right. I hired it for you, because you're not familiar with the roads around here."

She cringed, feeling chilled to the bone. She wanted to speak, but her lips wouldn't stop quivering.

She knew Xiao had been going out every day to inquire about Lian's whereabouts.

After a long pause, she summoned her courage and asked, "Have... you found him?"

"Yes."

His reply was short. Frighteningly short. And sharp as a needle.

Shen's expression looked like this needle had hurt her.

As a proper woman, she knew she should be pleased upon hearing the whereabouts of her husband.

Yet she simply couldn't make herself act pleasantly surprised.

After some time she asked, "Where is he?"

"The carriage driver outside knows. He'll take you there."

"Thank you." Her face finally formed a smile.

She knew the two words had come from her own mouth, but the voice sounded so unfamiliar and so distant, it was as if she were listening to a stranger talking.

She also knew she was smiling, but her face was so numb that the smile seemed to be on someone else's face.

"You're welcome," said Xiao. "It's the least I could do."

His voice was cold, and so was his expression.

Was his heart cold as well?

"Did you ask the carriage driver to wait?" Shen asked.

"Yes. It's still early. You can get a good start on the journey. And ... you don't have too many things to pack."

A strange smile spread across his face. "Besides, I know you must be in a hurry to go."

"Yes," she said, nodding slowly. "I haven't seen him for a long time."

"All right, go on! Perhaps we'll meet again in the future."

They both spoke extraordinarily softly and slowly, as though it took great effort to speak.

Were they saying what they really wanted to say? How many people could muster that kind of courage?

Since Old Heaven had allowed them to meet, why did it also make them lie to each other, deceive each other, and even hurt each other?

Xiao turned around abruptly. "You have a long journey ahead of you. I'd better not hold you up any longer. Good-bye."

"You're right. I have a long journey ahead. How about you? Are you moving on, too?"

"Yes, as long as one is alive, one has to keep going forward," he replied, starting to move away from her.

Shen suddenly bit her lip and spoke up. "There's another thing I want to do. Would you let me?"

Xiao stopped in his tracks, but he didn't turn his head around. "What?"

"I ... I want to buy you a drink."

She seemed to have mustered enough courage. "My treat, really. You've provided for me every day for so long. It's only fitting that you let me treat you once."

"But you—"

"I have no money with me, but I believe I can trade this thing for at least a few jars of wine. Right?"

She plucked the gold hairpin from her head.

The gold hairpin wasn't really valuable, but it was the thing she had treasured most. On the day after her wedding, Lian had put it in her hair.

She had never imagined that one day she would trade it for a few jars of wine.

But now she didn't care. Whatever it took to drink with Xiao one last time was worth it.

Xiao had sacrificed so much for her. She felt it was the least she could do to show her appreciation.

In this life, she knew she would never be able to repay him.

At length, Xiao turned around and looked at the hairpin in her hand.

He looked as if he had many words to say, but, eventually, he simply smiled. "You know me," he said, "I can never resist a free drink."

He got drunk. He got drunk really fast. When someone desperately wants to get drunk, it doesn't take much.

Even if a person isn't drunk, he can always pretend to be. The strange thing is that if he tries hard to appear drunk, eventually he can't tell whether he's really drunk or only pretending.

Xiao was humming that song again. Drunk people often find it hard to talk but easy to sing. Singing is easier than talking.

For a long time, Shen sat silently and listened to Xiao sing. She remained sober, afraid to get drunk, knowing that if she got drunk, she'd be unable to control herself. She was afraid she might do something she'd regret.

Those who are particularly afraid to die often end up dying sooner than others.

On the other hand, those who are afraid to get drunk won't get drunk, because of self-awareness. When they have drunk a certain amount of alcohol, they won't be able to continue anymore. If they drink more, they'll throw up.

When someone's heart rejects something, the stomach won't accept it either.

Xiao's singing was still so bleak and forlorn.

With tears brimming in her eyes, Shen couldn't keep from asking, "I've heard you sing this song many times, but I've never understood what it means."

The singing stopped and Xiao brought his eyes from the hazy distance back to her, staring straight into her face. "You really want to know?"

"Yes."

"You don't understand it because it's a Mongolian shepherds' song. Once you understand it, you may never want to hear it again."

"Why?"

Xiao's face showed his typical cynicism. "Because the meaning of this song can never be understood or appreciated by people like you."

Shen lowered her head. "Maybe—maybe I'm a little different from others?"

After staring at her for a very long time, Xiao said, "All right, I'll tell you."

He groped for his wine, found it, and drank it up. Then he began. "The song is talking about how people usually take pity on sheep and feel sorry for them, but few understand the suffering and loneliness of wolves. People see cruelty in wolves eating sheep, but they don't see how wolves endure loneliness and hunger and often wander in a world of ice and snow. When sheep are hungry, they eat grass. What if wolves are hungry? Are they supposed to starve to death?"

His voice was full of bitterness, and he was getting louder.

"Let me ask you this," Xiao went on. "If you wandered on the tundra in the bone-chilling wind for many days and hadn't drunk any water or eaten anything, and then you saw a sheep, would you want to eat it?"

Shen dropped her eyes and never looked up.

Xiao drank another cup of wine. Then he picked up his chopsticks and tapped on a cup, starting to sing aloud in Chinese:

It's March. It's early spring.
Sheep rejoice at the tall grass.
It's cold. The earth is frozen.
Who is going to feed the wolf?

Men's hearts take pity on the sheep.
Wolves' hearts are lonely and sad.
The heart of Heaven is hard to fathom.
The hearts of the world are cold as frost.

His pitch was very high. Upon singing the last word, his voice suddenly cracked.

Tears fell from Shen's eyes.

His head lying on the table, Xiao waved his hand saying, "I'm drunk and sleepy. Please go now! Go! *Go*! You have to leave eventually. Go soon, so that later I won't have to chase you out—"

Shen had never felt so unsettled.

Now, she knew she could make it back to the world she was familiar with, and that everything would return to normal and be secure and peaceful.

Now, after she went back, nothing and no one would ever trouble her again.

This is what she had hoped for. She should be happy.

But now....

She wiped her tears and asked herself, "If he had held my hands and asked me not to leave, would I have stayed with him? Would I have given up my stable and normal life, given up honor and status, given up those near and dear to me, and given up everything else, just for him?"

She dared think no further.

She knew she didn't have a strong will. She dared not test herself.

She dared not think about everything Xiao had done for her, his luminous eyes, and the affection in them.

Now, she only thought about Lian Chengbi.

She was determined to be a dutiful wife to Lian, because—

The carriage had stopped and she had returned to her own world.

This was a world of humans, not wolves.

It was quiet in the yard, so quiet she could even hear falling leaves.

It was late at night. This was a prestigious inn that only served important guests. Everyone was well-mannered. No one would disturb others.

Lian was staying in one section of the villa.

An inn servant, with a look of surprise in his eyes, led her to the courtyard in front of her husband's quarters. She waved her hand and he left, without asking a single question.

The first thing people working at the inn had to learn was what to ask and what not to ask.

The room in the west wing was still lit.

Shen moved quietly across the yard and started to ascend the steps.

There were only four or five steps, but it seemed to take her forever.

She felt an unspeakable fear in her heart, afraid to push the door open and face her own husband.

What was she afraid of?

Was she afraid that Lian would ask her: "Where have you been all this time?"

The light in the room was bright, but the volume of the voices remained low. Then someone spoke up, "Who is it?"

Though the voice was raised, it still sounded reserved, gentle, and so very polite.

She knew it was Lian's voice. Few people in the world could control themselves as well.

During that instant, everything good about Lian flooded back into her mind. She found herself missing him, too.

During that very instant, she thought about rushing into the house and running into his arms.

But she didn't.

She knew Lian didn't like emotional people.

When she ascended the steps, the door opened and Lian came out.

In the last two months, he had been searching relentlessly for his wife. He had been worried and fearful, and he had missed her greatly. Now, his wife appeared on his doorstep like a miracle.

However, even at a moment like this, he didn't show joy or excitement. He didn't even reach out to hold his wife's hand.

He merely gazed at her, smiled, and gently said, "You're back?"

Likewise, Shen simply nodded faintly and answered, "Yes. I'm back."

Only two sentences, nothing more.

Yet, her distraught heart suddenly calmed down.

She was once accustomed to this kind of calm and peaceful affection. Now, she found that nothing had changed.

What she didn't want to talk about, Lian would never bring up.

In his world, people always kept each other at a proper distance, even if they were father and son, brother and sister ... or husband and wife.

This distance might make them feel lonely, but it provided them with security, dignity, and peace of mind.

Lian wasn't alone. Zhao Wuji, Hai Lingzi, Tu Xiaotian, Li Gang, and Situ Zhongping were also in the room. Li Gang, also one of the so-called Six Ideal Gentlemen, was known as the True Gentleman Who Harbors No Lust Before Beauty. Situ Zhongping was joint leader of seventy-two security agencies from thirteen provinces. He was also known as Stable as Mount Tai. Mount Tai is the highest mountain in Eastern China. Situ got the nickname because he was such a scrupulous man that he had never been involved in any dispute, trouble, or controversy.

These five people were all well-known fighters with chivalrous reputations. They were Lian's friends. Naturally, they all knew Shen. Although they didn't say anything, they were all puzzled.

His wife was missing for two months, yet he didn't ask her where she had been or what she had been doing, they thought. It's also strange that she didn't offer an explanation.

They all thought Lian and Shen were a peculiar couple.

Shen was surprised to find that there were still wine and food on the table.

Lian was good at controlling his emotions, and he also paid close attention to his health. Shen had seldom seen him drink. Even when he did drink, he usually only had a sip. Since their wedding, this was the first time she had seen him drinking into midnight.

She didn't ask why. He must have his reason.

Lian started to explain. "We were having a discussion, before your return."

"Madame," Zhao said, "you know that men like to eat. Whenever we get together, we have to have something to eat or drink."

Shen nodded. "I know."

Zhao's eyes gleamed. "Madame, do you know what we are talking about?"

She shook her head with a smile. "How would I know?"

Ever since she was little, she had learned that if a woman wants to be a praiseworthy wife, she has to wear a smile constantly in the presence of her husband's friends.

Sometimes she smiled so long that her cheeks felt sore.

"Ten days ago, a major event took place here," Zhao said. "I invited Mr. Lian and the other four gentlemen over to discuss it."

"Oh? What happened?"

She didn't really want to know, but sometimes it's rude not to ask. If she didn't ask, it would imply that she didn't care about her husband's friends.

Therefore, she asked, even though she had never had a good impression of Zhao. She felt he was too sociable and too smooth-tongued.

Smooth-tongued people usually talk a lot; she didn't trust talkative people.

"There was a gentleman named Meng Sanye in this area," said Zhao. "Have you ever heard of him, Madame?"

"I know very few people," she replied.

"Mr. Meng was a well-respected philanthropist. His reputation for generosity could be compared to Duke Mengchang, a thousand years ago. Just over ten days ago, Meng Manor was robbed, and the entire family—over a hundred members—was slaughtered. Not a single soul was spared."

Shen frowned. "Who did such a horrible thing?"

"The Great Bandit—Xiao Shiyi Lang."

Her heart jumped. "Did you say Xiao Shiyi Lang?"

"That's right! Other than Xiao Shiyi Lang, who else could be so cold-blooded and brutal?"

She tried to stay calm. "Since no one survived, how do you know he is the murderer?"

"Xiao is not only ruthless, but arrogant. Every time he commits a crime, he leaves his signature on the scene."

Feeling heat rising inside her, Shen could stand it no longer. "That's impossible!" she blurted out. "Xiao Shiyi Lang can't be the murderer! You all wrongly accuse him. He's not what you think!"

Zhao's countenance changed. "You're a kind-hearted person, Madame," he said with a strained smile. "You prefer to think the best of everyone, no matter how evil they are."

"How do you know he didn't do it, Madame?" Li Gang spoke up, his piercing eyes staring at Shen.

Her body shaking, Shen wanted to run from the room and far, far away, to never hear these words or see these people again.

Yet, she knew she couldn't run away and that she had to stand up and speak for Xiao. She owed him that much. It was time for her to repay her debts.

She bit her lip and declared, "I know he couldn't have killed those people, because I have not left his side during the last two months."

Her words caught everyone off guard.

She didn't have to look to know the expressions on their faces, neither did she have to guess to know what they were thinking.

But she didn't regret it, nor did she care.

She was prepared to bear the consequences of what she had said.

After who knows how long, Lian said, "We may have made a mistake. I believe my wife."

His voice was still calm, and very gentle.

Tu nodded slowly and muttered, "It must have been a misunderstanding. It must have been...."

Zhao also kept nodding his head. Then he stood up and said, "You must be tired from your long journey, Madame. This is when we ought to excuse ourselves. We'll celebrate your safe return to-morrow."

Hai didn't say anything. He bowed deeply and walked out first.

Only Situ remained seated.

Consistent with his epithet, Stable as Mount Tai, he waited until Zhao, Tu, and Hai had left. Then, in a low voice, he said, "Brother Li, please wait a minute."

Li's mouth was still closed, but he stopped in his tracks.

"If Xiao Shiyi Lang didn't do this," Situ observed, "it's likely that he didn't do the other horrible things attributed to him either. If we have wronged him this time, we might have been wrongly accusing him the whole time."

His words made Shen feel an unspeakable gratitude.

She knew Situ started as an assistant in a security agency. It hadn't been easy for him to attain the position he had today.

Usually cautious and reserved, he seldom spoke, aware that talking too much could cause him trouble. With his current position and status, he couldn't afford to say anything inappropriate.

Since these words came from Situ's mouth, they carried enormous weight. Even if Li didn't like what Situ said, he could only listen.

Situ continued. "Since you and I are proud of our honor, whatever we do shouldn't violate the spirit of chivalry. I would rather let a thousand evil men go free than wrongly persecute one innocent man."

He sighed. "As the saying goes, 'Being pointed at by a thousand accusing fingers is enough to make one drop dead.' When a man is wrongly accused and powerless to defend his innocence, he must feel worse than death."

Listening quietly, Shen felt that never in her life had she heard such admirable and moving words.

Situ seemed to be a common person. With plain facial features and a balding head, he looked like an ordinary man who had experienced all the joy and sadness of life, who had no more ambition for anything ... who was merely waiting to die.

At this moment, however, he seemed indescribably noble and honorable to her. She almost wanted to go and kiss his bald head.

Situ went on. "If Xiao isn't the villain he's alleged to be, we mustn't wrongly accuse him, and, further, we should try to defend his innocence and clear his name so that he can turn over a new leaf."

He turned his eyes to Shen. "But judging one's heart is difficult. It's not easy to determine whether a person is good or evil in a few short months."

"He is not an evil man," Shen said. "I can vouch for him."

She lowered her head and continued. "In the last two months, I have gotten to know him well. He saved my life several times, but he has never asked for anything in return. When he heard that my husband was here, he sent someone to bring me here."

At this point, her voice choked with sobs and she could barely continue.

"In that case," said Situ, "you must do everything you can to clear his tarnished name, Madame."

"I thought I would never be able to make it up to him. I will do whatever it takes to clear his name and help him start a new life."

After a few moments of thought, Situ said, "May I ask when you parted from him?"

"Tonight, after dinner."

"In that case, he must be still around."

"Um-hmm."

Situ mused a while longer. "In my opinion, you should invite him here, so that we can see what he's like and get to know him."

He presented an earnest smile. "We have heard a great deal about him, but none of us have ever met him."

Shen appeared more cheerful now. "Once you see him, you'll know what kind of person he is, but—"

She suddenly frowned. "But today isn't a good day."

"Why not?"

"Today ... he's been drinking. He's incoherent at the moment."

"Does he get drunk often?" Situ asked.

"Yes, he does."

"Those who get drunk often have a high tolerance for alcohol, and they're often straightforward people. I would love the chance to have a drink with him."

Shen smiled pleasantly. "Everyone knows you have an ocean-like capacity for alcohol. No matter how much you drink, you're still Stable as Mount Tai. However, I don't think he would necessarily be the one under the table, if you two had a drink."

"Oh? How much did he drink today?"

"Over ten pounds."

"Over ten pounds? That's a very high tolerance, but it also depends on what he drank and where."

He smiled another smile and added, "A person's capacity for alcohol is determined by many factors."

"He drank in a small inn at the bottom of the hill outside town," Shen replied. "And what he drank was nothing but ordinary Burning-Knife liquor."

"It seems that he does have a high tolerance. I'm getting more and more interested in meeting him, but—"

Situ rose to his feet. "It's getting late. There's no hurry. When you've had a rest, you can invite him over. It's time for me to excuse myself."

He smiled and saluted to her in fists. "All this talk makes me thirsty," he said to Li Gang. "Brother Li, would you be interested in joining me for a few drinks?"

"Why not!" Li replied.

From the beginning until the end of Situ's questioning, these were the only words Li had uttered.

Chapter 17

The Heart of an Ideal Gentleman

EVERYONE HAD LEFT and the candle was almost burned out.

Flickering candlelight fell on Lian's handsome, gentle and serene face, making it appear slightly agitated.

But when he nipped off the extra wick and the flame stopped flickering, his face looked as serene as usual. Perhaps a little too serene.

Shen lifted a wine cup and then put it down. Suddenly she smiled and said, "I drank some wine today."

"So did I," Lian replied pleasantly. "The nights are getting colder. A little wine is warming."

She was quiet for a moment. "Have ... have you ever been drunk?" she asked.

"Only those who have a high tolerance let themselves over-imbibe and get drunk. It's not easy for me to become inebriated."

"You're right," she said. "Although getting drunk does free one from worry, not everyone lets himself do so."

A pause. Then Lian smiled again, as he said, "If you'd like a drink, I will be happy to join you."

"I know," she said, returning his smile. "Whatever I want to do, you always want to do it with me."

Lian slowly poured a cup of wine and placed it in front of her. "It's a pity that I used to spend so little time with you," he sighed. "All of this could have been avoided."

Shen was silent for a few moments before speaking again. "Do you know what has happened to me during the last two months?"

"I ... I know all of it, but not very clearly."

"Why didn't you ask?"

"You have told me plenty."

Shen bit her lip. "But why didn't you ask me *how* I met Xiao Shiyi Lang and *why* I saw him every day?"

Why? She suddenly became agitated, but Lian merely gazed at her with tenderness.

All he said was, "Because I trust you."

Only four words, but they said it all.

Shen was struck by Lian's unreserved faith in her.

During that moment, infinite tenderness and affection flooded her heart and seemed about to spill over.

She quickly drained her cup of wine, then placed her head on the table and cried.

If Lian had questioned her or even chided her, maybe she would have felt better, although she had never been unfaithful to him.

He was still so gentle and thoughtful. He trusted and cared about her, and he was forever eager to protect her from harm.

For some reason, she felt guilty.

In the past two months, she hadn't missed him as much as he had missed her.

She owed Xiao a great deal, but, now, she felt she owed Lian a great deal, too. Never in this life could she repay Lian either.

This feeling was like a knife cutting her heart in half.

Lian stared at her in surprise.

This was the first time his wife had revealed her true feelings and cried in front of him.

He didn't even know how to comfort her, because he didn't understand the pain in her heart. He suddenly realized that the distance between his heart and hers was vast.

After who knows how long, he finally rose to his feet and reached out to gently stroke her hair.

He soon withdrew his hand, however, and stood still for a while. "You're tired and need to rest," he said. "We can talk about everything tomorrow. Tomorrow ... tomorrow will be a fine day."

Tired from crying, Shen sat with her head on the table, as if asleep.

But, in truth, how could she fall asleep?

She heard her husband slowly leave the room and close the door. She had felt his hand stroking her hair, his every move and every act gentle and considerate.

She wished, however, that her husband would be rough with her just once ... maybe pull her hair, or swoop her up and gather her into his arms.

She was a little disappointed, but she felt grateful.

She knew Lian had been, was now, and always would be gentle with her. He would never harm her or force her to do anything.

After having a good cry, she felt much better.

Let bygones be bygones, she told herself.

As long as I can help Xiao clear his tarnished name and restart his life, I will have repaid him, to a certain extent.

From now on, I'm going to be a dutiful wife to Lian, and I'm going to do all I can to make him happy.

She had made up her mind.

When people have made up their mind, they usually feel more at peace.

However, tears trickled down Shen's cheeks ... again.

The night air was as cool as water.

The steps were also cool.

Sitting on the step, Lian felt a chill travel up his body, up his spine, and into his heart.

Nonetheless, he also felt a flame burning in his heart.

How did she meet Xiao Shiyi Lang?

Why was she with him every day?

What have they been doing for the last two months? Why didn't she come back until now?

These questions gnawed at his heart like a viper.

If he had confronted her with these questions, perhaps he would have felt better.

But he was a courteous gentleman. He never asked people to talk about what they didn't want to talk about.

But even if I didn't ask her, she should have offered to tell me, he thought.

Why didn't she tell me? What else is she hiding from me?

He tried to stay calm and trust his wife.

But he couldn't.

His heart could never be as calm as he appeared to be.

When he had seen how Shen had reacted to Xiao's name and how sad she had looked, he suddenly felt that Xiao might be much closer to his wife than he ever was.

This was the first time he had felt he didn't in the least understand his wife.

Was it because he had never had the opportunity, or was it because she had never given him the opportunity to understand her?

It was late autumn. The leaves of the firmiana trees were falling.

At that moment, he saw Zhao, Tu, Hai, and Li leaving the room in the east wing. They had all removed their long jackets and were dressed only in tight clothes.

When they saw Lian sitting alone on the step, they appeared surprised. They hesitated only a moment, exchanged glances, and then walked toward him.

Zhao was in front. "Why aren't you in bed yet, Mr. Lian?" he asked, with the semblance of a smile.

They usually addressed each other as "Brother," but now Zhao suddenly addressed Lian as "Mr." instead. People usually become overly polite when wary of the other person.

Lian only smiled in return. "And why aren't you in bed?"

Zhao's smile appeared more nervous. "We ... we have something to do. We must step out."

"I know," Lian said, nodding.

Zhao's eyes gleamed. "Do you know where we're going?"

A pause ensued. "No, I don't."

Zhao produced a legitimate smile. "Sometimes, it's better not to know."

A faint neighing came from outside.

They had ordered someone to prepare horses for them.

"Would you like to join us?" Hai asked abruptly.

Another pause ensued. "There are certain things I'd better not get involved in," Lian said.

They left.

These four gentlemen were first-rate fighters. They never made noise when they moved, but horses were different. Even a long way off, the sound of hooves could be heard.

Therefore, after leaving the inn, they walked their horses a long distance before mounting and racing away.

Why had they left in such a hurry and in such secrecy?

The room in the east wing was still lit.

For a long time, Lian continued to sit on the step, ostensibly waiting for the agitation on his face to fade. At last he rose and strolled toward the east wing.

The door was open. Situ was washing his hands in the room.

He washed them over and over, carefully, as if his hands were covered with irremovable stains of blood.

Perhaps he wasn't cleansing his hands, but his heart.

Lian stood outside the door, watching him.

Situ didn't turn his head around. "Did you see them leave?"

"Um-hmm."

"Do you know what they went out to do?"

Lian kept his mouth closed, as if refusing to answer this question.

"I'm sure you know," Situ said, "no matter what kind of person Xiao Shiyi Lang is, they won't let him live. As long as Xiao is still alive, they can't sleep in peace."

Lian smirked. "What about you?"

"Me?"

"If it weren't for the information you provided about Xiao's whereabouts, how would they have known where to find him?"

Situ stopped washing and held his hands in mid-air. After a long while, he finally took a towel from the rack and dried his hands. "I didn't tell them anything," he said.

"You didn't have to. When you were acquiring the information, you asked Li Gang to stay in the room. That was enough. You knew of Li's enmity for Xiao."

"I didn't go with them."

"As the joint leader of seventy-two security agencies, you have to be particularly cautious and avoid getting involved in anything risky."

"But killing Xiao will be regarded as eliminating a menace to the martial world," Situ countered. "It will be considered honorable, not shameful."

"Perhaps you don't want to offend Shen Bijun, or perhaps you're afraid that one day someone will learn that Xiao was killed unjustly, so you'd rather stay out of it than share the credit."

With a smile, Lian continued. "Your reputation for being Stable as Mount Tai is well justified."

Situ turned, and his eyes appeared strangely inquisitive. "How about you?"

"Me?"

"You knew I was trying to worm Xiao's whereabouts out of your wife, and you knew what the men were going to do, but you didn't stop me or them. How can you blame me?"

Lian said nothing.

"You didn't go with them, because you knew that since Xiao is drunk, they would definitely be able to kill him," Situ declared, with an unflustered smirk. "As a matter of fact, don't you want to have Xiao killed as well? You have more reason than any of us—"

At this point, his face suddenly changed color.

Lian followed Situ's eyes and turned his head.

Shen! She had been standing in the yard since ... who knows when.

She was shaking all over, tears trickling down her cheeks like pearls falling from a snapped string.

Taking a deep breath, Lian said, "You should be in bed."

As he walked forward, Shen backed away, step by step.

"It's cold out here," Lian continued in his gentle voice. "If you want some fresh air, you should at least put on a jacket."

"Don't come any closer!" Shen cried in a husky voice.

Her eyes glistened with tears and she spoke through clenched teeth. "I finally realize exactly what kind of heroes ... what kind of Ideal Gentlemen all of you are!"

She turned around and ran out of the yard!

Drunk. Really drunk!

When a man is really drunk, he feels neither pain nor joy. He doesn't think about the past, the future, or even the present, because his brain is completely blank.

When a man is really drunk, he doesn't think of others or himself, and the things he does seem to be done by someone else and have nothing to do with him.

When a man is really drunk, he does whatever he wants to do but never can while he is sober.

The reason a man does these things must be because of another person—someone whom he can neither forget nor let go of. Even if his brain has gone blank and he is blind drunk, this someone is still in his heart, in his marrow, and entwined with his soul.

Such a man will act by any means necessary, but he doesn't know what he's doing, because his heart is being held, in that moment, by someone else.

Only those who are in the habit of getting drunk can understand this feeling.

Out of the blue, Xiao jumped to his feet and dashed over to the counter. He grabbed the innkeeper by his collar, saying, "Give it to me!"

"What—give what to you?" the man said in a quivering voice, his face pale.

"The hairpin ... the gold hairpin." Xiao muttered.

Sober people are usually a little intimidated by drunk people.

Xiao seized the hairpin, stumbled a few steps, and then tripped and toppled over. He didn't get back to his feet.

He just slowly sat up, held up the hairpin, and stared at it.

Perhaps he didn't really know what he was looking at or what he was thinking about.

He only repeated Shen's name over and over.

He didn't have to think.

Shen wasn't in his brain. She was in his marrow, his blood, his heart, and entwined with his soul.

Seeing what was going on, the innkeeper sighed inwardly. "This man and that lady seem to be a good match and they love each other. Why did they have to separate?"

Xiao stared at the hairpin intently, whispering over and over.... Then he suddenly lay his head on the ground and burst out crying, like a child.

The innkeeper felt sorry for him.

If that lady had seen him like this, would she still have left him? he wondered.

He was glad he had never been so distraught and crazy over love. Anyway, he was too old to be lovesick now.

He didn't realize that those who have never experienced such passion actually have a void in their lives. This void can never be filled with anything else.

It's distressing to miss her so much.
Missing her consumes my soul.
This thought I cannot dismiss,
Yet still, would rather miss her.

There was a mixed sound of hooves pounding and feet running.

All of a sudden ... Bang! Bang! Bang!

The windows on three sides were smashed, and three people leaped in. A fourth person appeared at the doorway, holding a grayish-blue sword, his face bluer and colder than the blade. It was none other than Hai Lingzi, the finest fighter of the Hainan School!

Xiao stayed motionless. He was still sitting there, gazing at the hairpin in his hand and whispering Shen's name.

He was really drunk.

Zhao Wuji had leapt in through the window on the left side. "Who would've known that Xiao Shiyi Lang, the Great Bandit, is not only a mass murderer but also a sentimental lover?" he taunted, his eyes gleaming.

"No wonder Shen Bijun was leaping to his defense," Li Gang added with a sinister smile. "It turns out that they have ... ha!"

Shen Bijun! Did someone say Shen Bijun!

Xiao's head snapped up and he glared at Li.

Perhaps he wasn't really seeing anything, but his piercing eyes looked terrifying.

Li backed up a step involuntarily.

"Don't wait until he's sober. *Attack*!" Hai shouted.

While still shouting, Hai thrust his sword at Xiao's throat like a lightning flash.

Perhaps Xiao didn't realize this thrust could kill him, but the kung fu he had constantly practiced for twenty years was in his blood.

He waved his hand.

Clink! The hairpin in his hand met the tip of Hai's sword!

The famed top fighter of Hainan, staggered by the hairpin, was forced to back away two steps, his sword almost shaken out of his hand.

Zhao's face fell at the sight of this.

Since he had become the chief of Supreme Boundless Gate, he hadn't made much progress in kung fu, yet his title made him seem more imposing. Wherever he went, he was never seen carrying any kind of weapon.

Now, however, he pulled out a flexible steel rapier concealed in his belt. He drew an arc in the air as he brandished it. His footwork and movements looked graceful.

The axioms of Supreme Boundless Gate were:

Use still patience to check violent attacks.
Wait in comfort for an exhausted enemy.
Use the defensive as a way to the offensive.
Use the slow to counter the quick.

The moment Zhao thrust his sword, he heard a sound of wind and a long-stemmed tobacco pipe from Tu's hand shot past him, aimed at the Azure-Sea meridian point on Xiao's lower spine.

Tu looked countrified, clumsy, old, and weary, but the way he attacked was ruthless, precise, and fast!

Concerned about his social status, Zhao always tried to act as gracefully and relaxed as possible, so he was usually in no haste to deliver his attacks. However, when he saw how aggressive Tu was, he shook his rapier straight, swooping toward the artery on the right side of Xiao's neck. If this move worked, Xiao would bleed to death.

Hai didn't allow himself to catch his breath. He raised his sword and lunged forward again.

The swordplay of the Hainan School was swift and ruthless. The swordsmen of this school often delivered deadly attacks in the first few moves.

Since his entrance into the Martial Order, Xiao had never been defeated. Xiao's killer would earn himself a great reputation. If he weren't famous yet, he would become famous instantly. If he were already famous, he would become even more famous. With this in mind, these three were now scrambling to attack first, each fighting as if the others were trying to steal his rightful fame.

Clang! Sparks flew.

Hai's sword hit the tip of Zhao's sword.

Xiao rolled out from under the sword tips.

Both Hai's face and Zhao's face grew slightly red with embarrassment. They swung their swords in a graceful arc in mid-air, then turned and pursued.

Xiao's body flew up, hitting the counter with a thud! Blood oozed from his nose and mouth.

Xiao was so drunk, he hadn't seen Li, who had been standing in the corner.

Zhao, Hai, and Tu had fought to attack first, but Li had taken the opportunity to grab the credit.

With a sour smile, Hai said, "Brother Li, the reputation of your Great Slab-Smashing Hand is well justified. I look forward to taking some lessons from you."

There was no humor on Li's face. "No problem. Anytime," he said flatly.

Then they heard another *Clang!*

While Hai and Li were exchanging words, Tu had seen the opportunity to attack, so he had raised his pipe, aiming it at the Hundred-Meeting meridian point on the top of Xiao's head.

As it happened, Zhao's sword had been brandished, too. The blade shaved past the pipe and Tu missed his target.

But his steel pipe was fairly heavy.

Zhao's sword was knocked away and it flew upward. When their eyes met, though they both tried to smile, their expressions looked more unpleasant than if they had been crying.

"He was hit by my palm," Li sniffed. "Even without your further attacks, he won't live."

"I heard that if you want to make sure a person is dead," Tu said, with a strained smile, "the only convincing way is to cut off his head for close inspection."

Zhao forced a smile. "That's right. I've heard that, too, and I have never forgotten it."

"This is easy," Li said. "Right now, even a child can chop off his head."

Hai laughed cynically. "Not necessarily, I'm afraid."

"Not necessarily?" Li repeated, exasperated.

He turned his head and his face froze.

Xiao was grinning at them!

His bloodshot eyes still looked confused and unfocused, because of his intoxication, but they were wide open.

A dying man's eyes were not supposed to look like that.

Zhao rolled his eyes. "Mr. Xiao," he said, "you have been hit by Lord Li's Great Slab-Smashing Hand. You should close your eyes and wait to die. Why are you still smirking with your beady eyes?"

Xiao burst out laughing, laughing so hard that he could hardly catch his breath.

Li was usually rather composed, but now his face burned with anger. "What are you laughing at?" he asked, in exasperation.

Xiao smirked. "Is your Great Slab-Smashing Hand really as good as he says?"

Without waiting for Li's reply, Xiao rose and puffed out his chest. "Come!" he said with another laugh. "I'll let you hit my chest again."

Li's face changed color, from red to green. "You asked for it. Don't blame me!" he said.

His shoulders and waist remaining still, Li stepped forward and reached his fingers out to touch Xiao's chest. And then he suddenly pushed out his palm.

His palm-strength style was of the orthodox Small Celestial Star system.

Xiao withstood Li's palm attack without evasion.

Thump! It sounded like Li's palm had merely hit a piece of old leather.

Xiao still stood steady, without moving, as if his feet were nailed to the ground.

Li's face turned pale. He was speechless.

His Great Slab-Smashing Hand was ninety percent mature. Even though he couldn't pulverize rocks, when he threw out his fist, no flesh could bear it ... usually.

It was as if Xiao were made of iron.

When Li's fist hit Xiao's chest, he had felt a force pushing him back. If his legs weren't steady, he might have fallen backward.

Zhao and Hai glanced at each other. Although they gloated over

Li's setback, they were still on the same side. They felt more shocked than pleased.

Xiao grinned at Li. After a moment, he asked, "Is this really called Great Slab-Smashing Hand?"

"Humph!" Li responded.

"In my opinion," Xiao smirked, "it's not really Great Slab-Smashing Hand, but something else."

Zhao cast Li a glance and then deliberately asked, "What do you think it is?"

Xiao peered about before speaking. "I've studied this style before. Let me show you."

Xiao wasn't picky about food. He liked to eat anything made of soybeans: tofu, fried tofu, bean curd, bean strips, and so forth.

When he drank, however, he lost his appetite. Though he had ordered a plate of simmered tofu, half of it still lay uneaten on the table.

He staggered over to the table, picked up a few pieces of tofu, and then smashed it to the ground.

"This is called Tofu-Smashing Hand," Xiao declared with a dead-pan face. "It's very similar to Great Slab-Smashing Hand. The difference is that I learned it from my master's wife."

Not until Xiao said this did the others realize what he was doing.

Hai was the first to crack up.

It wasn't polite to laugh at a moment like this, yet he had never laughed so hard in all his life. When he saw the expression on Li's face, he couldn't help himself.

When Xiao saw them laughing, he started laughing, too. He laughed so hard that he doubled over.

Actually, he couldn't really laugh.

In the last twenty years, countless people had died under Li's Great Slab-Smashing Hand. After being hit by Li's palm twice, Xiao had suffered very serious internal injuries.

Drunk people, however, are often ignorant and fearless. They say what they aren't supposed to say and do what they aren't supposed to do.

Drunks are often overconfident. Five-foot tall people suddenly think they're actually eight feet tall. Weak people suddenly believe they possess superhuman strength.

As a result, drunks often pick fights. Whether they can win or not, they simply plunge headfirst into the fight. Even the smartest people become idiots, when they're drunk.

If Xiao were sober, he would never have tried to withstand the force of Li's palm with his chest. Unfortunately, when Xiao Shiyi Lang was drunk, he was no wiser than anyone else.

Tu was laughing, too, but he paid close attention to Xiao's every move.

As the proverb goes, "The older the ginger, the spicier."

Tu was older than the others by twenty or thirty years, which did make a difference. Though his face was laughing, his eyes were not. "I have studied this before, too," he said.

Xiao laughed loudly. "Oh? Would you like to have a try as well?"

"Certainly," Tu replied.

The instant he finished speaking, the pipe he was holding shot out.

He shook his wrist and his pipe seemed to split into three, attacking the Mystic-Ruse, Breast-Root, and General-Platform meridians on Xiao's chest.

Tu was regarded as the highest master of attacking meridian points. The move he had just used, called Projecting the Moon in Three Lakes, was virtually matchless in China.

Xiao's body didn't move. He stretched out his right hand as if to catch a fly. Then, somehow, Tu's pipe slipped easily into Xiao's hand.

Tu's face turned whiter than a sheet.

Xiao laughed. "I drink, but I don't smoke. This is useless to me."

He bent the pipe with both hands as if trying to snap it, unaware that it was made of steel. Unable to snap it, he suddenly let out a loud bellow, and *twang*! the pipe bounced out of his hand and hit the wall. Blood sprayed out of his mouth, showering Tu.

Tu had been stunned when his pipe was wrested away from him, but the sight of the blood gave him new confidence. He spun around and jabbed Xiao in the chest with his elbow.

This time, Xiao could no longer withstand the impact. His body was thrown, and with a flash, Zhao had thrust his sword into Xiao's side, under the armpit.

Shen couldn't find carriages or horses.

She was exhausted and hardly able to catch her breath.

However, she would rather die from exhaustion than stop.

I can't let Xiao die because of me. I have to save him, no matter what.

This was all she thought about. Nothing else concerned her.

It was a quiet night.

She got her bearings and raced as fast as she could. When she encountered a wall, she jumped over it; when she encountered a house, she hurdled it. She didn't care whose house or yard it was.

She would never have dared to do this before, but, now, she didn't care.

She would do anything to save Xiao.

Then a black cloud floated over her, blocking the moon and the stars.

She had lost her way!

Xiao crumpled into a heap in the corner, gasping for breath.

His eyes were so narrow he seemed unable to open them, but, in reality, he saw clearly.

He had finally sobered up.

Perhaps it would have been better if he hadn't, because his body began to ache all over, as if it were coming apart. The wine had been transformed into cold sweat and was starting to ooze from his skin.

Tu threw back his head and laughed. "This time, there is no doubt that even a child could chop off his head!"

"In that case, let me do the honor," Zhao said, with a smile.

Tu stopped his laugh. "Wait!"

"For what?" Zhao frowned.

"I'm the one who killed him. How could I trouble you to cut off his head?" Tu spoke graciously.

Zhao produced several loud guffaws. "Since when have you learned to use the sword, Brother Tu?"

Tu was silent for a moment before saying, "I may be too old to learn new tricks, but my tobacco pipe is no less useful than a sword."

"Anyone can tell his fatal wound was inflicted by a sword," Zhao said with a calm smile. "If you don't use a sword, where did the stab wound come from?"

"If I hadn't hit him with my elbow, your sword wouldn't have been able to touch even his robe," Tu sneered, his face grim.

Li also let out a derisive laugh. "If he hadn't suffered immense internal injury, your head might have suffered the same fate as your pipe."

"Xiao Shiyi Lang was standing defenseless, yet he had the audacity to attack him." Hai interjected, his voice full of mockery. "An Ideal Gentleman like him is truly unusual!"

"You're in no position to talk!" Li snarled. "Did you even touch a single hair on his head?"

"At least I didn't take unfair advantage of his current state and take all the credit," Hai shot back.

Just then, they heard Xiao heave a long sigh and mutter, "My head must be worth a lot of money; otherwise, why are these gentlemen fighting over it like dogs over a bone?"

Speechless, their faces changed color, from green to white and back again.

"I have a splitting headache. I'll be more than happy if one of you will cut it off," Xiao declared. "Whoever has the guts, come and take it!"

He suddenly smiled at Tu. "But are you still as confident that you can cut off my head? Why don't you come and try?"

Tu backed away half a step, his face pale.

Xiao shifted his eyes to Zhao. "How about you? You were fighting to be first. Why don't you try now?"

Zhao held the hilt of his sword tightly, his palm covered in cold sweat.

Turning to Hai next, Xiao taunted, "The people of the Hainan School usually have a black heart, but no guts. I guess you don't dare."

Hai shook with anger, but he still didn't dare to thrust his sword.

As the old saying goes, "Centipedes die without stiffening; critically injured lions and tigers are still awe-inspiring."

"As for you—" Xiao shot a piercing look at Li. "What a remarkable True Gentleman Who Harbors No Lust before Beauty! I saw through you long ago," he said with a chilling smile. "You come one step further, and I will lay you dead right at my feet!"

Li's face turned red and sweat poured off his forehead in a steady stream, but he couldn't move forward a single step.

Xiao burst out laughing again.

"Why are you laughing?" Zhao asked in bewilderment.

"I'm laughing at all of you cowards!" Xiao replied.

He laughed again and continued, "As a matter of fact, my head has been waiting for you to cut off. Whichever of you attacks, I have no strength left to defend myself. What's laughable is that none of you has the guts!"

Their faces changed color again, from red to white and back again. They were too embarrassed to raise their heads.

Xiao went on. "Though my head is waiting to be claimed, none of you are worthy of it!"

He suddenly pulled out the saber hanging from his waist, while throwing back his head and laughing. "Xiao Shiyi Lang! Xiao Shiyi Lang!" he lamented to himself. "You have such a fine big head, but no one dares to step up and lop it off. Alas, you'll have to do it yourself!"

"*Wait!*" Zhao yelled.

"Do you want to claim it now? It's too late," Xiao said, laughing and breathing heavily. "One day, people in the martial world will know that Xiao Shiyi Lang killed himself and that all of you four big heroes of chivalry just stood aside and watched!"

"We've never been real heroes of chivalry," Zhao said. "If we hadn't known you were blind drunk, we might not have dared to come."

"Well, that's true," said Xiao.

"But ... " Zhao smirked, "how did we know you were here? And how did we know you were drunk?"

"How *did* you know?" Xiao said grimly, his face darkening.

"Can't you figure out who told us?" Zhao taunted with a sinister smile. "Mrs. Lian hated you so much that she wanted nothing more than to have you carved up. That's why she made you drink until you got drunk. Yet here you are, holding her hairpin and indulging in your fantasies. You are much more laughable than all of us."

Xiao suddenly emitted a wild bellow and lunged his saber forward!

His wound had stopped bleeding, but, now, as he exerted his strength, it ripped open and blood spurted everywhere like a fountain.

Yet his saber strike was still overwhelming.

Zhao raised his sword to parry. *Clang!* The flesh between his thumb and index finger ripped open from the impact. He almost lost his grasp of the sword!

Shaken by the force, Zhao went limp and fell to the ground.

Xiao's saber came bearing down once more.

Zhao, frightened, discarded his concern for elegance, took to the ground, and rolled several feet away. He slammed his forehead against the corner of the counter with a bang.

Yet Xiao was coming after him again.

Zhao was scared out of his wits. Xiao raised his saber, but then it suddenly fell out of his hand and clattered to the ground. Xiao swayed unsteadily and collapsed.

Chapter 18

Hunted Down

XIAO SHIYI LANG was not made of iron after all.

His last remaining strength was drained from him.

Zhao rolled across the floor, picking up the saber and laughing triumphantly. "You will die by my hand sooner or later!"

At the moment, he heard a loud crash of thunder and rain started pouring down.

A violent gust of wind blew through the windows, knocking over the only two candles in the room.

Zhao raised his saber, but, suddenly, he couldn't see anything.

It was dark ... as dark as death ... as silent as death. Not even breathing could be heard.

Zhao held the saber tightly. He knew Xiao had been right under the blade!

But was he still there?

Cold sweat oozed from Zhao's palms.

All of a sudden, there was a flash of lightning.

Xiao was struggling to get up, but shaken by the thunderclap that followed the lightning flash, he fell again ... directly under the saber.

Zhao held the saber even tighter and waited for the next lightning flash.

When he chopped downward, the blade could only land on Xiao's neck!

There would be no mistake!

The rumble of thunder stopped. Who knew when the next flash of lightning would strike?

But when the next bolt did flash, Xiao Shiyi Lang's head would fall. Guaranteed.

When Zhao thought of how close this moment was, his heart raced faster.

It was a shame the candles had been blown out; he wanted to see Xiao's expression.

Just then, he heard the sound of hurried panting.

It was pouring outside. Someone seemed to have run in from the rain and then stopped still. Apparently, the incomer couldn't see anything either.

This person was also waiting for the next bolt of lightning.

Who was it?

Zhao couldn't keep from looking behind him, although he couldn't see.

The lightning flashed again!

Soaking wet and with disheveled hair, this person stood at the door with glaring eyes. The eyes were filled with shock, rage, hatred, fear, and bitterness.

Shen Bijun!

Zhao was stunned. Shen also saw him, and she suddenly raised her hand.

The lightning flash was gone in an instant, but during that instant, Zhao saw a string of golden needles soaring out from Shen's hand!

The deadly Golden Needles of the Shens!

Without time to kill Xiao, Zhao wielded his saber swiftly, to protect his face, and took to the ground and rolled away. *Thud!* He didn't know what he bumped into.

Another bolt of lightning struck. *Flash!*

Shen ran over to examine Xiao's body.

The darkness enfolded them again. In the rumble of the rolling thunder, she couldn't hear Xiao's breath. She felt something wet and sticky on a large area of his body.

It was blood!

"You killed him!" she wailed. "Which one of you did this?"

Her horrible cry of despair sounded more unnerving than the roaring thunder.

In the dark, a hand reached out to grab her.

When the rumble of the thunder died away, lightning flashed again.

She saw the bony hand, dark like a hawk's talon. It was Hai Lingzi.

Hai was holding his sword in the other hand. It looked like he was going to pull her away and then pierce Xiao's throat!

But he met her eyes—eyes more dazzling than the lightning!

Eyes burning like fire!

When the lightning flashed again, his hand was still hanging in mid-air. He dared not touch her!

"Go! Back off! All of you!" she shouted. "If any of you come any closer, I swear I will make you sorry for the rest of your life!"

While still yelling, she picked Xiao up and ran, carrying him out into the darkness.

"Wait!" she heard someone say.

When the lightning flashed again, light fell on Li Gang's face.

The blue lightning shone on his livid face, making him look indescribably grotesque.

"Get away!" Shen snarled. "How dare you stop me!"

Under the lightning flash, she appeared to raise her hand again!

Either shaken by her towering rage, or intimidated by the deadly needles in her hand, Li couldn't help but back away two steps.

Shen dashed past him.

Tu drew a long sigh. "We let the tiger return to the mountain. I'm afraid that after this, Xiao Shiyi Lang will kill us all, one by one."

"Why didn't you stop her?" Li snapped.

"Don't forget that Shen Bijun is Lian Chengbi's wife!" Tu sighed. "If she's injured, who's going to accept the consequences?"

"But if you were Lian, would you accept her as your wife now?" Zhao sniffed.

Tu hesitated for a moment and then said, "It doesn't matter. It's not too late to go after them. She couldn't have gone far."

"That's right." Li said. "Let's go!"

The rain was pelting down.

The raindrops beat upon them like gravel.

In the boundless darkness, the rain hung in front of Shen's eyes like curtains.

She couldn't see clearly which way to go, nor did she know where to run.

The world was broad and wide, yet there was nowhere they could go.

Fortunately, she hadn't seen any pursuers. She slowed down and thought: Which way should I go?

A lightning flashed, and she saw someone standing in the pouring rain and silently looking at her.

Lian! Why was he here?

Shen didn't see his face clearly, but who else had eyes that could express such tender affection?

She felt her feet pulled by an invisible but powerful force.

After all, Lian was her husband.

The lightning flashed again, and this time she saw him clearly.

He was dripping wet. Water streamed off his head and down his face. It dribbled from his eyelashes, but he simply stood there, silently looking at her.

There was no bitterness or anger in his eyes. He merely looked at her, quietly and intensely. Other than her, he didn't see or care about anything else.

Highly presentable most of the time, Lian was usually stylish and immaculately dressed.

But now—

Shen had never seen him so haggard and unkempt.

She felt heat rising in her, and her throat felt tight. "You ... have you been following me?" she said huskily, walking toward him.

Lian nodded his head slowly.

"But, you didn't stop me," Shen said.

After a moment's silence, Lian said, "Because I understand how you feel."

"You understand? Do you really understand?"

"If it hadn't been for you, he wouldn't have ended up like this," Lian sighed. "How could you *not* save him?"

Struck by his sincerity, she didn't know whether she was feeling sad or happy.

He understands me after all, she thought.

At that moment, if Lian had encouraged her to run away with Xiao, she might have stayed, though she knew she would regret it afterward.

At a moment like this, there was no way she could find it in her heart to leave Lian standing alone in the pouring rain.

"Let's go home," Lian said. "No matter how seriously injured he is, I will take good care of him and never let anyone harm him again."

Shen suddenly backed away two steps. "Do—do you believe he isn't an evil man?"

"When did I ever doubt you?"

Her body suddenly started shaking. "But when they left, you didn't stop them," she said, her voice cracking. "You knew they were coming to kill him, but you didn't say a word."

As she spoke, she kept backing away. Then, she turned and ran.

Lian couldn't help but call out: "Bijun!"

"If you really believe me, you must let me go," Shen cried out, "or else, I will never see you again, because I'll know you're just as hypocritical as the rest of them!"

Lian took a few steps forward, but then stopped.

The rain came down harder.

Shen disappeared into the sheets of rain.

Then he heard a voice say, "Mr. Lian's good temperament is indeed extraordinary. I truly admire you."

Even with the deafening rumble of thunder, Lian heard each word clearly.

A man holding an oilpaper umbrella emerged from behind a tree. The lightning lit his face. It was Situ Zhongping—Stable as Mount Tai.

He had a cryptic smile on his face. "If I were you, Mr. Lian, Xiao Shiyi Lang wouldn't have gotten away today. That's why I'll always be a bodyguard at best, and yet you have become an admirable, even legendary warrior of chivalry. Some day, you will certainly become a leader in the Martial Order."

Lian didn't reveal any emotion on his face. "What are you getting at?"

"Let me put it this way, Mr. Lian. Killing him now would have been a piece of cake for you. However, if you had killed him, when others found out you had taken unfair advantage of his weakened condition, wouldn't your reputation be tarnished? Besides, Mrs. Lian would be devastated. Nevertheless, even if you didn't kill Xiao, he won't live much longer anyway."

Lian didn't respond.

Situ continued. "Zhao and the others are going after them now. Mrs. Lian didn't see them, but you did. We are in the mountains. It's raining and it's dark. With Mrs. Lian's strength, how much farther can they run? Since someone else will take care of Xiao, you don't have to."

After a long pause, Lian said, "This is between you and me, right?"

"Mr. Lian, you know I'm very good at keeping secrets. Besides, I have a favor to ask of you."

"You must need a big favor, or you wouldn't dare to speak to me so honestly," Lian said quietly.

Situ laughed. "Nothing escapes your sharp eyes, Mr. Lian. As a matter of fact, the favor I'm asking will be quick work for you."

Lian broke into a smile. "Everyone in the martial world knows that Situ Zhongping is as stable as Mount Tai; however, I am not quite convinced."

Situ's countenance changed. "Mr. Lian, just like you, there's more to me than meets the eye," he said, with a strained smile.

Lian's face stiffened. "Do I look like someone who can be black-mailed?"

Situ cringed. He couldn't squeeze out a smile anymore.

Lian continued. "I know you don't have a choice, because the favor you ask is something I wouldn't otherwise grant."

Situ's features darkened. "Do you know what I'm about to ask, Mr. Lian?"

"If a man doesn't want others to know about something he does, he had better not do it in the first place. There is little about your affairs that I don't know. Yet all you know about me is that I have a good temper. You don't realize that I can turn against someone as quickly as I befriend him."

Situ looked at Lian as if this were the first time he had seen him.

"In fact," Lian said with a sigh, "everyone has two faces: one benevolent and one vicious. Otherwise, no one would be able to achieve great things, and everyone might have trouble surviving."

Situ couldn't tell whether the water covering him was rain or sweat. He suddenly dropped his umbrella and ran.

Lightning struck again!

But Lian's sword was faster than lightning!

Before Situ could let out a scream, the sword had entered his back and exited his chest, nailing him to the ground!

Lian peered down at him and said, "No one can be as stable as Mount Tai—except, perhaps, a dead man."

Slowly, he removed his sword.

The blood on the blade was washed away in the driving rain.

The mountain was desolate.

A lightning flash lit up a cave entrance at the seat of a saddle between two peaks.

Shen ran into the cave, without waiting for the next lightning flash or worrying about snakes or other beasts inside.

The cave wasn't spacious.

She held Xiao tightly, pushing herself as deeply into the cave as she could. Her back touched the cold and hard rock wall. She bit her lip, in an attempt to stop herself from panting.

The rain formed a curtain of crystal beads hanging over the mouth of the cave.

She felt like a wolf—a wolf being chased by hunters and dogs. Now, she understood how a wolf might feel.

Zhao and the others hadn't stopped pursuing them.

She couldn't see them, but she could feel them.

In life-and-death moments, people's senses become as sharp as wild animals, as if they can smell their enemy.

This was a survival instinct.

However, animals and humans share the delusion that they are much safer, after finding shelter.

Shen reached out a shaking hand....

Xiao's heart was still beating. He was still breathing.

She closed her eyes and heaved a long breath. After some time Xiao's body started to shiver, and his teeth chattered as if he were cold, terribly cold.

Having compassion for him, she held him tighter.

She felt Xiao gradually quiet down, like a frightened child who realizes he is back in his mother's bosom.

A mother's bosom is the safest place in the world.

It was still dark outside. The rain was heavy; the wind blew in great gusts; and she knew their enemies were still pursuing them.

She felt calm, however. A profound and indescribable maternal love had made her forget her fear and apprehension.

Children rely on their mothers.

Mothers rely on their children as well.

Just as a mother can make her child feel safe, a child can make a mother feel serene and blissful.

This was a strange feeling.

She didn't know why she felt this way.

Because she still didn't understand the true nature of love.

Just like mothers and children cling to each other ... so do lovers.

The thunder and lightning stopped.

Apart from the rain, there was no other sound.

Shen wondered whether she should run or continue to stay in the cave. Subconsciously, she felt that this was the safest place and that no one could ever find them.

Was she deceiving herself?

Sometimes people can survive because they deliberately deceive themselves. If they see through everything, they might lose the courage to live.

Her mind drifted back to the little hut in the deep valley.

Xiao had been building another hut alongside it. The raindrops beating on the rocks outside, at this moment, sounded like he had been hammering the wood with a rock.

The sound was monotonous, yet soothing.

Feeling her eyes growing heavy, she slowly closed them, seemingly ready to fall asleep.

She knew she shouldn't sleep now, but she couldn't hold out any longer.

Fear is not a bad thing.

People are the most vulnerable when they forget their fears and, thus, ignore danger.

Fortunately, Xiao started to make sounds.

His body stirred, and he breathed, "It's you?"

It was dark all around them. They couldn't make out anything.

Xiao couldn't see Shen any more than she could see him.

But he knew it was she. He sensed her presence.

"It's me," Shen whispered, feeling warmth rising within her. "Did you fall asleep?"

A long pause followed, before Xiao sighed softly. "You shouldn't have come."

"Wh-why not?"

"You know why. I don't want to drag you down."

"If it hadn't been for me, you wouldn't have ended up like this. It was I who dragged you down."

"Even without you, they would have found me. Even without you, I will survive. Do you understand?"

"I understand."

"All right then, you may go."

"I'm not going anywhere!" she declared. "No matter what you say this time, I'm not leaving."

Xiao had never heard her talk in such a determined manner.

She used to be a meek person. She had changed!

He thought about pushing her away by hurting her feelings, like he had done before.

Somehow, he couldn't speak those harsh words anymore.

Shen seemed to smile, and then she said, "Luckily, everyone has left. We're safe now. When the day breaks, I'll send you back. Then I can leave."

Xiao was silent again for a long moment, and then he smiled, too. "You don't know how to lie. Why bother trying?"

"Me lie?"

"None of them would give up so easily and simply let me live. I know this all too well."

Though his voice was still feeble, it contained faint sarcasm.

"Why do they have to kill you?"

"Because if I'm dead, they'll be able to live more securely and respectably."

She finally caught on to his sarcasm. "Is it because you know the foul deeds they've done?"

Xiao said nothing.

Silence was his reply.

"As a matter of fact," Shen said, sighing deeply, "you don't have to tell me. I've seen through those so-called heroes of chivalry."

"Oh?"

"What they say is completely different from what they do."

"They'll stop at nothing to kill me."

"That's for sure."

"You had better leave, Shen. You don't have to die with me."

"I'm not leaving!"

Shen's reply was the same.

These three words contained more determination than all the other thirty thousand combined.

Xiao knew even if he said three-hundred thousand words, she wouldn't change her mind.

So he chose not to say another word.

After a long silence, Shen spoke unexpectedly. "I know Zhao Wuji, Hai Lingzi, and Tu Xiaotian must have done many things against their consciences, but what's wrong with Li Gang?"

"You think Li is a True Gentleman Who Harbors No Lust Before Beauty, don't you?"

"Everyone says so."

"All I can say is that in the presence of men, he may be a true gentleman, but when he's alone with a beautiful woman, the only part of his body that would remain gentlemanly is his hair."

Shen was appalled and speechless.

It was still raining hard.

"Daylight is coming," Xiao said.

"Um-hmm."

"Are you sure you don't want to leave by yourself?"

"I'm absolutely sure." Shen remained determined.

"All right, then let's leave together."

Shen hesitated.

The sky was already light, and their pursuers were somewhere out there. She was afraid that after they went out....

"Can't we wait until the rain stops?" she asked.

"I know you hate the rain, but I'm grateful for it."

"Grateful?"

"The rain washed away our footprints. That's why they haven't found us. The rain gives us opportunities to escape."

"Opportunities? What opportunities?"

The driving rain gushed down the mountain path in torrents.

Li, Zhao, Tu, and Hai stopped at a fork in the road.

"The rain did them a big favor," Zhao sighed. "It not only washed away their footprints, but also their smells. Even if we had hounds, we probably couldn't find them."

"I don't believe they'll slip away," Hai said.

"Neither do I," said Tu. "Even we can't walk fast on this kind of road. Think about Shen; she's carrying a seriously injured man."

Tu smiled and went on. "And we all know Mrs. Lian's kung fu very well."

"Still, we don't know which road to take to go after them," Zhao said.

Li spoke up. "Let's split up!"

Zhao considered, and then said, "All right. I'll go with Father Hai. As for Brother Li—"

"I'll go on my own," Li said.

Before he had finished speaking, he had started to run down the left fork.

Zhao, Tu, and Hai stood there watching his figure disappear, until it was out of sight.

Tu observed, "That man has great strength and his Lightness Kung Fu isn't bad either, but he's not very smart."

Zhao smiled. "You mean he chose the wrong path?"

"Exactly. Shen and Xiao wouldn't have run down that path."

"Why?"

"Because that road is easier," Tu explained. "When people are on the run, they usually avoid the easy roads. They think if they choose the demanding roads, it'll be more difficult for others to follow."

"That's true. Most people think like that. I wonder why a veteran like Li Gang didn't think of this."

Tu watched the rain drip from the edge of his bamboo rain hat, and then he broke into a smile. "There's something else that puzzles me."

"What's that?"

"People call Li Gang an Ideal Gentleman. I wonder what dark

secrets Xiao Shiyi Lang knows about him. Why was Li so persistent about killing Xiao?"

"The reason he insisted on walking by himself is probably that he fears Xiao will expose him in front of us," Zhao concluded.

Xiao seemed lost in thought, so Shen asked again, "What opportunities?"

"They couldn't figure out which way we went, so they'll split up."

"Hmm."

"Li Gang is afraid that I'll reveal his secret in front of the others, so he won't want to go with them."

"But how about Zhao Wuji, Tu Xiaotian, and Hai Lingzi? They seem to have been working together recently."

"This time they'll split up, too."

"Why?"

"Fame." Xiao smirked. "None of them wants to share the credit for killing me."

"But aren't they afraid that one person's strength may not be enough?"

"They know I'm seriously injured and too weak to defend myself."

"But I'm not injured."

Xiao smiled. "Do you think your kung fu can match theirs?"

Shen bit her lip and said, "As far as I know, none of them dares to fight me."

"They're afraid of you," Xiao said, with a sigh, "because you're Shen Bijun—Mrs. Lian, not because of your kung fu."

Shen had no comeback.

"But they overlook one thing," Xiao added.

"Oh?"

"They don't know that a beast's ability to endure pain and injuries is stronger than any human's."

Shen smiled. "And they don't know your endurance is stronger than any beast's."

"If my calculations are correct, the combined strength of the two of us is enough to deal with any one of them. As long as they split up, we have a chance to kill them, one by one."

His words were chilling.

Shen appeared to tremble slightly. After a few moments, she asked, her voice filled with apprehension, "What if you're wrong?"

"We have to gamble," Xiao replied.

Although the day was bright, visibility was still low because of the heavy rain.

Shen helped Xiao stand up and exit the cave. "Which way are we going?" she asked.

"We're not going anywhere. We'll just wait here."

"Wait here?" She was baffled.

"We can't run too far, so let's just wait here until they come."

"B-but—"

"I know it's risky," Xiao explained, "but at least we're waiting in comfort for an exhausted enemy. We have very limited strength. We can't squander it."

Shen stared at him, her expression filled with admiration.

Xiao was truly a remarkable man with whom no one could compare.

Xiao suddenly smiled. "I'm guessing who will be the first one to find us."

"Who do you think it will be?"

"Tu Xiaotian."

"Why him?"

"He has the most experience in the martial world, and his Lightness Kung Fu isn't bad."

He smiled again before continuing, "The first one to catch the chicken is the old fox."

"If he comes, what should I do?"

Xiao reflected for a moment, then said, "Old foxes usually suffer a certain illness."

"What's that?"

"Paranoia."

"So we should take advantage of this condition."

Xiao beamed. "Exactly. All we need to do is...."

His voice became very low, so low that it was audible only to Shen.

As expected, the first one to arrive was Tu Xiaotian.

Also, as expected, he arrived alone.

Sitting on a rock in front of the cave, Shen looked numb. The rain was pouring on her, but she didn't seem to feel it. When Tu approached, she didn't appear to notice him.

Tu saw her, but he didn't see Xiao.

Was Xiao hiding in the cave?

Tu hesitated for a moment and then walked toward Shen. With a smile on his face, he feigned surprise and said, "What are you doing here, Mrs. Lian?"

Shen looked up at him and then smiled. "What took you so long?"

Tu's eyes gleamed. "Have you been waiting for me, Mrs. Lian?"

"I got lost. I've been waiting for someone to take me home."

"Where is Xiao Shiyi Lang?"

"He's dead," she said, sighing. "You must have known he wouldn't live long."

Tu nodded and sighed, too. "Indeed, he was critically injured, but if you get him a famous doctor, he might soon recover."

He suddenly grinned. "I wonder where his body is. Perhaps he still has some breath left in him."

Shen unintentionally glanced toward the cave, but quickly lowered her head. "After running half of the night, I had no strength left. I had to dump the body."

"Where?"

"I don't know. It was so dark. If you look carefully, you might find it."

Tu laughed. "We will find it."

His face tightened and he ran to the front of the cave, yelling,

"Xiao Shiyi Lang! It's over. There is no use hiding in there. Surrender and come out!"

No response came from the cave.

But Shen's face showed fear and panic.

Tu rolled his eyes, then ran over to Shen. "Excuse me!" he said.

He grabbed Shen's wrist.

"What do you want with me?" Her face changed color.

"Nothing, Mrs. Lian. I just want you to lead the way into the cave."

Shen hesitated for a moment before lifting her foot, her face pale with dread.

Tu pushed her into the cave, barking, "Xiao Shiyi Lang! Listen! Mrs. Lian is in my hands. If you dare play any tricks, I'll have you die a horrible dea—"

He didn't get to pronounce "death" completely.

It became a howl of pain!

He felt as if thousands of bees had stung his neck and back simultaneously.

Shen pulled away, plunging her palm into Tu.

Tu staggered backward and turned around at the entrance.

Xiao was grinning at him outside the cave.

Staring as if his eyes would pop out, Tu hissed between gnashed teeth, "You—you hideous devil—"

"Yeah, right. I'm a hideous devil ... but you're a stupid devil." Xiao smirked. "You thought I was in the cave, but I'm actually out here."

"Wh-what ... what vicious hidden weapons did you use?"

"Nothing but the Golden Needles of the Shens. The poisonous kind."

Tu's death-like ashen-gray face contorted violently.

Then, he fell.

Right after he collapsed, Xiao fell down, too.

Shen ran out and helped him up. "Are you all right?" she asked, her voice filled with concern.

"I was afraid I would give way. If I had fallen first, he might have been able to last long enough to kill me."

Shen inhaled deeply and said, "I'm surprised. You're no less skilled with the Golden Needles than I am."

"When it's life or death," Xiao sighed, "one often rises to the occasion."

Tu didn't move again.

Xiao, still out of breath, looked at Tu's body and muttered, "Luckily, old foxes are usually paranoid; otherwise, the chicken couldn't have survived."

"I'll drag his body into the cave. Is that all right?'"

"No, leave it here. His body is of use."

"What use?'"

Xiao closed his eyes. "The second one here will be Zhao Wuji."

Shen didn't ask him what his guess was based on.

She had complete confidence in him.

"Zhao is clever and sly," Xiao continued. "The weakness of most clever people is that they are overconfident in their cleverness, and a sly person is too timid to take risks."

"How are you going to deal with him?'"

"There's a knife in my boot. Pull it out."

The knife was sharp.

"You don't seem particular about what you use, but this knife is rather elaborate," said Shen in amusement, stroking the blade.

Xiao smiled. "I like knives."

"But not because they can kill," he added.

"I know."

"Like flawless jade, an excellent knife is a treasure in itself. Simply holding it brings great satisfaction."

"As a man's wealth often leads to his own destruction, a good knife often brings trouble to its bearer."

Xiao grinned wryly. "With or without a good knife, I've collected enough trouble for myself."

After this conversation, they both felt more relaxed.

"What are you going to do with the knife?" Shen asked.

Xiao took the knife and said, "Now turn away."

"I don't need to turn away," she said, staring at him. "I believe what you are doing is right."

Xiao avoided her eyes as he stabbed the knife into Tu's chest.

"With this," he explained, "Zhao will think I killed Tu face to face."

"Um-hmm."

"Did you see the two rows of trees across from us?"

"Zhao thinks you killed Tu, so he won't dare come over. Instead, he'll hide among the two rows of trees, right?"

Xiao smiled. "That's right. You catch on fast."

"But what do we do, when he hides among the trees?"

"First, go to the trees on the left side. Find some softer branches, bend them down, and then use your ... your hair to tie them to stones or tree roots on the ground."

He stared at her. "Can you do that?"

Shen touched her soft, silky hair. "Yes, I can," she said.

Xiao gazed at her, his heart filled with appreciation.

He knew how much women treasured their hair. Sometimes they would rather have their heads cut off than lose a single hair.

"What else do you want me to do?"

"The third tree on the right side has the densest leaves. Hide yourself up there."

"And then?"

"Then wait. When Zhao walks in among the trees and touches the hair, the tree branches will spring upward. He'll be taken by surprise and think there's someone waiting in ambush on the left."

Shen's eyes grew bright. "Then he'll run to the right side for cover."

"That's right. Then you can greet him with your golden needles."

"Got it."

"But you have to seize the right moment. When he's still in a state of panic and not ready to counter, deliver your attack."

"No problem," she said. "The Golden Needles of the Shens are not for embroidery."

Xiao took a deep breath and smiled. "There is an attractive bait waiting for him. I'm only afraid that he won't come."

Just then, they heard someone say with a sardonic laugh, "Great plan! What a great plan!"

Chapter 19

Brilliant Strategies

HAI LINGZI!

The next to show up was Hai Lingzi!

Xiao Shiyi Lang wasn't a god after all. There were times when he miscalculated.

A shiver of cold ran down Shen's back.

Wearing a rain hat and holding a sword, Hai stood less than seven feet away. Rain-soaked clothes clung to his gaunt body like snakeskin.

He looked like a vengeful ghost who had returned from hell to demand the return of his life.

Shen was afraid to look at him. She turned her head to look at Xiao.

Xiao was grinning!

"You didn't expect me next, did you?" Hai said.

"Didn't I?" Xiao laughed aloud. "I saw you lurking over there ages ago. I said what I did to trick you out of hiding."

He laughed so cheerfully and spoke so naturally....

Even Shen was tempted to believe him.

Hai's features darkened slightly, but he didn't stop.

He wasn't walking very fast. Each step was paired with a movement of his sword.

There was almost no weakness in his defensive moves.

He wasn't the type to be easily intimidated by a few words.

Xiao didn't wait any longer, knowing he couldn't afford to do so.

He used all his strength to pounce at Tu.

But he fell short.

His strength drained, he landed like a rock at Hai's feet.

Shen screamed.

Hai's sword leaped like a rattlesnake's tongue at Xiao's lower back.

Seemingly unable to dodge the sword, Xiao recoiled and met it with his right buttock!

The sword plunged into his body, producing a gush of blood.

A vicious grin spread across Hai's face. He was about to pull the sword out and stab again!

Suddenly, Xiao reached behind him and grabbed the blade with his bare hand.

Hai tried to pull it free, but couldn't. His body swayed slightly.

Then a string of golden needles shot toward him!

Xiao's quick wits and crisis-coping abilities were beyond anyone's imagination.

He knew he was too weak to fight his enemy face to face, so he had met Hai's blow with his own body, in order to disable Hai's snake-like sword.

He had to create an opportunity for Shen to attack.

He had been afraid that if Shen missed this opportunity, they would be doomed!

Fortunately, Shen had learned a great deal. In the blink of an eye, she had discharged seven bunches of golden needles!

Sky Full of Falling Rain.

The name of the move might not sound impressive, but it was one of the most powerful hidden-weapon techniques.

Xiao had fallen in such a way as to be out of the path of the golden needles.

Hai bellowed loudly and dropped his sword. Xiao rolled over, clasping his arms around Hai's legs. As Hai fell, a dagger was driven into his chest.

An almost flawless dagger was imbedded into the body of this revolting man!

Xiao lay on his back, gasping for breath. When the raindrops beat on his body, he didn't feel pain anymore.

Was it because the rain had subsided? Or was it because he was beyond pain?

Shen stood there gawking at Hai's body on the ground.

She couldn't quite believe it.

She appeared to be in shock.

Xiao struggled to get up.

Shen collected herself and rushed over to help him. "You ... your wound?" she whispered, tears pouring out of her eyes.

"My wound doesn't matter," Xiao assured her. "Help me sit up."

"But you ... I think you should lie down and rest."

Xiao produced a wan smile. "I have to sit up now, or I may lie here forever!"

The rain had subsided, but not completely stopped.

Xiao sat cross-legged beside Hai's and Tu's bodies, catching his breath.

Shen fixed her eyes on him, as if he were the only person left in the world, and as though she would fall to pieces if she took her eyes off him.

Xiao kept his eyes closed. Suddenly he spoke. "Zhao Wuji, since you have already arrived, why are you still hiding?"

Shen frantically searched the area with her eyes, but didn't see Zhao.

After an interval, Xiao said again, "Zhao Wuji, since you have already arrived, why are you still hiding?"

He repeated this four times.

Every few minutes, he repeated the same words. By the third time, Shen decided he was just bluffing, but after the fourth repetition, Zhao appeared.

Zhao walked calmly, but he appeared surprised. Confident that his footsteps had been lissome and quiet, he couldn't understand how Xiao had detected his presence.

Xiao opened his eyes, but he didn't look at Zhao. With a faint smile, he said, "I knew you'd come, but I'm surprised it took you this long. Even Hai Lingzi got here before you did."

Zhao glanced at the bodies on the ground. His face darkened. He goggled at Xiao with a look of shock and disbelief on his face.

"Don't look at me. I didn't kill them," Xiao said.

"Then who did?"

"I don't know. When they passed by here, they suddenly dropped dead."

Zhao's eyes gleamed. "Are you saying they killed themselves?"

"That's right. Come closer and take a look. Inspect their wounds for yourself."

Instead of walking forward, Zhao backed away a few steps. "I don't need to go any closer. I can see well enough from here."

"You don't believe me?"

Zhao moved his lips, but didn't speak.

"My strength is drained and I'm seriously injured," Xiao said, with a sigh. "I can't even run, let alone kill Lord Tu and the finest fighter of the Hainan School."

He sighed again. "I'm simply sitting here, waiting to die."

"Waiting to die?"

Xiao smiled wryly. "To tell the truth, if you still want to cut off my head, I don't have the strength to defend myself. What's worse, Ms. Shen has run out of golden needles."

Shen's mouth felt bitter. Extremely bitter.

Every word Xiao had said was true.

But ... why was he telling the truth? Was he out of his mind?

If Zhao came forward, they were doomed.

Instead of walking forward, however, Zhao backed away a few more steps.

"If you want to kill me, here is your opportunity," Xiao continued. "Why don't you come over and do it?"

Unexpectedly, Zhao threw back his head and laughed. He laughed so hard that he was nearly reduced to tears.

"Do you always laugh when you kill people?" Xiao said.

"You're both great actors," Zhao said, still laughing. "Unfortunately, I'm neither as gullible as old Tu nor as stupid as Hai."

"You think I'm deceiving you?"

"I don't want my chest stabbed quite yet."

"This is a great opportunity for you. It's a shame to miss it," Xiao said, in dead earnest.

"Thank you so much. I appreciate your offer, but I can't accept it."

"If you leave now, you'll regret it!"

Zhao laughed. "Living in regret is better than dying."

Before he finished speaking, he had turned and run.

Xiao shouted after him. "If you change your mind, you can always come back. I can no longer run."

They didn't know whether Zhao had heard Xiao or not.

He was out of sight before Xiao had finished speaking.

As soon as Zhao left, Shen's body relaxed. "I'm surprised Zhao was so easily fooled," she said, a touch of amusement in her voice.

Xiao heaved a long breath and said wryly, "Did you think I had absolute confidence?"

"I was scared out of my wits, but you were still so calm."

"Thanks to the rain."

"The rain?"

"In fact, I was covered in cold sweat, but Zhao probably thought it was rain water. And it helped that the blood stains on my clothes had been washed away."

Xiao smiled and went on, "The rain had thoroughly soaked all of us. We looked equally grubby. Otherwise, Zhao would have been clever enough to see through my bluffing."

Shen studied his face and suddenly showed a look of concern.

Xiao was still smiling, but his smile was grim and weary.

He knew what Shen was worried about.

Shen suddenly said, "It's been a while. Li Gang hasn't come yet. Maybe he won't come."

"Um-hmm, maybe he won't come."

When their eyes met, Shen suddenly grabbed his hands and held them tightly.

She wouldn't have done this before, but things were different now.

This might be the last minute they'd have together.

They were still lying to themselves, but, in their hearts, they both knew the truth.

Li would come ... soon.

Even if no one else came, it would be hard enough for them to hold out. If Li came, how could they live to tell the tale?

Li's heart was like a knife!

"I ... I just want you to know one thing," Shen said, staring at Xiao.

"What?"

She bit her lip and lowered her head. "No matter what happens, I have no regrets."

Seemingly spellbound, Xiao neither spoke nor moved.

After what seemed like an eternity, he said, "I have an idea for how to deal with Li, if you're willing to go along with it."

The rain had almost stopped.

Li removed his rain hat and wiped his face with his sleeve.

He had searched almost the entire mountain and was about to give up.

At that very moment, however, he found Shen and Xiao.

Xiao lay on his back. Hai lay next to him on the right, his hand holding a sword thrust into Xiao's hipbone.

Tu lay on his left, with his one hand on the impulse meridian of Xiao's wrist and his other hand pressed on the Mystic-Ruse meridian point of Xiao's chest.

It looked like they had all died during a fierce fight.

After a few more steps, Li saw Shen.

Her chest was heaving slightly; she was clearly still alive.

Her face was pale and her eyes were covered by her long lashes.

Her slender but mature body was tightly wrapped in rain-soaked clothes.

From the moment he saw her, Li's eyes fastened on her body. Although his feet had stopped moving, he didn't show any expression on his face.

She appeared to be either asleep or in a coma, unaware that someone was near her.

Li's stony face experienced a strange transformation, and his cold, piercing eyes started to burn like fire.

Breathing faster and faster, he expelled a faint sigh and murmured, "Indeed, she is a woman of matchless beauty—"

Before finishing this sentence, he had pounced on Shen.

Shen's body seemed to shudder a little.

Panting heavily, Li ripped open her clothes, the fire in his eyes burning hotter and brighter—

All at once, his eyes popped out of their sockets.

His body stiffened and straightened. His breath hissed in heavy puffs—

A little blood trickled from the corner of his mouth.

A knife was imbedded right between his ribs and driven into his heart.

Shen was shaking.

Her hands clutched the handle of the knife and Li's blood spilled over them.

She could feel Li's body gradually stiffen and turn cold....

She pushed him away with all her strength and stood up, breathless ... her teeth clattering and her lips drained of blood.

Suddenly, she bent over and threw up.

It isn't easy to go up mountains; sometimes, it's even more difficult to descend.

Shen struggled to support Xiao and stumbled along the mountain road.

She knew no one was coming after them now, but she still tried to run as fast as she could. The farther away from Li Gang, the better.

She had finally seen the real face of the so-called True Gentleman Who Harbors No Lust Before Beauty.

Xiao kept quiet, knowing whatever he might say would agitate her. He didn't want her to be hurt anymore.

If it weren't for him, she would have died before ever doing anything like that.

His heart was full of gratitude.

There were two figures lurking in the dense woods near the road.

But neither Xiao nor Shen noticed them.

They never knew they had run past ... Lian Chengbi.

Lian watched them go, but he neither spoke nor tried to stop them. His face appeared calm, as usual.

Zhao was standing by his side.

Zhao had always been proud of his ability to stay composed, but now he was about to boil over.

Realizing he had been fooled, he was about to chase after Xiao and Shen.

But Lian stopped him.

Baffled, Zhao asked, "Don't you want to persuade your wife to come back, Brother Lian?"

Lian slowly shook his head. "She'll come back sooner or later, if she wants to do so. If she doesn't want to, there's no use in trying."

Zhao kept quiet, trying to gauge Lian's intentions. After a while, the corner of his mouth formed a bizarre smile.

"You're right," he muttered. "Mrs. Lian will come back. Xiao Shiyi Lang won't last long."

Level ground wasn't far ahead of them.

Xiao covered his mouth, coughing weakly.

"Would you like to stop and rest for a while?" Shen asked anxiously.

Xiao shook his head, but suddenly fell down, and the hand he had used to cover his mouth fell away.

His palm was covered with blood!

Shen gasped and struggled to pull him up.

All of a sudden, she felt an indescribable twisting pain in her belly, as though her internal organs had twisted together and bile was being squeezed out of them.

Then she went limp, and she and Xiao rolled down the hill.

Xiao woke up before Shen did.

As soon as he came to, he thought of Shen and started to look for her.

He didn't have to look far, for she was lying right beside him.

However, they weren't lying on the grass at the bottom of the hill, but on a big, soft, comfortable bed with a silk canopy.

The comforter and the sheets were made of brand new and very smooth silk, elaborately embroidered with beautiful bright flowers.

Xiao and Shen were dressed in new silk robes, which were as elaborately embroidered as the comforter.

Xiao found himself in a strange place.

Was this a dream?

There weren't really any strange objects in the room. However, everything was ornate, some of them ridiculously so.

The candlestick was decorated with shining pearls and colorful gemstones, and the tassels of the bed curtains were made of golden thread.

Xiao knew the master of such a place was not a *nouveau riche*.

Everything was well-chosen. Though so many things were put together, the chamber didn't look cluttered or sleazy. Everything was perfectly matched.

The *nouveaux riches* don't have such refined taste.

Even if it were only a dream, it was a fancy, beautiful one.

Nevertheless, Xiao didn't like to dream.

He slipped off the bed so as not to awaken Shen. He didn't want her to wake up and find him sleeping beside her and become embarrassed.

The floor was covered with thick, soft Persian rugs.

Xiao walked barefoot across the floor.

It was a short distance, but it took him a long time. With every step, he felt as if his bones were going to cave in.

Nonetheless, his injuries had apparently improved a great deal; otherwise, he wouldn't have been able to even lift his foot.

How had his injuries improved so quickly?

Because he had some sleep or because someone had treated his wounds?

Who was the master of this place?

Why had he saved them?

Xiao had many other questions on his mind, but he was in no hurry to think about them.

The door was ajar.

He pushed it open and entered a wonderland more fantastic than any dream!

It was something he had never seen and could never have imagined!

The room was bigger than the one he had just come from; however, the only thing in it was a table.

The table almost filled the room.

On the table was a house. A dollhouse.

This dollhouse was more elaborate than any child could ever conceive.

The entire house was made of real wood and bricks. The tiles on the roofs were the same as those used for the royal palaces, except they were at least ten times smaller.

The house was surrounded by a big garden.

In the garden were pines, bamboo, flowers, grass, bridges, brooks, artificial mountains, pavilions, and so forth. Among the plants, Xiao could even spot yellow dogs, white rabbits, cranes, and deer.

The trees were real, and the flowers were fragrant, except they were all ten times smaller than ordinary ones.

The deer and the rabbits were carved out of wood or stone, but they looked alive. It was as if they would run to your feet if you simply beckoned to them.

The piece that drew Xiao's attention most was the octagonal pavilion behind the zigzagging bridge. The pavilion was composed of red columns, green tiles, and a stone table. On the table was an unfinished chess game. Two old men wearing caps were apparently playing chess. They seemed to be tired.

One old man, dressed in red, was sitting by the brook fishing. He supported his chin in his cupped hand. His face frowned slightly, as if he were still pondering over the unfinished chess game.

The other old man was dressed in a green robe. Sitting next to the man in red and looking at him out of the corner of his eye, he was holding his shoes, while washing his feet.

The man in green appeared confident that he would win the game.

These two figures were remarkably lifelike, their clothes well-tailored and made of luxurious silk.

Everything in the garden was extremely fascinating.

The garden, however, was nothing compared to the house itself.

The house had a total of twenty-seven rooms.

They included the main hall, side halls, bedchambers, guestrooms, storage rooms, and kitchens.

Through the windows, Xiao could see the interior of every room clearly.

Everything in every room looked real.

There were red sandalwood carved chairs in the main hall, and there were silk cushions on the chairs.

There were paintings on the wall of the main hall. The one in the middle was a landscape painting. It was a depiction of misty mountains, the atmosphere of which was relaxing. Xiao took a closer look at it and found that the signature, smaller than a fly's foot, was that of Wu Daozi, a renowned painter of the Tang Dynasty.

A couplet on the wall intrigued Xiao. It read:

I often get intoxicated without drinking.
And I often learn without studying.

How philosophical! How free-spirited! Xiao thought.

Two people were sitting in the hall, as if waiting to see the master.

A maid in red, who brought tea on a tray, was pulling open the curtains to enter.

Even the two teacups on the tray were real porcelain.

The maid wore a smirk on her face, as if she didn't really respect the two guests, knowing her master didn't think too much of them either.

The master was still lying on the bed in his chamber.

Four maids stood beside the bed prepared to wait on him—one holding a strange tall hat, one holding a yellow robe, one holding a fan, and the other crouching and polishing the master's boots.

The master wasn't old. Beardless, he looked rather handsome.

Behind the bed, a beautiful woman in a gauze gown was using a chamber pot. She appeared a little drowsy, as if tired from the passion of the previous night, but her face also showed a tinge of shyness and sweetness.

The servants in the kitchen were busy, obviously preparing their master's breakfast.

Xiao let out a sigh and muttered, "This man really knows how to enjoy his life."

There were people in every room. All of them were beautiful young girls—some strumming the zither, some writing, some doing needlework, some getting dressed up, and some still in bed.

Out of twenty-seven rooms, only one was empty.

It was in the corner. The covered walkway leading to it was lined with lush trees. The room was full of books. On the desk was a censer in which ambergris oil was burning.

Beside the censer was everything one would need to write. An unfinished painting lay on the desk. It was of a man admiring his sword under the lamp. The brushwork in the painting was excellent. Though not yet complete, it already looked impressive.

It seemed that the master of this place was not only a martial artist but also a refined scholar.

Xiao was no longer a child, but he couldn't help but marvel at such an exquisite dollhouse. He wished he could shrink himself and wander around in it for a while.

Only when he heard the voice behind him did he realize that Shen had awoken as well.

Her face was pale and bloodless.

But her eyes were gleaming with childlike joy.

She leaned against the doorframe looking at the dollhouse, apparently enthralled by it.

After a long, long time, she said, "What a beautiful house! If only I could stay in it for a few days; it must be a lot of fun."

Xiao smiled. "Unfortunately, no one has the power to shrink us."

Shen turned her head to look at Xiao. After a few moments, her face broke into a sweet smile. "Neither of us died," she said.

Xiao returned her gaze and nodded slowly. "Neither of us died." He repeated her words.

These words were not extraordinary, but they contained an immense amount of joy and appreciation.

Human desires are usually difficult to satisfy.

However, at that moment, merely being alive was more than enough for the two of them.

After another long pause, Shen asked, "Did you bring me here?"

"No. When I woke up, I was here already."

"So you don't know where we are either?"

"No, I don't."

Shen turned her head again to look at the dollhouse. "The master of this Manor must be eccentric, and quite interesting."

"That's true. Only an eccentric could put together something so special."

"Since he rescued us, why doesn't he come to meet us?"

Before Xiao could reply, they heard a tinkle-bell laugh from outside.

A voice said, "Because my master was afraid that he might disturb the sweet dreams of the Honorable Mr. and Mrs."

When Shen heard "Honorable Mr. and Mrs.," she blushed to the roots of her hair.

They had been mistaken for husband and wife!

With very convoluted feelings about this, she didn't know what to think. She thought about examining the expression on Xiao's face, but she didn't have the courage.

She bowed her head low, so she didn't see the speaker come in, but she smelled a faint fragrance. An orchid-like fragrance.

The speaker was certainly as refreshing as an orchid.

Dressed in a white gown, she wasn't wearing any makeup or jewelry. She wore her hair in a plain bun.

She had a fairly full mouth. When she wasn't smiling, she seemed stern and cold. However, when she smiled and revealed her delicate white teeth, she looked graceful and alluring.

Her high cheekbones added to her charm—charm enough to attract most men's attention.

This woman wasn't a dazzling beauty, but when she stood in this luxurious chamber, she looked radiant. If it weren't for Shen standing beside her, she would certainly be the center of attention.

Shen wasn't looking at her, but she was studying Shen.

When one pretty woman meets another, she tends to look her up and down, from head to toe.

Sometimes, women observe women more closely than men do.

Then, she turned her head to assess Xiao.

She wasn't a woman who became shy easily, but when her eyes met Xiao's cat-like eyes, she involuntarily lowered her head. In a shy but sweet voice she said, "My name is Susu. I have been sent to serve the Honorable Mr. and Mrs."

Honorable Mr. and Mrs. again!

Shen bowed her head even lower. She wished Xiao would explain.

However, if he had, she might have felt somewhat disappointed.

Xiao simply replied, "You're too kind."

"If you need anything, please let me know. If you have any questions, please feel free to ask."

"If I ask you questions, will you answer them?"

Susu smiled slightly. "I will tell you all I know."

"I want to know who saved us."

"My master found you while he was hunting, just after the rain stopped."

She smiled mischievously before continuing. "My master usually doesn't concern himself with other people's business, but you impressed him. You looked like a perfect match, and you seemed to be deeply devoted to each another. Even though you were unconscious and dying, you still held each other's hands tightly, refusing to separate...."

Hearing this, Shen's cheeks burned with embarrassment.

Fortunately, Xiao interrupted Susu by asking, "What's your master's name?"

"His surname is Tian. As servants, we are instructed to address him as Mr. Tian. We dare not ask his name."

"Tian? You mean the word for 'sky'?"

"Yes."

"Is there really such a surname?"

"Names are used to tell people apart. As long as you are comfortable with it, you can use any word you like, right?"

Xiao didn't respond.

Susu smiled even more pleasantly. "Take yourself for example. If I ask you your real name, you may not want to tell me. True?"

Xiao smiled, too. "I was wondering whether or not Mr. Tian is willing to see us."

"Of course, but...."

"But what?"

"But it's midnight now. He's in bed."

Only then did Xiao notice two things:

First, the room didn't have any windows.

Second, the light in the room came from the bronze lamps built into the walls.

Susu continued. "My master knows neither of you are ordinary people and that you must be martial arts masters, so he instructed us to give you the warmest reception."

Xiao smiled a little. "If I were a martial arts master, I wouldn't have ended up like this, would I?"

"You have four internal injuries and two external injuries. The two external injuries are not fatal ones, but the four internal injuries appear to have been inflicted by such kung fu as Great Slab-Smashing Hand or King Kong Palm. Ordinary people can't survive even a single strike of such kung fu, yet you have endured so many. Either you have great kung fu or you're incredibly lucky."

"Young lady," Xiao said, "not only do you have sharp eyes, but you must be a martial artist yourself. Otherwise, how would you know what kung fu caused my injuries?"

Susu replied, with a cautious smile, "Actually, I don't know anything. I overheard everything I have said."

She turned and left before finishing her words. She seemed to be hiding something.

Xiao neither stopped her nor asked her any more questions.

Shen stole a glance at him and whispered, "What do you think of that girl?"

"She is neither ugly nor stupid."

"She's not ugly at all." Shen chuckled lightly. "As a matter of fact, she's very pretty. Just by looking at her, you can imagine what kind of person her master is."

Xiao pondered this silently.

"It seems that everyone here is a little secretive," Shen added. "I wonder whether they have good or bad intentions toward us."

Right then they heard Susu say, "If we had bad intentions, you wouldn't be alive."

The rugs were thick and cloud-soft. When feet walked on them, there was no sound.

Shen blushed again and bowed her head low.

Susu walked in, carrying two cups of tea. "According to my

master," she said, pleasantly, "this is a potent herbal tea. Not only is it good for your health, but it will bring you a surprising benefit."

She cast Shen a glance. "My master offers this out of concern for your health," she said with a smile, "but if you don't want it, that's quite all right."

Xiao smiled. "Mr. Tian saved our lives. Even if the tea is poisoned, I'll drink it."

He took up the tea and drained it.

"No wonder my master speaks so highly of you," Susu commented. "Your heroic decisiveness is admirable."

She watched Shen drink up the tea.

She also watched Xiao pass out and then watched Shen fall down as well.

"As I said," she whispered, her smile still so pleasant, "the tea has a surprising effect. Soon you will see that I'm telling the truth."

Chapter 20

Doll Manor

THERE ARE MANY ways to sleep and also many ways to wake up.

You feel exhausted and go to bed. You sleep well. When you wake up, bright sunshine beams through the window, your beloved one is lying beside you, birds are chirping, children are giggling outside, and you smell ham and chicken soup simmering on the stove.

This is probably the most pleasant way to wake up.

You are in a bad mood, and you drink until drunk. After being unconscious all night, you wake up to find that none of your problems have been solved and now your head aches so much that you want to cut if off.

Waking up like this is worse than never waking up.

If you are drugged, your head is dizzy and heavy when you wake up, and you feel like throwing up.

When Xiao woke up, however, he felt very comfortable, like he was floating on air and as if he could fly, by simply waving his arms.

Shen was still sound asleep beside him.

He felt euphoric, as if he were completely content and all of his disappointments and misfortunes had been left behind.

Unfortunately, this sensation didn't last.

First, he saw many books. A roomful of books.

Then, he saw a censer.

A steady stream of smoke and scent was rising from the censer, which seemed to be burning ambergris oil.

Rising to his feet, Xiao saw that on the desk were a precious Duan ink slab, a rather old ink stick, and an exquisite writing brush.

Even the penholder appeared to be an antique from the Qin or Han Dynasty.

He also saw an unfinished painting on the desk.

The painting was of a man admiring his sword under the lamp.

Feeling a chill rising from his feet, Xiao shivered, as if he had fallen out of bed and into cold water during a harsh winter.

He stood beside the table for a while, then turned around.

The room had a window, a big window directly across from him.

It was a bright sunny day, outside the window.

The sunshine shone on a zigzagging bridge. The water below it was shimmering gold.

At the end of the bridge was a small octagonal pavilion, where two people were playing chess.

An old man dressed in red, with his fishing rod and other fishing gear beside him, supported his chin with one hand and held a chess piece in the other. He seemed to be pondering his next move.

Another old man, dressed in green and with a smug look on his face, was grinning at the man in red. He was barefoot. Beside his stone bench was a pair of shoes.

Weren't they the doll old man fishing by the brook and the doll old man washing his feet?

Feeling dizzy, Xiao almost lost his balance.

He couldn't believe his eyes.

There was green grass outside the window. A faint fragrance of flowers floated in the breeze.

A deer leaped out of the bushes, but it soon ran back when it sensed someone peeking at it through the window.

Behind the bushes was a high wall blocking Xiao's view of what was beyond.

Through the moon-shaped door in the corner of two high walls, he could see a tea table in the distance ... with two green teacups on it.

They were the two teacups he and Shen had just used. At that time, he could set the teacup in his palm.

Now, however, the two teacups appeared bigger than the octagonal pavilion. So big that he could bathe in them!

Xiao wasn't a man who panicked easily, but now he could feel his limbs trembling and his clothes were damp with cold sweat.

Shen let out a soft yawn. She had awakened.

Xiao turned around and blocked the window.

The experience of too many traumas and shocks had left Shen vulnerable, both mentally and physically. If she saw the strange sights outside, she might go insane.

Xiao himself was on the verge of losing his mind.

"How did we get here? Where are we?" Shen asked, rubbing her eyes.

Feeling strained, Xiao attempted to smile, but didn't know how to answer.

"What a strange man Mr. Tian is!" Shen said. "Since he meant us no harm, why did he have to drug us before sending us here? Couldn't he have sent us here while we were awake?"

Xiao smiled even more nervously, as he found the second question even more difficult to answer.

Shen noticed the discomfort on his face.

Xiao usually expressed himself freely. He seldom held back.

"Are ... are you all right?" she asked with concern. "Are you feeling ill?"

"I'm fine. It's just that ... I'm puzzled."

While he was talking, his eyes fell on the painting behind Shen.

He wished he had put away the painting. He wished Shen hadn't noticed.

Shen, alarmed, followed his eyes and turned her head.

Her face fell instantly. After a while, her eyes started to travel around the room.

Red sandalwood bookshelves lined the room on all four sides.

Xiao commented dryly, "Perhaps Mr. Tian is afraid that we'll be bored, so he sent us here. These books will take us many years to finish."

Her lips pale, her hands shaking, Shen sprang to the window and pushed Xiao away.

The zigzagging bridge, the brook, the old men, the chess game— Shen let out a soft cry and sagged against Xiao's body.

The ambergris oil in the censer was almost burned out.

But Shen had not calmed down yet.

It took her quite a while to speak again. "Is this place the ... the dollhouse?"

"Um-hmm." Xiao nodded.

"Are we ... *in* the dollhouse?"

"Um-hmm."

"But how were we shrunk?" she asked, in a wavering voice. "The two old men are supposed to be lifeless dolls. How did they come alive?"

All Xiao could do was sigh.

All of this was just too weird. Frighteningly weird.

No one would dream up something like this, and no one could explain it. This was more preposterous than the wildest fantasy.

Shen's lips were trembling. She bit her lip until blood trickled from it, to prove she wasn't dreaming.

Xiao smiled dryly. "We were just talking about taking a tour. Now our wish has come true."

Shen lost her self-control, grabbed his hand and cried, "We must escape! *Now!*"

"Escape to where?"

Shen was stunned.

Escape to where? Where could they go?

She lowered her head. A tear dripped onto the back of her hand.

Then they heard someone knocking on the door.

Who was it?

A maid dressed in red pushed open the door, which had been ajar, and walked in. Her eyes were bright, her face all smiles. Xiao vaguely remembered that she was the maid serving tea in the main hall.

She had been a figurine as well, but now she had come alive and was made of flesh and blood.

When Xiao stared at her, she blushed and dropped her eyes. "My master sent me to invite you for a drink in the hall."

Xiao followed her out without asking her a single question.

He knew it was useless to ask any questions now.

After strolling through the covered walkway, they came to the main hall.

Three people were sitting and chatting there.

The one sitting in the host's seat was an exceptionally handsome and luxuriously dressed man. Wearing a strange tall hat, he looked noble and dignified, like an emperor.

He had very fair skin that had an almost translucent look to it. His fingers were long and tapered, like a lady's. Obviously, he had never in his life performed hard labor.

He appeared rather young, but a closer look revealed some wrinkles around the corner of his eyes. If it weren't for the good care he had taken of his skin, he might look like an old man.

One of the two guests had a big head, a large waist, and a pock-marked face.

The other guest was much taller and bigger. His face was longer than that of a horse. The hand, holding his teacup, was as steady as a rock, but his fingers were chubby, and his little finger was as long as his middle finger, which indicated his external palm strength was fully mature.

Though their facial features looked rough, they were expensively dressed and acted confident. Apparently, they were both distinguished martial artists, with noble status and high reputation.

Xiao had seen them both.

When he last saw them ... they had been miniature dolls.

But now, they had come alive.

When Xiao and Shen walked in, the three of them rose with amiable smiles on their faces.

The man with a regal bearing was the master of the Manor. He left his seat with dignity and said, "The wine is still warm. Enjoy!"

His wording was concise and to the point. If he needed only nine words to say what he had to say, he wouldn't use a tenth.

His voice and manners were genteel and elegant, like a well-trained dancer whose movements were synchronized to the rhythm of the music.

This man's clothing, speech, appearance, and manners were all impeccable.

Nevertheless, Xiao had an unfavorable impression of him.

He thought this man was overly effeminate and almost smelled of facial powder.

When Xiao was with womanlike men or manlike women, he always felt uneasy.

A table had been set for drinking wine.

"Please have a seat," said the master, smiling and saluting them with fists.

"You are too kind," Xiao said. "This doesn't seem appropriate."

The pockmarked man smiled as he cut in, "The wine was prepared by the master especially to welcome the two of you. Please make yourselves at home."

Eyeing the master, Xiao returned his smile. "We have never met. How can we trouble you?"

The master was also inspecting Xiao. "Since you have come, that means we were destined to meet," he said kindly. "Please have a seat."

As their eyes met, Xiao noticed that the master was actually very short. Incredibly short.

However, he had a well-proportioned figure, and his manners were extraordinarily refined. When he sat, he appeared slightly taller than other people.

Few people would think that he was a dwarf.

Xiao immediately turned his eyes away.

He thought a short man wearing a tall hat must be more or less mentally imbalanced and afraid others would notice his height. If he looked at him too long, the man might think he saw him as a freak.

Short men often go to amazing lengths so that others won't pay attention to their height and will, instead, assume they're taller than they really are.

After they sat down, the master took up his cup first. "May I ask your name?"

"Xiao Shuyu," Xiao replied.

"Shu is the word for 'stone,' and Yu is the word for 'ease.' Is that right?" asked the pockmarked man.

"Yes."

"My name is Lei Yu. And this is Long Feiji," he said, introducing himself and the big horse-faced man.

A look of surprise flickered across Xiao's face. "Are you Lord Long, also known as Horse Flying in the Sky?" he asked.

The horse-faced man bowed and replied, "Yes."

Xiao turned back to the pockmarked man. "Then you must be Lord Lei, Cloud Floating Across the Sky."

The pockmarked man smiled. "My brother and I haven't been around the martial world for a long time. I'm surprised that someone still remembers our names."

"Everyone refers to you as Twin Invincible Palms and the Spirit of Dragon and Horse. Thirteen years ago, there was an earth-shaking event—the battle of Mount Heaven. I have always admired both of you."

Lei's eyes gleamed with some pride, but even with more sadness. "That was a long time ago," he said, sighing. "I'm afraid few people are talking about it now."

Thirteen years ago, with the strength of their iron fists, they had challenged the Seven Swordsmen of Mount Heaven. It had been a fierce fight. To everyone's surprise, they had come down the mountain in one piece. It had been a sensational event at the time.

"You both disappeared shortly after the battle of Mount Heaven," Xiao said. "Even now, people in the martial world are talking about you. No one could figure out where you had gone."

With a rueful expression on his face, Lei smiled bitterly. "Not only did others not expect this, but we ourselves didn't—"

He broke off, took up his wine, and emptied it.

The master let out a soft sigh. "This is not the human world. Whoever lands here will never be heard from again."

Xiao felt his palms getting cold. "This is not the human world? You mean—"

The master's calm face showed a look of wistfulness. "This is just a doll's world."

Xiao was taken aback.

"*Dolls?*" It took him quite a while to squeeze out this word in a hoarse voice.

The master nodded slowly. "That's right. Dolls."

He broke into a faint smile. "As a matter of fact, every creature in the world is a doll. Humans are dolls, too."

Lei added dryly, "The difference is that humans are Heaven's dolls and we are the dolls of humans."

He threw back his head and let out a hoarse laugh. "Who in the martial world would believe that my brother and I have become someone's dolls?"

Now Xiao's entire body went cold.

"May I ask your name?" he asked the master.

The master gave a bitter smile. "I have been here twenty years. How can I remember my name?"

"But—"

"In twenty years, you might both forget your own names as well."

"T-twenty years?" Shen echoed in shock.

She usually didn't like to talk in front of strangers.

But at this moment, her heart was sinking deeper and deeper.

"That's right. Twenty years," said the master. "When I came here, I thought I couldn't live like this for even one day. I couldn't imagine that I would have to stay here twenty years."

A sad smile appeared on his face. "But ... time flies. Twenty years have passed. From ancient times until now, the most difficult thing has always been to die in the right place at the right time. No matter how I live, it's better than being dead."

Shen was silent for a moment, and then suddenly turned away.

She didn't want others to see the tears that were about to roll down her cheeks.

Xiao thought for a while and then asked, "Do any of you know how you ended up here?"

Lei stared at him. "Do you know how you ended up here?"

"I have no idea how I got here, and I still can't believe this is happening," Xiao replied with a morose smile.

Lei drank his wine, put it heavily on the table, then let out a long sigh. "That's right. This is something no one understands and no one would believe. I have been here twelve years. I used to wish this were just a bad dream, but now ... now...."

Long also drew a long sigh. "But now we realize we will never wake up from this nightmare."

While still sipping his wine, the master suddenly asked Xiao, "Before you came here, was your life in danger?"

"Indeed, there wasn't much between death and me."

"Were you rescued by a man called Mr. Tian?"

"How did you know?"

"Like you," sighed the master, "all of us were rescued by Mr. Tian. However—"

"However," Lei broke in, his voice bitter, "he didn't save us out of kindness. He only wants us to be his dolls, his slaves!"

"Have you ever met him?" Xiao asked. "Do you know what he's like?"

"None of us have ever met him," said the master, "but by now you should understand what kind of man he is."

"He isn't human," Lei said. "He's a devil! He's more horrible than a phantom!"

Having said this, Lei turned to gaze out the window. The muscles in his face suddenly underwent indescribable changes that twisted his entire face.

"This man possesses an incredible magic," said the master. "He might hear every word we say and see everything we do. But I'm not afraid of him anymore! What in the world could be more frightening than what is happening to us here?"

"That's the truth," Lei sighed. "When people get trapped like this, they will no longer be afraid of anyone or anything."

"But isn't it appalling that whatever you do is constantly being watched by someone?" Xiao said.

"At first, everyone feels uncomfortable and embarrassed," said the master, "but little by little, they get used to it, become indifferent and eventually stop caring about anything."

"Whoever ends up here eventually becomes jaded and apathetic," Long lamented, "because living has no meaning and dying doesn't matter."

The master didn't talk much.

The words of those who don't talk much usually carry more weight.

Xiao didn't know whether or not he would become jaded and apathetic in the future. All he knew was that he needed a drink ... now—a large cup of wine.

He gulped it down. Then he asked, "Why don't you try to escape?"

Shen had asked him the same question.

"Escape to where?" Long answered with a sigh.

This was the same reply that Xiao had given to Shen.

"Right now," Long went on, "we're no different from ants or crickets, in the eyes of the other humans. Anyone can squeeze us to death with two fingers. Where would we go?"

Many jars of wine had been drunk.

"In fact," the master said brusquely, "escape is not impossible."

"Oh?" Xiao responded.

"Anyone who can break Tian's magic spell will go free."

"Who can break his magic spell?"

"We can only count on ourselves."

"Ourselves? What does that mean?"

"Magic is like kung fu in that no matter how profound a kung fu system is, it always has at least one or two weak points. Even the legendary Bodhidharma's *Yijin Sutra* is no exception. It is said that Supreme Priest Sanfeng found a couple of flaws in it."

"But the spell—"

"The spell has a loophole, and it has been left there by Mr. Tian himself."

"Why would he do that?"

"To challenge us! To challenge all of us!"

"To challenge us?"

"Life is like gambling in that there are always two possible outcomes: winning or losing. For Mr. Tian, a game without any possibility of losing is very boring."

Xiao smiled. "That's true."

"I guess Mr. Tian must be a man who likes excitement. He used his magic to confine us, but he deliberately left a loophole for us to break his spell. The loophole is in this Manor. Anyone who can find it will be able to break his magic spell."

Xiao pondered for a while and then said, "Is this what Tian said?"

"Yes. He promised me that if I could break his spell, he would release me with no hesitation."

The master heaved a long sigh before continuing. "I've been looking for it incessantly for the last twenty years, but I haven't succeeded yet."

Xiao thought for another moment. "This Manor has a total of twenty-seven rooms, doesn't it?"

"Including the kitchen, twenty-eight."

"If the loophole is restricted to the twenty-eight rooms, why can't you find it?

"No one can guess what form the loophole takes. It might be a grain of rice, a bean, a leaf, or even a particle of dust."

Xiao was wordless.

"Although it's nearly impossible to figure out the secret," added the master, "actually there is another way out."

"What is it?" Xiao asked.

The master rose and said, "Please follow me."

There was a small yard behind the main hall.

In the middle of the yard was a green rock, as big as a table and as smooth as a mirror.

Xiao was led beside the green rock. "What is this?" he asked the master.

"An altar."

Xiao frowned. "An altar?"

"If someone is willing to offer what they love and treasure most as a sacrifice to Mr. Tian, he'll release them!"

He stared at Xiao, his eyes growing brighter than usual. "What's the thing you treasure most?"

Instead of answering, Xiao asked him, "What do *you* treasure most?"

The master smiled wryly. "Everyone staying here is selfish. What each treasures most is his own life. No one wants to sacrifice his or her own life to Mr. Tian."

Then he added, "But some people may place someone else or something else above their own life."

"People like that aren't unusual," Xiao said.

"I've seen some myself. Ten years ago, a couple was confined here by Mr. Tian's magic. They loved each other so much that they both valued the other more than themselves. The husband came from a prominent family. He was well-educated and an excellent martial artist. He had been a promising and ambitious young man. But after coming here, he lost all hope."

"What happened to them?"

"Eventually," the master sighed, "the wife sacrificed herself to Mr. Tian, in exchange for her husband's freedom."

He regarded Xiao with intensity, as if to assess his reaction.

Xiao's face didn't betray any emotions. He simply listened.

Shen appeared encouraged, however. "Did Mr. Tian let her husband go?" she asked.

"Yes, he did," the master confirmed.

He added, "I didn't mention their names, because I think the husband must have prospered and attained high status after ten years and I don't want to tarnish his reputation."

After a long pause, Shen said thoughtfully, "They were an admirable couple."

Xiao suddenly laughed derisively. "In my opinion, they were fools."

"Fools?" The master was surprised at Xiao's comment.

"The wife sacrificed herself for the well-being of her husband," Xiao said. "But if her husband really valued her more than himself, how could he live in peace knowing his wife had sacrificed herself for him? What incentive would he have to do his best in his profession?"

The master was left without a comeback.

Xiao continued. "Even if the husband is still alive, his heart must be filled with regrets, and he must find it difficult to enjoy his life. Maybe he spends all day drinking, hoping to die more quickly."

A long silence ensued. At last the master broke it by saying, "Maybe it wasn't a smart thing to do, but I still admire the wife for her willingness to sacrifice herself for another person." His smile was strained.

The master didn't give Xiao a chance to respond. "On the other hand, it's not really so bad here. Every luxury from the human world is available for you to enjoy. Moreover, you won't be constrained by any rules of morality. Whatever you want to do, no one will stop you."

"That's true." Lei laughed aloud. "We're stuck here anyway. We should enjoy ourselves every extra day we live. To hell with honor and morality!"

Then he stood and yelled, "*Meizi*! *Xiaowen*! I know you're outside. Why don't you come in?"

Presently they heard a *clink-clink-clink*, like wind chimes.

Two girls dressed in silk stepped into the room with sweet smiles on their faces. They wore lots of jewelry in their hair.

Lei opened his arms to embrace a girl on either side. "These are my wives," he said to Xiao, "but if you're interested in either of them, I'll give her to you."

Shen's face became bloodless and as pale as a sheet.

Lei stared at Shen. "You don't believe me? I'll prove it to you."

He let go of the girl in his left embrace. "Xiaowen, which part of your body is the most beautiful?"

"My legs," Xiaowen replied, with a charming smile on her face.

She was tall and slim. Although her eyes weren't large, she was very attractive when she smiled. Under any criteria, she would be considered a pretty woman.

"In that case," Lei said, "why don't you show everyone your legs?"

With a coy smile on her face, she slowly hitched up her skirt.

With nothing on under the skirt, she revealed a pair of slender legs, which were firm, smooth, and fair.

Shen's fingers shook with both dread and anger.

Xiaowen still beamed proudly, as if she were the only person in the hall. Gracefully, she held the hem of her skirt and made a full turn.

Then she hitched her skirt even higher up.

The master smiled and took up his wine. "Let's drink a toast to such beautiful legs."

Xiao was holding a cup of wine at that time. To Shen's surprise... he drank it.

Patting the girl in his right embrace, Lei said, "What about you, Meizi?"

Her eyes twinkling, Meizi smiled alluringly. "What do *you* think is my most beautiful asset?"

"Every part of your body is beautiful," Lei said laughing, "but I would say your most beautiful asset is your waist."

Meizi started to unfasten her buttons with her orchid-like hands.

When the front of her clothes were pulled open, her slim waist was revealed. It looked as perfect as expected.

The master smiled. "You're wrong, Brother Lei."

"Oh?"

"The most beautiful part of her is not her waist, but the parts above her waist."

The parts above her waist thrust out from her torso, making her waist look relatively slim, so slim that it looked as if it might break at any moment.

Laughing, Lei took up his wine and said, "You're right. I'm wrong. I should punish myself by drinking a large cup of wine."

Meizi beamed radiantly, apparently rather pleased with herself.

Shen hung her head low, wishing she could run out of the house without ado. As long as she could escape from this evil place, it didn't matter where she went.

She thought even hell would be much better than this place.

"See? I wasn't bragging," Lei said, taking up his cup again and making a toast to Xiao.

"No, you weren't," Xiao said, his face still impassive.

"Everyone here is as generous as I am. I'm not the only one. Some of them may be even more generous than I am."

"Oh?"

"He's right," the master sighed. "When humans come in here, they are no longer human. They lose their sense of shame and stop caring about anything."

He stared at Xiao and continued, "You may be shocked now, thinking it's absolutely unacceptable, but in time, you'll become like everybody else."

Chapter 21

True Feelings Revealed

XIAO AND SHEN were led to their bedchamber.

In a place like this, they couldn't separate.

They had to pretend that they were husband and wife.

The chamber was comfortable and elaborate. Everything was where it was supposed to be. No necessities were lacking.

Whoever stayed here should feel content.

Nevertheless, Shen simply stood in place, feeling ill at ease. No matter how exquisite the objects in the chamber, she didn't want to touch any of them.

She felt that everything in the chamber was cursed by a devil's hideous spell and that merely touching them would make her go insane.

After an interval of silence, Xiao turned to face her. "You sleep. I'll keep guard."

Shen bit her lip and shook her head.

"You look frail," Xiao said gently. "We can't give way now."

"I ... I couldn't sleep."

"You haven't tried. How do you know you can't?"

Shen turned her eyes slowly to the bed.

The bed was big, sumptuous, and comfortable.

She suddenly recoiled. She wanted to say something, but her lips were trembling and she couldn't utter a sound, even after several attempts.

Xiao contemplated her. "Are you afraid?" he asked.

Shen nodded and then shook her head.

"Are you afraid of me?" Xiao sighed. "Are you afraid that I will become like those people?"

"I'm afraid, truly afraid," she said, her head lowered, tears running down her cheeks. "I'm afraid of everyone and everything. I'm scared to death, but—"

She lifted her face, staring at him. "I'm not afraid of you. I know your character won't change."

"If you trust me, then listen to me."

"But ... but...." she muttered.

She ran into his arms, holding him tight. "But what should we do? *What should we do?*" she said tearfully. "Are we really going to stay here for the rest of our lives, t-together with th-those people?"

Xiao's face turned pale, too. "We'll figure out a way to leave here. Don't worry. We'll figure out a way."

"But you're not a hundred percent certain."

There was a faraway look in Xiao's eyes. It was a long, long time before he finally let out a sigh and said, "No, I'm not a hundred percent certain."

"But," he added quickly, "there is still hope."

"Hope? What hope?"

"Maybe I can figure out a way to break Mr. Tian's spell."

"How long will it take? Ten years? Twenty years?"

Glancing up at him, she said through tears, "Please. Please let me do one thing."

"What?"

"Please let me sacrifice myself to that devil! I'd rather be an offering than stay here for ten or twenty years. If I have to stay here even one more day, I think I'll go insane."

"You—"

"I'm not your wife, but I'm willing to die for you. As long as you live, it doesn't matter what happens to me."

She had intended to hide these words in her heart forever.

Now, however, life had become humble and desperate. Everything in the world of humans was remote from them. What did she care? She saw no reason why she shouldn't reveal her true feelings.

Feeling the blood in his body rise to a boiling point, Xiao couldn't help but hold her tightly as well.

This was the first time he had held her ... like this.

Honor, disgrace, life or death—none of them mattered anymore.

Life existed only for this moment.

After a very long silence, Shen inhaled slowly and said, "You ... have you agreed?"

"If one of us has to be sacrificed," Xiao replied, "it should be me."

Her head snapped up. "You—"

Xiao gently covered her mouth with his hand. "You have a family and a future ... and you have hope. You should live on, Shen. I'm just a humble wanderer who has nothing. If I die, no one will care."

Tears slipped down her cheeks and fell onto Xiao's hand.

Xiao moved his hand away from her mouth to wipe her tears.

"You still don't understand how I feel about you ... not at all," Shen said, her voice sad. "Otherwise, you wouldn't say no one will care if you die. I ... I...."

"I do understand."

"Then, why did you say that?"

"I just said it. I'm not going to sacrifice myself to that devil!"

Staring into her eyes, he said solemnly, "And I won't let you sacrifice yourself either."

"In that case ... in that case, are you going to stay here for the rest of your life?"

Shen lowered her head and continued, "As long as I'm with you, even if we live in hell, I will have no complaints. But this place— this place is more evil and horrifying than hell."

"We'll try to get out of here," Xiao said, "but not like that."

"Why not?"

"If we do that, we'll be even more miserable."

"Don't you think Mr. Tian will keep his promise?"

"I think it's a trap. He wants us dead. More than that, he wants to manipulate us, toy with us, and make us suffer as much as possible ... before we die."

His eyes burned with anger. "I think he's a demon, a madman!"

Shen was silent.

"If we sacrifice our beloved and beg him for mercy," said Xiao, "not only will he not let us go, but he'll mock us and despise us."

"But you're not convinced it'll turn out like that, are you?"

Clearly, she still harbored some hope.

Most women are slightly more optimistic, because they don't look as far into the future.

"I'm convinced he's a madman," Xiao said. "Besides, the solution he provided is riddled with contradictions. Suppose a man sacrifices his wife so that he can go free. Doesn't that mean he values his own life more than he values his wife's? Since he values his own life the most, he should offer his own life as a sacrifice. If he offers his own life as a sacrifice, why does he need anyone to release him?"

He stopped there, gathering his thoughts. He seldom talked so much. Then he concluded, "If a man is dead, what magic spell can confine him?"

After a moment of silence, Shen took hold of Xiao's hand. "Since there's no hope for us, we might as well die now!"

Dying is a painful thing for most people.

As Shen spoke of dying, however, her eyes grew unusually bright, and her cheeks grew rosy red, for her death seemed to have become something to be enthusiastic about.

Leaning her head against Xiao's shoulder, she said quietly, "I don't know what you think, but I feel that living is so painful that dying is the best way to relieve our suffering."

"Indeed, sometimes dying is a way to relieve suffering, but it's only for cowards and the weak. Besides—"

His voice suddenly became determined. "We haven't gotten to the point where we have to take our own lives yet. We should at least try to see if we can find a way out."

"But what the master said is true. In the eyes of others, we're no different from ants or crickets now. Anyone can crush us with a small stone."

"I know it won't be easy to escape. I have to do three things first."

"Three?"

"First, I have to wait until my injuries have improved more."

He smiled a little and continued. "Apparently, Mr. Tian doesn't want me to die too soon, because he's treated my wounds. I don't know whether he used magic or medicine. Anyway it's working like a charm. Maybe I'll be fully recovered in a few days."

Shen took a breath. "I hope so."

"Second, I have to discover the secret of his magic and break his spell."

"Do you believe the secret is hidden in the Manor? Do you believe he has been telling the truth about this?"

"Gambling is part of human nature. Madmen are especially fond of making bets. I believe Mr. Tian has purposely left a clue for us, betting on our not finding it."

Shen sighed. "What's the third?"

Xiao turned his head to peer out the window. "Do you see the two men in the pavilion?"

The two old men had just finished a game of chess. They were drinking and chatting. The man in red tugged the sleeve of the man in green and pointed to the chessboard. Obviously, he was trying to convince the latter to play another game.

Losers always want to play again ... until they win.

"I think these two old men are special," Xiao said,

"Special?"

"I believe they must be distinguished martial artists who disappeared from the martial world many years ago, and I think they pose a greater threat than Lei Yu and Long Feiji."

"So you want to find out who they are."

"I hope my guess is wrong," Xiao said gravely. "Otherwise, we'll be in serious trouble."

Patient.

Shen had learned to be patient ever since she was a little girl.

Most people in her world think the first thing women need to learn is patience. A woman's lack of patience is considered sinful.

Therefore, Shen had always thought it was a woman's duty to be patient.

Nevertheless, she had found, in time, that there were situations in which it was difficult to remain patient.

She had once thought she couldn't live in this place for even a single day.

Now, several days had passed.

She hadn't died or gone insane.

Patience has its purpose. People can endure almost anything, for their loved ones.

It's especially so for women.

Most women don't live for themselves, but for their loved ones—their husbands and their children.

Shen felt that she had, in the past few days, grown more mature.

The layout of the Manor was basically square, just like the quadrangular compounds in Beijing.

There was a courtyard between the gate and the main hall.

Behind the main hall was another courtyard.

On either side of the second courtyard was a row of rooms.

The row of rooms in the rear was used as bedchambers by the master and his wives.

Around the corner was a much smaller compound, which contained kitchens and servants' rooms.

Lei Yu lived in the east wing. He and his two wives and four maids used four rooms and a small hall.

The other two rooms in the east wing were used by Long Feiji.

Long was a strange man. He wasn't interested in women or wine. The only thing he liked to do was eating, and he ate a lot.

He didn't care whether he was eating chicken or duck, whether the food was delicious or not. He just kept stuffing all kinds of food into his stomach.

Strangely enough, the more he ate, the thinner he got.

Five of the rooms in the west wing were always closed. The two mysterious old men were said to live in them.

But Xiao had never seen them go in or come out.

The other two rooms in the west wing were used by Xiao and Shen. One was their bedchamber and the other was the dining room.

Meals were delivered to them promptly, every day.

The food was delicious and there was always wine.

The wine was mellow and there was enough of it to get several people drunk.

Alcohol helps one avoid facing reality.

Xiao seldom saw a completely sober person here.

After a couple days, he had become fairly familiar with this place.

What the master had said was true. As long as Xiao didn't cross the boundary of the Manor, he could go anywhere and do anything, and no one would interfere.

However, since the day they first drank together, Xiao had not seen the master. The others said that he was rarely around.

When one has more than ten pretty wives to take care of, the days are short. One doesn't have time to spare.

Every day, after breakfast, Xiao wandered around in the Manor, as if interested in everything. He greeted everyone with a smile.

Aside from Lei Yu and Long Feiji, he seldom saw any other man.

Most of the girls around the house were intrigued by his large eyes. Every time he smiled at them, they smiled back sweetly.

The moment Xiao left their chamber, Shen closed the door.

She was not afraid to be alone.

She had spent most of her life alone.

It was the fifth day.

The dishes on the dinner table included stewed pork with bamboo shoots, scrambled eggs with parsley, hibiscus chicken, stir-fried mixed vegetables, smoked pickled pork innards, and cabbage and fish ball soup.

The cook on duty this evening was a master chef from the north.

Shen was in a better mood today. She knew Xiao liked to eat northern Chinese food. These dishes would be to his taste.

She was prepared to have a drink with him.

Xiao usually showed up soon after the meal was delivered. He always talked a lot when he was eating.

She liked to listen to him talk.

This was the only time she could forget her fears and worries, forget how dreadful this place was, and forget how miserable they were.

But, today, all the food had gotten cold, and Xiao had still not returned.

As a matter of fact, she had experienced plenty of similar incidents.

Within two months of her wedding, she had often waited for Lian at dinner time. More often than not, she had reheated the food several times before he finally returned. Most of the time, she had dinner alone.

She was used to it.

Today, however, her heart was unsettled. There were several times when she picked up the chopsticks and then put them down again. She craned her neck, but couldn't see Xiao coming back.

Xiao had never kept her waiting. What was wrong with him today?

Had something terrible happened to him?

Anything could happen in a place like this.

She suddenly realized that she had become so attached to Xiao that she couldn't stand to be without him even for a couple hours.

The sauce of the hibiscus chicken had gelled and the soup had gotten cold.

She clenched her teeth, stood up, opened the door softly and quietly walked outside.

Every few steps down the covered walkway, she saw a gauze lantern. Then she saw a man leaning against the railing grinning at her.

It was Lei Yu.

It was too late for her to turn back.

He had greeted her with a smile. It was rude to turn back now.

Under the lantern, the pockmarks on Lei's face appeared denser and darker.

Each pockmark seemed to be grinning at her suggestively and repugnantly.

Nodding slightly, she intended to hurry past him.

She had to go look for Xiao.

However, Lei stopped her. "Have you had your dinner?"

"Um-hmm," Shen responded.

"Today the chef on duty is Old Gao. I heard that he was the master chef at Lumingxiang, in the capital. He has excellent culinary skills."

"Um."

"The courtyard isn't large, but if you don't have someone to guide you, you might still get lost, Miss. If you mistakenly enter the master's bedchamber, it will be most inappropriate."

Her face turned cold. "Who is this 'Miss?'"

"You're Mrs.?"

"Um-hmm."

Lei grinned. "Madame, do you know where your husband is?"

Her heart missed a beat. "Do you?"

"Of course I do."

Shen tried to make herself look calm. "I'm looking for him."

"You'd better not go further, or you might get upset."

Her heart jumped. "Why?"

Lei grinned even more hideously. "Do you want the truth?"

"Of course."

"You know, there are many beautiful girls here. They're young and lonely and your husband isn't at all a bad-looking man."

His eyes narrowed into a smile. "Madame, you're a gorgeous woman, but you know, sometimes those who incessantly eat rich and exotic food would like to have something different just for a change—"

"Stop talking nonsense!" Shen cried out, shaking with anger.

"You don't believe me?" Lei grinned. "I can take you to see for yourself. The girl isn't as pretty as you are, but she is younger. Men are always interested in younger girls."

Shen was so furious that her lips quivered.

"Take my advice," Lei went on. "Don't take anything too seriously. For the people here, things like this are as common as eating rice. If he can fool around with other women, why can't you fool around with other men? Everyone is looking for fun. If you get even with him, you'll feel better."

His eyes had narrowed into a thin line and he was about to take her hand. "Come on! Don't be shy. Anyway, sooner or later you'll go to bed—"

Shen didn't let Lei finish, but gave him a slap in the face instead.

Lei was stunned. He hadn't expected her to be so swift.

Hiding her hands in her sleeves, Shen glared at him and started to back slowly away.

Lei touched his face and said with a sinister smile, "You're asking for trouble. No matter how chaste or virtuous a woman you were, after arriving here, you'll have to give in. There's no way out."

He advanced toward her.

"Freeze!" Shen called out loudly. "One more step and my golden needles will kill you!"

"Golden needles?" Lei echoed in surprise.

"You were once in the martial world for several years. You must have heard about how deadly and accurate the Golden Needles of the Shens are. Are you sure you can dodge my golden needles?"

As expected, Lei stopped walking. "What relation are you to Lady Shen?"

"She is my grandmother—"

Before finishing her words, she had backed into her chamber and banged the door closed.

For a long while, there was no sound coming from outside. Lei seemed to have been scared away.

She leaned against the door, panting.

Her heart was aching, so much so that she almost forgot the fear and anger she had just felt.

She is younger than you. Men are always interested in younger girls. Your husband is fooling around with other women. Would you like me to take you there to see for yourself?

These words tore at her heart.

Xiao wasn't her husband, but, somehow, even if she knew Lian were seeing another woman, she wouldn't feel as miserable as she did now.

I don't believe it! I don't believe it! I don't believe it! … He wouldn't do such a thing!

But … why hadn't he come back?

There were more than thirty girls in this place. They were all pretty, and all had beautiful smiles.

Only one of them had never smiled at Xiao or given him so much as a glance.

This girl's name was Su Yan.

Xiao was lying in Su's bed.

She was resting her head on his broad chest.

Her eyes were closed, her lashes were long, and the corners of her eyes curved up slightly. Apparently, when her eyes were open, she was very attractive. A pair of charming eyes is enough to conquer a man.

Moreover, the other parts of her body were charming as well.

She was partially covered by a comforter, but it was clear that her legs were beautiful, neither too plump nor too thin. They were firm, and their curves were nicely rounded.

It had been quiet in the chamber a moment ago, but now there was a sweet laugh, like the tinkle of a faraway bell.

There are many types of women's laughs.

Most women can only laugh with their mouths. Their laughs are nothing more than sounds. Some women's laughs are so unpleasant that they even give their listeners goose bumps. Women who can laugh with their whole face are rather rare.

Those women who can laugh with their eyebrows or eyes, or even their noses, often leave men gawking in wonder.

There is a kind of woman who can laugh with her whole body. She has all kinds of facial expressions and laughs with her chest, her waist, and even her legs.

Men can't help submitting to the charms of such a woman.

Su Yan was a woman of this kind.

Her chest was heaving up and down, her waist was writhing, and her legs were rubbing.

Xiao wasn't a wooden man. He couldn't ignore her seductiveness. "What are you laughing at?" he couldn't keep from asking.

"I'm laughing at you."

"Laughing at me?"

"You have such a pretty wife, and yet you're still fooling around."

Xiao smirked. "What man doesn't?"

"I heard that a man is like a tea kettle and a woman is like a teacup," Su giggled. "A kettle always goes with several cups."

Xiao laughed. "That's a brilliant metaphor. Who told you that?"

"A man did, but—"

She sat up, supporting her body with her elbow, and stared at Xiao. "Every girl here is pretty. Why did you pick me?"

"When a man wants to sneak some food out of the kitchen, he always picks the most delicious."

Su bit her lip. "But I never even looked your way. How did you know I would take your bait?"

"Every man knows that the more a woman pretends to be indifferent, the more easily she gets hooked."

Before he finished, Su had pounced on him. "What? You're saying I pretended to be indifferent? You think I would go to bed with any man? You know what? Lei Yu is crazy about me. But every time I see his pockmarked face, I feel sick."

Xiao stifled a laugh. "What's wrong with a pockmarked face? Nine out of ten pockmarked men are cute. Some women are even particularly fond of pockmarked men! Besides, when the lamp is out, what difference does it make?"

Su gave him a gentle slap in the face, chiding him playfully. "I thought pockmarked Lei was bad enough, but you're worse."

"I guess, other than Long Feiji, none of the men here are decent."

"That's true."

"What about those two old men? They do nothing but play chess all day."

Su pursed her lips and sneered. "That's where you're wrong. Those two mummies' bodies may be old, but their hearts are young. They have molested all of us, except those reserved for the master."

"Including Lei's wives?"

"Those two sluts offered themselves to the two old geezers."

"Doesn't Lei mind if his wives sleep with other men behind his back?"

"Pockmarked Lei likes to throw his weight around in the Manor, but in the presence of those two, he's afraid to even fart."

"Lei is young and strong, and he's a martial artist; why is he afraid of them?"

Su didn't answer.

"Are the old men better than Lei in kung fu?"

She still didn't answer.

"Do you know their names?"

"No, I don't."

Xiao smirked. "At least you know when they arrived, don't you?"

"No, I don't. When I arrived, they had been here already."

"When did you come here?"

"Several years ago."

"How did you end up here?"

"Like everyone else, I ended up here without knowing what happened."

"But you're still young. Are you willing to stay here for the rest of your life?"

"Under these conditions," Su sighed, "I can only resign myself to fate."

She leaned on Xiao again and cooed, "Everyone here is happy. Why are we talking about this? Come on...."

No sooner had Xiao held her in his arms than he cried out in pain.

"What's wrong with you? Have you got a cramp?"

"No. No...." Xiao gasped. "My wounds ... my wounds haven't healed."

Blushing and biting her lip, she poked at his nose lightly with her index finger, chiding him, teasingly. "I was so picky. Turns out I picked a feeble sickly man like you!"

Shen sat at the dining table, with her head hanging. Her eyes were red from crying.

The dishes on the table hadn't been touched.

Xiao knocked on the door for a long time, before the door finally opened.

When he returned, Shen usually smiled like a flower when she greeted him.

Today, she bowed her head low and asked, "Did you have dinner elsewhere?"

"No. Did you ... ? Why didn't you start?"

"I ... I'm not hungry yet."

She kept her eyes down, scooped a bowl of rice, and placed it in front of Xiao. "The dishes are all cold. Have some if you want. These are all your favorites."

Xiao suddenly felt that as long as she was beside him, even this wretched place was filled with the warmth of home.

Shen scooped half a bowl of rice for herself and ate slowly.

For some reason, Xiao felt a little guilty. He wanted to say something, but didn't know what.

A husband who fools around outside the home, often becomes extra gentle with his wife when he returns. The more his wife keeps silent, the more guilty he feels.

After a long silence, Xiao spoke. "I have measured this place thoroughly in the last few days. There should be at least thirty rooms, but I can't find the two extra rooms."

A moment passed before Shen finally responded, in a small voice,

"There are many girls here. Girls like to gossip. Why don't you ask them?"

It was then that Xiao realized why she was upset.

She was jealous. Jealous over him!

Men are always pleased to find women jealous over them.

Xiao had a sweet feeling in his heart. Never in his life had he felt this way. After some silence, he decided to tell the truth.

"I tried to ask," he said with a wry smile, "but I didn't get any useful information."

A pause. "But the more they keep their lips sealed, the more I'm convinced that they're hiding something and that there are some dark secrets here."

After another moment's silence, Shen asked, "You're not going to ask them again?"

"No, I won't ask them again," said Xiao, gazing at her.

Though Shen lowered her head even more, the corners of her mouth curved into a smile.

She tried to keep a straight face, but this smile was from the bottom of her heart, and she couldn't suppress it.

At the sight of her smile, Xiao finally felt hungry and quickly shoveled rice into his mouth. "I'm done with the girls. Tomorrow I'm going to ask the old men," he said.

"I suppose," Shen said cheerfully, "tomorrow you'll be back earlier."

She started to blush even before she had finished speaking.

When women are overly jealous, men get headaches; however, if women didn't get jealous at all, isn't it possible that men would have much less fun?

The sixth day was a fine day.

When Xiao walked to the front courtyard, he noticed that the surrounding wall was very high. Almost six times a man's height. The small gate in the corner between two walls had once been open but was now closed and locked.

Who locked the gate and why? Xiao mused.

In Mr. Tian's eyes, the people confined here were no different from ants or crickets. Even if they escaped, he could just pick them up with two fingers and toss them back. Why did he have to impose such tight security?

The corner of Xiao's mouth curved up in a faint smile.

The two old men were drinking and playing chess again in the pavilion.

Slowly, Xiao walked toward them, his hands clasped behind his back. He stood beside them and quietly watched them play chess.

With their attention focused on the game, the old men didn't seem to notice someone standing beside them.

The wind was blowing the leaves to and fro, the brook was babbling, and everything was quiet and peaceful. The two old men looked relaxed.

Xiao, however, sensed some intensity in the air about them, as if he were near two unsheathed swords.

Extraordinarily sharp weapons always have a vengeful air about them.

Similarly, those extraordinary martial artists who have no respect for life usually have a callous aura about them, too!

Xiao could sense that these two people had killed countless others.

The man in red, holding a chess piece, was pondering his next move. The man in green, supporting his chin with his left hand and holding a cup with his right, was sipping his wine. Judging from his expression, he was apparently more proficient at chess than the man in red.

When the man in green finished his cup of wine, the man in red still hadn't decided where to place his chess piece.

The man in green suddenly looked up at Xiao, held out his cup, and gestured at a strange-shaped wine kettle on the stone table.

His meaning was clear: He wanted Xiao to pour wine for him.

"Why should I pour wine for you?"

This was how others might respond, if they were in Xiao's place. Even if they refrained from cursing loudly, they might just turn and walk away.

Nevertheless, Xiao didn't say anything. He picked up the wine kettle.

The kettle was raised and tilted, but the wine had not flowed out.

Xiao slowly aimed the spout at the old man's cup.

If he tilted the kettle a little more, the wine would flow into the cup.

However, his hand just hung there.

The hand of the man in green also hung in midair ... waiting.

Xiao stayed still, and the old man also stayed still.

The man in red froze as well.

It was as if the three of them were abruptly frozen by magic and had become lifeless dolls.

The shadows on the ground kept shortening as noon approached.

Three hours had passed.

None of the three people had moved their bodies, or even their fingers. Their hands were as steady as rocks.

Then the shadows gradually elongated.

The sun was setting in the west.

If Xiao's hand wavered a bit, the wine would spill.

But his hand was still as steady as a rock ... after six hours.

At first the expression of the man in green had been calm, his eyes showing a slight contempt. But, now, his expression had changed. He looked slightly astonished and somewhat impatient.

He didn't suspect how uncomfortable Xiao really was.

Xiao felt the kettle in his hand getting heavier and heavier. It was as if the kettle weighed more than a thousand pounds. The feelings in his arm changed from sore to numb, from numb to aching—so much so that it was like thousands of needles pricking his arm.

His head stung, and his clothes were drenched in sweat.

But he clenched his jaws and endured, trying not to think about the pain.

He knew he had to remain motionless ... now.

Although none of them moved, this fighting was more danger-ous than the clashing of swords or sabers.

If the wine flowed, Xiao's blood might flow as well.

This was a duel of endurance, patience, and internal and physical strength.

It was a duel of absolute stillness.

It was also an unprecedented duel.

It was dangerous, but not fierce or tense, not exciting either.

It started in the morning and lasted until dusk. It had gone on for almost ten hours, but not a single person had come to watch.

The residents here only cared about themselves. They didn't care what others were doing or whether others were dead or alive.

Chapter 22

The Longest Day

THICK DUSK HAD descended.

The lamps in the main hall and the gauze lanterns in the covered walkways were all lit.

Light reflected on the face of the old man in green.

His face was pale; the muscles around the corners of his eyes were twitching.

But his hand was still as steady as a rock.

Disheartened, Xiao felt he was going to give way.

His confidence was shaken and, soon, his hand was going to start shaking as well.

He could hardly hold out any longer. If the duel lasted even one more moment—

Just then, the man in red shot out the chess piece he was holding, slicing the spout off the wine kettle. The spout fell and clanked on the ground.

Wine flowed into the cup.

When the cup was filled, the man in green withdrew his hand and sipped his wine. He didn't give Xiao another look.

Xiao set down the kettle, strolled out of the pavilion, and walked over the zigzagging bridge. Lifting his head, he noticed that it was dark and there were lights everywhere in the Manor.

He stopped at the head of the bridge, gazing at a gauze lantern glowing in the far distance. He stood there for a long time.

Never had he noticed that lamplight could be so restful and appealing.

It wasn't a bad thing to live after all.

Only when someone has experienced the fear of dying does he understand the preciousness of life.

Dinner is probably cold, Xiao thought.

He rubbed his arm quietly and strode back toward his chamber.

Today had probably been the longest day of his life, but this day had not been wasted.

He had gained something.

Every muscle in his body was sore, but he felt invigorated. He was ready to have a big meal, a few cups of wine, and a good sleep.

Tomorrow, he would have many things to do. Anything could determine his fate.

The door was ajar.

Shen must be waiting anxiously.

I hope she won't think I've been fooling around again, he thought.

Xiao pushed the door open quietly, hoping to see her radiant smile.

If he had known what he was about to see and what would happen next, he might not have opened the door!

There were five dishes on the table: steamed crabs and fish heads, a spicy combo of vegetables, thickly stewed eels, fried shrimp and bean sprouts, and a big plate of deep fried shrimp to go with the wine. The soup of the day, in an earthen pot, was stewed pork balls.

The cook on duty today was a master chef from Suzhou.

All the dishes were cold.

Beside the table, a person sat ... waiting.

The person was not Shen but the master of the Manor, who had not been around for several days.

The lamp in the room wasn't lit.

The light of a gauze lantern shone through the window lattice, casting scattered shadows around the room. Sitting quietly among the hazy shadows, the master looked surreal, mysterious, and elusive, just like a spirit.

He was contemplating a painting on the wall. The painting was about the folk story of Zhong Kui fighting ghosts.

Xiao's heart plummeted. He had an ominous feeling, like a wolf has when it smells an upcoming disaster but finds it unavoidable.

The master didn't turn his head.

Xiao hesitated for a moment before sitting down across from the master.

He decided to remain silent and wait for the master to speak first. Not knowing what might have happened, he couldn't guess what the master was up to.

After who knows how long, the master sighed and observed, "Old ghosts are never completely eliminated, and yet new ones keep coming up. There are all kinds of people and all kinds of ghosts. Ghosts can never be destroyed. Why does Priest Zhong bother?"

Xiao poured a cup of wine and gulped it down.

The master also had a cup of wine in his hand. At last he turned his eyes to Xiao. After a long pause, he suddenly smiled. "You look tired," he said.

Xiao smiled, too. "Not too bad."

"No matter how you fought them, it must have been a daunting challenge."

"Not too bad."

The master's eyes gleamed. "After this fight, you must know who they are."

"I had guessed their identities beforehand."

"But you still dared fight them?"

"Um-hmm."

The master threw back his head and laughed. "Good! You have guts. Let me make a toast, to you."

"Cheers," Xiao said.

The master drained his wine, then his face tightened abruptly. "What else do you know?"

"Neither too much nor too little," Xiao replied.

"I hope you don't know too much yet," said the master. "Those who know too much often bring death down upon themselves. It's better to know nothing at all."

"Where is she?" Xiao asked, rotating the empty cup round and round in his hand.

"Who?"

"My wife."

The master produced an eerie smile. "You mean Ms. Shen?"

Xiao stared at the cup he was toying with. His pupils appeared to contract suddenly and his eyes became unspeakably blank.

After an interval, he nodded slightly.

The master stared straight into his eyes, asking emphatically, "Is she really your wife?"

Xiao didn't answer.

"Do you know what happened?" the master asked. "Do you know why she's so frail?"

Xiao took a long breath. "What happened?"

"She was going to have a baby in a few months, but it's gone now."

Smack! The cup Xiao had been rotating flew out of his hand, crashed against the wall, and broke into pieces.

Xiao's eyes were still fixed on his empty hand. His fingers looked rigid, unimpressive, and uncharacteristic ... as if frozen stiff.

The master grinned. "If you weren't aware of this, how could you possibly be her husband? How could you even qualify to be her husband?"

At last Xiao turned his eyes away from his fingers and stared at the master. "Where is she?" he asked again.

Ignoring his question, the master said, "Have you noticed something? In this place, the most beautiful women, the most comfortable chambers, and the best of everything ... belong to me."

He fixed Xiao with his sharp gaze. "Do you know why?"

"Why?"

"Because I'm the strongest!"

He smiled again and went on. "I told you before, neither integrity nor morality means anything here. Whoever is the strongest and the most powerful owns the best."

"You mean—"

"Now that you're here, you have to follow the rules of this place. Ms. Shen is neither your wife nor anyone else's, so whoever is the strongest will own her!"

He pressed the empty cup into his hand and continued. "She belongs to me now, because I'm stronger than any other man, including you."

His delicate fingers were more graceful than most women's fingers.

However, when he finished the last word and opened his hand, the cup had become a pile of powder. Powder finer than salt!

Xiao bolted to his feet, but then slowly sat down again.

The master didn't glance at him. "This is your strength. You know more clearly than most young men that I really am stronger than you. You're also more patient than most young men. That's why you're still alive."

He smiled and went on, "It's not easy to find a good sparring partner like you, so I don't want you to die too soon. As long as you're smart, you might live—for a very long time."

"My trouble is that I'm too smart," Xiao sighed. "Smart people don't live long."

"Not necessarily. I myself have lived quite a few years. If you're really smart, you'll talk less and drink more. If you still feel compromised, I'll make it up to you."

"Make it up to me?"

"I mean Su Yan. Although she isn't as pretty as Ms. Shen, she has many merits that Ms. Shen doesn't have. As a matter of fact, didn't you choose her yourself? You lost one, but you gained one. You see, you suffer no loss. Once you stop taking things so seriously, you can live happily here for the rest of your life, like everyone else has. Perhaps you'll even be happier than if you lived outside."

"What if I don't want to stay?"

The master's face turned hard. "You must stay, because you have no choice. You can't escape!"

Xiao smiled. "What if I find the way to break the magic spell?"

The master's face stiffened slightly, but soon broke into a broad grin. "Impossible. No one can find it."

"If I find it, will you let me take her away with me?"

"How much time do you need?"

"Not much. I can find it right now!"

"What if you can't?"

"Then I'll stay here and be your slave until I die!"

The master's smile suddenly became very tender. "The stakes are high," he said kindly. "You had better think twice."

"The higher the stakes, the greater the thrill. Otherwise, there's no point in gambling. Let's see whether you dare take my bet."

"I'll accept any bet, no matter how high the stakes. You can trust me on this."

"Promise?"

"My word is my bond!"

"Good!"

The moment Xiao finished speaking, he jumped up and smashed against the wall. *Boom!* A cloud of dust rose up. A hole as big as a table was smashed into the nine-inch-thick wall!

Xiao had stormed into ... the neighboring room!

The room was big, but it had no windows. There was nothing but a big table in it. On the table was ... *a dollhouse!* In the garden of the dollhouse, there were pavilions, bridges, brooks, an old man in green washing his feet by the brook....

A grin flickered across Xiao's face. "This is the secret of your magic, isn't it?" he said, still panting slightly.

The master's face went pale. He didn't say anything.

"The dollhouse is a miniature replica of your residence," Xiao said. "You made us see the dollhouse before taking us out of the room, so we'd have the illusion that we'd been shrunk by magic and become dolls."

He added, "This is a preposterous but brilliant idea. No one would ever imagine that there's a madman like you who'd do something so diabolical."

"It's true." The master laughed aloud. "No one could imagine this. I've used the same method to fool countless people. Many of them either went insane or slit their own throats."

"So ... you find this method not only effective, but also *entertaining?*"

"It's definitely entertaining," the master said. "If you had seen the expressions of those who were shocked to find themselves 'shrunk,' and how they kept drinking or using other ways to numb themselves until they finally went insane, you'd agree that nothing in the world is more entertaining."

He laughed loudly and continued. "In order to survive, those people discarded everything they'd once believed in, including morality, integrity, reputation, or social status. Sometimes, they'd even trade their wives for a mere jar of wine."

"Do you think everyone is like them?"

The master smirked. "If you'd seen the people I'm talking about, you'd realize that humans aren't really as smart as they think. Sometimes they're more lowly than dogs and more stupid than pigs."

"Don't forget that you're a human yourself!"

"Who says I'm human? Since I can determine the life and fate of humans, I'm a god!"

"Only a madman looks upon himself as a god," Xiao sighed.

A gentle smile spread across the master's face again. "Don't forget that you're still under my control. I can still determine your life and fate."

"And I haven't forgotten your promise."

"What if I have?"

Xiao smiled. "I don't believe you have. Since you regard yourself as a god, you won't go back on your word. Otherwise, wouldn't you be as worthless as a mere human?"

The master stared at him and muttered, "You're exceptionally intelligent. I've underestimated you!"

"Where is she? You promised to let her go."

"I still have some questions for you."

"I knew you would. Go ahead and ask."

"How did you guess the secret?"

Xiao grinned. "If we were really in a doll's world, we wouldn't be able to see the sun. But there is sunlight here."

"I noticed this loophole as well," the master said, with a sigh. "But people who come here usually become so disoriented they never notice it. Gradually, even I have forgotten about it."

"Most people think they can see far ahead, so they don't pay attention to the small things around them. You know this human weakness very well, so you arranged for me to stay in this particular room. You thought it would never cross my mind that the key to the secret might be in the room right next to mine."

"How did this idea occur to you?"

"I had a vague feeling that there were two hidden rooms in this place, but I wasn't sure where they were. I was merely trying my luck."

Xiao grinned, as he added, "I was lucky."

The master was quiet for a few seconds. "Well, no matter how lucky someone is, his luck will run out, sooner or later."

The long night was almost over.

The master was still sitting in the room, which remained unlit.

In the gloom, a small hazy figure appeared and slowly came up behind him. She started to massage his back with her gentle fists. Her voice was tender, sweet, and unbelievably charming.

The master neither responded nor turned around.

The window paper was whitening. The dawn light lit the figure.

She wasn't tall, but her figure was perfectly proportioned and its curves were smooth. With a round face and large twinkling eyes, she appeared to wear a constant faint smile, even when she wasn't smiling.

Her smile was not only sweet, but also naïve. Whoever saw her smile would surely leave all worries behind.

It was ... *Little Mister*!

Why was *she* here?

"You're right," the master said. "Xiao Shiyi Lang isn't an ordinary man. I should never have underestimated him."

"You shouldn't have let him go!" Little Mister said.

"I want it to be known that every word I say carries sacred weight!"

"But ... you let the tiger return to its mountain—"

"It's true that they have left," the master cut her short, "but they'll be back within ten days." A broad grin flickered across his face.

"Back? Are you saying they'll come back here?"

"Yes, I believe they will."

Little Mister smiled. "Do you think Xiao needs to return?"

"Xiao might not, but Shen certainly will."

"How can you be so sure?"

"Have you ever seen me do things I'm not confident about?"

"Why would she want to return?"

"Because I have captured her heart."

Little Mister winked and giggled.

"You don't believe me?" the master asked.

Little Mister grinned. "I merely want to know *how* you have ... captured her heart."

"There are two ways for a man to win a woman's heart."

"Which two?"

"The first way is to make her love you. This is the best method, but it's more difficult."

"What's the other way?"

"The second way is to make her hate you. If a woman really hates you, she'll think about you so much that she can never erase your image from her mind."

He smirked. "This method is much easier."

Little Mister rolled her eyes. "But if a woman has never really loved you, she'll never really hate you."

"You're wrong," the master said, with a smile. "There may be only one kind of love, but there are different kinds of hatred."

"Oh?"

"If someone killed your loved ones, would you hate them?"

Little Mister was powerless to contradict him.

The master continued, "I told her that I'm the person who destroyed Shen Manor and killed her grandmother."

"But, this kind of hatred—"

"This kind of hatred is hatred as well. The more she hates me, the more she'll try to come back to me. Only when she is by my side will she have the chance to kill me and have her revenge!"

"If that's the case, why did she leave?"

"Because she didn't want to drag Xiao down. She knew if she didn't leave, Xiao wouldn't leave either."

Little Mister's eyes sparkled. "So you know she's in love with Xiao?"

"Anyone who isn't blind can see when a woman is in love with a man."

Little Mister bit her lip. "Are you sure you can win her heart?"

"As long as she's with me, I'm convinced I can."

"But, she loves someone else. What's the point in bringing her back?"

He smirked. "As long as I can possess her body, I have a way to make her forget other men."

Hearing this, Little Mister stopped her massaging hands and lowered her head.

The master turned his head around, held her hands, and smiled an eerie smile. "Other people may not understand how I do it, but you should know."

"Ohhh!" Little Mister purred sweetly and fell into his arms.

Chapter 23

A Stunning Bride

XIAO FELT THE distance between Shen and him widening again.

When they were in Doll Manor, their hearts had been connected.

They had forgotten many things and many worries.

But, now, everything was different.

There are certain things people will never forget as long as they live.

The road, long and desolate, was obviously an abandoned and ancient one.

The grass along the road was brown and withered. The leaves rustled in the wind.

Instead of walking by Shen's side, Xiao trailed two steps behind her.

Shen didn't wait for him.

The danger had passed; their wounds would soon heal; they had escaped from the clutches of the devil. They should be rejoicing, but, for some reason, their hearts were heavy.

Was it time for them to part ways again?

Couldn't they just stay together?

Suddenly, they heard the sound of wheels and the neighing of horses. A big carriage was swiftly rolling toward them!

Just as Xiao was about to make way for the carriage, it came to a standstill near him.

The carriage horse was a fast steed, and the ebony black surface of the vehicle was as shiny as a mirror, shiny enough to reflect the crestfallen expressions on Xiao's and Shen's fatigued faces.

The windows of the carriage had silk curtains.

All of a sudden, the curtains were pulled open to reveal two faces—the faces of the two mysterious old men.

"Please get into the carriage," the man in red said.

"We'll give you a ride," added the man in green.

Xiao hesitated. "I dare not trouble you."

"We have to see you off," said the man in red.

"Yes, we must," added the man in green.

"Why?" Xiao asked.

"Because you're the first person to walk out of there alive," the man in red said.

"And the first person to survive a duel with me," added the man in green.

They both wore deadpan faces, but their eyes gleamed with enthusiasm.

This was the first time Xiao had felt that they were living, breathing human beings, complete with emotions.

He smiled and opened the door.

As with Doll Manor, the interior of the vehicle was sumptuously furnished. Any exhausted passenger would certainly find it comfortable.

Shen, however, appeared impassive.

She sat rigidly and stared out the window.

Xiao also felt somewhat uneasy, because the old men kept their eyes on Shen.

The man in red spoke first. "Now that you have escaped, never go back!"

"Never ever go back for any reason!" the man in green added emphatically.

"Why?" Xiao asked.

A hint of trepidation appeared in the eyes of the man in red. "Because he's a devil, not a human being. No, he's a monster more menacing than any devil. Whoever crosses his path might as well lie down and die!"

"You surely know who we're talking about," the man in green said.

Xiao took a long breath. "Yes, and I know who you are as well."

"You certainly do," said the man in red. "With your kung fu, only three people in the world are your match, and we are among them."

"However, the two of us combined are not his match!" said the man in green.

The mouth corners of the man in red were quivering. "No one can last more than thirty moves with him," he said.

"You probably could withstand only fifteen, no more," said the man in green.

Shen bit her lip. There were several times when she wanted to speak but held back.

After a moment's thought, Xiao said, "I think I know who he is."

"You'd better not know who he is," said the man in green. "All you need to know is that he can kill you at any time, but you can never kill him."

"No one in the world can kill him!" added the man in green.

"Have you both fought with him?" Xiao asked.

The man in red drew a long breath. "How else would we get stuck there playing chess all day?"

"Do you really think we're that crazy about chess?" asked the man in green.

The man in red smiled bitterly. "Honestly speaking, I get a headache every time I touch the chess pieces. But what else can we do to kill time?"

The man in green said, "We haven't made a single friend in the last twenty years. No one has been worthy of our friendship. You're the only exception. But we can only give you a ride as far as the intersection. Then we have to head back."

"Can't you refuse to go back?" Xiao asked.

The two old men exchanged glances and then shook their heads grimly.

A gloomy smile formed around the mouth corner of the man in red. "We're too old," he said with a sigh. "We don't have the courage to escape anymore."

The man in green smiled even more bleakly. "We tried before. But no matter how far we ran, when we stopped, we always found him waiting for us."

Xiao pondered for a long time. Eyes gleaming like swords, he gazed intensely at the old men. "If the three of us work together, perhaps—"

The man in red cut him off. "No! No way!" he warned.

"Don't even think about it!" said the man in green.

"Why not?"

"Because if you get this idea into your head, you'll try to kill him," said the man in red.

"And if you try to kill him, he'll kill you," added the man in green.

"But—"

"Why do you think we came to see you off?" the man in red interrupted. "You think we're afraid that you would be too tired too walk? You think it's easy for us to come out whenever we want?"

"We came to make you understand that it was pure luck that you escaped this time," said the man in green. "Stay away from him as long as you live! Never come back again! And never think about killing him. Otherwise, even if you survive, you would find living worse than dying."

The man in red sighed and repeated the same words: "Just like us, you would find living worse than dying."

"Other people will definitely get killed, if they try to kill him," said the man in green. "But you ... he might let your live, just as he has let us. And when he's bored, he'll use you as a sparring partner for a little entertainment."

"He can only find pleasure by fighting with people like us," said the man in red.

"But we don't want you to repeat our fate and end up his plaything," said the man in green. "Otherwise, why would we care whether you're dead or alive?"

The man in red gazed at the mountains far in the distance. "We're old and dying," he said. "When we're dead and he can't find other sparring partners, he'll be very lonely."

The eyes of the man in green gleamed. "That will be our revenge! Other than this, we can't think of another way to have it."

Xiao listened quietly, not knowing what to say.

The carriage stopped, and the man in red opened the door.

"Go! Go away! The farther the better!" he said.

"If you dare come back, even if he doesn't kill you, we will!" warned the man in green.

There was a thoroughfare ahead.

The carriage drove away, kicking up dust in the distance. Xiao and Shen stood at the end of the road, staring after the vehicle for a long time.

"Do you think they might have been sent by *him* to scare us?" Shen suddenly asked, her face pale.

"No, I don't think so."

"Why not?"

"They may have killed hundreds of people for no reason, but they'd never lie."

"Really? Why? Who are they?"

"In the last twenty years, no one in the Martial Order has been more notorious or ferocious. Whenever people hear their names...."

Before he could say their names, they heard gongs and loud music coming from afar.

Xiao looked up and saw a procession of people snaking their way down the road.

Behind the horses, the gong beaters, and the oboe players was a palanquin, a bridal palanquin.

At the head of the procession was the bridegroom, dressed in a wedding robe, wearing golden flowers on his head and riding on a tall, pure-white horse.

Bridegrooms usually look happy and proud, especially when their brides are already inside the palanquin.

Unlike most people, Xiao usually wasn't loathe to see how happy others were, when he was in low spirits himself. Today, however, was an exception. Whether by accident or by design, he suddenly bent over to cough.

Shen continued to walk, looking straight ahead, but she wasn't really seeing anything. The only thing the palanquin reminded her of was her own bridal palanquin.

At that time, her mind had been full of beautiful dreams and hopes.

What had become of her since then?

She hoped the bride sitting in this palanquin wouldn't repeat her fate and fall in love with a man other than her husband.

The bridegroom was holding his head high.

Those in a merry mood usually like to look at the expressions of others, hoping others are looking at them as well. They want to share their joy.

But this bridegroom was an exception. Though he was still riding on the horse, his thoughts had drifted into the palanquin. His bride was all that mattered to him at the moment.

He had fought long and hard to win his bride.

He couldn't remember exactly how much humiliation he had endured.

Nor did he know how much weight he had lost over her.

Just when he was about to give up, she had nodded her consent.

"Alas! A woman's heart!" he sighed.

His days of suffering were over, and she finally belonged to him.

The palanquin was going to arrive at his house, and his bride was going to enter the nuptial chamber.

Thinking of this, he thought his heavy body would float off the horse.

He looked up at the sky and then at the ground.

"Thank heaven and thank earth!" he whispered.

After eight pairs of steeds and sixteen gong beaters and trumpeters, the bridal palanquin appeared, carried by eight bearers.

The curtains were drawn.

Brides usually sit still in their palanquin, no matter how energetic or mischievous they really are.

But this bride was an exception as well.

She pulled the curtains open a little and peeked outside.

When Xiao raised his head, he saw a pair of rolling eyes behind the curtains.

Quite amused, he thought to himself: She's still in the bridal palanquin, and she's already having a hard time controlling herself. How much more trouble will she get into in the future?

Such brides were unusual enough, but something even more extraordinary was yet to come.

The curtains were suddenly pulled open.

Out of the palanquin flew the bride, dressed in a red wedding robe, wearing bridal headgear on her head and red silk shoes on her feet.

Xiao was stunned.

The bride landed in front of him, reached out her hand, slapped him on the shoulder, and said excitedly, "You little bastard! Where the hell have you been for the past couple of months?"

Xiao had been almost thrown backward by the slap, but the voice astonished him even more.

The oboe players, the gong beaters, the bearers, the attendants— everyone in the procession stopped and gawked in wonder. They looked as if a hot-boiled egg had been stuffed into their mouths.

Shen was stunned as well. She had never dreamed of something like this.

"I've only got a pound of powder on my face," the bride quipped. "Don't you recognize me?"

With a wry smile on his face, Xiao sighed, "Even if I didn't recognize your face, I should have guessed who you were. Other than Feng Siniang, what bride would behave like this?"

One pound was certainly an exaggeration, but it was true that the powder on Feng's face weighed at least four ounces.

This was the achievement of Feng's maids of honor. It was said that a professional maid of honor could not only *bleach* the face of a dark girl but also fill every small hollow on the face of a pock-marked girl. Therefore, all brides were beautiful, and they all looked alike.

However, no amount of powder could cover the sweet and play-ful smile on Feng's face or hide her air of boldness and buoyancy.

Unlike ordinary brides, Feng was still herself, even when a hundred pairs of eyes were staring at her.

Still giggling, she slapped Xiao on the shoulder again. "Did it ever occur to you that I might be the bride? Did you believe that I would ever get married one day?"

"It's an absolute bombshell to me," Xiao said, with a cynical smile.

Feng didn't feel there was anything wrong, but Xiao was very embarrassed. "You're a bride now," he whispered. "Better get into the palanquin. See! Everyone is waiting for you."

With widened eyes, Feng said, "What's the big deal? They can wait a little while!"

She hitched up her skirt and made a full turn. "Look! I'm dressed up for the wedding. Do I look pretty?"

"Pretty! Pretty! Very pretty!" Xiao said. "Such a pretty bride is a rare sight."

"You know what?" Feng poked at his nose with her index fin-ger. "You're not lucky enough to have a bride like me!"

Xiao touched his nose. "I'm afraid I'd be overwhelmed by such good luck."

Feng gave him a glare and then beamed again. "Guess who I'm going to marry?" she asked, cheerfully, winking at him.

Before Xiao could reply, the bridegroom had rushed over.

Xiao finally saw the bridegroom's square face and square mouth clearly. Though the groom looked anxious, he still walked steadily. Even the gold flowers on his hat barely shook. He looked like a freshly-made pancake.

Xiao saluted to him with fists. "Congratulations, Brother Yang!"

Yang Kaitai was taken by surprise. After a moment's confusion, he returned Xiao's salute, trying hard to smile. "Thank you. Thank you. Our wedding preparation is a little hasty this time, so we didn't have time to send invitations to many friends and relatives. Next time—"

"Next time?" Feng stamped on his foot and chided, "How could you say something like that! Next time? You're such a silly goose."

Realizing his mistake, Yang nervously wiped his brow. The more nervous he became, the harder it was for him to speak. He tugged at Feng's sleeve and stuttered, "At a m-moment like this ... h-how could you come out of the s-palanquin?"

Feng glared at him. "Why can't I? I can't even greet an old friend?"

"But ... but you are a b-bride now—"

"So what? Isn't a bride human?"

Yang's face grew red. "You—" He turned to the spectators. "Please be my judge, everyone! Have you ever seen a bride acting like this?"

"I have always been like this," Feng snapped. "If you don't like my style, you can get a new bride."

Yang stamped his feet with rage and huffed, "Unreasonable! Unreasonable! You're absolutely *unreasonable*!"

"Well ... well," Feng cried out loudly, "Now you're saying that I'm unreasonable. Why did you never say so before?"

Yang wiped his brow. "Be ... b-before...."

"I wasn't married to you before, so whatever I said was reasonable. Even my farts smelled wonderful. But now I've gotten into the bridal palanquin and become a Yang, you think you can start ordering me around, is that what you mean?"

Yang softened again. "That's not what I mean," he sighed. "It's... it's just that...."

"It's just what?"

Yang stole a glance behind him, seeing over thirty pairs of eyes goggling at him. His blushing face was on the verge of turning black. "It's just that people will laugh at the way you act," he whispered.

The more he tried to keep his voice low, the louder Feng barked. "So let them laugh! What's the big deal? I'm not afraid of being laughed at!"

Yang's face changed color. He was a breathing human being, not a lifeless clay statue. He couldn't help but yell, "B-but the way you act, h-how am I supposed to keep my d-dignity?"

"You think I have brought shame upon your family?" Feng questioned, angrily.

To her surprise, Yang kept his mouth shut, acknowledging the truth of her words with silence.

Feng's smile was cold. "If you think I'm not worthy of being your bride, then I'm not going to marry you."

She pulled off her bridal headgear, hurling it onto the ground. "Don't forget this! Although I stepped into the palanquin, I haven't passed through the gate of your house. It's not up to you whether I will marry into the Yang family. It depends on whether I feel like it or not."

The bearers, the attendants, the oboe players, and the gong beaters all wore the same openmouthed look. Their eyes had almost bolted from their sockets.

Some of them had been working as palanquin bearers for several decades and had escorted countless brides to their future homes, yet none of them had ever seen or heard of anything like this.

Yang was crazy with panic. "You ... you ... you...." he stammered.

He always stuttered when he got nervous. At a moment like this, he found it even more difficult to articulate his thoughts.

Xiao thought about stepping in, but then he thought better of it. He knew Feng's temper very well. When her rage detonated, no one could pacify her.

Feng took off her wedding robe and threw it at Yang's face. Then she turned and grabbed Xiao's hand. "Let's go!" she said. "I'm not going to become a daughter-in-law of the Yangs. Let's see whether I will be crushed without him!"

"You can't leave!" The three words jumped out of Yang's mouth. He ran over to grab Feng's hand.

"Who says I can't leave?" Feng slapped his hands away and yelled, "If I feel like it, no one can stop me!"

Pointing at Yang's nose, and with glaring eyes, she shouted, "Listen! Stay away from me from now on, or else you'll be asking for even more humiliation!"

Yang stood as stiffly as a wooden dummy, with sweat trickling down his face.

Xiao felt sorry for Yang. He was considering whether to say something to ease the tension when Feng pulled him hard and strode away.

He couldn't shake off her hand or jerk his hand out of her grasp, neither could he get mad at her, so he could only let her drag him along. He pleaded with a sour face, "Please! Let go of me. I can walk by myself!"

"I just love to pull you. So what? I'm not afraid. What are you afraid of?"

Not knowing what to do with Feng, Xiao could only mutter, "But ... but I have a ... a friend with me."

Only then did Feng remember that she had indeed seen someone standing beside Xiao. She turned her head and said, "Young lady! Why don't you come with us? Mr. Yang is rich and powerful, but we don't have to stay here and put up with his snobbery."

Shen hesitated for a moment before finally walking after them.

She didn't really want to go with them, but she couldn't stay. She couldn't bear to see how pitiful Yang looked.

Her own expression wasn't any more pleasant than Yang's.

After talking to Shen, Feng gave Yang another cold stare and yelled, "Listen, Iron Rooster! If you dare latch onto me again, as you did before, I swear I'll pluck every feather on you!"

"Don't worry, witch!" Yang yelled back. "Even if all other women in the world were dead, I'll never look for you again!"

Finally, Yang was infuriated.

Feng was taken aback. After a pause, she said icily, "Good! Don't forget what you just said."

Now Feng's face had darkened as well.

They walked on and on. For a long time, Feng didn't say anything, but she kept looking back.

"You can stop looking," Xiao said. "He's not coming."

"You think I was looking for him?" Feng said crossly, her face reddening.

"Weren't you?"

"Of course not!" she protested. "I ... I was merely looking at this young lady."

After saying that, she turned to take a serious look at Shen.

Though Shen hung her head low, anyone could tell that she was in a bad mood as well.

Feng loosened her hand, which had been dragging Xiao. "What is your honorable surname, miss?" she asked warmly.

"Shen."

Though Shen finally spoke, her voice seemed to have come from her nose. It was barely audible.

Feng smiled. "This young lady must have been surprised to see me acting like that."

"What would really be surprising is if she *hadn't* been surprised," Xiao said dryly.

"Please don't be upset, young lady. Xiao is my old friend and my little brother, so every time I see him, I like to tease him."

Her explanation was worse than no explanation at all.

Xiao could do nothing but smile his wry smile.

Feng's words were meant to lighten up the mood a little, but Shen's face didn't show the slightest humor.

Feng studied Shen intensely, with her eyes wider than those of a letch who sees a beautiful woman. She pulled Xiao over and whispered, "Is this young lady your ... your special someone?"

Xiao shook his head with an uncomfortable smile.

"You don't have to deny it," Feng giggled, rolling her eyes. "There's nothing embarrassing about it. If she isn't, why is she so jealous of me?"

Her lips almost touched Xiao's ear, as if she were showing off in front of Shen. Nine out of ten women have this terrible habit of showing off their men in front of other women.

Shen lowered her eyes, pretending not to see anything.

The volume of Feng's voice had never been low, and now she raised it even higher. "I wonder which family this young lady is from. If you really like her, beg me. As your big sister, I can serve as your matchmaker."

Xiao's heart quivered.

He was afraid to look at Shen, but he couldn't help it.

Shen happened to lift her face, but she looked away at once, when she met his pain-filled eyes. "Why don't you explain it to your big sister?" she said coldly.

"Explain what?" Feng's face turned to Xiao.

Shen looked calm. "We're just ordinary friends. Besides, I'm ... someone else's wife."

Feng was dumbstruck.

Shen went on, her voice drained of feeling. "From what I see, you and your big sister look like you're made for each other. My husband and I can serve as matchmakers, if you like. No matter who her parents are, I believe they will give serious consideration to our proposal."

She spoke calmly and politely.

However, each word ripped Xiao's heart like a knife.

He appeared numbed by heartache. Beads of sweat trickled down his taut face.

Feng found no voice with which to speak.

She couldn't think of any other time in her life that had been more embarrassing.

"My husband is Lian Chengbi," Shen said to Feng. "I believe you have heard of him."

Feng held her breath, unable to believe that Lian's wife had been walking alone with Xiao.

Shen seemed to have become even calmer now. "As long as you agree, my husband and I will—"

"Stop it!" Xiao shouted.

He ran over and grabbed Shen's hand.

Shen eyed him, as if she had never seen him before.

In an even colder voice she said, "Could you please let go of my hand?"

Xiao's voice cracked. "You—you can't do this to me!"

Shen gave an indifferent laugh. "Who are you to me? What right do you have to hold my hand?"

As if jerking from the lash of a whip on his back, Xiao loosened his hands and involuntarily backed away. His once sharp bright eyes became unspeakably blank and empty.

Feng's heart was aching, too.

She had never seen Xiao so distraught. Only then did she realize how deeply Xiao loved Shen and how much he was being tormented. Feng wished she could swallow the words she had just said, even if each word were a stone.

Only when he had backed away to a tree beside the road did Xiao start to make sounds. In an empty voice, he kept repeating the same words: "Who *am* I? What *right* do I have?"

Averting her gaze, Shen said, "It's true that you saved me a few times. I'm grateful to you. But I have repaid you, to a certain extent. We owe each other nothing ... now."

"Yes. We owe each other ... nothing," Xiao repeated blankly, with a vacant expression on his face.

"You haven't completely recovered from your injuries. I was supposed to accompany you for some distance along the road. Now that you have someone else to take care of you, it saves me the trouble."

At this point, her voice trembled slightly and she paused....

When she had regained her composure, she continued, "Remember that I'm a married woman. I have to be particularly cautious in whatever I do. If there is any gossip floating around, it won't do either of us any good."

"Yes ... I understand," Xiao muttered.

"It's good that you understand. We can still be friends...."

She trailed off and suddenly turned around.

"Miss Shen!" Feng called out.

Shen's shoulders seemed to shake. "I am ... Mrs. Lian ... now," she said after a long pause.

"Are you going to see Mr. Lian, Mrs. Lian?" Feng said with an unnatural smile.

"Aren't I supposed to see him?"

"But you may not know where to find Mr. Lian. You can walk with us for a while, to avoid any dangers, if you'd like to."

"I don't need you to worry about me. Even if I needed someone to escort me, I wouldn't ask either of you."

Then she added, "Mr. Yang Kaitai is a gentleman and an old friend of my husband. It's far more appropriate to ask him for assistance. No one will gossip about him and me."

Feng could neither smile nor speak. She seldom found it difficult to speak. She was usually the one who left others tongue-tied. Now, however, she couldn't even show the slightest anger in front of Shen.

Feng hadn't expected a woman who looked so quiet and gentle to be so uncompromising.

"In the future," said Shen, "my husband and I may have the chance to invite you to Flawless Manor for a visit. But ... I think such occasions will be rare."

She walked away with firm steps, without looking back even once.

It looked like she would never turn back!

Chapter 24

An Affair to Remember

THE WIND WAS cold. Heart-chillingly cold.

In the wind, brown and withered leaves were falling off the trees.

Xiao stood under the tree, making no sound, no facial expression, no motion.

After what seemed like an eternity, Feng released a deep sigh. "It's all my fault. Why am I always saying the wrong words and doing the wrong things?"

Xiao didn't seem to hear her, but after another long silence, he suddenly said, "This has nothing to do with you."

"But—"

"Those who have to leave will leave sooner or later. Perhaps it's better this way."

Feng reflected for a moment before saying, "You mean, pain is better cut short than drawn out?"

"Um-hmm."

"That is a great saying, and whoever coined it must have been a genius, but human emotions are just not that simple."

She gave a wan smile and continued, "Some problems aren't solved so easily."

Xiao closed his eyes and lowered his head. "What can I do if I can't solve this problem?"

A few moments later, Feng said at last, "Perhaps you're right. Even if you don't know how, you have to solve it. No one really knows how to deal with this."

After another silence, Xiao lifted his head. "Well, the problem has gone away. Why are we still worrying about it?"

Smiling, he grabbed Feng's hand and said, "Let's go. Today I will make an exception and let you treat me. Let's go have a drink."

As he smiled, Feng smiled, too.

But both their smiles carried an indescribable poignancy and an unspeakable loneliness.

This moment might have become an affair to remember,
Only, at the time, you were already lost and bewildered.

Shen had read these two lines of a poem long ago, but she had never understood them.

Now she realized that the sorrow they described could be so dense that it would never dissolve.

Tears trailed down her cheeks.

Xiao Shiyi Lang, Xiao Shiyi Lang, I didn't want to do this to you, but you're young and you have your whole life ahead of you. I don't want to drag you down.

Now you may be sad and even angry, but you will forget me, in time.

Forget ... forget ... forget ... Was it really so easy to forget? So simple?

Her heart twisting in pain, she knew she would never forget Xiao.

Deep in her heart, she hoped he would never forget her either. She'd rather die and be chopped up and burned, turned to ashes, than to be forgotten.

There was a patch of woods near the road.

All at once, she dashed into the woods, threw herself to the ground under a tree and started to cry.

She wished she could cry until she passed out, or better yet, she wished she could cry herself to death.

She could no longer endure such excruciating heartache.

She had thought she was doing the right thing, and that she could bear it, but she hadn't expected the pain to be so violent, so profound.

After who knows how long, she suddenly felt a gentle and assuring hand stroking her hair.

Xiao Shiyi Lang? Has Xiao Shiyi Lang come for me again?

If Xiao had indeed come for her, she would run into his arms and never part with him again. Even if she had to give up everything and run away with him to the end of the world, she wouldn't hesitate.

She turned around.

Her heart sank.

It was gloomy in the woods. The dim moonlight shone through the branches, falling on a face—a handsome, refined, and gentle face.

It was Lian Chengbi.

He looked distressed, but his eyes were still as warm and endearing as before.

He gazed at Shen with immense affection.

Shen felt a lump in her throat and in her heart.

At last Lian said, "Everyone is waiting. Let's go back."

His voice was still so calm, as if he had forgotten everything. As if none of this had ever happened.

But how could she forget? Every scene and every moment of joy or sorrow had been branded into her mind, injected into the marrow of her bones.

She could never forget any of this.

The spring silkworm's thread ends only with death;
The candle's tears will not dry until it turns to ashes.

She had a far-off gaze in her eyes, her mind drifting back to the remote past.

Long, long ago, in the dusk of a similar autumn day, they had strolled in a patch of withered woods. They had watched the setting sun through bare branches, lamenting over how fleeting life is. When darkness closed in on them, she was still lost in thought, oblivious to time.

At the time, Lian had whispered to her, "Everyone is waiting. Let's go back."

The same words, said in almost the same way.

On that day, she had gone home with him without hesitation.

But now, everything had changed, and she had changed as well. No one could bring back times gone by.

With a rueful sigh, she said, "Go back? Go back where?"

"Home. Let's go home."

"Home? Do I still have a home?"

"You have always had a home."

"But things are different now."

"Nothing is different. It's all over. Once you return, everything will be the same."

After a long interval of silence, a sad smile formed around the corner of Shen's mouth. "I finally understand."

"What do you finally understand?"

"What you want is not me, but my return."

"How could you say—"

"The reputation of the Lians is paramount and mustn't be tarnished. A daughter of the Lian family should never do anything disgraceful."

Lian didn't speak.

"So I must go back," she went on. "As long as I go back, everything can be forgiven, but—"

Her voice suddenly filled with agitation. "Has it ever occurred to you that I'm a person, not an accessory in your house?"

"Do you ... do you think I did something wrong?" Lian sighed gravely.

Tears streamed down her face again. "No, you didn't do anything wrong. I'm the one at fault. I let you down."

"Everyone makes mistakes. I have forgotten all of that."

Shen shook her head slowly. "Maybe you can forget them, but I can't."

"Why?"

A long pause followed. Then, with a sudden determination, she said, "Because my heart has changed."

Her words drained the energy from his body. Lian could barely stand.

Shen bit her lip and continued, "I know the truth hurts sometimes, but it's always better than a lie."

Lian clenched his fists. "Do ... do you really ... love him?"

Shen bit her lip so hard that blood trickled from it. She nodded slowly.

On the spur of the moment Lian reached out to grip her shoulders. "Tell me. What does he have that I don't?"

His voice cracked; his body quivered with agitation.

He had always thought he could stay calm in any situation. He knew staying calm was the best way to deal with problems.

Now he realized he had been wrong.

Like everyone else, he was a breathing human being, and his blood was warm.

Shen felt as if her shoulders were being crushed, but she endured the pain, refusing to let tears flow.

"He may be inferior to you in every way," she said, her jaw clenched, "but he would give up everything for me, and even *die* for me. Would ... would you do that?'

Lian, stunned again, loosened his hands slowly, starting to back away, step by step.

Averting her eyes, Shen said, "You once said that when a woman's heart has changed, there is no way to make her turn back. Any man who tries to bring her back will only suffer more."

Lian's bright eyes became blank and empty. In a daze, he stared at her, muttering, "Good! Good for you . . .!"

He repeated the same words again and again until he suddenly ran over and slapped her hard across the face.

Shen remained motionless, as if she had become a block of stone. "You can beat me or even kill me, and I won't blame you," she said, staring straight ahead. "But you can never make me come back to you."

Lian turned and stormed away.

Only then did Shen turn her eyes to him.

She watched his figure disappear in the distance, tears trickling down her face like beads.

I'm sorry. I'm so sorry, but I have to do this. I'm not the cold-hearted woman you think I am, but I can't drag you down.

I can only repay you—both of you—with my death.

She wished she could rip her heart and body into halves.

But she couldn't.

She had no choice other than death.

Night came.

She appeared to have run out of tears.

There was only one road for her to take now—the road to Doll Manor.

She could picture that hideous grinning face saying, "I knew you'd come back. You had no choice."

Xiao didn't drink very quickly.

He felt a lump in his throat. Even wine couldn't go down smoothly.

Feng was in a gloomy mood as well. It was even more difficult for her to talk about the thoughts in her mind.

What was worse, they were drinking at a very small wine stall. The wine sold here was sour, bitter, and spicy.

She could hardly swallow it.

Feng wasn't a stingy person, but what bride carries money with her? And she couldn't find a place in this small town to pawn her jewelry.

Xiao didn't fare any better. He was perpetually penniless.

Feng broke into a faint smile and said, "It seems that we always drink at wine stalls."

"I don't mind drinking at wine stalls," Xiao said distractedly.

As he sat drinking, his thoughts drifted far away.

While Shen and he had been together, though they were always getting into trouble and suffering all kinds of hardships, they still had their sweet moments of joy.

Now, however, all of the joy and sweetness had transformed into painful bitterness, and the thought of those wonderful moments only served to make his heart ache more acutely.

Feng drank another cup of wine and griped, "I heard no matter how bad the wine is, as long as you drink it faster, you'll eventually get used to it. But this wine seems to be an exception."

"As far as I'm concerned," Xiao said, "any wine that can get you drunk is good wine,"

He was trying to get drunk fast, but, somehow, he remained clear and sober.

Pain is fairly effective at keeping one sober. Even if one has become stone cold drunk, the ache in one's heart remains.

Feng stared at Xiao, at the end of her wits.

She had tried many ways to divert his attention, but all to no avail.

Apparently, no matter what she said, his mind was still fixed on that particular someone.

"I think she must have her reasons for treating you like this," said Feng with a sigh. "There must be some special reason. She doesn't look like a cold-hearted woman."

"Women's hearts are never cold," Xiao said. "They just change once in a while."

His voice sounded distant, as if these words didn't come from his mouth.

"I don't think she's that kind of woman," said Feng. "It's just that—"

"Who do you think is the finest martial artist alive?" Xiao interrupted and asked.

Feng was baffled by such an out-of-the-blue question, but she thought for a moment and replied, "As far as I know, Count Carefree."

"You know him, don't you?"

"Um-hmm."

"What's he like?"

"I've never seen him."

"Didn't he give you two fine swords?" Xiao asked, with some surprise.

"Yes, but I've never seen his face."

Xiao smiled wryly. "You've gotten me confused here."

Feng smiled, too. "Every time I saw him, there was a curtain between us. One time, I couldn't keep from pulling open the curtain to look at his face."

"Did you see him?"

"I thought I was fast," Feng sighed, "but when I ran through the curtain, he had already disappeared."

"Turns out that he isn't really your friend," Xiao sniffed. "He doesn't even want to see you."

"It's because he's my friend that he doesn't want to see me."

"What does that mean?"

"There are only two types of people in the world who will get to see his face."

"Two?"

"The first is someone he wants to kill. They don't live long."

Xiao was silent for a while before asking, "What's the other type?"

"Women—women he has his eyes on. No woman he's interested in can escape from his clutches. Eventually they all become part of his collection."

Xiao's countenance changed a little. Then he poured a cup of wine down his throat. "That means he doesn't have his eyes on you," he taunted.

Feng's face changed color as if her temper were about to explode. But she quickly changed her expression and said with a pleasant smile, "All right, I admit that he doesn't have his eyes on me. Today, whatever you say won't make me mad."

She went on. "There are many rumors about him circulating in the martial world. Some say that he's afraid to let people see him, because he's blind and has an ugly pockmarked face. Some say that, like the Great King of Chu, he's a bulky man who has a large waist and a full beard."

"No one has ever said that he is good-looking?"

"If he is good-looking, why wouldn't he let people see him?"

"Maybe it's because he's very short and he doesn't want others to look down upon him."

Her eyes growing wider, Feng stared at Xiao. "Have you seen him?"

Xiao didn't answer. Instead, he asked, "Are you planning to travel north of the Great Wall again?"

"Um-hmm."

"Did you see him last time when you were up north?"

"No, I heard that he has come south."

"Is the strength of his kung fu really unfathomable?"

"Even if everything else is discounted, his Lightness Kung Fu alone is peerless."

Xiao suddenly smiled. "Do you think I'm not his match?"

Feng stared at him for a moment, and then said, "It's hard to say."

"Why?"

"Your kung fu may not be as good as his, but I have always felt that you have a spirit of stubborn resilience that few can match or imitate."

She smiled faintly at Xiao. "The key may be that you have no fear of death. When people are prepared to risk life and limb, their opponents are intimidated, at least to a certain extent."

Xiao gazed into the distance and muttered, "You're wrong. I have never really risked life and limb before."

"I'm not saying you risk your life. I'm just saying that there is a burst of energy within you at crucial moments."

"You're wrong again." Xiao smiled. "When the right time comes, I will risk everything."

His face was smiling, but his eyes were not.

Feng's face stiffened. "Why are you asking me all this?"

"Nothing, just asking."

He appeared calm, but his eyes and brows had hardened.

This didn't escape Feng's attention.

"Are you planning to challenge him?"

Looking Xiao straight in the eye, she said, "Because you want to die!"

She pressed on. "You think only death can solve your problem, don't you?"

Every muscle in Xiao's face seemed to tighten suddenly.

Unable to control himself anymore, he started to his feet and said, "I have drunk enough. Thank you."

Feng grabbed his hand and cried out, "You can't go!"

"When I want to leave, no one can make me stay," Xiao said coldly.

Just then, they heard someone say, "I will make you stay."

The voice was graceful and steady, but unspeakably cold.

From the darkness emerged a person with bright eyes and a pale face. His walk was steady and his manners seemed elegant. He looked like a young scholar in every sense, except that a sword hung from his waist.

Its scabbard was sable black, shining chillingly under the lamp.

"Mr. Lian?" said Feng in surprise.

"Yes," Lian said. "Perhaps I'm the only person in the world who can make Xiao Shiyi Lang stay."

Xiao's features darkened. "You really want me to stay?"

Lian gave a wan smile. "I'm in a bad mood. I would like you to stay and have a drink with me."

His pupils seemed to contract before focusing on Xiao's face. "I fell into such an ugly mood, because of you. If I insist that you stay and drink with me, you shouldn't refuse ... should you?"

Xiao was staring at him, too. A long silence passed. At length Xiao sat down.

Feng took a breath and said warmly, "Please have a seat, Mr. Lian."

The light seemed to dim.

Under the lamp, Lian's face looked dead.

Lian scrutinized Xiao's eyes, as if trying to fathom what he was thinking.

But Xiao's blank eyes gave nothing away.

The wine vendor had been watching them, paying special attention to Feng. He had been selling wine all his life, but he had never met a female customer like her.

He wasn't a gentleman. In fact, he hoped the three customers would all get drunk soon, so that he'd have the opportunity to grope Feng's hands. If he could grope other parts of her, it would be even better.

But now—

He noticed that since the refined young man had joined them, a disquieting tension hung between the two men.

He didn't realize that this tension was what people called "the air of killing." All he knew was that when he walked near them, sweat materialized on his palms and his heartbeat almost stopped.

As she poured wine for them, Feng said with a smile, "The wine isn't any good. I hope Mr. Lian won't find it too hard to swallow."

Lian took up his cup and said, "Any wine that can get you drunk is good wine. Cheers!"

These were the exact words Xiao had used.

If Shen were here now, she'd be surprised to hear Lian and Xiao saying the same words as well, because they were very different people.

Perhaps they were the same type at heart, but their environments had shaped them into completely different personalities.

Or, it might be because they were thinking about the same person with the same emotions.

Feng's head was full of many different thoughts. Suddenly the image of Yang's face popped into her mind.

She had never felt sorry about Yang before. She had never loved him. If he insisted on wasting his affection on her, he deserved to suffer. It was not her fault.

Now, however, she understood his sorrow. She realized how miserable it was for him to have his love rejected and despised.

There was a sour and bitter feeling in her stomach. She raised her cup slowly and drained it.

Lian's cup was filled again. He made another toast to Xiao. "I drink to you."

He seemed to be trying to make himself drunk so that he could relieve himself of his unbearable helplessness and heartache. Numbing himself with alcohol seemed the only viable solution.

Why was he doing this?

Feng tried to explain. "Mr. Lian, perhaps you're not aware of it yet. She—"

As Feng was thinking about how to enlighten him, Lian interrupted her, "I know everything."

"You do? You know she's looking for you?"

Lian smiled bitterly. "She didn't have to look for me. I had been following her the whole time."

"You've seen her?"

Lian peered into the distant darkness. "Yes, I have."

"Where is she now?"

"She left. Those who have to leave will leave, sooner or later."

Again, the same words Xiao had said.

Feng was becoming more and more puzzled. Did she leave him? she mused. She said she was going back. Why did she leave him? If she had already decided to leave him, then why did she break Xiao's heart?

Though Feng was a woman, she couldn't understand all women's hearts.

Sometimes, she couldn't understand her own.

But Xiao suddenly understood. His whole body went cold, from his heart and his stomach, to his feet.

Yet, his eyes started to burn like fire.

He knew Shen's heart had been more torn and aching harder than his. She couldn't evade the problem, nor could she solve it.

She could only choose the only way out ... death.

But she wouldn't die for nothing. She wasn't an ordinary woman; her death must have a value. Before dying, she would use blood to cleanse herself of all the disgrace and injustice that had been imposed on her.

Xiao clenched his fists; he finally understood her intention. He hated himself for not having figured this out earlier and for not stopping her in time.

He wanted nothing more than to go look for her right away and trade his life for hers.

But not now. He'd have to do this by himself.

He didn't want to owe anyone else anything.

Lian turned his eyes back from the distance and stared at Xiao. "I thought you were a pathetic man, but now I realize you're much luckier than I am."

"Me ... lucky?" Xiao eyed him questioningly.

Lian smiled again. "Because I finally realize that I never completely won her heart."

His smile was bitter and slightly cynical. Was he cynical about life, about others, or about himself?

After a moment's silence, Xiao said solemnly, "All I know is that she has never been unfaithful to you."

Lian stared at him, then he suddenly threw back his head and laughed loudly. "What's faithful? What's unfaithful? Nothing in the world is absolute. Why do people have to search for a precise definition for everything?"

"You don't believe me?"

Lian stopped his laugh and stared at the wine in his cup. "Right now, I don't believe anyone. The only thing I believe is wine. Wine is more reliable than anything. At least it can make me drunk."

He drained his cup, then started to sing loudly, while tapping the table:

Feng Siniang!
Xiao Shiyi Lang!
I'm going to make a toast to you.

Don't stop your cups.
Today we're going to drink three hundred cups.
I wish I could be drunk eternally, never sobering up.
Saints and sages have always been lonely.
Only drinkers leave their names.

Even when people have difficulty drinking fast, they're able to immediately speed up, when challenged to a drinking contest.

Lian's head was resting on the table, but his hand was still holding his cup. "Drink more! Drink more!" he mumbled. "Are you afraid to drink more?"

Feng was a little tipsy herself. "All right," she called out loudly. "I'll drink. No matter how much you drink today, I'll drink as much as you."

The more intoxicated she became, the more sorry she felt for Lian.

It's always heartrending to see a once calm and strong man suddenly become depressed and disconsolate. The more drastic the change, the stronger the contrast.

Feng realized that, like everyone else, Lian was a person with emotions.

Xiao appeared drunk as well.

"Xiao Shiyi Lang," Lian grumbled. "I should kill you."

He suddenly stood up, drew his sword, and glared at Xiao.

But he couldn't even stand steadily. When he tried to wield his sword, he fell down.

Feng rushed over to help him up, but she fell down, too. "He's my friend," she yelled. "You can't kill him!"

"I should kill him, but he's drunk." Lian gave a mirthless laugh. "No, I still can't do it—"

Feng and Lian spoke in turns, appearing very serious about their conversation. In reality, only they understood their words.

Eventually both fell silent.

After a while Xiao rose to his feet. Under the dim light, he stared down at Lian thoughtfully.

The expression on Lian's face made him look like an injured wild animal that was covered with wounds and bruises and that knew he was dying.

Though still drunk, Lian suddenly yelled, "You owe me! You owe me...."

Xiao clenched his teeth and muttered, "Don't worry. I'll bring her back. Please treat her well. My only wish is that the two of you will live more happily than before."

Chapter 25

Splendid Sunset

XIAO ENTERED DOLL Manor again.

The first thing he saw was Little Mister's naïve, sweet, and tender smile.

Little Mister was reclining on a high branch of a pine tree, as though waiting for him. "I knew you'd come back, too. No one who comes here can bear to leave."

Xiao appeared calm, but his face was ghostly pale. "Where is she?" he demanded.

She blinked. "You mean *Lian* Shen Bijun?"

She deliberately put the stress on "Lian."

"Yes," Xiao replied, still expressionless.

"She came back before you did. I'm afraid she has retired."

Xiao glowered so fiercely at her, with his eyes so wide and hard, it seemed as if the corners of his eyelids would rip.

Little Mister was afraid to look into his eyes again. "Would you like me to take you to see her?" she asked.

"Yes."

Little Mister giggled. "I can help you, but how are you going to thank me?"

"You name it."

Little Mister rolled her eyes. "If you kneel down and kowtow to me, I'll take you to see her."

Without saying anything, Xiao dropped to his knees and kowtowed to her. There was no look of hurt or bitterness in his eyes.

Other than Shen, nothing else mattered to him at the moment.

The two old men were still playing chess in the octagonal pavil-ion.

Neither of them turned to look. It seemed that nothing in the world concerned them anymore.

Little Mister leaped off the tree and stroked Xiao's hair. "Good boy!" she cackled. "Now come with me."

It was quiet in the room.

Count Carefree was reclining on a big, comfortable bed, staring at Shen with an eerie smile in his eyes.

Seated in a chair across from him, Shen was so nervous that she felt like throwing up.

Being stared at in this way, she felt as if she were completely naked. She wished she could rip out his eyes, crush them between her teeth, and swallow them whole.

After who knows how long, Count Carefree asked brusquely, "Have you made up your mind yet?"

She took a long breath, bit her lip, and shook her head.

"You should make up your mind more quickly. You know you must do it . Only if you listen to me will you get your chance. Otherwise, you've returned for nothing."

Shen was trembling.

"I know you want to kill me, but if you refuse to get close to me, you won't have an opportunity. You know very well that I never let clothed women near me."

"But you already know I want to kill you. I have no chance," Shen said hatefully. Her voice quivered.

The smile on his face grew even more sinister. With narrowed eyes, he said, "Don't forget that I'm a man. Men often lower their guard, when their desire is aroused. When men lower their guard, women can seize this opportunity...."

His eyes narrowed to mere slits. "Now, the problem is whether you are good enough to arouse my desire."

Her body shook more violently than ever. "You—you're not human!"

"When did I ever say I was human?" Count Carefree laughed. "Killing humans is easy. Killing me will exact a high price."

A glare of hatred flashed from her eyes. After a very long time, she suddenly clenched her teeth, stood up, and started to unfasten the front of her clothing.

She wasn't moving very fast, because her body, especially her hands, was still trembling.

When the upper part of her clothing was removed, half of her flawless body was revealed to Count Carefree.

With a glint of satisfaction in his eyes, he said, "Good! You haven't disappointed me. Even if I am killed by a beauty like you, it will be worth it."

Shen bit her lip so hard that blood trickled from it again. Against the red blood, her skin appeared even more radiant.

Her chest appeared fairer and more translucent, and soon her legs—

All at once, the door burst open.

At the door stood ... *Xiao Shiyi Lang*!

Xiao's heart exploded from his anguish.

Shen appeared completely stiff and numb. Standing stock-still, she gazed at him blankly. All of a sudden, she collapsed onto the floor.

Count Carefree didn't look surprised. He let out a sigh and muttered, "Haven't you heard that those who spoil the romance of others take thirty years off their lives?"

Xiao clenched his fists. "If I must die now, I'll take you with me."

"Oh? Are you challenging me to a duel?"

"Yes."

Count Carefree smiled. "There are many ways to die. The one you just chose is not very smart."

"After you!" said Xiao.

Count Carefree stared at him for a moment, before smiling again. "No one has ever dared to challenge me. You certainly are an exception. So I will make an exception for you as well. I'm always especially tolerant of a man who is about to die."

He had been reclining, but now he flew out of the room like a cloud. His Lightness Kung Fu was frighteningly superb.

Yet, Xiao took no notice. He slowly walked toward Shen. Bending over, he gazed at her with a look of pain in his eyes.

His heart was crying out: "Why did you do this? Why did you debase yourself like this?"

When he opened his mouth, however, his voice was steady. "It's time for you to go home, Shen. Someone is waiting for you."

Tears streamed like a fountain from the corners of her closed eyes.

"You can't think only of yourself," Xiao went on. "Sometimes you must think about the suffering of others as well. Lian's heartache may be more profound than anyone else's."

"I know he's suffering," Shen cried aloud, "but it's only because his pride is hurt, not because of me."

"That's what you think."

"What about you? You—"

"Whatever happens to me has nothing to do with you. I have never had anything to do with you."

Shen's eyes flew open. She stared at him through her tears.

Xiao was trying with all his might to keep his emotions in check, but when her eyes stared into his, he felt as if he were falling apart and his heart were going to be crushed—

He wanted to take her into his arms, and she wanted to bury herself in his embrace.

For two people so deeply in love, they have more than enough, as long as they can live and stay together. Nothing else matters. Even if they have to die together, they are delighted, because it's at least more bearable than the pain of separation.

Right then, however, Feng Siniang barged into the room.

"I knew you'd be here!" Feng stormed, with vehement agitation. "Did you really think I was drunk?"

Xiao's face turned hard as he asked, "How did you know I was here?"

Then he realized that he didn't have to ask, for he spotted Little Mister hiding behind the door chuckling.

"Where is Lian?" he asked Feng.

"He's in no danger, but you ... why did you do this?"

Xiao didn't respond to her question. After a long pause, he said, "It's just as well that you came. Since you are here, take her away with you."

"No, I'm staying with you," said Feng, her eyes red.

"I have always thought you understood me, but you disappoint me."

"I certainly understand you."

"If you really understand me, then take her back with you."

He didn't say another word.

Staring at him for a long while, Feng sighed ruefully, "Why don't you ever leave anyone a second option?"

There was a distant look in Xiao's eyes. "Because," he said, "I have only one option left myself."

Death road!

When someone has absolutely no way out, they can only choose the death road. *Death road* is a Chinese expression, which means "dead end" or "a road of no return." It was true that Xiao was stuck at a dead end, and it was also true that he had gone on a road of no return.

Feng helped Shen put her clothes back on. Shen tried to rise and follow after Xiao, but Feng put her arms around Shen's waist, holding her back.

"Once he decides to do something, no one can stop him," Feng said. "Otherwise, he might do something even more reckless."

Shen understood what Feng meant.

She cried so hard that her heart almost stopped beating.

Suddenly, they heard someone speak with a laugh like the tinkle of a bell, "What a sad girl! She's breaking even my heart. Actually, you don't have to feel miserable for Xiao. You will certainly die before he does."

Feng glared at her. "Don't you dare touch her!"

"Why not?" Little Mister smiled disarmingly.

Feng smiled, too. "You're such a sweet little witch, even I am charmed. Unfortunately, I'm an old witch. In front of this face, those petty tricks of yours are merely childish pranks."

"Oh? Really?" Little Mister's eyes grew wider, as if she were surprised.

"Try me!"

"Now? I'd love to. Unfortunately, I already have."

"You have?" Feng responded, in great alarm.

"I tried, and it's working pretty well."

Feng's face broke into another smile. "Your bluff is quite convincing, but it won't work on this face."

"It might not work on your face, because you're too thick-skinned, but it worked on your hand, because the skin of your hands is more delicate than a little girl's."

Feng couldn't help but raise her own hands and take a close look at them.

"When I led you in by the hand, you weren't wary of me at all. All your thoughts were fixed on Xiao Shiyi Lang," said Little Mister with a bewitching smile. "I didn't know so many women had fallen for him. Dying for your beloved is noble. Your death won't be for nothing."

"Little witch. You do know a lot," said Feng, also with a charming smile.

She attacked before finishing her words.

The people in the martial world usually considered Feng more dangerous than Xiao, because she was much more vicious and unpredictable. Her attack always came at a moment when she smiled the most delightfully.

Nevertheless, Little Mister had foreseen this, because her style of attack was similar.

This would have been an exciting duel. Unfortunately, with her hand stung by Little Mister's poison needle, Feng became paralyzed.

The duel ended before it had even started.

Eyeing Feng, who couldn't move a muscle, Little Mister said condescendingly, "I won't kill you. You're too old to be worth my trouble."

She turned her eyes to Shen. "But you're different. You're much more attractive than I am. How can I leave you alive?"

Her heart frozen in sorrow, Shen didn't care about her own life.

"Xiao is on the road of no return," Little Mister said. "He can't come to your rescue. And you're afraid to fight me by yourself. Don't you care at all?"

Shen still didn't move, listen, or make any sound.

"Oh, I see." Little Mister winked. "You're waiting for someone else to save you. Are you waiting for that drunken pussycat? Would you like to see him now?"

She clapped her hands. Two giggling maids helped someone into the room. A strong odor of alcohol could be smelled from quite a distance.

Lian had been led to Doll Manor by Little Mister, too.

The sight of Lian shook Shen out of her trance. She had never seen Lian so miserably drunk. It made her even more heartsick and distraught.

Little Mister walked over and patted Lian on the shoulder. "I'm going to kill your wife now. I know you must feel sad. It's a shame that you can only stand by and watch. Perhaps you won't even see it clearly."

Then, without warning, Lian bent over and threw up. He vomited all over Little Mister.

The maids cried in disgust and backed away, covering their noses.

Little Mister frowned and sneered, "I know you want to die, but I—"

Suddenly, there was a flash of white.

A dagger was stabbed into her heart!

The sword had been amazingly fast.

Feng was awestruck.

Then she remembered that Dagger in the Sleeve was the secret move of the Lians. Neither she nor anyone else had ever seen it. Even Shen had never seen it before.

Those who had seen it were all in their graves now.

Lian had practiced this move millions of times. He could use this move even in his sleep.

He had never had the chance to use it ... until today.

Little Mister collapsed, staring at him as if she still didn't believe this was happening.

She had never imagined that she would die as easily as others.

Then a faint sweet smile suddenly formed around the corners of her mouth. She stared at Lian and said softly, "I think I should thank you. I didn't know dying was so easy. If I had known it, perhaps I would not have tried so hard to stay alive. You know what I mean?"

Gasping, she turned her eyes to Feng. "The antidote for your poisoned wound is in my bosom. If you want to live on, take it. But listen to my advice. Being alive isn't as comfortable as being dead. Just think about it. Which living person has no worries or frustrations...."

The road snaked ahead.

An old man in red and an old man in green stood there side by side, gazing toward the end of the road. Both with somber faces, they seemed unaware of the three people coming up behind them.

Lian was not completely sober yet.

Either he didn't want to sober up or he was afraid to, because, as soon as he sobered up, he would have to face reality.

Reality is always ruthless.

Shen trailed behind the other two, her face cast downward. She was afraid to lift her head, because, as soon as she raised her head, she would have to deal with the things she was afraid to face.

They were both evading truth ... but for how much longer?

Feng approached the two old men. After a long silence, she asked in a low voice, "Did they take this road?"

"Um-hmm," replied the man in red.

"Are you waiting for them to come back?"

"Um-hmm," replied the man in green.

Feng took a long breath. "Who do you think ... will come back?" She was afraid to ask, but couldn't help it.

After a moment of hesitation, the man in red said, "There's little chance he will be able to come back."

Feng's heart sank. She knew what he meant by "he."

"Perhaps neither of them will come back," said the man in green.

The man in red nodded slightly. "I hope so."

Feng suddenly cried out defiantly, "You think he won't be able to match Count Carefree, right? You're wrong. His martial arts may not be as good, but he has courage and a fierce spirit of resilience. Many people can beat a stronger opponent when they possess this kind of resilience."

The two old men simultaneously cast a glance at her, and then turned their heads back to continue gazing toward the end of the road, the expressions on their faces still solemn.

Feng wanted to say something more, but her throat felt choked.

Shen suddenly lifted her head and walked toward Lian. When she stood in front of Lian, she said to him, word by word, "I am going, too."

"You're going, too?" Lian repeated in bewilderment.

"Whether he is dead or alive, I'm going to be by his side," she said with a calm face.

"I understand," Lian said.

"But I still won't do anything unfaithful to you. I won't disappoint you."

Then she turned and ran toward the end of the road.

They knew she wouldn't come back either.

In the dusk, the sunset was splendid.

Almost everyone had left. There was no point in waiting.

This was a road to death.

No one who took this road would ever return.

Only Feng was left gazing toward the end of the road.

"Xiao Shiyi Lang will come back. He will," she told herself.

Lian had already left. He was completely sober at the time.

Feng hoped he'd pull himself together and face up to life. And she hoped Xiao would survive. She couldn't bear to see both of them ruined by love.

She had confidence in them.

But, did she have confidence in herself?

"I will never be tormented or heartbroken by love, because I have never loved anyone ... and no one has ever truly loved me."

Did she really believe that?

The setting sun was reflected in the tears glistening in her eyes.

" Xiao Shiyi Lang! Xiao Shiyi Lang ... please don't die! As long as you live, that's more than enough for me. Nothing else matters."

The setting sun grew even more gorgeous.

A wind sprang up. The disturbed crows took off.

Feng turned and saw ... Yang Kaitai.

Yang stood there silently, still so straight and so very steady.

It seemed as though he would never falter.

He gazed intently at Feng. "I decided to follow you here after all," he said. "Even if you beat me up, I will still follow you."

His words were plain and simple, neither suave nor romantic.

Yet, so much affection was hidden in them.

Feeling a heat within her, Feng ran into his arms. "I want you to follow me. I want you to follow me ... forever. I will never break your heart again."

Yang held her tightly. "Even if you break my heart, I will still follow you, because if I don't, I will only be more depressed and more heartbroken."

Feng murmured, "I know ... I know...."

She suddenly realized that it is better to be loved ... than to love.

But, if so ... why were her tears still falling?

THE END

 *More Titles from Homa & Sekey Books*

Flower Terror: Suffocating Stories of China by Pu Ning
ISBN 0-9665421-0-X, Fiction, Paperback, $13.95

"The stories in this work are well written." – Library Journal

Acclaimed Chinese writer eloquently describes the oppression of intellectuals in his country between 1950s and 1970s in these twelve autobiographical novellas and short stories. Many of the stories are so shocking and heart-wrenching that one cannot but feel suffocated.

The Peony Pavilion: A Novel by Xiaoping Yen, Ph.D.
ISBN 0-9665421-2-6, Fiction, Paperback, $16.95

"A window into the Chinese literary imagination." – Publishers Weekly

A sixteen-year-old girl visits a forbidden garden and falls in love with a young man she meets in a dream. She has an affair with her dream-lover and dies longing for him. After her death, her unflagging spirit continues to wait for her dream-lover. Does her lover really exist? Can a youthful love born of a garden dream ever blossom? The novel is based on a sixteenth-century Chinese opera written by Tang Xianzu, "the Shakespeare of China."

Butterfly Lovers: A Tale of the Chinese Romeo and Juliet
By Fan Dai, Ph.D., ISBN 0-9665421-4-2, Fiction, Paperback, $16.95

"An engaging, compelling, deeply moving, highly recommended and rewarding novel." – Midwest Books Review

A beautiful girl disguises herself as a man and lives under one roof with a young male scholar for three years without revealing her true identity. They become sworn brothers, soul mates and lovers. In a world in which marriage is determined by social status and arranged by parents, what is their inescapable fate?

 *More Titles from Homa & Sekey Books*

The Dream of the Red Chamber: An Allegory of Love
By Jeannie Jinsheng Yi, Ph.D., ISBN: 0-9665421-7-7, Hardcover
Asian Studies/Literary Criticism, $49.95

Although dreams have been studied in great depth about this most influential classic Chinese fiction, the study of all the dreams as a sequence and in relation to their structural functions in the allegory is undertaken here for the first time.

Always Bright: Paintings by American Chinese Artists 1970-1999
Edited by Xue Jian Xin et al.
ISBN 0-9665421-3-4, Art, Hardcover, $49.95

"An important, groundbreaking, seminal work." – Midwest Book Review

A selection of paintings by eighty acclaimed American Chinese artists in the late 20th century, *Always Bright* is the first of its kind in English publication. The album falls into three categories: oil painting, Chinese painting and other media painting. It also offers profiles of the artists and information on their professional accomplishment.

Always Bright, Vol. II: Paintings by Chinese American Artists
Edited by Eugene Wang, Ph.D., et al.
ISBN: 0-9665421-6-9, Art, Hardcover, $50.00

A sequel to the above, the book includes artworks of ninety-two artists in oil painting, Chinese painting, watercolor painting, and other media such as mixed media, acrylic, pastel, pen and pencil, etc. The book also provides information on the artists and their professional accomplishment. Artists included come from different backgrounds, use different media and belong to different schools. Some of them enjoy international fame while others are enterprising young men and women who are more impressionable to novelty and singularity.

 *More Titles from Homa & Sekey Books*

Ink Paintings by Gao Xingjian, the Nobel Prize Winner
ISBN: 1-931907-03-X, Hardcover, Art, $34.95

An extraordinary art book by the Nobel Prize Winner for Literature in 2000, this volume brings together over sixty ink paintings by Gao Xingjian that are characteristic of his philosophy and painting style. Gao believes that the world cannot be explained, and the images in his paintings reveal the black-and-white inner world that underlies the complexity of human existence. People admire his meditative images and evocative atmosphere by which Gao intends his viewers to visualize the human conditions in extremity.

Splendor of Tibet: The Potala Palace, Jewel of the Himalayas
By Phuntsok Namgyal
ISBN: 1-931907-02-1, Hardcover, Art/Architecture, $39.95

A magnificent and spectacular photographic book about the Potala Palace, the palace of the Dalai Lamas and the world's highest and largest castle palace. Over 150 rare and extraordinary color photographs of the Potala Palace are showcased in the book, including murals, thang-ka paintings, stupa-tombs of the Dalai Lamas, Buddhist statues and scriptures, porcelain vessels, enamel work, jade ware, brocade, Dalai Lamas' seals, and palace exteriors.

Musical Qigong:
Ancient Chinese Healing Art from a Modern Master
By Shen Wu, ISBN: 0-9665421-5-0, Health, Paperback, $14.95

Musical Qigong is a special healing energy therapy that combines two ancient Chinese traditions-healing music and Qigong. This guide contains two complete sets of exercises with photo illustrations and discusses how musical Qigong is related to the five elements in the ancient Chinese concept of the universe - metal, wood, water, fire, and earth.

More Titles from Homa & Sekey Books

Breaking Grounds:
The Journal of a Top Chinese Woman Manager in Retail
by Bingxin Hu, translated from the Chinese by Chengchi Wang,
Prefaced by Professor Louis B. Barnes of Harvard Business School
ISBN: 1-931907-15-3, 256 pp, Hardcover, Business, $24.95

The book records the experience of a Chinese business woman who
pioneered and succeeded in modernizing the aging Chinese retail business. Based on her years of business experience, the author recounts
the turmoil, clashes of concepts and behind-the-scene decisions in the
Chinese retail business, as well as psychological shocks, emotional
perplexes, and intellectual apprehension she had gone through.

The Haier Way: The Making of a Chinese Business Leader and a
Global Brand by Jeannie J. Yi, Ph.D., & Shawn X. Ye, MBA
ISBN: 1-931907-01-3, Hardcover, Business, $24.95

Haier is the largest consumer appliance maker in China. The book traces
the appliance giant's path to success, from its early bleak years to
becoming the world's 5th largest household appliance manufacturer.
The book explains how Haier excelled in quality, service, technology
innovation, a global vision and a management style that is a blend of
Jack Welch of "GE" and Confucius of ancient China.

"The book throws light on a number of important issues about China's
development path...comprehensive and up-to-date...highly readable."
— Dr. N.T. Wang, Director of China-International Business Project,
Columbia University

www.homabooks.com

ORDERING INFORMATION: U.S.: $5.00 for the first item, $1.50 for each
additional item. **Outside U.S.:** $30 for the first item, $15 for each additional item.
All major credit cards accepted. You may also send a check or money order in
U.S. fund (payable to Homa & Sekey Books) to: Orders Department, Homa &
Sekey Books, P. O. Box 103, Dumont, NJ 07628 U.S.A. Tel: 800-870-HOMA;
201-261-8810. Fax: 201-384-6055; 201-261-8890. Email: info@homabooks.com

CPSIA information can be obtained
at www.ICGtesting.com
Printed in the USA
LVHW111533040319
609417LV00001B/267/P